The Under-study

A NOVEL BY

STEIN AND DAY/*Publishers*/New York

ELIA KAZAN

The Under-study

"Toot Toot Tootsie Goodbye"
W/M: Ernie Erdman, Gus Kahn, Dan Russo, Ted Fiorito
Copyright c 1922, 1949 Renewed 1950 Leo Feist Inc.
Used by Permission.

First published in 1975
Copyright c 1974 by Elia Kazan
Library of Congress Catalog Card No. 74-78538
All rights reserved
Designed by David Miller
Printed in the United States of America
Stein and Day/*Publishers*/Scarborough House,
Briarcliff Manor, N.Y. 10510
ISBN 0-8128-1731-1

To Sol

who saw
what I didn't think possible

The Under-study

I

IN EVERY SHOW," my friend Sidney used to say, "there's a payoff scene. You don't have to kill them along the way if you bring off your finish, and it doesn't matter how great you are up to then if you don't. The end is everything."

Years ago he said this, and I must say I thought it strange coming from him. Dear old Sidney Schlossberg—Mr. Sidney Castleman, quite a star in the forties you may remember—he'd try to break the bank every scene he played. He became quite a ham, my old friend.

'In the depression," he'd say to me, "when there was nothing else, I used to play the burlesque wheel. I'd go through those old bits, most of them for shame, no script, nothing. But everybody out front knew that next to closing I'd walk down center and spill my crazy guts. The Rave Act they called it. Before your time, my boy, you never saw Rags Ragland. That was the comic's big moment, and that's how I was judged, by what I did when I was out there at the end, alone.

'The legitimate? No different. Take *Lear*, which I first played when I was twenty-seven. It's a natural for Second Avenue, *König Lear*. All those scenes, in Yiddish you see what they are, old momma-jerkers which Mr. William Shakespeare, a true thief, cribbed from his guild brothers—family stuff, father and children, bad daughters, good daughter, in-law troubles, best friend is blind, all kinds cheap stuff. But then, at the end, Willy-boy didn't know what to do so he throws on the stage his headliner. His daughter part too, but her he don't give jokes. Not a hell of a lot to the old man either. Read the book sometime. So it's up to the actor. 'Go out there save my ass!' the author says.

"Well, the first time I played that part I knew if I put over the scene on the heath, if they listened to me and not the property man banging the thunder sheet, I had it made. That's the Rave scene in *Lear*. Are you listening, my boy?"

He was always at me, Sidney, my father by adoption. He started me in the theater and never let up. Even later when they were fighting over me, the producers, and he couldn't get a job, he was advising me not only about show business but about everything else.

"I watch you," he'd say, "and I'm waiting. When's he going to cut loose? All right, his makeup is good, he speaks very nice, he's got a voice even if the customers in the last row balcony can't hear him he does his business well, handles his laughs, and he's got a short nose that turns up at the end, everything he needs to be a star on Broadway. Except what? The main thing. Has he got that fire? Yes? So when am I going to see it? When do I see the mensch in the man?

"What I'm worried," Sidney used to say, "is that it may not be there, my boy."

That used to worry me, too. Did I have the big emotions? Did I have what I needed to bring off my climaxes? Sure, I worked every season, but a big star I did not become. I was always convincing, even excellent, but you know those words, they mean mediocre.

Old Sidney was really after something else, not only that I lacked temperament on stage, I lacked passion in life. I didn't behave as Sidney thought an artist should. "You're too goddamn nice all the time," he'd say. "Nobody's afraid of you. You're a getalongnik."

I told this to my wife Ellie.

"Why should anybody be afraid of you?" she said.

"You're missing his point," I said.

"What's wrong with being nice to people? He's such a fraud, your friend."

Ellie didn't agree with Sidney about a thing in the world. She's a Yankee, lean as a plank out of an old Hartford, Connecticut, family tree, her father and mother look-alikes. Ellie is very hard on exaggeration, calls it lying. "You don't want to end up like him, do you?" she'd say. "Besides, how does he know you lack passion? Was he ever in bed with you?"

"I know what he means," I'd say.

Sidney used to make fun of the way I dressed, said I came on like a stockbroker, not an artist.

"Garbage!" Ellie said when I told her. "What's an artist supposed to look like, Abbie Hoffman? Or Sidney, that rancid old goat? You tell him I don't like the way he dresses. And why doesn't he patronize his dry cleaner? He's carrying last year's borscht on his lapels."

Ellie reminded me of the time we ran into Laurence Olivier on the street. "If you didn't know who he was, wouldn't you think he was a teacher or a lawyer, something respectable? What's wrong with being what the British call well turned out? Clean? Yes, neat? I don't even see why an actor can't have civilized standards of conduct."

Ellie had trained for the piano but, due to a tragedy in her life, had given up her hopes for the concert stage and stopped practicing. She had few friends, wanted fewer. My mates in the theater hinted I might have made a more passionate second marriage—well, Sidney said it outright. They see Ellie's rather clenched face and her steel-rimmed glasses but never the delicate flush that makes her face glow when she takes those glasses off—her signal that I can approach—or the no-one-but-you light in her eyes when she turns on. Ellie takes time to heat up, but when she's ready, she's shoo-shoo baby under the electric blanket.

At the same time, she's an immaculate person who will not give up an inch of her home convictions, detests the easy familiarity— "darling!," "sweetheart!"—of theater people. "I will not play their 'Look, everybody, see how happy we are,' game," she'd say. "What you and I do in private is private."

Now my first wife used to be all over me in public, an actress, that one, on and off stage. Also a human sieve, passed money like water. When I married Ellie my bank book read owe owe nineteen. Ellie organized my life for me. I used to hand her my paycheck each week, and she did our bills, made sure we were on time with Blue Cross and Blue Shield, gave me my allowance. Don't laugh. Sidney could have used someone like that.

Sidney is a prime example of what lack of order can do. He was one of the top stars on the Street once, Mr. Sidney Castleman, have you forgotten? He had his apartment in the Plaza Hotel, and I used to borrow it during the day to meet Ellie for our matinees. We were both married elsewhere then and—

By the way, Ellie managed even these on-the-sly meetings like a perfect lady. "This is the last lie I'll ever tell," she'd say, referring to what she'd told her former, an investment counselor, about her day's calendar. "Shopping," she'd say.

Ellie pointed out to me that when people's places are as messy as Sidney's was in those days, it means only one thing, demoralization has set in. And so it turned out. Sidney was already on the greasy chute. Evidence: the bathroom sink was full of shaving sludge, his clothes lay on the rug where he'd dropped them the night before, and the laundry was two feet deep in the back of his closet. Ellie predicted what was going to happen to Sidney—on the nose!

When I tried to warn Sidney that he was getting too careless with the big agents, the prominent producers, the influential critics and columnists, he'd say I was paranoid. "They're all my very very good friends, ' he'd say.

Well, when the time came, one by one, those very very good friends ate his living body. So—am I paranoid?

And suppose I am. Who wouldn't be if he was a member of a vanishing profession? Nothing is permanent with us. Success for instance. The distance between the top and the bottom is the distance between the top and the bottom of one of Fat Clive's columns. "Our very, very good friends!" We've all had their knives in our bellies.

So there. I'm paranoid. Every professional actor is.

Ellie was the first person in my life who made me feel something might last awhile.

Don't get me wrong. I used to make a good living on Broadway, and Sidney finally couldn't get a job except through me. I was sort of a star. If the play was by an unknown, I went above the title. And with a voice-over now and then and a commercial announcement, hell, I did fine.

But I had the good sense to get out. I live in Florida now.

Sidney died up there. In the trenches.

I'll tell you one reason I survived: because of the kind of actor I was. I could play anything from a mature thirty to any kind of eighty. I was born with an old face, but I still wear belt size thirty-four. A day I remember: I was in my mother's dressing room, watching her make up, and became aware that she was observing me in the mirror and smiling.

"What are you laughing at?" I demanded. I was pretty touchy even at twelve.

She kissed me first. "Because you have an old man's face, Sonny, and I love it."

Sonny was my nickname, and did it ever stick!

Six years later I was playing fathers in the Yale Dramat. My first jobs on Broadway were understudying old men's parts like those Sidney did. Later I played them. My comfort was Paul Muni. In time his age caught up with his face. As I got older I played straighter. At thirty-seven I got the girl.

So from the first all my parts were character parts. I was a craftsman, not just a stage personality that might suddenly go out of style like Sidney did. No one knew better than I the uses of a well-fitting wig or how a little hair, added here, taken off there, can change a person's appearance. In England the great ones live by that, Olivier and Guinness, Gielgud and Richardson. No comparisons intended.

Old Sidney now, he was strictly a type. But who needed a sixty-six-year-old potbellied Jewish bull for a hero? On Broadway? In our time?

But oh Sidney, oh Schlossberg, I miss him. I do.

When I came down from Yale in 1942 I was committed to acting, perhaps only because my mother was in the profession, although it generally works the other way, doesn't it? Anyway, I can't remember making a decision. I simply accepted that's what I was, an actor.

So despite the fact that I was army-bound, the first thing I did when I hit the big city was go backstage to the Ethel Barrymore Theatre and present my letter, now more than a year old, to the person my mother had assured me would "get me rolling." This personal contact was my mother's most valuable bequest. After Yale, she gave me Sidney Castleman.

Sidney's play was about to be performed the last matinee and evening of a year and a half's run. I expected a minute, hoped for ten, was with Mr. Sidney Castleman from noon till two the next morning.

That night I learned what a star is.

Sidney's dresser, a portly black named Oliver, escorted me through a hushed backstage space, over a red runner laid down from the stage door to the star's dressing room.

Sidney was taking off his street clothes to put on a green China-silk robe, the front stippled with makeup. I remember how thick-through he was, how fully rounded his shoulders, how straight and strong the back of his neck, how rich his hair—mine was going fast —and how flat his belly, a contrast to the tub of lard he lugged around at the end of his life.

We sat side by side in front of his long dressing-room mirror as he made up. He spoke affectionately of my mother, grieved that she had not received the public recognition she deserved, told me how much she'd meant to him because, just when he needed to hear it most, she'd promised him he'd be a star, not downtown where he already was, but on Broadway, the goal of every Jewish actor in those days. I suppose he meant to remind me of what I knew, that he'd been her lover, but he never put it baldly.

When the respectful knock on the door and the call boy's voice announced, "Half hour, Mr. Castleman," Sidney sent for the stage manager and asked him to put a chair under his signal console so I could watch the show, a sell-out, from backstage.

I remember how, in the last instants before he strode on the set to meet his applause, Sidney paced back and forth in the darkest corner of the stage house, seemed to be talking to himself, nodding, turning, preparing for the scene he was about to play by playing in his imagination the scene that preceded it.

I have never forgotten his climax scene, his "Rave," when he shocked his fellow board members in a large industrial corporation, told them it was a new world, one world, that the needs of the workers had to be respected equally with those of capital. Those were the days! I remember how the balcony kept interrupting his speech with applause. The orchestra was silent at first, even resentful, but in time those four-forty ticket holders broke out in a storm of applause, admiration for the man's passion and his artistry.

After the show, Sidney did an unheard-of thing. He called a rehearsal between matinee and evening, the last performances of that play. The fact that the run was over was no excuse, he told those of his cast he'd ordered on stage, for sloppiness and "faking." He particularly began to coach a young actress from radio, a recent replacement. In a close whisper, he lived through her role for her, showing her how far short she'd fallen. All this on the last day of the play's run!

One particular bit of business with a pad and pencil he went over and over, illustrating for her benefit how much could be told by the way she handled these props. Finally he worked on an instant they had together, taking the girl by the shoulders and "turning her out" so the audience could see more of her face, "giving" her the scene. "Talk to my downstage eye," he said.

Then he begged her to have faith in her talent—was he also talking to me?—to believe that if she gave herself a chance, "it," the emotion, the magical thing, would happen. "You may even surprise yourself," he said, shaming her, inspiring her. "What? Well, what?"

Before she had a chance to reply, he strode off the stage, leaving her in turmoil.

A reporter was waiting in the wings, come from a paper that had roasted the play when it opened. In light of the play's long run, he wanted to know, would Sidney still say what he'd said then, that the critics had too much power?

Sidney looked at him a long time, as if he was making up his mind about something else. Then he said, "My friend, I know what you are, a whore, and you know what I am, a whoremaster."

A masseur was in his dressing room. "I don't eat before a performance," Sidney said to me as he took off his clothes. "We'll have supper later." He responded to the kneading and stroking like a lover, a groan, a sigh. Before it was over, he was asleep. The masseur covered him with a soft blanket. Oliver turned off the lights, asked me if I wanted to step outside.

I didn't. I sat in the twilight, the sting of the alcohol in my nostrils, and listened to Sidney's heavy, even breathing. It was there and then that I made up my mind what I wanted to be. No, not *like* Sidney. I wanted to *be* Sidney. I wanted to be the man himself. It was the most profound confluence of love and longing, of admiration and envy, I've ever felt in my life.

I watched the evening's performance from the same place. The young actress burst into tears when her exit was applauded. In the wings she leaned against me and whispered, "How did he do that?"

Sidney, playing his big speech, his Rave, for the last time, gave the kind of show you don't see anymore. Like a tightrope walker, he edged the precipice of overdoing. He was in some kind of transport, telling off, it seemed to me, a whole generation, the men who'd made the depression, and at the same time giving heart to a whole other generation, the young upcoming, telling them that America by its strength and courage and basic goodness could solve all its problems, in fact all the problems of the world. Who believes that anymore? But they did that night in 1942, they took it from Sidney.

The curtain had a part in the middle, a foldover. It did not lift for the first call. An assistant stage manager parted it and held it open, wide enough for one man. This promise sent the applauding audience into the frenzy that only ballet arouses today. But if you think Sidney let himself be rushed, you're mistaken. He was at the stage manager's console, near me, where Oliver had given him a comb and was holding a small hand mirror. Sidney straightened out his hair, sprinkled Pinaud's Eau de Lilac Végétal on his hands to slap on his face and neck. Then he winked at me and slowly went to where the curtains were being held apart.

As he approached this opening, he seemed suddenly depleted. Before the audience, he stood with his head bowed, letting his worshipers know he'd held back nothing. Their applause seemed to revive him. With a grand gesture, he ordered the curtain lifted to reveal his company. He gave each of them his moment. The fervor of the audience, still mounting, seemed to surprise him. He made a gesture, parting his arms, to express his wonder. Was he acting? Was he exaggerating his exhaustion and his gratitude? What's the diff? It was all theater.

Visitors to his dressing room were entertained graciously, of course, but there was something faintly mocking about the way Sidney received their praise. "You can't possibly believe I was all that good," he seemed to be saying. Then there was his laughter, the laughter only a young and completely assured male can produce.

Once more we sat in front of the long dressing-room-table mirror. He slapped a fistful of albolene on his face, asked Oliver to pour me a long Scotch, his a little longer, and side by side, we smiled at each other. He asked me what I thought, and I told him that I was particularly impressed with the way he listened on stage.

"Just as important as speaking," he said.

"That's a rule they give you in drama school," I said, "but I never saw it honored before."

A knock. The young actress, dressed to leave, had come to thank him. "I learned so much this afternoon, Mr. Castleman," she started, "I want to—"

"You can do better," Sidney interrupted.

"Do you really think so?"

Sidney indicated a chair. "We're going to have some supper," he informed her.

"Oh," she flustered, "excuse me then." She ran out of the room.

Peetie, the property man, and his assistant had come to say goodbye. "We just hope we're lucky enough again—"

Half an hour later, when we left with the accumulation of a year and a half's run, I carried Sidney's makeup case. At the stage door the young actress was making a difficult explanation to a handsome young Ivy Leaguer. As soon as she saw Sidney, she added a quick final word, kissed him lightly, and hurried to join us. The distressed young man was able to respond properly to Sidney's nod.

Still, despite the triumph and the glory, there was something forlorn about us as we huddled in the back of a cab. We were gypsies again, homeless refugees, looking for a safe place in a heartless city. The streets we passed through were dark and empty and somehow threatening. The young actress said it, "I can't believe I will ever again be in a successful play."

In the two rooms under the roof of the Plaza Hotel where Sidney lived, a table had been set up, and Sidney's regular waiter was in attendance. Sidney disappeared into the bedroom, reappeared in a red velour smoking jacket over an ascot and a pair of opera slippers. Lobster Newburg, a cold Rhine wine, cherries and pears.

Inevitably Sidney got talking about the theater so inevitably about himself.

"True tragedy," he said, takes place not because of outside circumstances and events. It takes place because of what the person to whom it happens is. The tragic hero brings his tragedy with him. Because of what he is, he is doomed. In the Heroic Theater it is perfectly believable that a man will kill for honor. Can you imagine any character in today's plays doing that? Now our central characters behave reasonably. Good sense solves all, so our plays come to nothing. Medea, in the Theater of Common Sense, meets Jason in the divorce court with her lawyer, Lou Nizer no doubt! What? What?"

"I see what you mean." I said.

"Shakespeare's Shylock cannot be paid off except by the pound of flesh. Today he'd sue for damages, sit down with Portia in the judge's chambers, an out-of-court settlement, there goes the quality-of-mercy bit! Hamlet? He'd rush back to his analyst. Lear? Miami Beach, still kvetching but eating very, very good!"

The girl said something for the first time.

"What about you, Mr. Castleman?"

"My darling, I am Prometheus, bound to the rock by the gods of my time because I have, year in, year out, defied them. Don't you think," he said turning to me, "that vulture from the paper is waiting for the chance to get back at me for what I said tonight?"

"I think he is," I said.

"When they go for my entrails, I hope I have some of the strength I have now." He looked at the young actress. "And the friends."

She was getting the idea. There was that light in her eyes.

Sidney looked at her a long time. "I think you have to make a choice," he said. "Now! Tonight!"

"What do you mean?" She seemed frightened. Also thrilled.

"Can you imagine Eleanora Duse, if she didn't have a crust of bread, doing one of your radio commercials?"

"Never," the young actress said, her eyes full of wonder.

"When Duse died her pride had never been violated," Sidney said. "She never permitted that. Nor have I! Nor will I!"

He hit the table top. The plates rattled.

I don't think Sidney Schlossberg was as good an artist as Eleanora Duse.

But with the lobster and the wine and the shaded lights, the rumble of his voice and the pitter-patter of the waiter, I believed every word he said that night, and some he didn't. The girl, I saw, was hopelessly enraptured. She wanted to be his as I wanted to be him.

As I listened to him predict the bitter end of his life, I knew, yes, that will happen to him. But he won't grovel, he won't beg off. He's a man of that stature, a heroic person.

"Have you understood a little of what I've been saying?" Sidney said to the young actress.

"A little—I think—yes!"

"The gods will see to it that I pay for my hubris, do you know what that means, young lady, hubris?"

"No, Mr. Castleman."

"I will presently explain it to you."

My cue. I got up to go. Sidney put his arm around me, walked me to the door. The waiter was there. Sidney told him to leave the table, the maid would clear it in the morning, but to bring another bottle of the wine, quickly please.

As we said goodbye, he asked my plans. I told him I was scheduled to go into the army any day. Sidney laughed at my misfortune. A lumbar condition, he said, rubbing his back gratefully, had saved him.

"But I'll be waiting for you when you get out. Tell me now, what do you want to be?"

"I want to be you," I said.

"Oh, well, we'll see, we'll see. But rest easy. We'll have a job for you when it's over, a part, yes. Won't we?"

He included the young actress. Was he trying to impress her with his kindness to newcomers in the profession? Or me with how simple seduction was?

"Oh Mr. Castleman," I said. "I'll probably be gone so many years, I won't blame you if you forget all about me."

He swore however long it might be—who knew then? Remember 1942? The Germans were invincible, the English begging, the French had quit, and our ships were on the bottom—whenever it was that I came back from the war, I wouldn't have to ask. His help would be waiting.

"Don't worry," he said. "You're with me now, kid!"

I didn't really believe him, I'll confess, but on the chance I wrote Dear Mr. Castleman from the coast of Southern California, where we were practicing landings through the surf, and later I wrote him from

Hawaii, where we were doing the same with live ammo. I wrote him from Hollandia in New Guinea, where I was part of MacArthur's HQ Company, assigned to shepherd visiting USO troupes come to keep our boys from going batty on that moist mountain top. I wrote him—it was Dear Sidney now—from Biak, where I was in charge of films as well as cooking up some kind of self-entertainment for our bogged-down troops, and I wrote him from Tacloban, where I got the clap. Finally I wrote him from Manila the day after the city fell, told him about the trolley car I'd come upon in the center of the city and the strong smell that came from it, quite sweet it seemed until I realized what it was. Then it turned my stomach. I held my nose and breathed through my mouth as I looked through the windows at the three Japanese who'd died there. "Defending what, Sidney, tell me?"

And Sidney answered, wrote promptly so I'd get his mail before I left each of MacArthur's stepping stones, kept me up-to-date on our profession—"our," he said, I loved that—sent me Sam Zolotow's "News of the Stage" columns, wonderful in those days, and the notices of the big hits, above all the accounts of his own triumphs. They were coming fast those years.

Sidney kept my faith alive.

Finally when I did come back, still in uniform, there he was in a different theater but the same dressing room, numero uno. Again it was full of show people, praising him for another triumph, agents, their faces agleam with venal shine, envious actors spouting praise that he mocked as excessive, and a very sincere young actress, not saying a word, sitting in a corner, waiting.

He asked everyone to leave his dressing room—except the girl in the corner—and again asked his dresser, the same Oliver, to pour me a long Scotch, his a little longer, and again we sat side by side looking at each other in the mirror. He looked the same, but I looked older, my hair much thinner—you could see where it was going to go—while his was still as thick as that of a young Italian woman.

"Don't worry," he said. "You're with me now, kid!"

A month later, when I was discharged, he had a job waiting for me, got rid of someone in his supporting cast, a little ruthlessly, but I didn't care.

I was working on Broadway.

Those were the years! Sidney was an idol on our Street. I followed him around like a puppy.

When he chose me as his understudy, I was in heaven.

For twenty years we were as close as the pages of a rain-soaked newspaper. And I want to say it plainly, Sidney did a lot for me.

But I also want to say this. Later, when he began to fail, I paid him back. In full.

There's a certain guilt that comes with success, and for the last ten years of his life every time I looked at Sidney Schlossberg, I felt guilty. Exactly why I don't know. There was that quick thing I had with his wife, Roberta. But I told Sidney all, or almost all, about that, and he laughed and said, "My boy, you were neither the first nor the last." Then he said that was the least of his troubles, and I shouldn't worry about it.

But the guilt is there and for no good reason. I carried Sidney every chance I got right to the end. His last three jobs he was my understudy. Part of my deal was that I could consult on, which is to say, choose, my understudy. No other actor ever had that kind of arrangement. That's how anxious they were to sign me.

Of course Sidney didn't want it known that he was my understudy, asked that the "credit" not be printed in the program, and to oblige me, the management did leave it out.

But like they say, lend money, lose a friend.

One day, not so long ago, he passed me on Broadway and barely nodded. Then, when he got twenty feet up the street, I heard him call, "Say there!" I turned, and it's like twenty-five years ago, he's the star, and I'm the lucky fellow. He's standing there, can you believe it, crooking his finger at me, not even saying the words, "Come here," just crooking his long middle finger and not taking a step in my direction. I had to walk to him. And all the time he had that twist of a smile, like the one that made Franchot Tone, the actor, so sexy for a while, and he says, Sidney, not Franchot, says not asks, "Prepare for the worst. I am wondering if I might once again get into you for a twenty. I mean borrow of course."

At that particular time, Sidney was pulling down two two five as my understudy, a man without a wife at service and with a self-supporting kid who teaches college out west and a brother, Myron Castle, very big in ladies wear. Sidney had no responsibilities, not a single one. I had a wife and her kid and my first wife, who was still benefiting from those little drains her lawyer stuck into me, like they stick into maple trees in the spring, only I had to produce the golden sap twelve months a year.

Later I told Ellie about the incident.

"What absolutely bewilders me," she said, "is that he never seems the least bit embarrassed."

"Why should he?"

"He lives entirely by the charity of one person. Wouldn't that embarrass you?"

"I guess it would," I said, "but it's a matter of loyalty, simple kindness."

"I'm very suspicious of your kindness," she said. "What are you paying him off for?"

Anyway, I gave Sidney the twenty, and when he looked fish-eyed at me and gave me that sneer-smile, another ten. He nodded, as though making a judgment on my generosity that was not favorable, added an insulting sort of thanks, and left me standing there to watch him stroll up the avenue with his snap-brim black Borsalino and that gold-headed cane he always sported.

That isn't what got me sore at Sidney. Hell, I was accustomed to that, very gracious about it actually. What got me was his use of the word "borrow." A few years before, in an effort to slow the pace, I'd told him that any money I gave him I didn't expect back. He knew that. Still he always said "borrow," extra clearly, "can I once again borrow," giving me that phony bow, then standing there waiting for me to deliver like he was some old-time movie star with a castle in the south of Ireland and eager hounds and jumping horses as well as a wife and a mistress and a mistress to cheat on his mistress with when he gets sore at her, and he says, Sidney does, "I wonder if I might once again borrow"—the son of a bitch! Then when I accommodate him with half of what I had in our pocket—

Did you get that? "Our"?

Actually it wasn't much, what was in our pocket. Already nobody was walking around with a lot of cash because of the muggings.

Where had Sidney's salary been going?

For the last five years of his life he was putting down option money on *Titan*, a play. Every actor lives for a part, dreams of playing Hamlet at thirty, Macbeth at forty, the Merchant at fifty, Lear at sixty, Prospero at seventy. Sidney had *Titan*. It was his conviction that *Titan* would, with one boost, raise him—restore him, Sidney would have said—to his rightful place in the history of the theater.

Actually the play was *Prometheus Bound*, ripped off by a freak named Lester Brown, self-styled Paul Prince. When someone called this man's attention to the fact that Theodore Dreiser had written a novel called *The Titan,* his response was, "History will remember only one of us."

The hero of *Titan* was a man to Sidney's scale, a great scientist who regretted having had a hand in inventing the Bomb and now, with a new formula in his head for the release of a force even more devastating, refuses to accede to the demands of the Pentagon that he yield up his secret. He is imprisoned on false charges, but does not crumble, rather becomes more defiant—and more garrulous. He also finds the opportunity to fall in love with Io, a campus rebel, and the daughter of the warden. When the president of the United States himself comes to place patriotic reasons before Sidney, our hero still does not give in. He is placed in solitary confinement. But the cell is bugged, so when Io comes to visit him and he tells her that he wants her to carry his secret to the weakest nation on earth, thereby making the weakest the strongest, the Pentagon generals find out. The Supreme Court condemns Sidney to death for treason. This occasions another salvo of defiant oratory, taken shamelessly from Aeschylus. The play ends on a blackout of all light on earth, then a tremendous flash, Prometheus's revenge. Doomsday!

For the last six years of his life, Sidney was never without a copy of *Titan.* It was as much part of him as his hand or his tongue. He would recite parts of it. "Listen to those words," he'd say, "those glorious words!" He'd suddenly change the subject in a conversation. "I've finally made up my mind what the style of my production will be," he'd say, then show a book of reproductions of paintings, once Hieronymus Bosch, another time Edvard Munch.

He'd even use *Titan* as an aid in courtship. Over a hundred girls in his last five years read the part of Io for Sidney, allowed themselves to be coached by the old actor, usually in their apartments or in a top-floor dressing room of an afternoon when the theater was "dark," trying to imitate his way with words and phrases and passion, then putting off or submitting to his sexual demands.

My next to last job on Broadway, and his last ever, was in a play about the president of a girls' college, me, and the problem he was having with his "now" students. The two top floors of dressing rooms were wall-to-wall "college girls," actually a rather unlikely group of students when you got to know a little about them. This area became Sidney's domain. The girls had a special wingback chair for him in the big chorus dressing room, and Sidney would sit there like a caliph from the time the girls came in to make up and dress, throughout the performance, and until after they'd dressed to leave. The girls would pet him and twit him and play their little games with him. Like his hair had gone completely white. The girls dyed it a rather reddish brown and touched up the roots as they came out. They sewed his buttons when they got loose, bought him ties and matching handkerchiefs, massaged his neck and shoulders. When they bought new dresses, they'd try them on for him, get his advice. They undressed freely in front of Sidney—girls have never done that for me—consulted with him about their lovers, and when they found a new one, showed the young man to Sidney for his approval.

He in turn let them read—"try out," he said—for Io. There were several strong candidates for the part as the season passed and whoever was for the time being closest to "getting" the role, Sidney would fall in love with, not as you or I might, but romantically, the kind of love more intense because unrequited.

Damn if one of those girls didn't ask him home with her one night when he was complaining that the chill of death was settling over him. Sidney told me later that the sympathetic young lady took him into her bed so he'd be warm.

When he made his move she said, "Sidney, I'm sorry, but I don't like you that way."

"My dear," he replied, "to an old man that doesn't make any difference."

He was still, you can see, behaving like an old-time leading man, Thomashefsky or Jacob Adler, oh the backstage stories about those old Jewish giants! Sidney felt every girl in that cast belonged to him by right of talent. His, I mean.

I knew the truth, of course. Sidney didn't have any interest in girls. He just liked to feel that last bit of the power he used to have.

To the very end Sidney talked about *Titan* as if it would certainly be done when everybody got his head on straight. He was talking about Merrick's head, or Robert Whitehead's, both newcomers in the theater as Sidney saw them. Of course he couldn't even get into the offices of these men, but he carried on as if he was in constant touch with one or the other and fighting off Joseph Papp. They were all seriously considering *Titan,* he declared, making budgets and cast lists. It was he himself, he led you to believe, who was delaying production until he'd assembled the perfect set of elements. We pretended to believe every word.

Sidney's problem was with the author and with that quality the author had in common with all members of the Dramatists Guild, impatience. Paul Prince was a small man who, while waiting for the great day, worked in the New York Public Library. He was the picture of a stack rat with an uneven complexion and hair that was long, tangled, and cellar white. A long, insistent neck thrust forward a face loaded down with very heavy lenses.

"Talented men " Sidney used to say, "invariably have a ludicrous aspect."

Their relationship was based on distrust. They were always together, not for reasons of companionship, but to keep an eye on each other. Sidney always suspected, correctly, that despite his years of "work" on *Titan,* Paul Prince would give the play to the first producer who'd promise him an immediate production and that he would not insist that Sidney play Prometheus.

Paul Prince's distrust was equally realistic that Sidney Schlossberg didn't have any source of production money and never would have, that he was bluffing all the way.

They stayed together for the reason most couples do. They had no one better to turn to.

What did Ellie think of all this? "Baby, he is simply not your responsibility," she kept reminding me. But I went right on as though he was.

For instance, when I take a vacation I like to have a job to come back to. Before this college play closed I was already having meetings on a comedy for the spring. And I asked what I always asked every producer, that he pay for my dresser and that I have the right to consult on, read, choose, my understudy.

The producer said O.K. on the dresser, but on the understudy, he said that was up to the director.

The director was one of those thirty-day-wonder geniuses first time uptown. His name was Adam something, "Gosh-man" it sounded like. He didn't want Sidney Schlossberg around.

He said Sidney was on drugs.

I got outraged at that—you know what happens once that gets around—and the whole thing almost blew up right then, would have except for my agent. He slid between. These new directors, he told me later, they're the future. I'd have to learn how to get along with them.

My agent is a mover, smooth as a snake, skinny as Sinatra, he wears a slim-line black suit of some material made especially for agents. He saw me getting worked up and said to all assembled, "Look it's unimportant," then to me, "Let's give Adam a chance to think it over." Then he turned to Adam and said, "We've always consulted on our understudy," and before Adam, who looked like he had a pretty hot head could say anything, he got up, my agent, dropped his balls into place with a shake of his left leg, and told me he was going to take me to lunch.

Over a corner table at Sardi's he conveyed the information to me. I wasn't Adam's first choice. I was being offered the job only because the producer insisted.

"Never start a fight you can't win," he added.

"Who says we can't win? Fuck 'em, let's walk."

"Your nerves are showing, Sonny," he said.

"Don't call me that, do you mind?"

"Christ, I've been calling you Sonny for twenty-five years."

"Well, for twenty-five years I haven't liked it, so stop."

"O.K., but you just proved my point. You need a beach and a very dumb broad."

"I'm going to take a vacation," I answered, "right after this lunch."

"Who you protecting, anyway? Sidney Castleman? A guy who bad-mouths you every chance he gets?"

"That's my business. That's a private thing."

"His taking drugs ain't so private. One night I saw him start into Frankie and Johnnie's and hit the wall four feet one side of the door."

"What Sidney takes is Miltown, by the handful, agreed, and sleeping marbles in all colors—"

"And booze."

"A bad combo, I know, but he does it to steady his nerves."

"Where do you think he's been the last three weeks?"

"I don't know and I don't care."

"For instance, did he show backstage to fulfill his duty as understudy?"

I couldn't lie. "No."

"Don't you think Adam found that out? No secrets on this Street, kid."

"I know what you mean," I said. "But I am the only friend the guy's got left, and I am not going to—"

"I wish I knew what neurotic goddamn thing makes you so nice to someone who's cutting your throat—"

"That's my problem," I said. "I don't care what—"

"But Adam does. He's green but not slow. He called the stage manager of your last show, and Eric tried for a fast minute to defend Sidney too. But when Adam pressed him, Eric had to admit that Sidney never really got the lines of your part. When Eric asked Sidney why he had so much trouble learning those jokes, Sidney said he didn't like the way they were written. Then he laughed and said Eric shouldn't worry because in the moment of crisis old Sidney would be there, ready on cue. Eric was sort of laughing when he told Adam all this, but he admitted he was pretty relieved you never got sick. Are you paying attention?"

"Actually, Sidney learns lines very quickly."

"And another thing, Sidney refused to confine himself to the same moves and business you used. Want a direct quote? 'Our present leading man,' he told Eric, 'is not overloaded with temperament, while I am a member of a more expressive tradition.' "

"That's true, what he said."

"It's also bullshit. 'Please, Eric,' he demanded, 'allow me a certain freedom to express in my own style the essence of this sorry play and provide it with a little of the stature it does not now have.' How do you defend that?"

Actually I'd been in the back of the house that day, had dropped by for my mail and heard the whole thing. I had to admit, to myself only, that I felt hurt, even a little angry.

Later I told Ellie about the incident.

"How dare that man talk about you that way! And you took that?"

"What would you have done?"

"Gone up on stage and cut his throat."

"He was not altogether wrong, you know."

"God! Where do you get your control?"

I defended him, sort of, but the truth is I didn't know why they didn't fire him.

Well I know one reason.

There's a comradeship among people of the theater, even producers, and what it's born of is desperation. Since memory began, we've watched our own and our best play their hearts out, then disappear into the discard, die before they die. I felt proud that I was able, against all opposition, to take care of Sidney, to keep him going.

Not that he made it easy, he made it as hard as he could. But why shouldn't he? Charity is charity, it's demeaning. It should be taken for what it usually is, a head trip for the donor. That's the way

Sidney took my handouts, with a measure of saving scorn. Perversely, no doubt, I rather admired him for behaving as if he was doing me a favor to accept my help.

There were lots of actors who looked up to Sidney because he wasn't so crawling grateful when some producer stooped to notice him. They told stories about Sidney's impertinences. There was one about an audition that became a legend. Two bright young Dartmouth boys were producing their first play. When Sidney strode on the stage to read for them, they asked the routine, "Mr. Castleman, would you please tell us what you've done?"

Sidney's response was, "You first."

Stories like this one crackled up and down the streets of Times Square, messages of hope for the rest of the profession. All Equity marveled that Sidney was able to get away with what he did, asked how come, and got the answer. He had me looking after him.

Maybe that was why I did it. I was admired for it.

Actually, I bawled Sidney out pretty good when that story reached me. These boys, I told him, were bringing nothing but money into the theater, not many like that left. The worst they could have been guilty of was naïveté and ignorance. Why make them the laughingstock of Broadway?

But the truth was I envied Sidney his chutzpah. I might have thought, "You first," but never have said it. Hell, I wouldn't even have thought it.

While I was reminding myself of all this, my agent was going on and on about my sick relationship with the Schloss and how the guy had made a masochist of me.

"Face it," he said, "your friend Sidney is unemployable."

Why? Why was Sidney unemployable? I mean aside from his arrogance and the fact that he sometimes came to auditions with the shakes. After all, most directors know that arrogance is nothing but a cover and every actor is nervous. Mr. Alfred Lunt once told me he got more nervous as he got older, not less.

What made him unemployable was his art, the Art of Sidney Schlossberg.

If you are not in the profession, you've never heard of the Schlossberg Shiver.

Let's say you're getting near the end of an act, and the scene is building to a confrontation. Sidney, instead of standing there like a regular human being, he's standing with his back three-quarters to the audience, his head tilted at an angle to his body, his chin tipped up, looking sort of as if he had a ruffle under his chin, wore boots and garters, and was really the exiled prince in disguise.

The other fellow says the words that are supposed to tip the bucket of emotion, and what Sidney's been directed to do is cross over to his acting partner and tell him quietly and sincerely what he feels. Curtain.

But Sidney does not do this. There is a long pause. It's time for him to make his move. But nothing. Maybe he's forgotten his lines, you think. Then you notice that he's shaking. It starts in his foot—Sidney wore Adler elevators—works up through his knee and so on up. Then when this miniparoxysm has come to its climax and all of Sidney is vibrating like an organ pipe, he sort of ducks his head and crosses stage to the waiting actor, in a move a little too reminiscent of Jackie Gleason's famous bit, and once there gives him the eye-daggers and unloads. And even this, it's not like recognizable human speech. It's declamation. I don't mean loud, not necessarily. I mean it's from an older time and tradition.

I've seen them in their darkened auditoriums, the producers, the directors and their sucks, turn their faces away in the middle of an audition by Sidney Castleman, drop their heads behind their chair backs, and smile at each other. Then when he was through, they would turn their heads back or lift them up, and one of them, whoever could control the giggles, would say in an elaborately polite tone of voice, "Thank you very much, Mr. Castleman." And the stage manager, who is usually kinder than the bunch out front if only because he sits on stage with the suppliants, would say, "You'll be hearing from us, Mr. Castleman."

Sidney knew he shouldn't wait that long to take his next bath.

So I felt for him. Other actors felt for him. "Just stand there and take their shit," we'd tell him. "Just be simple, talk and listen and keep your body still."

Sidney smiled. He pitied our bad taste.

But still, why did I, particularly I, feel for him? It was more than simple gratitude, of course, it was what Ellie called it, sick, an obsession.

I was not born in a dressing room but in the theatrical hotel across the stage alley. I never got acquainted with my father, a theatrical accountant who got into difficulties accounting for where the money went. When he disappeared one pay day—I was five—the management realized that where the money had gone was with him. Apparently he'd chosen Copenhagen for sanctuary because we got a lovely card from there the first Christmas, all frills and gilt, expressing his best wishes for our happiness. It was unsigned. Father had finally learned discretion, so much so that we never heard from him again.

My mother was a very giving person and, being in the theater, mobile. She kept me in boarding schools while she lived out her life here and there. When I was nineteen she died between the Saturday matinee and evening shows in the number two dressing room of the old Studebaker Theatre in Chicago, where she'd been playing one of the last road companies of *Life with Father*. Mother had been having an intimate relationship with "Father," but he was married and the show was booked ahead, so I had to go out and bury her. I saw more of her that one day than in the year before, giving everything she wasn't wearing in her coffin to the cleaning woman, settling her last bills with her last pay envelope, and so back to college with her makeup box, a sack of stage jewelry, and some yellowing tear sheets, all that was left of her.

One other thing. Sidney once had a short thing with my mother. He was twenty-two and I was ten, and my old lady used to take me with her when she went calling. She'd put me in the movie across the street while they did whatever they did. Mother liked them young, and she had an instinct for who would be successful in the profession and, so, useful to her in time. She told me Sidney was going to be a big star, which he did become. And it was useful, in fact the best inheritance I had from my mother.

Now can you see why I had this exaggerated concern for Sidney? No? Well, it puzzled me too.

After lunch I took a cab to where Sidney lived in the Village. He didn't answer his bell so I dug out the owner, a person of delicacy who lived in the garden apartment.

"Oh, I'm so glad you came," he said, looking terribly relieved, "because I haven't seen Mr. Castleman in three weeks and I—"

"Where did he go?"

"I wish I knew."

"His stuff, it's still upstairs?"

"All of it. Come up, I want you to see."

He unlocked the front door, and as I followed him I heard the siren of a prowl car in the distance and glanced back.

"See any of them coming?" the owner asked.

"What? Who do you mean?"

"He's been keeping very strange company these last two months."

He closed the front door, tested that it was locked.

"I'm frightened for him," he said as we started up the stairs. "He's had some guests here, very what we call mixed, rough trade, black, in the middle of the night. Sometimes it looked like the Tombs had been emptied here. Honestly, if it had been anyone else, I'd have asked him to leave, but Mr. Castleman—artists have to study all kinds, don't they?"

"Drugs?" I asked.

"My dear, everyone is on drugs. You know that."

"Not everyone."

"Shall we say everyone I know?"

He unlocked the door to Sidney's apartment, and we peeked in.

It looked like the jumble firemen leave after they've put out a harmless fire with that furious energy that builds up in the station-house playing cards.

"He said I could have everything here. You know I've been carrying him for three months—"

"Everything?"

"Furniture, clothes, oh, don't mention his clothes! His underwear, see? Rags."

"Whatever he owes you, I'd be glad to—"

"Oh, no. I'm not a romantic myself, but I can afford an occasional gesture for someone like Mr. Castleman."

The floor around the window table was littered with script pages torn to bits. I picked up a scrap.

"The only thing he took with him," the owner said, "was that horrible plaster of paris death mask of himself. He went down the street carrying that dreadful white mask and his toothbrush."

"*I placed in them blind hope,*" I read aloud. "*A greater gift than power!*"

"Oh, *Titan.* He used to recite parts of it when I came up to pass time. Lord, he's got a great voice! The line he loved, 'There is no torture you can devise that will make me reveal what I know.' You should have heard him do that one."

"I have. Well, I imagine he'll be back."

"I don't think so. He sent for his collection."

"His what?"

"His boxes of clippings and notes, his old character shoes and hats, you know."

"Who took them?"

"Blacks. The last thing before he left, he made quite a profound observation. 'It's important to know when one phase of your life is over,' he said. 'Abandon the old before it abandons you.'"

"Those blacks, did you ask them where he—?"

"They wouldn't speak to me. I asked Mr. Castleman before he left, 'Suppose a friend of yours wants to know where you've gone?'"

"What did he say?"

"'I have no friend,' he said."

I must admit that hurt me.

I took a cab home. One thing was certain. I had a good excuse for not fighting to get Sidney the understudy. "I couldn't find you," I'd say. I'm always having imaginary conversations with the man, even now, when he's dead. "Why the hell didn't you leave a forwarding address for your friends? Oh, I forgot, you have no friends."

I had another excuse. Of course I couldn't really push for Sidney to understudy this new role. Adam "Gosh-man" was right. In his last years, Sidney had run to lard. The more he drank, the less he ate. The more he drank, the heavier he got, like many men at a certain age and level of self-disgust.

I warned Sidney a year ago he was putting on too much weight. I learned the lesson from Elliott Nugent, another of my heroes. I suppose he's been forgotten now too, but not by me. Mr. Nugent in his middle forties was still playing "boys," the love interest. I learned from him that it's simply professional to control your appetite and keep your belly flat. To be slim is to prolong your career as well as your life.

I told all this to Sidney. His reply was, "You will not make your point with Elliott Nugent. He was strictly stock." His look bracketed me in the same scorn.

"I came from another tradition," he'd rave on, "the tradition of Werner Krauss and Emil Jannings. I don't suppose you're familiar with their work. All the leading men of the German and the Yiddish and the Polish Theater—and even the French till they became Americanized by our films—they were built like bulls. Raimu, Michel Simon, Gabin, you must remember them? Only in America do we have the idea that boys can be sexy."

I think the fact that I'd been looking out for Sidney gave him a false sense of security. He strutted up and down the Street, that subsidized rebel, publicly scorning me, still eating my bread, like one of those lefty kids. It's easy to be a big radical when daddy's hoisting the bill.

Perhaps the day has come to pull the rug out from under him, I thought. Fuck the fact that understudying is such a terrible come-down. If it's the best he can do at this time, then it's the best he can do.

"So stop being so goddamn superior, Sidney." I was scolding him. "Eric is just doing his job, and maybe Adam 'Gosh-man' is right. Why make it so tough on everybody? Be grateful for once. Thank some-body occasionally. Because it's not easy to be your friend, Sidney, believe me. And don't ever crook your finger at me that way again. When you want to talk to me, you son of a bitch, walk up to me, you and that phony cane. When you want money from me, you arrogant bastard, ask for it nice. Don't give me that sneer-smile, and don't pretend you ever will or ever have paid me back. So don't say 'loan,' don't say 'borrow,' say 'please,' you leaky old balloon. Next time, beg a little."

In the cab going up traffic-logged Sixth Avenue, I was perspiring like a murderer.

This was my chance to relieve myself of the man. Whatever our past together had been, I'd repaid everything and anything he'd done for me one hundred times. I was not responsible for his whole life. I was responsible for my whole life and Ellie's and—

That was it. I'd tell Ellie my problem and let her decide.

I knew what she'd say, of course.

Then I'd get out, out of town, out of the country, somewhere, quick. South America, that was it. I'd never been there. No. The Caribbean, into one of those beautiful ads. Cozumel. That warm clean water! I had three big weeks before rehearsals. I could even go to Africa. Why not? No one could reach me there, way back in the Bush. I'd been to Kenya, years ago with Ellie, but had never seen what I wanted, a big kill of one of the Big Six, never been close to the migration of wildebeest, never gone to the Northern Frontier and Lake Rudolf to tie into those hundred-pound perch, never been through Savo to Mombasa, never swum off Melindi, never seen Marsabit, and Ahmed the biggest elephant in the world, never got what I wanted out of that awesome dark continent. If I went alone now, alone with one hunter, I could go way back and lose myself there, lose everyone else too. Yes, I'd cable tonight, and I'd forget, really forget that ungrateful, self-righteous suck.

I began to laugh. Ellie should see me now, I thought. Controlled?

I stopped by the theater a minute to see if there was any mail, held the cab at the curb, clock down. Actors keep going back to the theater where their last play closed like cubs nuzzle their dead mother.

Rudy, the doorman, was dozing in his little booth. "Someone in there," he said, pointing toward the darkened stage, "waiting for Mr. Castleman."

Curiosity got me.

He came out of a shadow, passed the seventy-five-watt pilot bulb, becoming a silhouette, the rays behind long and dark.

I'd seen him once before. The last week of the run of the play Sidney didn't even show up to collect his pay. He'd called in to ask me to sign for the dineros and give them to someone he'd send. The one he sent was this man, a tall black who wore reddish brown cord-du-roi trousers tucked into boots of oxblood red, knee-high with hooks not eyes and built on platform soles and heels that made him look even taller. Over his shoulders hung a cape of midnight blue with white piping. On top of his Afro was a broad-brim hat of psychedelic purple, a feather in the hatband. The compulsory dark glasses were worn even here on this stage, which was darker than night. This freak had come to my dressing room on that payday and asked for "Sid's bread," held out his hand with a suggestion of impatience. I surrendered the envelope. I didn't hear from Sidney afterward so I supposed he got the money.

Now here was this same man approaching me on three-inch heels at the same time completely ignoring my presence.

"Where Sid at?" he asked.

'You tell me," I answered.

He looked at me as if I'd committed an impertinence, said, "He's late," as if that was some way my fault, then walked back into the shadows.

That was the last push I needed out of this city.

On our dining-room table there was a note from Ellie: "We've gone to class. Back at six with makings."

The class was jujitsu and met a few blocks away at a karate "institute."

'We" included her ten-year-old son, Arthur. "Little Arthur," his mother called him.

He was the son of Ellie's former, Lewis Doyle, one of those nun-stunned urban paddies you can still find in our police and fire stations, also in banks. Lewis was an investment counselor. He wore his hair exactly as his mother had first combed it at the age of seven months, slicked straight down from a center part and glazed with a tonic. "Lace Curtain Louie," Sidney had dubbed him, adding that his mother got her terms mixed, ordered her son castrated at birth instead of circumcised.

Little Arthur has a problem. Me. When Ellie divorced his father, enter the Intruder! Every time I touched the kid, offering friendship, he edged away. "Don't rush it," Ellie advised. "It's going to take time." But I was never sure Ellie wanted this relationship improved.

Well, that's not a very kind thought. But I firmly believe that Ellie would let anyone, me included, bleed to death at her feet in order to hustle down to the corner drugstore for a Contac pill if Little Arthur sneezed. They were birds in a nest.

For a while I thought the boy was getting too attached to his mother. He was always fondling her and hugging her while looking at me as if he wished I'd vanish. But just when I was convinced she was making a sissy of the kid, Ellie did one of those things that surprise me, pleasantly. She took him and herself to this karate institute.

Jujitsu is self-defense, so they say. Ellie took to it for the same reason she revered *The Well-Tempered Clavier*, it boxed the strongest kind of feeling—murder, isn't it?—in the most controlled and precise form. She admired its aesthetics, she said.

Ellie told me after the first month that I should come see "the work," I'd be proud of Little Arthur, she said. So when I decided that afternoon to get out of Schlossberg country, I also decided to do that one thing before departing. Maybe then I wouldn't feel guilty about leaving the two of them alone in this nine-million-member street fight.

It was test day at the institute. The new pupils were being examined, one by one, for form and dexterity. Those who had, in the opinion of their instructor, made sufficient progress were to be awarded belts of a heavy yellow cloth.

I sat on the floor near the entrance to the large room at the feet of an elderly Japanese gentleman who wore a robe of the old culture. This austere patriarch, whom Ellie adored, faced the action but at no time responded, any more than a stone lantern would, to what happened on the floor. He seemed to be looking only within himself. Thus he created the dominant mood of the room, devotion to form and tradition.

Ellie and Little Arthur were two of perhaps thirty, dressed in white and sitting on their buns in two lines across the length of the floor. One by one, the instructor was putting the acolytes through a series of throws and falls, grading them on a card but showing no reaction.

Ellie had her fine red hair pulled straight back and under her glasses. She looked immaculate in her whites, a teen-ager.

As soon as she saw me she found a way to crawl over without attracting attention and kissed me.

"You look tired, baby," she whispered. "Did you have a bad day?"

"I did."

"Well, don't mind. Watch. You've got a surprise coming. I'm so glad you came."

The instructor had started on Little Arthur. "He might get a yellow belt today," Ellie held up her hand, crossed two fingers.

As we watched, I dropped a whisper that I'd decided to take the role in the new play. That didn't thrill Ellie. She didn't think much of that play or most plays I got myself into. In fact she didn't think a hell of a lot of what she called "the commercial theater."

I added that my young director-to-be would not accept Sidney as understudy.

"Sounds to be a very sensible young man," she said.

Then she hooked her arm through mine, pulling me close. "Now!" she pointed.

Ellie's Arthur was the youngest and the smallest in the class. But, zap!, he flipped his partner, a plump boy four inches taller, over his shoulder. When he had his practice victim on his back, he thrust his fist at the older boy's neck, pulling it up just a fraction of an inch from its target. The cry he released at this instant—"Aieeee!"—was so savage I could not believe it came from the kid to whom his mother had been reading *The Wind in the Willows* the Sunday previous.

"What do you say to that?" Ellie whispered.

"Wonderful," I said.

The instructor made a mark on his card and Little Arthur sat again, in perfect form, his heels under his butt. As he did he caught my eye, tossed off my admiration, turned his head straight ahead, and didn't move again until the tests were over.

Ellie's face was shining.

"God!" I said to her, woggling my head. "What happened to him?"

"I told you"—she was beautiful to see—"he's some kid!"

Then she looked at me, must have liked that I was so pleased with her son, or maybe she was sympathetic because I looked pooped, because what she said was spoken with loving concern.

"Why don't you go off for a vacation, baby? Now that you've got that job?"

"I think I will. I thought I might even go to Africa for a couple of weeks, you know, a complete change."

"Do that," she whispered. "You need it." She was still looking at Little Arthur proudly. "Don't worry about us. We can take care of ourselves."

"I can see that," I said. "I am just a little worried what will happen to—"

"Damn Sidney," she whispered through her teeth. "Go to Africa, go somewhere—"

"I thought I would, tomorrow."

"Good! And when you get back and are feeling better, can we have a new look at the whole thing—"

"What whole thing?"

"Oh. My turn." She hopped to her feet, trotted into place.

It wasn't the first time Ellie had hinted she wanted to have a "real talk."

Her partner was a Mrs. Horowitz, a horse of a housewife. Ellie immediately flipped this oater over her shoulder, which was quite a trick considering that my redhead breaks a hundred only after a spaghetti dinner.

A new look at what whole thing?

Ellie's generally a blurter, speaks straight and speaks quick. But for several weeks now, I'd had the feeling she was not saying something, or waiting for the right moment to say it.

Mother and son got yellow belts that afternoon. I congratulated them *con brio*. As we went out the door, I said, "I'm proud I have two great samurai protecting me in the streets."

"No cause to fear," Ellie winked at the kid, "Little Arthur's here!"

The boy winked back. He even smiled at me.

We charged down the stairs, all pleased with each other. There, at the street entrance waiting for us, was the man Sidney called "Lace Curtain Louie."

Ellie's former went from his mother's arms to a parochial school, then directly to his investment bank. Traveling that route he developed an ability to absorb punishment that I've never seen equaled in a human. I'd often told Ellie she should not have left this remarkable person. "He's the new man," I'd say, "uniquely adapted for yielding to strength in a woman."

Ellie didn't think my joke funny. "Lewis is a very decent human being," she'd reply.

In the catalog of this man's virtues, there was this special one: he loved his son every waking moment, worried about him steadily and painfully. He thought Ellie far too permissive, comparing her, unfavorably, with his mother.

He didn't approve of the jujitsu classes. What he approved of was trebling the police force. Long before their divorce he'd given up trying to influence Eleanor, feared crossing her on anything. But he kept calling on the phone to make sure Little Arthur went to bed when he was supposed to, that he gargled for his postnasal drip, and that his stool was firm. All this was not easy to check on because Ellie would not let him into the house and the telephone still cannot peer into a toilet bowl.

The terror of this good person's life was the "neegro." Lewis was an encyclopedia of details for every new mugging on the Upper West Side.

Tonight he had a new tale, told as he bought us ice cream cones. An old woman in the building next to his had entered the passenger elevator to find herself alone with a "big black neegro." She had immediately blocked the closing door, following instructions of the organization known as the Concerned Citizens of the Upper West Side. Out in a flash, she found the stairs and began running down, a remarkable feat for a woman her age. She must have done it in some extraordinary style, pulling up her skirt to free her flabby old gams, because she heard her assailant laughing as he chased her down the stairs. Actually the amusement she provided this man broke his stride and saved her purse. She managed to get to the front door ahead of him. As she pulled it open, he caught her arm. She turned and bit his hand—dentures holding fast—then ran out into the street where her luck had brought a neighbor, male, with a large German Shepherd on a leash. She ran to the side of this person, whispering as much as she could get out before the black joined them.

He strolled up, as Lewis acted it out, with all the swagger of a motorcycle cop, nodded to the man with the dog, patted the animal on the head. Then he looked at the old lady, rubbing his hand where she'd bitten him, said, "Another time, baby," and ambled down the street.

"I hate this city," Ellie said.

"Did they call the cops?" I asked Lewis.

"There are no cops," he said. "They're spread out too thin."

"Their hands are full," Ellie added.

"Their hands are full of payola," I said.

"That's unfair," she said. "They do the best they can but—"

"There should be three times as many," Lewis said. "Actually one did come running out of that apartment house on my corner, just too late."

"Was he zipping his fly?" I asked.

"I don't know what you mean," Lewis said.

"I mean he was probably laying the janitor's daughter or watching the Knicks' play-off, or both. Simultaneously."

"Stop it," Ellie said, indicating Little Arthur.

"I really don't think," Lewis said, "that a man as intelligent as you should give the police of this city a bad name."

"The police of this city have a bad name," I said, "because they've earned it. That's how someone gets a bad name."

Lewis threw his empty cone into the gutter. "This ice cream," he said, "is all chemicals. Don't finish it, Arthur."

"I notice you finished yours," Little Arthur said, taking a big lick.

Lewis smiled proudly. The fresher the kid got, the bigger the man's smile.

"The police of this city," I said to Ellie, "are part of its underworld."

She started to reply, then swallowed whatever she was about to say. Again I had the impression she was postponing—what?

"We're at the mercy of those black neegroes," Lewis said. "I heard another story yesterday—"

"I'm afraid, Lewis," I said, "you're bigoted."

"I am not. Look," he pointed, "look at that girl!"

Nobody knew what he was talking about.

'What's that with her?" he asked.

No one answered.

"All right," he said. "It's a dog. Is it a big dog or a small dog?"

No one would say. Finally I couldn't stand the suspense. "It's big," I said.

'Now look there, what do you see?"

"Another girl," I said.

"What's she got with her?"

' Another dog."

"Big or small?"

"Big."

"Do I have to explain the significance of—"

"I don't think so," I said, "unless there is something you read into this recurring phenomenon that I am too naïve to—"

"Don't make fun of Lewis," Ellie said. "On this point he's one hundred percent."

"It's gotten so bad," Lewis said, "that if you're attacked on the street and want assistance, you don't holler help."

"Don't holler help!" I couldn't resist mocking him.

"What do they do, our neighbors, when you call for help?"

"They don't come out of their houses. Right?"

"They lock their windows. So how do you get them to come out?"

"I'll bite."

"Holler fire." He burst out laughing, then sobered with a crunch. "Arthur! Watch out crossing the street."

He grabbed the boy's hand and rushed him across the street, just making the light.

When Ellie and I caught up with them on the other side, Lewis was kneeling in front of his son holding up two quarters.

"So if any of them bother you," was the first thing we heard, "give them these."

"What are you doing, Lewis?" Ellie asked.

"I'm trying to protect my son," he said to her with a vigor that surprised me. He started to push the quarters down into the watch pocket at the front of the boy's trousers. "Mugging money," he explained to me. "Some of the fathers at the last meeting of the Concerned Citizens recommended this. The little neegro hoods when they get these quarters, they're temporarily satisfied and leave the white child alone."

"I don't want them." Little Arthur threw the coins in the gutter and ran down the street, making like a broken-field runner.

Lewis's eyes followed. "Isn't he beautiful?" he said. "Ellie, look at him go." Then he flipped over. "Don't leave him alone on the street, Ellie. It's getting dark. Stay with him!"

Immediately after Ellie had left, Lewis took my arm. "Let's take turns," he said. "I'll watch the boy one day, you do it the next. I mean only after he gets out of school in the afternoon. Or else he'll simply have to stay home. What do you say?"

"I'm going away for two or three weeks," I said.

"Going away? What for?"

Suddenly his eyes shifted down the street. "Mother of God!" he said and ran off.

There was a small crowd under the street lamp in front of our brownstone, Ellie and Little Arthur, two black men, and a heavily built older man in a snap-brim black Borsalino.

As I hurried up I saw that Ellie was unloading on Sidney as only she can.

One of the two blacks I recognized. Known as "Boots," he was the one who'd come for Sidney's pay.

At the curb was a man I'd not seen before, a short, thin fellow in his thirties, his small head perfectly shaped, a chocolate egg. His nose, if anything, was too small, too fine, his eyes, peepers without expression. He affected the clothes of an English country gentleman, dark brown ankle-high chukkas, gray flannel trousers under a brown jacket of houndstooth tweed with a small notched flap off one lapel, provided in case our squire, caught in a sudden squall, should wish to button under the neck.

Sidney was taking Ellie's tirade, as he did everything about her, with a big show of amusement. But I saw he was ill at ease. He kept glancing toward the small black, who held his eyes averted from the embarrassing spectacle of a friend, male, being scolded by a woman.

As I got close, Ellie saw me and stopped speaking.

"What were you people talking about?" I asked.

"I was telling Eleanor how well she looked," Sidney said in a sweep of gallantry. "Not like a girl, pretty, but like a woman, beautiful."

That must have come from one of Sidney's old plays.

Ellie, without a sound, mouthed, "Fuck yourself."

Sidney burst out laughing. "Charming," he said. Then he turned to his small black companion and introduced him. "This is my friend Frank Scott," he said.

When I offered my hand, Frank Scott reached out his, which was surprisingly limp.

"Your wife was telling Mr. Castleman to get off your back," he said. "What's the matter with her?"

Pulling Little Arthur by the hand, Ellie said to me, "I'm going in."

When Lewis started to follow, she turned on him. "Where are you going?"

"I thought I might come in. Just for a minute. About his leaving you alone, shouldn't we talk?"

"No," she said, digging for her key.

"Lace Curtain Louie," Sidney said, "I have guessed why you're so anxious, and I am going to help you."

Lewis gave him the look reserved for Christ-killers, said, "I will not be responsible for what happens here," and slithered away.

Ellie had the door of our building open. "Coming, dear?" she called to me. It was more than a hint.

"In a minute," I said.

The door closed on her and the boy. I heard the bite of the bolt.

"She's very nervous," Frank Scott said, "even for a white woman."

"Nervous is not the word, Frank," Sidney said. "Apprehensive. And with reason. These are parlous times. A woman alone in an apartment is at the mercy of every villain. That's why I rushed here," he turned to me. "I heard you were leaving the country."

"I decided that only an hour ago, how did you—?"

"My boy, I have a network of informers throughout the decaying corpse of the theater. I always know everything."

He hooked his arm through Frank Scott's, pulling him close, just as he had me thirty years before, the day I first heard, "You're with me now, kid."

"Rudy told you," I said, "Rudy, the doorman."

"Rudy is one of the faithful, yes. I gather that your predecessor in felicity"—he looked up at the front windows of our apartment, one story up—"is concerned that there might be an incident of some kind, a mugging perhaps or some other unfortunate occurrence while you're overseas."

"Lewis is afraid of everything."

"How would you like it if I stayed in your home while you're away? I just might be able to arrange to do that."

"Sidney, that's very kind of you but—"

"Then you can enjoy your vacation." Sidney turned and smiled at his new-found black buddy. "He looks exhausted, doesn't he, Frank, dangerously tired?"

"Sidney, thanks, but no thanks."

"You will certainly not get the rest you so badly need if you worry the whole time you're away. By the way, is it absolutely essential that we have this conversation on a sidewalk?"

He looked up again at our front windows. Little Arthur was watching us.

"I really have to pack, Sidney," I said.

"My point is that with me here, guarding your treasures"—he indicated the child in the window—"you should be able to rest easy. Do what I say, my boy, you'll be grateful later."

"Sidney," I said, "you know Eleanor can't stand the sight of you."

"In a woman, my friend, that generally masks an attraction."

"Not in this case, I assure you."

"Then there is nothing for you to be concerned about, is there? I will occupy that tiny study over the garden. I may rearrange some of the furniture, but—"

"Sidney," I said, "cut it out. Stop."

He looked at me, nodding a few times, promising—I knew his every sign—that I was going to pay for my impertinence.

"Frank, are we of the same opinion," he said, "that my friend here allows his wife far too much say in the management of his home?"

"My home is all right, Sidney."

"I certainly hope so. By the way, can you now afford to return that twenty dollars I loaned you?"

"I don't remember any—oh, yes. Sorry. Here." I slipped him a bill.

"Thank you." He blew at the edge of the money, found it to be only the twenty he'd requested, and gave me his sneer-smile. "I hear you've been looking everywhere for me, my boy."

Frank Scott consulted a very thin wristwatch.

"Yes, we haven't much time," Sidney said, "so tell me what it is you want."

I took the plunge. "Sidney," I said, "I've got bad news."

"After a certain age, all news is bad news."

"So right," Frank Scott said.

"I couldn't do it this time, Sidney."

"You can't do many things. What now, in particular?"

"I have a new play for the spring, a comedy. I don't think much of it but—"

"Come to the point, if you have one. What is it you couldn't do?"

"Get you—you know—the understudy."

Sidney's eyes flitted to Frank Scott—I'd never seen him so strung up—then back to me.

"Understudy!" he said. "What led you to believe I would ever understudy? I can't recall asking you to—did I do that?"

"Well, no, but—"

"You have exposed me to rejection for a kind of work I wouldn't accept under any conceivable circumstance. Who is the management? Answer!"

"Sol Bender."

"Sol Bender!" He turned to Frank with a laugh. "He used to be my stage manager."

"Well, he's not your stage manager now," I said.

"You mean to say that there is no part in that despicable little comedy that a Sidney Castleman might play?"

"They didn't think so."

"And you?"

"I didn't either. I mean, it's all the star's play. He never stops talking."

He looked at me a long time with that half smile, then he said, "Even you must see how the theater has disintegrated when you are offered a star role and I—" he turned to Frank Scott. "You see, Frank, now that the theater has crumbled into its final disintegration, they don't need actors anymore. What they need"—he pointed to me—"is zombies with memories, machines programmed to say tasteless lines on mechanical cues—"

"Sidney, what is the point of knocking everybody and anybody including me?"

"Somebody sooner or later has to say the truth. That's the point. Jokesmiths, all of you, laugh carpenters. Frank, the Theater of Theme and Poetry is dead."

I started for the house.

"Just a minute!" Sidney ordered in the voice he used to climax his big shiver scenes, "I'm not through with you."

I stopped. For another reason.

Ellie was at one of our front windows now, watching my humiliation under the street lamp. How long had she been there?

"Before you go," Sidney said to me—and his knee was quivering—"tell me what I did to give you the impression you could go around this city offering my services to assistant stage managers so I will not ever again—"

"Oh, fuck off, will you, Sidney?"

"Why do you insult my friend?" Frank Scott said.

"I've been trying not to."

"Try harder."

"Friendship doesn't give him the right to humiliate me, does it, Frank?"

"Mr. Castleman," Frank Scott said, "let's split."

"Do you think I'm in need of charity?" Sidney said, his foot tap-tapping the pavement in a rhythm I knew very well. "Is that it? Tell me."

"For chrissake, Sidney, you always took the goddamn jobs."

The instant I said that I knew I'd made a mistake.

Sidney was trembling all over. "Strictly as a favor," he said. "I assumed you knew that."

"Boots," I heard Frank Scott say, "get the car."

'It's right across the street," Boots said. He indicated a long gray Mercedes, a 400SL, and when I saw it I knew who Frank Scott was and why Sidney had been playing up to him so frantically.

Three weeks before, on the day Sidney dropped out as my understudy, he'd told me of a large group of black men, neocapitalists, doctors and dentists and anonyms, after "their share of the pie," who'd provided the backing for a new show on Broadway. The show had come up roses. Sidney, ever alert to the movement of money, had struck up a friendship with the nominal producer and through him, with one of its leading investors, this Frank Scott. I could see that Sidney had captivated this nifty little man, and I could guess the bold plans Sidney had to rechannel the moneys coming to Frank Scott from the new hit.

"I'm sorry, Sidney," I said, "but I went to see your landlord, and he told me you'd given him all your furniture to pay for three months' back rent. I mean, we might as well face facts, no?"

"Where you staying now?" Frank Scott asked Sidney.

"He's staying with me," Boots said from the middle of the street. "On the sofa. He told me not to tell you. Just for a night or two, he said. He's been there three weeks."

Sidney looked destroyed. But, the most resilient of men, he came back with, "It's only temporary. I am going to look for another accommodation directly after lunch tomorrow. It's not easy, Frank, to find anything satisfactory. My requirements are rather special. Meantime, since our show has closed, my income has been—its flow has been interrupted. I could go on relief, of course," he laughed heartily. "That might be an interesting experience for me, but I really wouldn't know how to go about arranging—"

"I'll get someone to help you," I said, trying to sound very off-hand.

"So, you want me to go on relief?"

"I didn't say that, but—"

Sidney put a heavy hand on my shoulder. "My old friend," he said. "I've been aware for some time now that beneath all your protests of concern and appreciation for what I've done for you, there is an underlying desire to destroy me, to see me dead."

"Sidney, stop it. Please!"

"Despite that," he said, "I have tried to be your friend—"

And then his eyes filled with tears, and it seemed he couldn't go on.

But I'd watched Sidney, year after year, from the wings, and I knew this was a trick of acting, one which Sidney had always been able to bring off. His tears did not mean he was in emotional distress. What emotion he was feeling was pride in his technique.

"What is it, Sidney?" I obliged by playing the supporting role.

"I have no place to stay," he said. "I must confess this to you, my two closest friends. I can't go on at Boots's place, occupying the sofa in his living room. It's not fair to him."

Again he looked toward the windows of our apartment, where Ellie was waving for me to come in.

"Frank," Sidney said, "do you see that lovely lady in the window?"

"Did you say you're sleeping on Boots's sofa?" Frank asked.

"Yes," Sidney said quickly, "a sort of bench." Then, back on his track, "I have lived an irregular life, Frank. At one time, years ago, I also had a lovely wife, the loveliest of the three I've enjoyed. Her name was Roberta." He looked at me. "You remember Roberta?"

"Yes," I said, "I remember Roberta."

"She had the longest hair, Frank, of raven's hue, light as silk threads in a breeze. And she used to— Frank, are you listening?"

Frank looked at the old actor, whose eyes were heavy with tears. "I'm digging you, dad," he said.

"She used to wait for me to come home from rehearsals," Sidney went on, "as eagerly as Eleanor is waiting for him there now. Well, let's not exaggerate, we did have one good year. Then the pressures of my libido became uncontrollable. When she found out, of course, she behaved as women must. Infidelity is their only reprisal."

"Sidney," I said, "didn't it cut both ways?"

He ignored me. "I have forgotten and I have forgiven, Frank, the way Roberta behaved because I understand the lady is dead. But it is more difficult"—he turned to me—"to forgive some of my close friends who cooperated with her, men who've been jealous of me all my life and would and did use any means to get the better of me. You remember," he said to me.

"I remember Roberta. I just told you I did."

"But in our first great days," Sidney rolled right over me, "I used to come home from rehearsals and there she'd be at the window. When she saw me, she'd make a sign with her hand that was barely perceptible but promised everything and caused my heart to beat like it did just now when I saw his wife, Eleanor, beckoning him to come in. Where did she go?"

Ellie had disappeared into the house.

Sidney turned and looked at me in the most mysterious way. "Go on in," he said with his half smile. Was he jealous? "She's waiting for you."

He dropped his head. "Frank, oh, Frank," he said, "how I have devastated my years. I'm a fool, Frank. My friends laugh at me, and they think I don't know it."

Frank Scott put his arm around Sidney. "I don't laugh at you, daddy," he said. "I'm going to take care of you."

He turned to Boots, who had driven the Mercedes close, and he said, "Go get Mr. Castleman's stuff and bring it to my place."

"You sure?" Boots said. "Because, man, there's a mess. All kinds of papers and books, old magazines, shit out of the newspapers, boxes of shoes and hats, you don't know!"

"Go get it," Frank said. "Put it in my room. Go on, Boots. What are you waiting for?"

"Yes," Sidney said. "You're a new friend, Frank, but a good one. Where did you say we were going from here? I am at your disposal."

"To my place," Frank said. "You're with me now, kid." He laughed with pleasure to be using the old man's phrase.

"Oh, now, now," Sidney said, "that's extremely generous of you, but it's not necessary."

"I don't do nothing because it's necessary," Frank Scott said.

"But you hardly know me," Sidney said, and he looked at me.

"How much more would I know about you, daddy, in a year?" Frank Scott said.

"Well, all right, Frank. Since you insist, I accept. I hope it's not too crowded. All right! There. You have me."

Then he turned to me and touched my cheek. Triumphant, he was.

"I'm sorry," he said, "that you won't invite me into your house, even for a drink. I'm sorry, that is, for you. Your wife has you terrorized."

"My wife has me what?"

"Terrorized. I know you as a more generous man than the one Frank has been observing. He is, Frank. I love this undistinguished-looking person, even now when he's betrayed me again. You can see—look at him, Frank—you can see how ashamed he is."

Just that bit of truth. I believe I was blushing.

Frank Scott saw that I was. "You got to stay on top of 'em," he said. "You got to be boss."

"I'm boss," I said.

"You don't look it," he said.

"This man," Sidney went on, tasting and retasting triumph, "believe it or not, plays leading roles on stage, heroes yet! Still he is so intimidated by his wife that he won't invite me, his lifelong benefactor, into his home for liquid refreshment and a moment's peace."

"It's because I'm with you," Frank Scott said. "Schwartzuh!"

"Like hell it is," I said.

"Then why is it?" Sidney asked. "I'm puzzled. Why have you never, not once over all the years, invited me into—"

"This is not a good time," was the best I could come up with.

"It's her loss, of course," Sidney said. "Women, you should know by now, once they marry, scrunch up into defensive postures, become increasingly timid and wary. They suspect everyone is after their husband, if not his cock, his money, if not his money, just his time. But"—and he waggled his finger—"you are still aspiring, are you not, to be some measure of an artist? If so you should remember that kind of uxorious supervision—'Coming, darling?' " he imitated Ellie—"is anathema! Now Frank, who is an artist by temperament, not by trade, he knows what I'm talking about. Were you ever married, Frank?"

"Never," Frank Scott said.

"Unimaginable!" Sidney said. Then, referring to me again, "Of course you were never what one could in good conscience call an artist. You are, at your best, a technician. There have never been any surprises, any unexpected illuminations in your performances. They have always been, I regret to say, completely predictable. That is why you've never become a true star."

I had no answer.

Before dismissing me with a wave of his cane and going off with his new captive, Sidney gave me the following instruction: "Find Paul Prince immediately. From him obtain a copy of *Titan*. I had only one clean copy left. Someone broke into my apartment and stole it. the third I've lost that way. Leave the script backstage with Rudy the doorman. I will pick it up in the morning. Tell Rudy he must keep it under lock. Everyone in town is conniving to get hold of that manuscript. Is that clear?"

"Sidney, I don't think I can—"

He didn't hear a word, riding that high. "Tell Prince," he said, "that I suddenly see daylight on the problem of financial sponsorship."

He turned, hooked his arm through Frank's, and started toward the Mercedes 400SL.

"Sidney"—I was looking at two backs—"I really can't run your errand tomorrow. It's my last day in the country, and I want to spend it with Ellie."

He wheeled on me.

"You are going to spend the night with her, are you not?"

"Yes, but—"

"So! I assure you there is nothing you might do tomorrow as important as what I've asked. I will expect the manuscript."

I think I nodded.

Frank Scott enjoyed the traditional moment of largess before departure. He pulled some little cards out of his pocket. "Your family bowl?" he asked, handing me the slips.

"No," I said.

"See that they learn," Sidney said. "It's the perfect family sport."

On the slips was printed, "Scotty's Lanes." Then in smaller print, along the bottom, "A Division of Frank Scott Enterprises." Diagonally across the cards in open red print was stamped "Complimentary."

The Mercedes disappeared effortlessly, leaving a memory image of my friend Sidney and his friend Frank sitting side by side in the back seat, at ease together.

As I opened the door I heard Chopin. Ellie was lying on the sofa, listening to Brailowsky playing one of the Preludes.

"Don't ever bring any of that riffraff into my house," she said.

"I'll bring anyone I want into my house," I answered, ready for battle.

But there was no return fire.

"Did you hear what I said, Ellie?"

"Yes."

I, terrified? She was the one, she looked frightened.

"What got you so worked up out there?" I asked.

"Oh, I'm sorry. I can't bear the man, but that's no reason to scold him in front of his pals, is it?"

"Well, so?"

"When I came up, he put his arms around me and kissed me."

"He was telling us how seductive you looked in the window."

She laughed.

"Imagine being stuck in an elevator with that man."

"What put that thought in your head?"

"Could you ask your friend not to kiss me on the mouth? I had to gargle."

She looked at me, seemed about to say something, then closed her eyes.

I took my coat off and stretched out on the sofa.

The prelude was the "Raindrop," one of Arthur's favorites. Big Arthur.

Arthur was the other presence in my life, even though his name was never mentioned.

When Ellie was nineteen, she'd left Swarthmore and her father's home, defying every standard propriety with a boldness only the pure in heart have, to move in with a young man, Arthur, a student at the same school whose passion for music equaled her own. At the back of Carnegie Hall there are apartments. They'd taken a small one. Ellie had described the place to me. It contained two grand pianos, fitted to each other, and one narrow bed. There they'd spent their days playing the great symphonies and concerti arranged for four hands and their nights fitted like the halves of the Zen egg.

That was their perfect time. How could anything afterward match it?

Arthur was a youth who lived only for music. Nearsighted to the point of blindness, he knew no other experience, except Ellie. He walked the streets of the city, on the rare occasions when he left their musical heaven, head held high, as Ellie described him, seeing nothing clearly beyond the tip of his nose.

Then one day he disappeared. Ellie found out where he'd gone from the morning paper. He must have been holding his head high when he stepped off the curb into the path of a marauding U.S. mail truck.

This disaster was the genesis of her anxiety about safety and her hatred of the city.

A year later she'd married the most dependable man she could find, Lewis Doyle, first warning him that she had little love to give, he'd have to take her, if he wanted her, as she was.

When she began to see me, she told me the whole story, without tears, promised when we married she'd never mention Arthur's name. She asked one favor, that she be allowed to keep a photograph of Arthur in the house. It was in our bedroom. I'd respected her loss.

She'd sold her piano but placed Arthur's in storage for safekeeping.

I had the same thought you must have had, that Little Arthur was—but the dates proved it. Little Arthur was Lewis Doyle's son. Lewis had agreed to the name Ellie wanted to give the baby.

A living "in memoriam." No wonder we didn't get along, Little Arthur and I.

I'd come to accept this perfect ghost's presence in my life, but it rankled me in times of tension. When she stared at the ceiling as she was now, I knew whom she saw there. When she referred to "the commercial theater," my profession, I knew what the opposite comparison was.

"He's taken over Sidney," I said, breaking the silence. "Frank Scott has."

"I wish him luck," she said, not moving.

"Can you hear me all right?"

"Yes."

"Mind if I turn this thing down a bit?"

"Switch it off if you want. I don't like the way he plays."

I tempered Brailowsky.

"Did you give him money?" she asked.

Is that what was troubling her? She must have seen something from the window. Nevertheless I lied. It was none of her business.

"He didn't ask me for any," I said.

"Why do you lie about that, baby?"

"I'm not. He didn't ask me for any money."

Chopin reproached my lie. Ellie looked at the ceiling.

"Oh God, all right, oh, all right," she said. "It doesn't matter."

"What he did ask was to come live here while I was away."

"When's he moving in?"

"Oh, Ellie, come on."

"Well, you have to admire the man's gall," she said.

"Then he said he forgave you."

"For what?"

"I don't know. What did you do to him?"

"Turned him down once. I told you about that."

There were all kinds of reasons we call instinctive for the way Eleanor felt about Sidney, but looking back I see a single incident.

When Eleanor and I were matching up, before she left Lewis and while I was still married, not biologically but by living at home, Sidney let us use his place at the Plaza to meet. It was high above the park, high enough so we didn't have to pull down the shades. We'd go there late mornings while Sidney was indulging himself at the Luxor Baths and Baby Arthur was in the park with his nanny. We'd pleasure a few hours, then Ellie'd do some of what she'd told her husband she was going to spend the day doing, shopping. I'd go to the Lambs, chew my cud till it was time to hoist one at Sardi's Little Bar, then inside for a cannelloni or a butterfly steak. Those were the good times! I had the joy of Ellie without the grief. Every time we saw each other we blessed the day.

Anyway, the incident. It was one of those miracle mornings at the end of March that promise a perfect summer, the sky a wash of the purest blue and under it a breeze like warm silk. I thought our date was for the day following, but Ellie still maintains— O.K., it's my fault. Girls are so uncertain, they have to be right.

When Ellie arrived that morning, she pulled back Sidney's green velvet curtains, threw his windows up as high as they'd go—it was such a soft spring day! Then she took off her clothes and laid herself out in front of the open window to let the breeze wash her. When she heard the key in the lock, she was in the state of perfect anticipation. Wishing to prolong those delicious moments, she didn't bother to look up.

In walks Sidney.

And he did like Sidney. Without saying a word, he went into his bedroom, undressed, and suddenly there he was, beside her on the sofa, beginning what preliminaries he bothers with, which, from what girls have told me, are minimal.

You'd think the fact that Ellie was my girl might make a difference, but it probably never crossed Sidney's mind. We were that close those years and several times had shared a secret acquaintance.

"Well, what did you do?" I asked Ellie later that day.

"What could I do? He was clamped to me. 'Mr. Castleman,' I said, 'may I ask what in the hell you think you're doing?' Guess what he said."

" 'Relax, kid, you're with me now.' "

"Can you believe it?"

"What did you claw his face for? He's got to go on stage tonight."

"I did just what daddy taught me."

Ellie's father was Air Force, one star (now retired to Florida), and he'd instructed his daughter how to take care of herself in a one-on-one combat situation.

When Sidney pulled his face back from her nails, she gave him her knee.

All men are old-fashioned when they get it in the jewels. All will respond the same way. But when Sidney clouts a girl, it's a matter of principle. He's putting her back where he's convinced she belongs. And he went further. In his biggest manner, he informed her that he'd made a careful study of her personality—they'd met exactly once before!—and she was definitely not the type of girl I should switch to, if I was going to switch, because she was competitive and a stone crusher, so born, so bred. What I needed, Sidney said, holding his sack, was a peasant, a girl-lady, not a man with a cunt.

The next day Sidney had completely forgiven her. That too was part of his code, the generosity of the superior male animal. But he told me again I should have a peasant for a wife. Why the hell, he wanted to know, did I always go for dominant bitches, intellectual pseudos? O.K. to fuck, but for a wife, look out!

"I suppose he wanted another shot at it," I said over the sound of Brailowsky's piano. "You want a drink?"

"No, thanks," she said as she got up. "I can't stand the way this man plays Chopin," she moved in on the machine. "All that mush!"

Ellie, and Big Arthur, thought of Chopin as a classicist and a contemporary. None of that "consumptive genius playing his heart out in an abandoned monastery on rain-swept Majorca" crap for them! They'd played Chopin, she told me, as if he was living today. In Hartford, no doubt.

"Sounds all right to me. Leave it on if you like."

She cut Brailowsky down in the middle of a run.

"Anyway, I'm glad he's off your back," she said.

"Actually, he has no money coming in, and he will not go on relief."

"For chrissake," she said, "half this city is on relief!"

"Sidney will not stand in line for anything."

I poured for myself. I needed a fight.

"Well, maybe I will," she said, "have a drink. Half."

I stalled over the pouring, drank mine, poured me another. Then I did hers.

"Why the hell do you feel totally responsible for his welfare?" she said when I gave her her drink. "He hasn't an honest bone—"

"Will you stop asking me that. You've asked me that one thousand times."

"All right."

"Maybe it's illogical, but it's my goddamn—"

I gave up. She wasn't listening.

"Every time we run into that man," Ellie said, "we're both upset for days."

"I'm not upset."

"If you say so."

"I just can't stand the way actors are treated."

"Did you notice his eyes? Glazed? Sort of fixed?"

I'd noticed. But to Ellie I said, "Nonsense."

She dropped the lid of the record player. "What's that you're holding?" she asked.

It was a tiny cardboard box that Frank Scott had given me with the complimentary tickets to Scotty's Lanes.

Ellie came up as I opened it. "A sample of his wares?" she asked.

Frank Scott had given me a pair of tortoise shell cuff links in the shape of bowling balls. I freed one from its cardboard clasp and showed it to her.

"Pretty," I said.

"Throw them away. I won't have you wearing that man's gifts."

"You won't have me! I'll wear any goddamn thing I want."

So much for "terrified."

I knew as soon as I got into bed that it was going to be one of those nights. My wife is easy to read in bed. When she lies on her back, staring at the space above her, I know who's up there. And she was still wearing her glasses.

But it was my last night home, and I decided to make an effort to break the ice. This is not my strong point, warming a cool. There is something obdurate in my foolish nature that makes it impossible for me to make the first move.

"You go around all day apologizing to everyone else," I said to myself after she'd turned off the light and lay stiff as a plank on her side of the bed. "Why the hell can't you say a sweet word to your goddamn wife?"

"Because there's nothing to apologize to her for," I answered myself. "She should apologize to me for what Sidney said."

"I really admire," I said out loud, "what you're doing with Little Arthur."

She didn't answer, didn't move.

"I mean, for a sensitive kid who I always thought was afraid to mix it up with other kids, he amazed me."

"He's not afraid of other kids. Why do you think that?"

"I didn't say exactly that, afraid. But you know what I mean. He's just not physical."

"He has his own way of being physical. Why do you want him to be like other kids?"

"I don't want that," I said, working the one sure road to her heart. "The way he threw that other kid around! He's a terrific boy."

"I always told you that," she said.

"How did you get him to do it? Last I heard, he was saying he wouldn't go."

"You've always underrated him."

"Not true. I've always liked that kid despite the fact he doesn't give me the time of day."

She was still looking at the ceiling. I began to consider going to sleep.

"He can do anything when it's got a form to it," she said.

I didn't know what she was talking about. "I know what you mean," I said.

"And he loves his Sensei."

"Sen—what?"

"Sensei. Teacher. Instructor."

"Yeah, he seemed like a terrific guy."

"You see, Arthur's had to look for a substitute father. I mean Lewis is Lewis, and you're always somewhere else, rehearsing or on the road or whatever you do all day."

"Of course, you're absolutely right," I said. Craven, craven! But I didn't want to fight that night. I wanted to be a lover that night.

"He needs a father image," she went on, "every kid does, especially these days, and the time's coming when he has to go out in the park alone. He's getting up to eleven years old and—"

"I can take him to the park."

"Oh, come on." Her face was tense, and she looked paler than I'd ever seen her. How women vary in their appearance, how they suddenly look old! "We don't expect anything from you," she said.

"Well, I don't have control of my hours, you know that."

"I know what hours you rehearse," she said. "I know when you have time and when you don't. You just don't want to. By the way, did you read that article I put on your bureau?"

"What article?"

"Out of the *Village Voice*. I put it under your hair brush. About that couple who made a marriage contract. Division of duties."

"Baby, both those people work."

"It said work which brings in money is no more privileged than work in the home."

"Is that what you've been getting ready to lay on me?"

"I've been—what?"

"I've had this eerie feeling for days that you've been rehearsing a speech to be directed at me when the right moment came."

"That's your guilty imagination."

A denial tells you when you've hit the bull in the eye. So that's all it was, that fucking *Voice*.

"All I ever started to say was that I really admire what you're doing with the kid, and that you looked pretty good out there yourself."

"And I was never physical-ed minded in school either."

"At least ten years younger than those other tomatoes."

"Don't try to get around me that way."

Still it worked. She becomes like a little girl when she's praised.

A minute later she turned to me and said, "You know that Chinese restaurant below the institute? That fellow has been held up three times."

"Three times! No."

"Yes, and they never got a cent. You saw him, the owner, that squinty little man."

"That little nothing?"

Actually, I couldn't recall him.

"And they never got one cent."

"How does he do it?"

I could hear myself sounding a lot more interested than I was. After all, I'm an actor, and it was in a good cause.

"I'll show you," she said. "Get up."

"You mean now? Out of bed?"

"Now. Come on." She was out, wearing panties and glasses but no bra. Her breasts are small but in great shape for a lady with a kid.

I was bare-ass naked.

"Come at me," she said, "as if you have a knife."

"In which hand?"

"Either one. Come on. I won't hurt you."

My acting performance would not have won a Tony.

As I came at her she grabbed my wrist, stepped to one side, twisted my arm over and across my body, and when I pulled away, instead of backing off she came toward me, put a foot behind one of mine, and pushed me over her ankle. I was on the floor, she standing over me, twisting my wrist.

"I've dropped the knife," I shouted.

She laughed. "That's called tai-saba-kee," she crowed.

"That was great," I said.

"Did I hurt you?"

"No. Well, maybe a little."

She took off her panties and her glasses, jumped back in bed, pulled her pillow near mine, and was suddenly very girllike. When I got into bed, cautiously, she gave me her most reassuring smile, scooted over to my side, put her leg over mine, and offered her face.

"I want you to know," I said, "about this African vacation. I feel a little guilty leaving you here. I mean this city is getting pretty dangerous."

"Oh, don't worry about that now," she said, climbing on top of me. Oh, when this Yankee lady goes on the offensive!

Now I must describe certain gymnastics.

Without interrupting what was happening, I had the cunning to make one quick adjustment. I turned us around so I could brace my feet against the headboard. Our bed has no barrier at its base.

Then everything was perfect, she holding me around the chest and the back of the head, I holding in cupped hands where she was busiest. And—

I was looking into the eyes of Arthur, no, not the living ghost, the photograph in its place of honor on the little shelf above and behind our bed.

He wasn't looking at me, oh no, way past me, head held high.

This was not the moment to be generous.

I had to turn us over.

But she resisted. That is her favorite position, on top, and she wasn't about to give it up.

Arthur watched the skirmish with perfect composure. For the first time I noticed that a slight smile lifted the ends of his lips and that his eyes, those treasures, were veiled, in disapprobation, no doubt.

Ellie fought like a cat, reviving the memory of the encounter where I'd come at her holding a "knife" and been humiliated.

I finally had to say, "Ellie!" Meaning, "Please!"

At this she gave in, a gracious victor.

But in the struggle our friend has slipped out. When I went to reengage, there was only half left.

I did the best I could with what I had.

"I'm sorry," I said when it was over.

"Oh, that's all right," she said. "It's happening all over now."

"What is? Happening all over?"

"Our liberation, it's got men sort of uncertain. They can't get it up or if they do, they get it up like you did, you know, half, then they come right away. They're not used to women, the way we're becoming. They're used to those oh-you're-just-wonderful type girls."

"I like the way you are."

"You didn't act like it." She laughed and kissed me. She seemed pleased with herself, even with me.

"Well—" I was completely stymied.

"You know," she said, "I read in the *Voice* that impotence has become fashionable among French intellectuals."

"I wasn't impotent."

"I didn't say you were. But you were, you know, you have an adjustment to make. But with these French intellectuals, it's their way of fighting back."

"Fighting what back?"

"Us."

She smiled in a way I didn't altogether like, but it was my last night, and I didn't want another argument.

"It's a whole new thing between man and woman," she said.

"I see what you mean." Final surrender.

"Now, I want to ask you something."

"Go ahead."

"Don't get sore. Just try to tell me why you feel so apologetic to Sidney Schlossberg."

"Apologetic?"

"Yes. You're not responsible that he can't make a living. Maybe Mr. Schlossberg should get a job, a real job."

"Like what?"

"He'd make a great headwaiter at one of those snooty places."

"There is absolutely nothing else that man can do."

"The commercial theater is O.K., I guess, if you're on top, but for a man like Sidney, it's an illusion. *Titan!* Christ! The truth is, even you're lucky to get the work you get."

"I know I am," I said.

But I didn't like that remark.

"I don't mean to hurt you," she said, "but I must tell you I sometimes wish you had another profession."

"Too late, Ellie."

"You know who I met on the street yesterday? Jack Deming? Remember him?"

"Sure. A pretty fair actor."

"You know what he's doing? Taking a course in motel management, and he's older than you are."

"I know, and Tommy Collichio, remember little Tommy in that play? He picked me up in a cab the other day. He was driving it. A lot of actors are driving cabs now."

"That's what I mean."

"But those guys never got anywhere."

She let that one hang.

"I'm not going to drive a cab, Ellie."

"Who said you should?"

"And I'm not going into motel management."

"I don't want you to, but suppose things get worse. You're successful now, O.K., but—"

"Are you all that worried?"

"Because I love you, I really do. I guess I was taken in, when we met. I saw you up there on stage, the big he-man and all. But you're not as strong as I thought. I mean—"

She kissed me.

"I mean you're human, and I'm glad you're the way you are, because I know you need me."

"I'm still not going into motel management."

"Oh, sweetheart," she said, "all I really want is for you to stay home every day all day"—what she and Arthur used to do—"in bed with me. O.K.? Like this."

But I knew the facts. She had no respect for my profession. The only true art for her was music, and the only true artist a memory.

For whatever perverse reasons, this made me want her again.

"You don't have to—" she said.

"But I want to."

"No, you don't, not really."

She was right. What I wanted was to lie close and sleep.

Which I did. For a while.

Gunfire woke us. From the street. Three shots, then two more, that made five. Six. Seven.

"What's that?" she asked.

"Just a sidearm, I think."

"Just a sidearm!"

"Nine. Ten."

"Has it ever occurred to you that we don't have to live in this rotten city?"

There were the sounds of someone shouting and running in the street along the park.

"Have to read the paper tomorrow," I said.

"There won't be anything in the paper. You call that news?"

She cuddled close, wrapped her slim arms around me.

"There are too many people," she said.

"In the city?"

"Everywhere. If everybody in the world had an acre of ground, there'd be no more wars."

"They'd want two acres."

"I guess so." And she fell asleep.

In the morning she was still close against me and very warm, smelled of sleep and love and I—oh, God, I hate this word, it's for circus animals!—I did perform better.

After, she was simple and loving, the way she used to be at the beginning, said she'd go shopping with me and pack for me and stay with me right till the plane left.

We declared the day a holiday.

She took her bath slowly and carefully like she used to when we were first together and fucked a lot and, afterward, her body was sore all over.

I lay in bed and thought.

Here I was, connected with two perfect idealists, as different as hot and cold, but both lofty and superior and patronizing. "Everything I do is beneath them," I thought. "Still, they take their daily bread from me."

Then I thought, "Why should I give a damn what that man says about me? To the point where I get all worked up and can't make proper love to my wife and Ellie and I have to talk about it seriously as a family problem?

"Christ, we survive by forgetting, so this one's easy, forget Sidney Schlossberg. Blot him out."

I went for orange juice. It didn't loosen the knot in my stomach.

I took out a piece of paper, found a pencil. Maybe, I thought, if I wrote all his slurs down, then tore up the paper, that magic would make it possible for me to forget the poison and enjoy the holiday Ellie and I had declared.

"Just a mechanic," I wrote. "Everything you do is predictable," I wrote. "If only once you'd give us some illumination into the soul of—" I wrote, and "Zombie with a memory," "Laugh carpenter," "Audience whore," and so on. Everything I could remember that monster had said.

Then I tore up the paper, ritualistically, and flushed it down and away.

And felt worse.

"What's the matter, baby?" Ellie said. She'd come to make coffee.

"Nothing."

She put her arms around me. "You've had bad thoughts. Were they about me?"

"I was going over the things that old man said about me yesterday with that coco-head bobbing his coco as if he had the least idea what Sidney was talking about and him making a goddamn fool of me there—"

"You're a little late," she said. "He's only been saying stuff like that about you for twenty-five years."

"Well, I'm fed up with it."

"Praise the Lord!"

"And you were right about his eyes. They were glazed."

"Of course they were."

"That man is out of control. He shouldn't be allowed to wander around carrying a cane with a sword in it, insulting people."

Ellie laughed. "Has he got a sword in that cane?"

"He sure has, and I'm going to take a bath."

She put her arms around me again. "Don't be sore at me today, sugar, if you can help it."

"What makes you think I might be sore at you? Something you're thinking but haven't yet said?"

"Where did you get that idea?"

"Don't put down my profession, Ellie, that's the one thing I've got."

"I wasn't doing that."

"You said you wished I was in another profession."

"Every once in a while I do but—"

"And if you possibly can, stop all that two-bit psychologizing and heckling and criticizing. You think you could maybe stop that?"

She turned away.

"And if you want to give me a real thrill sometime, relax that Yankee ramrod you've got up your ass. I mean, admit you're wrong about one thing, just one small thing."

I got a yogurt from the ice box, went into the bathroom.

I was looking into the mirror trying to puzzle out why the hell I'd said what I'd said, when I heard her come in the bedroom to dress.

"Ellie," I called out, "I'm sorry."

No answer.

"Sidney said something yesterday that upset me."

I could hear her curse.

"What did you say, baby?" I asked.

"I said upset you about what?"

"About the way we were, you and I."

She stood in the doorway. "Have you really found a way to take that man seriously?"

"He did get under my skin."

"You know I love you to death. You know I'm going to miss you every day you're gone and ten times more at night. You know that."

"I know," I said.

"So don't eat that yogurt. I'm making you a big breakfast."

I made my bath Japanese-hot, sat in it, and ate my yogurt, slowly.

I could hear her. She'd heated up the record player. *The Well-Tempered Clavier* again. I was bloody tired of her Arthur, even though she'd kept her promise and never spoken his name.

Goddamn it, what Sidney said was true. I couldn't invite him and his friends into my house, and it was because of her.

I got up and began to dry my body. Then I got back into the tub and soaped myself. I'd forgotten to soap myself.

She was reading the paper, sipping coffee.

"Why do you read that?" I asked her. "It ruins your day every day."

She put the *Daily News* on the table and slid it to me.

"No thanks," I said. I could read the headline upside down, something about a cop killing a kid by accident. "Our finest are at it again," I said.

She didn't pick up.

"These are good," I said. I was putting away her specialty, French toast covered with honey and dusted with nutmeg.

No answer. She looked very uptight.

"I know I look simply awful today," she said, "but I don't know a thing in the world to do about it."

"Don't start your day every day by reading that kind of shit, that's what you can do about it."

She made no sign, but again I had the impression there was something on the tip of her tongue she wasn't saying.

"You know," I said, "there are some people dressed in blue who all you got to do is look at them and you know they shouldn't be given guns to use whenever they get that itch in the finger."

Now she looked at me.

"I want a favor of you before you go," she said.

"What favor is that?"

"I want you to go somewhere with me."

"Where? I mean sure, but where?"

"Just up the street from the travel office."

"I've got to go see—"

"Your agent. I know. This'll only take half an hour."

"Where you planning to take me?"

"You'll see."

She didn't say anything more. When I looked at her, she started to clear the table.

"Ask me to be true to you while I'm gone," I said.

"You ask me to be," she said, disappearing in the kitchen.

When she came back, I put it to her.

"Come on now. What's the big mystery? Tell me where you want me to go."

"If I told you now, you'd find a way to get out of it."

"I'm going to do it to the first lioness I find in heat."

"I know you've been planning something like that—and not with lions. And I know the reason."

"And what is that?"

"To prove you're no French intellectual, Sonny," she said. Then, quickly, "I'm sorry. That was below the belt."

She has an enchanting smile when she scores.

In Abercrombie and Fitch, filling out my safari wardrobe, I remembered how cold it gets on the equator at night when you're up seven thousand feet.

"What I'd really like," I said, "is a pair of flannel PJ's. It's going to be cold at night without your little ass in bed."

"Oh, you have someone all lined up for that duty. Shall we find her a pair, too? How big is she? Her boobs, for instance?"

We were both on edge. So in the elevator leaving Mr. A. and Mr. F.'s PJ department, I put my arms around her and said, "I really do love you."

"I love you, too," she said.

"You're a beautiful woman."

"I know it."

Suddenly she hugged me hard and said, "I am worried about you and I'm—I'm worried about me. Now remember this. I'd never do anything bad to you. Whatever I do it's because you don't. You understand?"

"I don't know what you said or what it means."

"It'll come to you."

"Fuck that, no more of that! Now tell me what the hell is eating you?"

The elevator stopped, and two old boating buffs got in.

At the travel office we stopped to pick up my ticket. Mr. Jeffers, an old-style gallant, broke out a split of champagne.

"Why don't you take her with you?" he said.

Before I could figure out an answer, Ellie said, "He doesn't want me to go."

"Of course he does," old Mr. Jeffers persisted. "You both look like you could use a change and a rest. I can still get another seat on the plane, and the hotel room in Nairobi is big enough for two when they're as close as you two."

"You don't want to go, do you?" I asked her when we were on the sidewalk again.

"I wanted you to ask me," she said.

"But?"

"But that's not what I really want from you."

I'd be damned if I was going to ask her any more questions. I looked for a cab, but she took my hand and turned me up Fifth Avenue.

"Just up here a ways," she said.

The streets around St. Pat's were clogged with charter buses, parked and double-parked, and in front of the cathedral there was a great crowd.

"This is it," Ellie said.

She took my hand and pulled me through a side entrance into the cold gray stone house and the crowd of mourners. I couldn't see the service. It was two blocks distant.

"I can't see a damned thing," I said. "What's this all about?"

"A mass for the police killed in the East Village last week," she whispered.

She pulled me forward, but we didn't get very far.

Then I noticed. "Ellie," I said, "the joint's full of cops."

Most of them were dressed in civilian clothes, but you could see what they were. Some had long hair and were dressed like hippies. Others were "dealers" and "prosperous Mafiosi" and "pimps" and "old cons." Once you got the idea, you could see they were all cops. "And look at those black guys, Ellie " I said. 'Like the mug shots on page four of the *Daily Neus*. They're cops too. And dykes, they got dykes!"

She was watching me closely now. In fact she made me damned uncomfortable. How the hell was she expecting me to react? What was she waiting for?

"Christ," I said, "everybody in this city could be a cop."

The crowd got thicker as we squeezed forward. Finally we had to stop, still too far away to hear anything but a murmur of ritual spoken by unseen priests.

Then there was a tinkle of altar bells and a sudden flooding of light, and the service was finished. We both turned and saw the enormous, saint-encrusted front doors of the cathedral swing open.

People began to file out.

"Hey, Ellie," I whispered, "let's get out of here!"

"I want you to see the widows," she said.

We were going against the cop current now, like bucking an avalanche of soft boulders.

"All this crowd," I said, "they're not here because they want to be. It's just a big P.R. show, orders from the top."

"Wait'll the first time you get mugged," she said. "I want to hear you holler help."

"Ellie, believe me, you're hysterical about this."

"There are two widows in that aisle whose men were shot down without warning," she said. "They hysterical too? You just have a hangover of Sidney's old liberal crap, all cops are bad."

She pushed me toward the aisle. I could make out two funeral clusters, one all white, the other black, friends and relatives offering their sympathies to the bereaved.

The white mourners began to move slowly up the nave, and as they went by I turned my head. The front portals were entirely open now, and I saw a broad aisle had been provided through the crowd on the front steps by facing lines of police in uniform. Through this opening I could see into the street, and there, standing in the formal postures of professional respect, were the police brass, out to demonstrate their grief and their anger.

Ellie was off talking to Mrs. Horowitz, the horsewife from the karate institute. I didn't want to socialize with that woman, so I edged toward the aisle. The white widow was opposite me now, guarded by the men of her tribe and padded on all sides by hefty Italian-kitchen women accustomed to demonstrating grief publicly.

I heard the rustle of sleeves. The phalanx of honor outside had seen the white widow group approaching and, on command, saluted.

Ellie came back. "Mrs. Horowitz told me. They shot them down. Then they danced around their bodies."

I looked at Mrs. Horowitz, who nodded her head in confirmation, then disappeared into the crowd of—

Of course. Her fellow cops.

"Jesus," I said to Ellie, "she's a cop, too. Everybody in this town is a goddamn cop."

"They shot them sixteen times," Ellie said, "where they were lying in the bloody snow. That's the kind of person your friend Sidney is going around with."

That remark wasn't worth correcting.

Now the black woman and her group were coming up the aisle. She was uncertain on her feet and had to be supported.

Outside a trumpet called for attention.

Nobody in the cathedral was moving except the cluster of blacks moving slowly up the aisle.

"They brought some of the people who live down there in for

questioning, Mrs. Horowitz told me. You want to know what they said?"

"Yes. As soon as we get out of here."

"What they said is they didn't think the killers had anything against the two policemen. They were shooting at the uniforms. What do you say to that?"

They were holding the black widow up now, lifting her by the elbows. She was overweight and without will.

The bugler was playing something slow and severe.

"Well," Ellie was demanding, "what do you say?"

"Why blame it on Sidney?" I said.

It was then the black widow collapsed, slumping against one of the men holding her, her legs' strength dissolved by grief.

Everyone in the church stopped whatever they were doing. There wasn't a sound.

Then I heard sobbing. It wasn't only the widow, but all the women around her, shouting and moaning and crying out their pain.

A primitive rite had broken out, something out of Africa, warm and true and heavy-scented, had taken over that cold stone church.

I felt a pinching at the ends of my eyelids that I couldn't hold back. I turned away so Ellie wouldn't see my face.

Outside the trumpet sounded again.

The blacks, carrying the sobbing widow by her bent arms, progressed slowly past me.

I tensed to keep from crying.

Ellie put her arm through mine. I didn't look at her.

Priests rushed up, asked in whispers that the women choke down their grief and observe the decorum of silence.

I grabbed Ellie's hand and pulled her through a small side door.

In the street a lane had been held open for the funeral limousines, the first of which had just accepted the white widow and those with her.

Directly opposite the long Cadillacs stood the mayor of the city and his police commissioner.

As the black widow was supported down the steps of the cathedral, the lines of blue on either side saluted.

The trumpet was silent now.

Slowly, step by step, they moved the dead weight of the widow down to where the long black car was coming to take her.

All I could hear was the shuffling of bodies and the scraping of shoes.

As the bereaved came down the last steps, the mayor of the city and his police commissioner saluted.

The trumpet commemorated the instant.

The door of the car was opened. The black widow fell back into the upholstered limo seats. Then she leaned forward, her face turned up. She looked at the spires of the cathedral. I don't know for how long—it was a while. No one moved. Then she fell back out of sight.

I couldn't look at Ellie. I was crying.

She reached up and kissed me.

We had to walk blocks to find a taxi. It was heading in the wrong direction, but we were lucky to get it. "I'll have to go roundabout," the hackie said when I gave him our uptown address, "the streets are blocked."

"Christ," I said to Ellie after we'd gone a few blocks and I'd recovered, "they could make you cry at Hitler's funeral if they had that kind of pageantry and the right music. The power of that kind of—"

"Oh, shut up," Ellie said. "Get away from me." She slid over the seat, crouched in her corner of the cab.

She wasn't talking so I picked up with the driver.

"We just came out of that funeral," I led.

"No-good bums," he came back.

"Who, the cops?" The hackie was a black man of about fifty.

"No. Those animals who shot 'em. When them niggers is bad, they the worst there is."

I looked at Ellie. She was pale as paper.

"Hell, you were crying," she said. "Why do you deny your feelings?"

"They don't mess with me"—the driver was warming up—" 'cause when they do, they don't have any face left directly."

"All right," I conceded to Ellie, "I was ridiculous. Hitler for chrissake! But you know what I mean, about the pageantry?"

"No, I don't. I think what you said was horrible. I think you're heartless, you're cold, and you're a liar."

"Because I don't wait for them to get bad with me," the driver said. "All they got to do is look funny at me one time, and I tell 'em to get on out."

"What's the matter," I said to Ellie, "can't I express an opinion?"

She was looking at me in a very strange way. She always had fits, I remembered, whenever I left her, even for overnight.

"Ever ask Sidney about that key?" she asked.

A year or so ago, while Ellie was at the beach, I'd loaned Sidney the key to our place in the city so he could go in and borrow my copy of Robert Graves' *The Greek Myths*. Sidney had returned the key if not the book, but Ellie had always worried he might have had a duplicate made.

"Change the lock if it worries you," I said.

"You gave it to him," she said. "You change the lock."

"There was one of them in the cab last week," the driver persisted. "Give me your money, he says to me. Come and get it, I said. I stopped the car and got out. He had a knife, too."

"Did he get your money?" Ellie asked.

"Lady, what do I look like to you, an old man?"

"Yes," she said.

"All I got to do is get 'em off their feet. Then they're done for. This one I'm telling about, he come at me, throwing his knife open—"

"You listening?" Ellie said to me.

I was fed up with Ellie. I didn't want to be scolded anymore.

"Where you going?" I asked the driver. "We were on Forty-second Street."

"Going cross Thirty-ninth. The streets are choked. Like I was telling you, I grabbed his arm, and I threw him over, and he never got up, because, lady, I was on him with my shoes. He needed a new head when I got through with him. And something else new, he needed."

"I can't live here anymore," Ellie whispered.

"He never had a chance to use that knife. Here." The driver reached into a compartment under his dash, pulled out a knife, and flipped out a seven-inch blade. "See?"

"I can't live in this goddamn city anymore," Ellie said.

"I kicked that boy, lady, where I can't tell you, but I destroyed that boy."

"Tell him to shut up," Ellie said, "because I can't take any more of this."

"I saw him click this knife open, like so, and I didn't wait for any developments. That was all the developments I needed to see. He didn't have a face his mother would kiss when I got through with that boy."

"Can't you shut him up?" Ellie wasn't whispering now.

I tried to close the sliding glass panel.

"That stuck!" the driver said. "I kicked his eyes in. He couldn't see nothing when I—"

Ellie began to scream, then to get out of the cab. "Let me out of here!" she commanded. I grabbed her. The cab was still moving. She flailed at me wildly, pulled her arm loose, opened the door.

The struggle had given the driver time to stop. The car behind, pulling up short, hit us, not a crash, a bump.

Ellie was out and on the sidewalk.

Our driver hustled around to inspect the damage. It didn't amount to anything. Peace was declared.

He checked his clock, came to be paid.

"She's all upset today," I said to him. "You know how it is."

"I think you made her nervous," he said, as I paid him off.

Ellie was standing in the middle of the sidewalk, trembling, her body tense as piano wire. I touched her to quiet her, but she pulled away.

The air was full of smoke. We were on Seventh Avenue in front of one of those gyro places. I could smell the flesh of a heavy animal browning.

I didn't know what to do. Ellie was shaking, her eyes staring, unseeing. There was no way to move her.

Trucks rumbled. Pedestrians scrambled for safety to sidewalks where handcarts, their racks jammed with identical frocks, scattered them again.

"I'm sorry," I had to shout. "Ellie, I'm sorry."

"I'm not going to live in this city anymore," she said.

I didn't answer.

Still not looking at me, her face twisted in distrust, "Did you apologize to him?" she asked.

"To whom?"

"To the cab driver. I saw you talking to him."

"About what, apologize?"

"About my screaming and—"

"I just paid him off," I lied.

The air was heavy with smoke swirling off the turning cylinder of meat. It reminded me of campfires and the bush, where I'd be within a day, and relieved, God, yes, relieved of her and of Sidney and of this city, at least for a couple of weeks. "I don't want to come back here ever," I thought. "I want out of this."

"I got to eat something," I said. "Want one?"

"Of that? No, thank you very much."

But she took a piña colada and backed off from the fat-heavy smoke.

"There's no reason why you should be frightened all the time," I said.

"It isn't even that. You know I don't scare easily."

"You certainly don't, baby."

"It's Little Arthur I'm worried about and—well—goddamnit, it's humiliating. It rankles my pride. Can you understand that? Pride?"

"What rankles your what?"

"You don't have any pride. Why did you apologize about me to that cab driver?"

"I didn't really."

"I saw you speaking to him. And smiling that way! I know you. Tell me, will you tell me why I should put up with all this? Can you tell me that?"

"No reason in the world."

"Then why don't you do something about it?"

"I'm not responsible for this city."

"Let them have their goddamn city. Let them all kill each other. It's a civil war? O.K. I'm getting out."

She looked white and tense, and I thought, "I've got to get her under control because she's going to crack any minute."

"Ellie, listen," I said, "suppose, when I get back, suppose we look around, Ellie? Maybe we'll move. Remember that house we saw up in Scarsdale? I'll commute every day. Remember that house?"

"It's the same up there, Scarsdale, Mamaroneck, Harrison, Rye. Didn't you read *The New York Times?* Stamford is the venereal disease capital of this country."

The wind had shifted, and the smoke swirled toward us.

"Let's get away from this," she said. "I hate that smell."

Ellie hadn't enjoyed our trip to Africa. She was fighting flies and ants the whole time, and the pit toilets disgusted her. The flies from there, she said, came to dinner with us.

"I need an aspirin," she said.

There was a drugstore in sight.

"Well, what's your idea?" I asked after she'd taken four little white ones and washed them down with Seven-up.

"Well—"

"Come on. Tell me."

"I didn't intend to say anything," she said, "till you came back." She was calmer now, but you could see she was determined to go through with whatever, wherever it might lead.

"I didn't want to spoil your vacation," she said.

"Spoil my vacation. Let's find out where we stand."

"They serve food here," she said. "That sandwich you had looked terrible. Have something clean."

"It was a good sandwich," I said.

"I want to live in Florida," she said.

So that was it!

"Don't get mad at me now. Oh, get as mad as you want. But, well, here! Since mother died, dad's been all alone down there and—"

"So that's what you've been cooking?"

"He's got a room where I can practice and—"

"What about me? That's a problem, don't you think?"

"Whose problem is it, yours or mine?"

"What did you say?"

"I said whose—you heard me very well."

"Well, I'm fast finding out whose."

"I didn't mean that quite as it sounded."

"I'm an actor, Ellie, goddamn it! A professional, commercial, Broadway actor."

"I admit I haven't figured out that part of it, but let me finish my part. Florida is safe, if there is such a thing in this country. They have a very good school down there, daddy says. And the school bus comes right down North Robbins Key Road, picks up the kids every morning and brings them home every afternoon and, well—I don't care if you're mad at me. I don't intend to be panicked anymore, and I won't have my son living that way either. So there. I've said it."

"And you don't lie. I lie but you don't."

"Yes, I don't and you, I'm afraid, do."

"But in your own way, don't you? You didn't really tell me the truth last night. Jack Deming is studying motel management, Tommy's driving a cab. What's your plan for your meal ticket? Why didn't you tell me that?"

"Because I don't want to hurt you."

"Go ahead. Hurt me."

She finished her Seven-up.

"Well, for one thing," she said, "I fail to see how you take it."

"Take what?"

"The daily life of the actor in the commercial—"

"You don't have to take it, I do."

"How do you think I feel when I see you kissing the ass of some crummy agent? Or when a producer passes you on the street, neglects to say hello, and you shake?"

"Arthur wouldn't do that, would he?"

"No, he wouldn't. And remember, I didn't say his name, you did."

"But he lived off your money didn't he, your old man's money?"

She had no answer to the truth, just looked at me as if what I'd said was contemptible.

"Since you've been investigating everything so thoroughly you know there's no show business in Florida."

"Jackie Gleason works there."

"Jackie Gleason! You must be kidding. I'm in the legitimate theater."

"What legitimate theater?"

"What's left of it, I'm in."

"What's left of it, what's that?"

"So what do you recommend, going into real estate, teaching drama at the Sarasota High School? What've you got lined up for me? Oh, fuck it, I've had it. I'm going to clear the decks tonight. All around. You go live like you want and I'll—come on."

"Where?"

"I told you. New deal all around. Fresh start. For everybody."

"I mean where are you going now, right now?"

Out on Seventh Avenue, I turned her south.

"First stop The Castle Mode."

"Which is what?"

"The place of business of Mr. Myron Castle, the brother of Mr. Sidney Castleman. That's the first deck I'm going to clear."

"Let's take a cab. I'm tired."

"It's two blocks."

"Well, slow up. You're making me run."

"I'm not moving to Florida, Ellie."

"I may not be here when you get back."

"If you're not, you know what it will mean to me."

"What will it mean to you?"

"Do it and find out."

"Don't threaten me. Don't ever threaten me. I'm not going to be intimidated anymore, I told you that, not by anybody, not even by you."

Then, after these brave words, she stopped, dropped her head, and turned away. She was going out of control again, trembling and shaking. "Goddamnit," she said, "goddamnit."

I cannot resist her when she breaks up.

"Ellie, come on. Don't be like that, Ellie. I'm your friend, Ellie."

She couldn't answer. Then she said, "I must get over being afraid to tell you what I feel."

"Baby, that's not your problem," I said. "Look, I won't go anywhere. O.K.? I don't need a vacation. Forget it!"

"That's not what I mean," she said, "but—" She didn't look at me. "But I've never ever seen you do one single thing just because it was good for me. Every way we've ever lived, it's because it was good for you."

"Well, I bring in the bread. I got to do that, don't I?"

She had no answer for that either.

"Ellie," I said, "if it's a matter of Sidney, I told you that—"

"It's nothing as silly and trivial as Sidney. But I saw you giving him money yesterday. You lied to me about that too. Didn't you? Yesterday?"

"Yes, I did."

"Still you complain about what Little Arthur's karate lessons cost. How do you think that makes me feel?"

"I know."

"You don't protect me, but you certainly protect Sidney, every way you know how."

"Well, what the hell can I do? About this city—?"

"Mrs. Roberts next door, her husband's got a pistol by their bed."

"I will not fire at another human being."

"I don't like that idea either, but that's the situation which prevails."

"Ellie, come on—"

"I simply must learn to look after myself. I must learn to do what's best for me."

"Come on, Ellie, it's only another half block."

"I'm going to find a job," she said. "That's the first thing. I'll give piano lessons. I can do that."

I took her arm and got her walking again.

"Stop treating me like a hysterical woman," she said, pulling her arm loose. "Because I'm very calm now. I'm making sense, you're not."

I turned her in to the lobby of the building where The Castle Mode has the entire seventh floor.

"Leave me a little more money before you go," she said as we went up in the elevator.

"Money for what? I gave you your regular."

"For emergencies."

"What kind of emergencies?"

"Any kind. Use your imagination. Suppose something happens to—"

"Suppose you suddenly decide to go to Florida?"

"Suppose that, too."

"You expect me to pay for you to leave me?"

"Husband, dear, I expect you to pay for everything I need and do and want."

"O.K.," I said, "I'll leave you the money, a fare and a half to Sarasota, Florida."

"Mr. Castle has some people in his office with him at the moment," Myron's secretary said, "but he wants to see you very much. He's been trying to get you on the phone all morning."

There was no one else in the paneled waiting room. I looked at the pictures of Myron which covered the walls. He was the new breed of dress man, a graduate of Syracuse University, had played guard on the football team that beat Colgate that famous game. You wouldn't guess it to look at him now, he'd run to blubber, but on the walls were the action shots to prove it.

Ellie was repairing her face.

"I'm ashamed of myself," she said. "I promise you I'll never carry on that way again."

She looked altogether recovered.

"I know I'm a fool," she went on, "but I'm not patient Griselda. I know we can find a better life. Well, to be perfectly honest, I know I can. What do I actually need? The few people I love, a room, a piano, and—what else? Nothing. A little food. That's all. Then why have I been suffering all this? For you, my friend. Forgive me, but I think I know what's good for you better than you do."

"That," I said, "is the most conceited remark I've ever heard."

"Yes, it is, isn't it? But it's also true."

At which Myron Castle blew in, shaking off apologies like a dog does drops of water.

He went directly to Ellie and began his pitch for girls, telling her how glad he was to see her, how sorry he was that he'd kept her waiting, how well she looked, and so on.

Having spewed this all over her, he turned to me. "I've been trying to get you on the phone all morning," he said.

Now somebody else was scolding me!

Myron's private office was pretty snazzy, paneled in white birch and dominated by a half-moon desk. On the walls were photographs of our hero shaking hands with almost everybody.

Myron closed the door after us, turned to me, and said, "Sidney's here."

"Sidney's where?"

"Inside, asleep. Knocked out. I don't know from what. He smells funny."

"Well," I said, "what about it?"

"What are we going to do?"

"Me? Nothing."

"Well, now, listen," Myron said, "listen."

"For chrissake, Mr. Castle"—Ellie couldn't hold it in—"he's your brother."

"Myron," Myron corrected her. "Eleanor," he went on, "I've spent my whole life looking after that man and I—"

"So has he." Ellie indicated her beloved.

"And never got a word of thanks."

"You think he did?"

"I've reached the limits of family loyalty."

Myron was beginning to perspire heavily.

"Nevertheless," Ellie said, "you are his family."

"That is a bond that can be dissolved."

"Since when? It's your responsibility—"

"Ellie, shut up." I broke up the fight. "Myron, I saw Sidney around five, and he'd just accepted an invitation from a new friend to go live with him."

"He said the apartment smelled of pig fat. Also it was full of boisterous people, and Sidney, so he says, needs absolute quiet for his work. What work? Damn if I know. So he walked out. What are you going to do with a man like that? Come, look."

He slid open a door with a concealed handle and indicated we should follow him on tiptoe.

"I have a little room here where I nap"—Myron smiled seductively at Ellie—"and occasionally entertain a visitor in the later afternoon. My nookery. I don't generally show it, but you're sort of family. Come."

"I don't want to see him," Ellie turned away.

She missed a sight. Sidney was on his back, sprawled over a large tufted sofa done in mauve velvet, the kind of piece they call a casting couch in show business and a workbench in the cloak and suit trade.

Asleep with his eyes open, Sidney might have been dead except that he was snoring heavily.

Myron saw the look, horror, I guess on my face, laughed silently, and closed the door. "I imagine," he turned to Ellie "you'd prefer if I didn't wake him."

"Right as usual," Ellie said.

"He's been sleeping that way since midnight," Myron said, going behind his desk and sitting on his Itkin throne. "I didn't have to take a second look at the ugly schwartzuh with him to know he was under the influence."

"A short thin man, was he?"

"A big booger, had red boots on. You know who he is?"

"No," I lied.

"So anyway, I rescued him, practically carried him to that couch. Then I had to hire a watchman to sit here all night so he wouldn't wake up and set fire to the office or open it to every quick thief on the street."

"He takes sleeping pills to quiet his nerves," I said.

"That is not sleeping pills in there," Myron said.

"Right as usual," Ellie shot in.

"Now listen to this." Myron's voice dropped to a dewy whisper. "That goniff Sidney brought in here, or was it vice versa, he was a dealer. He claimed Sidney was into him for ninety bucks, wouldn't leave until I paid him."

"So it's not just a sedative Sidney takes to steady his nerves," Ellie said for my benefit.

"Now this criminal knows where my business is and any time he needs cash, I'm worried he'll blow in here and threaten me something bad with Sidney or my stock or, Jesus, anything. My mother on West End Avenue."

"He knows where we live too," Ellie said, again mostly to me.

"So you see, it's not only my problem." Myron leaned back, and his eyes softened. "I remember," he said, "many a day long ago, when my brother would come in here and tell me his concerns about you. 'Sonny has some talent,' he'd say. 'He may make it.' Other times he'd say, 'I'm afraid the boy is going to disappoint me. He doesn't work hard enough on his voice.' Oh, yes, my brother Sidney spent many a long hour through many a year worrying his heart out over you. So what happens? Now when he's in desperate trouble, all you can say is, 'Get him off my back.' "

"And quickly, please," Ellie said.

"What about his son Irving," I said, "in California? He's got a good job teaching."

"Irving stopped talking to Sidney five years ago."

"Well, Myron," I said. "I've supported your brother for so many years that I—"

"I know," Myron said, "and now I see it was out of guilt."

"Oh, get off it, Myron."

"If you really liked him, you wouldn't be defecting out of this emergency."

"He has an emergency every other week," Ellie said.

"After ten years. You got some nerve, Myron. Really!"

"I think he belongs in an institution," Ellie said.

Nobody said a word.

"Then you could both forget him," Ellie said.

Myron slowly wheeled his throne around and beamed on her. "Why are you always so right, little girl?" he said. "I mean, we are in perfect agreement."

He got up and went over to her, and I guess he meant to do something that involved touch, because she shivered, then stiffened, a dramatic effect worthy of Julie Harris. Denied her he wheeled on me—you could see where he'd been a hell of a linesman, he was nimble as a fighting bull—and said, "Is that agreeable to you?"

"Absolutely."

"Then we can both forget him."

"Really."

"Now that's settled," Ellie said. She turned to me. "What time is your plane, darling?" She knew when the plane was.

"Wait a minute wait a minute," Myron exploded. "I want to talk about this. Maybe we've found the solution. I'm going to pour me a drink and—"

"We don't drink in the middle of the day," Ellie said.

"Speak for yourself," I said. "Scotch over ice. Myron."

He'd opened a concealed bar and was digging for ice.

"Because I'll tell you, Myron, I'm going on a vacation and when I come back I'm starting life over this time without your brother Sidney. I'm not going to give him money or get him jobs, worry about him or cover for him. Nothing."

Ellie burst into applause.

"In fact I don't want to hear about him except like news about an old friend who's moved to Australia. There are a lot of Jews in Australia, and he's going to be one more—"

"Forgotten," Ellie said as I took my drink.

"A thing of the past." I poured my drink down my throat.

Myron was slowly mixing himself a vodka martini. "I'm going to tell you how right you are, Eleanor," he said. "I had the same thought over a year ago. Then you got him that job in your last play, and I forgot about it. But I did have a chance to find out what the rates in those places are."

"Honey," Ellie said, "don't you have to see your agent?"

"I imagine they're pretty high," I said.

"How high can you imagine?" Myron asked.

"You can afford it," Ellie said.

"Seven hundred dollars a month. That kind of financial burden I don't propose to carry alone."

"Let's go," Ellie said to me.

"Just a second," Myron said.

"What kind of a man are you?" Ellie was beginning to boil over again. "How can you—"

"Ellie"—I pointed—"go look at those sketches."

A coarse-cork display board, one side of the room, was covered with sketches, Myron's hopes for the fall.

There was a silence while he waited for her to get out of range.

We could heard Sidney snoring.

Then Myron said in a voice he hoped only I could hear, "Call it intuition, call it the result of my analysis, but I always felt you didn't really like Sidney."

"Now, Myron!"

"That you resented him—"

"That tactic will not work, Myron."

"Every step up the ladder," Myron went right on, "you made by climbing up his back. That understudy job he gave you, you used to get him drunk so you could go on for him. Your first big part in that film, you connived to take that away from him. The whole history of you two is a case study, the jealous upstart and the—"

"Myron, go back into analysis."

He poured himself another drink, this one neat. "What do you think of those sketches, Eleanor?" He was buying time.

"Hideous," she said.

"Well, get used to them because you're going to be wearing those hideous little numbers this winter." He sounded very miffed. "I'll tell you something"—he turned to me—"goddamn if I'm going to pay eight hundred dollars—"

"You went up a hundred," Ellie said.

"That is all I have to say on this subject." Myron stood up, an executive concluding an interview. "Eight hundred dollars a month I am definitely not carrying alone. The deal is off."

"Myron," I said, "it was not my proposal."

"We're going," Ellie said quickly. "Myron, can I steal this magazine?"

"Take anything you want." He turned to me again. "So you're going to leave him here? On my hands?"

"As far as I'm concerned, he's in Australia."

I remembered later that my heart was beating as if I'd had a physical encounter, my breath was short and my voice vengeful. And it all felt so good.

"It's your final triumph over him," Myron said, "isn't it?"

"Oh, fuck off, Myron."

"Yes, do that please," Ellie said, her hand on the door knob.

"There's no charity left in mankind," Myron said, a mournful quaver in his voice, "no pity in this city. Haven't you even got a suggestion for me? I mean what kind of profession is this where you don't protect your—?"

"Try the Actors Fund," I said.

"What is that?"

"A suggestion. They have a home."

"Well, talk to whoever is over there for me," Myron said. "I'm not conversant with your field." He was rather pathetic suddenly.

"Call Mr. Ben Polito at Actors Fund. He's a real nice guy."

"You call him. You be a nice guy, too."

"Look out," Ellie said.

"This is the last thing I'll do," I warned, "if I do this, it's the—"

"Right," Myron said, "the last thing. Do it."

"Don't ever ask me anything again." I picked up the phone.

"I'll never ask you, just get him in there."

I dialed information.

"Do you think he'll agree to it? Sidney? Suppose he won't go?"

"What choice does he have," Ellie said, "now that you've both come to your senses?"

"That's right." Myron looked heartened. "What choice?"

I had the information, dialed the number.

"Would you postpone your vacation and—" Myron started.

"Look out!" Ellie said.

"I mean just a few days, long enough to take him to—"

"No. This telephone call is the last thing I—"

"All right."

"Will you remember that?"

"Don't worry about it."

"I want you to say it. Say 'I agree.' "

I pretended to hang up.

"I agree. I agree."

I told Mr. Ben Polito—he knew me, of course—what the problem was. He was a peach, Mr. Polito. He said that Sidney Castleman, in his day, had given Mrs. Polito and himself a great deal of pleasure so he was delighted for this opportunity to show his gratitude. I put Brother Myron on, and they charmed the hell out of each other.

Ellie came and kissed me. "I feel better," she said.

When he'd hung up on Mr. Polito, Myron was euphoric. "What a great, great person!" he crowed. "What a superb human being!" He kept on and on with that kind of TV talk, all the while performing a sort of executive's ballet around his half-moon desk. "That takes care of Sidney," he whispered very loud in my ear as he hugged me. "Now we can both forget him."

If to perspire is healthy, Myron was in the pink.

To celebrate he insisted on taking Ellie into his stock room. "I owe this sudden peace of mind to you," he said. "I must express my gratitude." Ellie told him she didn't want any free dresses, and I suppose she meant it, but, fired by vodka, he pulled her into the stock room, and they disappeared like that old-fashioned eloping couple, she prim and decorous but willing as hell.

It was quiet in the paneled office. I poured myself a refill and threw it down.

I found myself wondering how Myron would break it to Sidney. Would he tell him it was my idea? What would Sidney think of me then?

Precisely the habit of mind I had to kick!

I could hear Myron yelling at an underling. "Summer weight, she said. Cottons. She's going to Florida."

So then I laid down the law. To myself.

Everybody's got a right to live anywhere and in any style they want. There is no reason why we should all be tied to each other, me to Ellie, she to me. Let her go to Florida and live with her daddy if she'd be happier there. And Sidney, he's not my blood. And if he were, he'd still have the privilege of fucking up his life any way he chose. Let everybody float free, find their own level, go their own route. I was going to Africa, a free man.

From the stock room, sounds of revelry. Myron, from what I could hear, was pressing Ellie hard, piling on dresses. "Give her that one, too," he was ordering an assistant. "Go on, Eleanor, take it. The more you take, the happier you make me. I'm a rich man who has no way of pleasing his friends. Grab that one too. Go on, grab it. You don't like the trim? Pull it off. Here."

There was the sound of ripping stitches.

I walked to Myron's nookery, found the concealed handle, and slid the panel open.

Sidney was snoring massively, his arms thrown over his head.

I tiptoed to the body.

I don't think he really woke, but his eyes were open and he did talk to somebody.

"Did they call half hour? I'm ready. Stop worrying. I don't wear makeup. Start the overture, relax my understudy. I'll be there."

He smiled his absolutely confident smile—it was so absurd under the circumstances—then he fell back into sleep, or whatever it was.

I could hear them whispering and laughing in the stock room, Ellie saying, "No, Myron, that's enough. Myron, don't do that, Myron. Cut it out, Myron. Stop it. Oh, Myron!" Then both of them laughing like lovers. It was obscene.

The friendliest thing I could do for that woman was set her free.

And the friendliest thing I could do for myself?

"Goodbye Sidney," I whispered.

"Don't worry, son," Sidney smiled serenely. "Sidney will never let you down."

I pulled the sliding panel door till it clicked shut.

II

In THE INSTANT you step from a night flight into the land of Kenya, you find a festering in the air and that the illumination is faint. Imagination, of course, livened by alcohol, but what I smelled that night were cannibal fires, and the light, feeble and spotty, was the light from those fires.

Inside Nairobi Terminal, the officials making entry difficult or simple were black. They were extremely courteous in a style out of fashion in our society and inherited from the colonialists they'd booted. But this show of manners made the power they had over me more threatening. They treated the white man as an equal, a terrible comedown for the Caucasian accustomed to favored-race status. Equality is not what he wants.

I'd been drinking. The only thing more salutary than being alone, I'd discovered, was being alone in alcohol. Now it suddenly concerned me that these health and security people might find my wobbly presence undesirable. I tried to control my sway and my totter. I needed help, but from someone who would recognize that my disarray was basically spiritual and that I might wish to enjoy it a bit longer.

Then there he was, a man who did. "I'm Piper," he said, "Jim Piper, your white hunter."

[text obscured by overlapping card] the customs man going [...] swered. They were old [...] the official, who now [...] with a chalk mark.

[...] e pointed the direction, [...] you?" gesture, led me, [...] e, my hat and raincoat, [...] ed.

[...] d over his shoulder with

[...] hy, so not asking for it.

'Sorry about that, sir " he said as if he was responsible and had goofed.

'I know you must be very sleepy," he said as we got into a VW box. "We'll have you in your room within ten minutes. The hotel Kimani." he said to the driver.

"The last time I came to Nairobi," I said. 'it was also the middle of the night, and all I found was a note directing me to take a taxi to the New Stanley Hotel, where there was a room reserved. I was with my wife, and I—"

'How could anyone allow you to arrive in a strange continent at two in the morning and not be met?"

"What safari company?" Kimani turned to ask.

"Don't tell," Jim Piper said. "I don't want to think badly of our rivals."

"Is this room quite all right?" he asked. We'd not paused at the desk. Jim had registered for me.

'Oh, fine, fine." I was asleep on my feet.

'I'll have a peek at the bed. It's traditional, make sure the linen is—yes, it's fresh. Now, goodnight and thank you. I look forward so much to our days together. In this envelope"—he offered me a large English-style Manila-brown—"you will find three items, a map of the region where we'll be going, a sort of schedule of times, places, and distances, which please consider no more than something to depart from, and finally, here, a list of what I think you might want to have with you in the way of clothing and personal effects. I'm sure you've thought of them yourself, but just on the chance that you or your wife have overlooked something, there it is. I will be here at noon, and we'll go shopping for whatever you may want to add to your gear. That shouldn't take too long, so we'll get you a nap in the afternoon." He quickly pulled down both shades. "You've lost seven hours, you know."

He came by exactly at noon and had a second breakfast with me. He was tall, blond, and handsome. If that sounds like the hero of an old-time novel, that's exactly what he looked like, perfect in the same way. So were his manners, taught him at a guess by a maiden aunt who'd learned hers from a maiden aunt. Jim Piper did everything quietly and easily but with rigid attention to correctness. I used to make the mistake of considering an Englishman gay if his bearing was gentle and his manners irreproachable when all it had been was that they're bred to the graces, including a consideration for others we Americans neglect. Jim, for instance, asked if I wanted my rolls warmed and did I prefer cream to milk in my coffee. He made sure my eggs were as I liked them, sent them back when they weren't.

He informed me he no longer killed game, refused shooting safaris. "I regret every animal I've killed," he said. "I've done all I ever will of guiding people who come to Africa to get their Big Six and when they see a larger head than one they have, kill it too. I don't want this part of the world changed, it's the last of it, you know."

On the shopping go-round he made sure I wasn't overcharged or given inferior goods, offered recommendations which I accepted. I actually didn't need all the extra stuff, but I was enjoying his company and how he handled the Indian shopkeepers.

I noticed he wore sandals over bare feet, asked did I really need socks? He was very positive about that, thought I should have at least four pair, always a dry set available. The only real hardship in the Bush, he reminded me, was the ants. They'd crawl up a man's trouser legs if he stood still for more than an instant next to one of their marching columns. It was best to have long socks with elastic tops and keep them up and over one's trouser bottoms.

In the course of all this I dropped that my wife generally did my shopping and asked, "Are you married?"

"Oh, dear no," he said. "Almost once. Decided against it when I began to lose sleep over her. Haven't time for that."

Had I found a man without a "personal life"?

"If a woman wants to stay over at my place now," he went on, "I make it quite clear that I intend to get a full night's rest and if she wants to stay up and chatter to please look elsewhere."

That was the first time I noticed what I came to call Jim's voice of command. When he was recalling his conversation, imagined or real, with the young woman who wanted to talk after intercourse, he impersonated himself in that situation, not as he was with me, but suddenly very commanding, a person who protects his elite order by laying down rigid rules of acceptable conduct. Then he smiled at me, and there again was this comforting, companionable voice and his air of affable gentility.

He took me back to the hotel and, looking at his watch, said, "Now I want you to take your catch-up nap. Lack of sleep can make one a bit edgy in the Bush. Meantime I have to get together with Kimani and the other two boys. We have three hundred items to check and double-check before we set out. Why here"—he handed me two typewritten sheets—"suppose I give you a copy of our list, just for sweet curiosity's sake."

"God, you're organized," I said, after a quick look.

"There's no way to correct mistakes in the Bush, you know. Now one last thing. We generally try to provide some proper entertainment for our clients the night before we set out, a sort of get-to-know-each-other party, not that you and I need that any longer, do we?"

"Oh, no, but fine."

"Well, there's a rather nice place, Indian, of course, but clean. I'm confident you won't get any tummy trouble. Quite a nuisance in the Bush, that can be. Do you like curry?"

"I like curry and I like it hot."

"They'll make it as hot as you can stand. Well, now then, there's this other matter. I hesitate to bring it up because of the very affectionate way you spoke of your wife, but here! I am prepared to bring along two ladies, one young, the other less young, and if you care for either—they're not too bad actually and I know from experience that they're agreeable—" He stopped, seemed to have lost his way. "Oh, yes, if you care for one or the other—you see I was so impressed with the devotion you expressed for your wife—but this may be our last contact with whatever benefits urban civilization has to offer, and it's possible young women are one of those, would you say?"

"I imagine," I said, joining the conspiracy, "they can be quite a nuisance in the Bush."

"Indescribable. The mind balks at the thought." He came back to procedure. "Well?"

"You were about to tell me how I might indicate a preference?"

"Oh, yes," Jim said, "order the same drink the one you prefer ordered."

"I'll have a beer too," I said to the very swarthy Indian who was, Jim informed me, the owner as well as the waiter and the cook.

Then I turned my face to the sandy-haired, blue-eyed sabra, the excessively healthy employee of El Al Airlines, one of the two women Jim had brought along.

It was so simple, the first step out of my married bind. She looked so clean, El Al, nifty! Perhaps we would do nothing but talk. I've done that, I really have. No, I'd go with it, come what may. I was entering a new phase. Let Ellie go to Florida and lug Arthur's piano with her. El Al! She had blue eyes, looked very clean. I'd fallen into luck, and I had Jim to show me the way. He was, I could see, what I wished myself to be—unconnected.

"So, it'll be two whiskeys," Jim said to the owner-cook-waiter, "without ice, please remember, and two beers. I imagine the local will do." He turned to me. "I think you will find it acceptable. If not we will have a word or two with this gentleman." He smiled, a little threateningly I thought, at our host.

The tone of his instructions to the Indian, an older man of a sodden yellow complexion, brought back certain salients of British history and the sound of martial brass. But when he turned to me, his voice switched over to that of a member of our elite, clubby, softly spoken, almost girlish.

If Jim had any reaction, disappointment or pleasure, because I'd preferred one woman and left him the other, he showed it not at all. Actually the girl who'd become "his" scared me. Darkly handsome with excellent features and long chestnut hair, she would have been quite attractive except for her eyes. They bugged out of their sockets. This lady, perhaps thirty, was quickened by an excessive flow of thyroid that gave her the threat of instant hysteria. I'd had all I could take of that.

My sabra was as clearly uncomplicated, no threat of tears in the corners of those agate eyes, no lines of affront around their casings, no disappointment erosion tracks off the ends of her mouth. She wore a military skirt of the same sandy color as her hair and a blouse that was loose and light. Through its panels her breasts were offered. My sabra promised an evening of simple pleasure.

Nothing turned out as I'd anticipated.

In the first place there was no question of whether we would or would not, no problem of my place or yours. After the curry, Jim dropped us off at her home without asking either of us. He was riding a well-worn track.

Then? Nothing. I didn't turn on.

And El Al? She sat on the armchair, perched on the sofa, finally waited on the bed, like a fish on a plate, ready to be consumed, promising no resistance, looking at me with neither desire nor apprehension.

That became the challenge. Could I rouse this girl?

And myself?

Finally her indifference got to me. But—

When one caress didn't work, I tried another. When one area didn't yield a response, I shifted my efforts. I went lower. I parted the petals. When my hand didn't do the job, I used my mouth. When that failed, I introduced my member.

She didn't seem excited or repelled by anything I did. To judge by the expression on her lovely face, she might have been behind the counter at the El Al office.

When I came, if she was relieved to have it over with, that didn't show either.

"Don't you come?" I asked after she'd washed off my contribution.

"Of course," she said, "whenever I care to."

"How is that accomplished?"

"It's very simple, you kneuew." This was her only mistake in English pronunciation, this *you kneuew.*

"You mean you do it to yourself?"

She smiled, crinkling her eyes.

"Why didn't you give me some hint, a suggestion?"

"That wouldn't have accomplished anything."

"Then why did you allow me in the first place?"

"I wouldn't want you to go away disappointed on your first night in East Africa."

"Are you sure that you—?"

"Of course. I please myself. Very much."

"So then, you need no one?"

"I like the whole thing better that way. I don't have to douche or wash off. I don't have a big body pounding hell on me in a rhythm that has very little to do with my own and leaves me much too tired to do a good morning's work in the office. By God, I've seen some chaps who want to keep putting me on my back again and again all night and in the same way. I wonder what pleasure they think we—?"

"But still you do it?"

"A social gesture, you kneuew."

"It isn't that you like girls?"

"They're as bad as the men. We have very strong girls in Israel. They pound hell on you and, excuse me, chew on you, worse than the men. For longer."

"So then, all you really need is—yourself?"

"It's not a big problem, is it? Just a body function for you, so a body function for me. Alone I never have to plan it or go through a lot of nonsense first. Sometimes I take myself by surprise. Suddenly I'm playing there, and continue till satisfied. Then I sleep. Immediately. No damned neurotic woman with her stories of failures with men, no anxious man who wants me to wait till he's raised what's necessary to try again. That can be a long wait, you kneuew."

"Yes, I know."

"You're not offended, I hope. Some men take it as a slight on their—"

"Not me. I understand you perfectly. Thank you."

"How did you get on with El Al?" Jim asked the next morning as he helped me carry my bags to where our jeep was parked.

"Did you ever make it with her?"

"Everyone in our organization has. But if you mean shoot her down, no one has accomplished that. Still it's very nice to have that kind of person around, don't you think? She's quite companionable and certainly not tiring, and she can always get you on a flight, one way or another. You slept well, did you not?"

"Perfectly."

"What more can you ask?"

"And the other one, yours?"

"Oh, my God, she, how do you Americans say it, she flips her bloody wig as soon as you touch her. At first you get an overwhelming sense of potency, you find yourself as she finds you, irresistible the completely exciting man. But after a while, all that becomes quite exhausting."

"So you're tired this morning?"

"Oh, God no," he reassured me, brother to brother. "I told you I do not allow any woman to trouble me. For instance, last night, she wanted to come to my place and so forth. But I—"

"But then you would have had her all night." Was I getting the idea?

"No, no, you Americans are so romantic, so polite. I would have told her the evening was concluded just when it was concluded at her place, after my second discharge. But at my place, I would have had to get up and be rather persistent that she do likewise. I can't stand last night's woman around in the morning. Can you? I would have had to dress her, that's a bit of a problem with an unwilling woman, don't you find? Then lead her to the street against her will, possibly with a bit of resistance to boot. I have no time for that."

"But at her place?"

"I get up when I'm ready, my car is below."

I'd cabled the safari company that I wanted to go out as simply as possible, with one man in one tent. But the jeep we were approaching had a trailer in tow which bulged with equipment and supplies, and I certainly had not anticipated that three small black men would come tumbling out to snatch up my luggage and call me bwana.

I watched Jim going over the trailer coupling, testing each rope and knot to make sure it was taut and hard. He had the massive forearms of a tennis pro.

Satisfied, he commended his crew.

Then we rolled out of Nairobi.

Street by street, the city shook off Europe. In Karen, the suburb named after Isak Dinesen, Jim told me there were still lion and, even closer to human habitation, leopard, heard at night, seen never. Leopard were the great adapters, he said, could live on anything, our cats and dogs, our leavings. They would survive men. Behind me the "boys" were laughing their assent.

"They understand more English than they let on," Jim said. "But say whatever you wish and quite openly. They're good boys."

"Kikuyu?" I asked.

"Oh, God, no, Kikuyu! Civilization has reached them. The Jews of Africa! Much too clever for their own good. No, these boys are Wakamba."

Then he made the introductions, a C.O. presenting his staff, Kimani the cook whom I had already met, Francis the waiter, and Obowatti the spotter, all smiling and I at them. They were packed into a space so full of baggage and gear, of extra fuel and hyena-proof lockers that I would have said there was no room for them except there they were, knees pulled up under their chins, looking like saucer-eyed bush babies.

"I thought the short rains would be over by now," I said an hour or so later. We were going down the side of a great escarpment into the Rift Valley, and a huge cloud, lowering its black belly over us, began to drop its load.

The boys were out before Jim stopped the vehicle, putting up the side screens.

"If you're tired," Jim said, "this might be a good time to nap."

"I don't want to miss anything."

While Jim, on request, was telling me about the Great Rift, what it was and how geologists say it happened, I fell asleep.

When I woke it was still raining and I spoke the thought that woke me. "About last night," I said, "what we were discussing, don't you think if you exclude from your experience all relationships that cause you pain or inconvenience, aren't you denying yourself the most real—?"

"What is real?"

"Deepest?"

"Because they hurt you, they're deep? My God, you're a Christian saint, complete with stigmata."

"They're bound to be painful often, yes."

"I've never had a deep experience with another human. I avoid that sort of thing. You have to be careful whom you admit to your life, wouldn't you say? I'm sure that sounds shameful to you, quite un-Christian."

He'd said precisely what I wanted to hear.

"Most of the women I know," Jim continued, "are pleased to have it brief and impersonal. The protestations of everlasting love I've heard are generally for quite a practical purpose."

"So we'll pay the bills?"

"For one thing. There's an awful lot of sentimental brush to clear away. Sexual pleasure, when you've tasted it for a while, is not that precious. To tell you the truth, neither is life. When you've lived in the Bush awhile—"

"But doesn't that way of living—leave a rather large hole in your life?"

"Which way of living?"

"The arm's-length way?"

"I didn't say that. I said clear away the false concerns, the sentimentality. Accept things as they are."

I was tempted to bring up Sidney.

"The deepest experiences I've had are not with women, what they call love. That's an American obsession, love. You're looking sleepy again. And just when I was getting to the deepest experiences of my life."

Jim would have forgotten Sidney years ago.

When I woke the rains had stopped, and I saw animals grazing.

"The gazelles," Jim pointed, "are Grant's. And there's a—"

"A Tommy." I remembered the little Thomson's gazelles with affection. "The cattle? Belong to the Masai?"

"Yes. We've reached the border," Jim said. "The meat producers for humans have begun to give space to those for cats. Oh look!" He pointed. "See. He's only got three legs."

The Tommy had lost one leg behind. He was grazing apart from the others, pulling up a couple of quick teeth-crops, then looking up, then down for more, then up, all the time his short white-tipped tail twitching nervously.

"How come he's separated from the herd? I should think he'd—"

"His fellows probably drove him off. He's bad magic, don't you know, a spook. Anyway, he's safer here with the cattle. The Masai hold off the lions."

We'd stopped so our boys could remove the rain panels.

Standing in the middle of the field were two very young Masai of the area whose ear lobes had been pulled down and opened into long loops. Their faces were daubed with reddish clay. On end, at the sides of their tall, slim bodies, were long spears. One of the boys, pre-pubescent, was naked.

Jim waved. The boys waved back, looking at us with neither deference nor hostility.

Ahead the plains rolled like the open sea.

"That's the way it all used to be," Jim said, "I can remember."

We were moving again.

"How does he survive, the Tommy, on three legs?"

"He does, as you see, for a while."

"Someone should take him in."

"How like a god!"

"What does that mean?"

"Forgive me, but that's what I mean by sentimentality. It's our special arrogance that we humans decide who survives, even who deserves pity. Nothing personal, but who are you to say that particular Tommy should be saved?"

"It's only an impulse to help the weak."

"That's very Christian and very dubious. You're an American. You know that the strong survive by killing the weak."

"You in favor of that?"

"Of course not."

"Against it?"

"Of course not."

"Then what? It's the law of nature?"

"The law of life. Every man for himself." He smiled at me.

"Actually I wasn't thinking of those less strong. I was wondering about—aberrations. I don't know the proper word applied to animals. For humans it's eccentrics, freaks. Did you say 'spook'?"

"Yes. They're killed."

"Why?"

"They threaten the rest of us."

"But why?"

"That's the unanswered question. The Greeks killed messengers who brought bad news. By killing the man you kill the news. Animals believe in the same kind of magic. They're no less savage than we are."

Midafternoon we came up to a complex of low-lying buildings.

"Keekorock Lodge," Jim announced, "part of Kenya's national effort to lure the dollar—well now it's the Deutsche mark."

"That where we're going to stay tonight?"

"We could. We could also press past here to the spot I have in mind for our permanent camp. It's about twenty miles into Tanzania, well off the road in an unmarked valley that—"

"Let's go on."

"I was hoping you'd say that, but before I take you up on it, let me warn you that this lodge is your last chance for a sitting-down defecation, and a bath with unlimited hot water. We have a shower, but theirs is better."

We did the twenty miles to the Tanzania border in silence. It was that hour of the afternoon when the predators begin to hunger and stir and, if they are lion, stalk off from their pride, their legs stiffened in the heavy walk peculiar to cats, their heads lower than their shoulders. We made a turn in the road, and there were three cheetah, a mother and two, Jim said, walking not trotting, business on their minds. They moved off the road for us, not hurrying, then watched as we passed, perfect beasts, the king's hunting companions of old, the frown of royalty etched into their face fur.

"Why are they traveling the road?" I asked. "Isn't that dangerous?"

"This is a photographic area. No shooting allowed."

"They know that?"

"Of course."

"Still, why on the road?"

"Small game stay close to where man is, feel safer there. So the cheetah—"

"Know that?"

"Of course."

Some ten miles later, Jim turned off the gravel road and into the

Bush. There was no sign anyone had gone over that ground before, open country without track, rut, or marker. Jim was navigating by a hill, a gully, a brook, a special tree, a great rock.

The jeep astonished me. It rolled over brush and small trees, climbed at sixty degrees, forded streams.

"It's a Toyota, actually," Jim said, "a Japanese copy of the British Land Rover, which, like many of their imitations, is better than the original."

I asked about a herd in the distance. "Zebra," Jim said, "and so, of course, lion." He pointed out a pile of white bones.

"How do you know, lion?"

"Hyenas don't leave bones. Leopards don't feed on the ground."

The area was an old battlefield littered with the final traces of those who'd perished.

The secret camping site was at the bottom of a long, even slope. A stream ran among heavily leafed trees, giants.

"Fig trees," Jim said.

He drove under the great boughs into the dark.

"Isn't this great?" Jim said, jumping out where it was most heavily covered. "Precisely the kind of place you want, I'm sure."

Behind us the light flared, then failed. Rain began to fall, but under the spread of trees it was still dry.

"It sure is," I said, wondering what it would be like at night.

I watched them uncouple the trailer, Jim moving swiftly here and there in a kind of lope, never seeming to hurry, still everywhere, pointing where he wanted our tents, where their kitchen, speaking his orders in that unchallengeable tone. It seemed perfectly in place here, his voice of command, not excessive or unnecessary. It was reassuring to hear.

"Come on." He started for the Toyota. "We'll look around."

Birds were scurrying for shelter.

"It's raining pretty hard," I said.

"Going to be a beauty. Great sport! Let's go."

"The boys have guns?" I asked as I got in my side.

"We don't carry guns on this kind of safari," he said. He spun his motor, shouted some final instructions in Swahili, and we drove off.

The rain was falling in glazed sheets.

Climbing, we'd reached a nob of high ground. Jim whipped his Toyota around like a movie cowboy his mount and flipped off the ignition.

"Now, will you please look at that!" he said.

I'd never seen the anatomy of a storm before. In open country a storm has dimensions and contours, it has movement. We could see where this one was going, and where it had been the light of the sun was again touching the earth.

Then the belly of the cloud came over us and gutted itself. We could see nothing, ahead or behind. A sheet of water covered the ground.

"How do the animals survive this?" I asked.

"They turn their backs," he said. "Isn't it beautiful? Don't you find it beautiful?"

"Yes. Even though it makes me feel helpless."

"Cuts you down to size, doesn't it?"

He was looking at me, appraising me. Then he changed the subject, questioned me about New York, knew street names, buildings, statistics.

I told him about the muggings, about the terror in which middle-class whites live and the poverty in which most blacks live, finally about Ellie and her karate class, about her determination to protect herself.

When I was through, he asked, "Why do you live there?"

"It's where my profession is. And it's my country. That's the way it happens to be now."

The rain was coming down even harder. Still we heard distant barking. Dogs?

"What do you consider your country?" I asked. "This one's ruled by blacks. You're merely tolerated here."

"The old man, President Kenyatta, still needs the white man's brains and knows it, so he's been fair to us, so far. But when he dies, I haven't decided where I'll go. I lived in Rhodesia for a time—"

"Rhodesia?"

"I was in their police. There's a lot I liked about Rhodesia."

"Of course you saw it from the police point of view."

"I imagine you must be for that since they're protecting your wife while you're here."

"My generation was brought up to disapprove of the police."

"Why ever?"

"I wish they didn't have to be so many and so—brutal."

"Brutal! You are a sentimentalist. Really! Forgive me, but—what do you think civilization is? Strength provides order. Nothing else can. Actually Rhodesia is the only country which will survive what's coming."

"Which is?"

"The holocaust, the great black revolution. This is Africa, and the savagery of our animals is nothing to the savagery of our natives when they're not controlled."

I've noticed that when you talk to the boys your tone of voice is—"

"In Rhodesia the police are trained to be very definite and very loud, in that way exercising a sort of control by voice over our inferiors."

Then it's an acquired thing?"

"I also come by it naturally. My father, deceased, was a general in the army when this was British East Africa. Our family went through the Mau Mau time, and while it wasn't as bad as your sporting novelists make it out, nevertheless the ones who were hairy-back came through while the sentimentalists perished or fled to the mother country. May I ask you something?"

Of course."

"In the situation you describe, the one in the streets of your city, don't you feel at the mercy of your blacks?"

"I suppose I do. Sometimes.'

You can't possibly like that feeling."

"What would you do in my place?"

'Go to Rhodesia. Perhaps.'

"If you liked it there so much, why didn't you stay?"

"There was a threat of marriage," he said. 'I escaped. Are you getting hungry?"

He'd changed the subject abruptly.

"I am, but it's not important."

'Our client's comfort is always important," he said.

Apparently he'd noticed a diminution in the force of the storm which I had not. I wouldn't have moved on a superhighway, but Jim proceeded slowly yet without hesitation through what seemed to me to be a cloudburst. I could see no path, no marks, but in a short while we were rolling down that long, even slope, at the bottom of which I could see our camp. He put the Toyota right up against my tent.

"I imagine." he said, "since you're so happily married, a woman can't possibly seem a threat to you?"

"It's happened."

"I know you'll disagree with this, but here it is. I believe the wave of the future is the herd concept, not the family."

"Are you serious?"

'That's how most of us live now, isn't it?"

"And you're satisfied that way, to be alone?"

"Above all when I consider the opposite choice. The family, to begin with, is an invention of man. It's not natural, is it?"

He looked at me and waited, but I didn't pick up the subject.

"When you're ready," he said, "we'll have a drink."

I dashed through the rain into my tent and zipped the flap.

I hadn't exerted myself, but I was tired. I found a narrow cot made up with bulky blankets, and I fell on it. The only other furnishing was a small table holding a large field lamp. It was lit and hissed. The tent was made of a fine cloth which glistened, a synthetic. Waterproof, it also seemed airproof, a perfectly sealed container, like those small ones they use to pack frozen foods or those other enclosures where some of the sick spend their last hours.

I decided to have that drink. I jumped the puddles to the front of Jim's tent. The little waiter, Francis, came trotting through the rain to ask what I wanted.

"Whiskey, please," I said.

"With soda, sir." A statement, not a question. "And no ice."

"Actually I'd like it with hot water, but with the rain—"

Francis was gone.

From inside Jim's tent I heard BBC, the news. "They're having a freak snowfall back home," Jim called out. "Yours. That ought to cool those streets."

The rain was still coming down. "Under the circumstances," I said to Jim when he appeared, "I'd be quite content to have something cold and simple, like a peanut butter sandwich."

"I'm not sure we have peanut butter," Jim said.

Francis came trotting back with a glass containing three fingers of Scotch whisky and a small white pitcher full of steaming water.

"How do they heat the water?" I asked Jim.

"By fire," he said.

Francis's head was as wet as that kind of hair can get. He asked Jim what he wanted and trotted off through the break in the bushes. Jim had placed the kitchen so it was concealed. Almost immediately Francis reappeared with Jim's drink and a plate. He stood in the rain just outside the shelter made by the canvas overlap and reached in. The plate contained cashews, and they were warm and crisp.

"This is all very gallant, this running back and forth in the rain,"

I said to Jim when Francis had disappeared, "but why did he stand that way? Why didn't he come in out of the rain?"

"And get us wet? I wouldn't have cared for that." Jim passed the nuts. "They don't take rain the way you do," he said. "They live in the weather."

"How do they keep a fire going?"

"They do. Several. Please don't show surprise at what they're able to put on the table. At the end of the meal, if you feel so inclined, say a word of commendation. They'll merely nod, but a word like that, correctly spoken at the right moment, holds the whole thing together down here. It pays their pride."

"Which is all they have?"

"What more have you? Sorry."

The dinner was excellent. There was even a kind of béarnaise sauce for the steak and three kinds of vegetables. Considering the conditions under which it was prepared, the meal was a miracle. But I'd already learned to accept miracles with the same exaggerated casualness Jim did.

When it was over, I chose what I thought might be the right moment and spoke some words of praise in a tone as close to Jim's as I could manage.

Francis nodded and ran off. Kimani, the cook, who'd come to our end of the kitchen path, nodded, then turned back.

"Spoken like a true white African," Jim burst out laughing. "Now, let's have a liqueur. Francis!"

Francis was already bringing a tray of bottles from among which I chose Drambuie. As I sipped, I heard the first lion.

Jim didn't, apparently.

"He sounds hungry," I said, to call his attention to the distant roar.

"It's the rain," said Jim. "It makes them anxious and disgruntled."

"Will that go on all night?"

"Till they make a kill. When their mouths are full of meat, they don't roar."

"I'm perfectly safe in my tent, I know," I said. "But by what magic? It's a very light piece of cloth, actually—"

"No self-respecting gourmet lion would choose you if there was wildebeest available. We'll have some of that steak in a day or so. It's almost as good as British beef for flavor."

I had another Drambuie, just to keep up with Jim.

"Besides," he went on, "lions have nothing against humans at night. During the day they know we have guns and can see to use them. You can't like someone you fear, can you? But at night—"

"There's another one. Hear? Seems closer."

"He is. Tell me. Why did you come here? Particularly? I've been meaning to ask."

"Just for a vacation, a change. What do you mean?"

"People from superior civilizations keep turning up here. Some to experiment with danger, but most don't really know why. I can guess. The tension at home has become unbearable. The trap has been sprung, poor buggers. The least they can do is restore through this shock of the elemental—Africa!—some sense that life is not—their lives—bound between two converging steel rails which lead to the edge of a cliff. But I rather think you're like me. You pretty well know what you're doing and why."

"I did something just before I left the States I haven't yet figured out."

"Then there has been something on your mind, I was right."

I didn't want to talk about Sidney.

"Well," Jim said, "except for our neighborly lions, you'll have lots of peace tonight to puzzle out whatever it is."

"Are you suggesting I should go to bed now?"

"I've begun to recognize your sleepy look."

He walked me to my tent like a host should his guest, checked my bed, inspected the floor for ants, found none, showed me how to turn the hissing Gaz light off and on, said a perfect goodnight, and zipped me in.

Being alone was a new experience for me. That sound unbelievable? I've always had somebody with me, my mother, my first wife, Ellie and Little Arthur, the cast of whatever play I was in, my agent, the Lambs, the Players, Equity Council, the handball players at the West Side "Y," my tax man, my lawyer—and Sidney.

Work is my drug. Whenever I'm alone for more than a few days, I do something drastic, I get a job of some kind. When I'm working I have no time to wonder if I'm happy or miserable. That is why I never take a vacation unless I've a job to return to. I don't dare.

Now, here I was, as I'd wished, me and my Gaz light and a couple of books, *Future Shock* and *One Hundred Years of Solitude,* that I carry everywhere but never read and probably never will.

I heard the lion again. Another lion? The same? He sounded different, perhaps because he was closer?

A word about a lion's roar. It's not. It starts like a roar, then there's a succession of sounds you never hear in a zoo. It goes like this, in a sort of diminuendo, "I'm hungry, I'm hungry, hungry, hungry, hungry, hung, hung, hung, huh, huh, huh, hu, hu, h, h, h, h, gh." Finish. Silence.

What's he doing now?

The natives tell you the lion is saying "I'm boss," over and over. Maybe the fucking lion has an identity problem, has to reassure himself he's boss all the time.

The lion—or lions—I was hearing may have been uncertain, but he was—or they were—also advancing.

An actor is not a brave man. I suppose there are exceptions, but I don't remember meeting one. They're all very brave on stage and on the screen. Burt Lancaster has never lost a war. Kirk Douglas has never even lost a battle. John Wayne gets straight up after a heavy chair's been broken over his skull. Every picture since *The Great Train Robbery* has celebrated the courage of these men. They've been a great ad for our sex!

But in life, as I've known them, actors are rather cautious. They don't want their features mashed or misplaced. They don't even want their hair mussed.

For instance, I'm an absolute coward. Yet on stage, I play people of unwavering courage, not only physically dauntless, which is comparatively simple, but morally. I've played moral leaders!

Yet if I'm without a job or some close friends close by or a loving bedmate even for a day or two, I begin to wonder why I live.

Add an advancing lion to that and—

I sat up. Why the hell should I lie in bed with the covers pulled up over my head, trembling? If I couldn't sleep, I'd do what I do at home, read. I got the Gaz lamp going, although it hissed in a way it hadn't when Jim lit it, and found my place, the one I'd had for the last two weeks in *Future Shock*. I began to read about modular man.

Suddenly I put the lamp out. Why call the lion's attention to which tent I was in?

I'd spotted a roll of toilet paper on the bedside table. I pulled a piece loose and compacted it into a pellet. I stuffed the pellet into one ear, made another, plugged the other ear.

I still heard the lion.

I wetted the pellets with saliva, stuffed them back into place.

I heard the lion less.

I kept my fingertips in place behind the pellets.

I could not hear the lion.

Was he silently sneaking up on me? Did predators of that size come into camp? Did they smell the meat smoke from our dinner? Meat smoke! Christ! There were five very smelly humans in that camp, and the most powerful odor of all was the one from my frightened and disconsolate soul.

I turned over. The pellets fell out of my ears.

Fuck Sidney Schlossberg! I'd avoided thinking about him, and I would not think about the bastard now. I had no time for Sidney Schlossberg. He deserved what I'd done, and asked for it. I'd taken years and years of his shit and now—fuck him! Feel guilty? Why should I? All right, I do, a little. Ellie doesn't feel guilty. Myron his brother doesn't feel guilty. My producer, Mr. Sol Bender, who used to be his assistant stage manager doesn't feel guilty. Adam, the first-time-uptown director, doesn't feel guilty. The president of Actors Equity, Mr. Frederick O'Neill, I'm sure he doesn't feel guilty. Cardinal Cooke, a real-life moral leader he doesn't feel guilty. Why should I feel guilty?

Because I'm a goddamn freak that's why. There was no reasonable basis for the guilt I felt.

And what the hell did it have to do with that lion outside, the one who was looking for me?

Imagine what Jim would say about Sidney! I knew goddamn well what he'd say. He'd laugh.

I'd make sure. I'd ask him in the morning.

That fucking animal was getting closer and closer. Hugh, hugh, hugh, ugh, ugh, ugh, gh, gh, gh, h, h, h, you ugly son of a bitch!

I tried the pellets once more, but they were dried and misshapen. I'd call Ellie in the morning and tell her to send me a box of those rubber things Brando wears in his ears. I read he wears them even when he acts so he won't hear the actors he's working with. So much for the Actors Studio.

With that, I fell asleep.

What phone? How could I call Ellie?

Which reminded me, I hadn't seen my agent before I left.

I woke.

No, the lion woke me. He must be right in camp, the sound was that close.

I listened for footfalls, didn't hear any. Of course not. Their feet are padded.

The rain was gentlenow, the storm had moved on. From a

distance came a crack of thunder followed by the barking of many animals.

Suppose I had to take a piss now. That would be something! Then I realized why I'd had that thought. Because I did. Have to piss.

I sat up. I really had a problem.

It was all that goddamn liquor I'd put down. What the hell did I drink all that Scotch for? And the Drambuie? Three shots? And Sanka? Why? To prolong the dinner, the time I'd be with Jim? To postpone the moment when I'd be alone in my tent? To make sure I'd sleep soundly, that was it.

Another theory shot to hell.

Outside someone, something had moved. Which is to say, some animal had knocked over—what? There was a washstand with a bowl on it at the entrance to my tent. I thought I'd heard the metal bowl ring. Now some heavy scuffling movement. Then silence.

I really had to go. The hero of stage and screen had to pee.

I put on the Gaz light, listened. I got out of bed. Slowly. Without, I hoped, a sound.

Suppose, I considered, I kneel at the entrance, zip up the zipper just enough so I could—no, that wouldn't work.

Note to my lady readers. The member tends to shrink when the bearer is frightened.

Also, I remembered a story Jim had told me about a tall "tripper" who'd fallen asleep with his feet outside the tent and lost one of them to a passing hyena. At one clomp! The pressure in a hyena's jaws, Jim had informed me, was equal to nine hundred pounds. Or was it seven hundred? What the hell's the difference?

Better a foot than my dear little friend.

I wondered what Jim would do? Why, he'd go out and do his business. He'd told me another story about going to our little canvas field toilet, there meeting a lioness coming out. Jim had laughed at the surprised look on her face. She'd run away, of course, but then Jim gives off confidence and I give off the opposite. "Never back off," was Jim's advice. "If you turn and run, you're finished."

What I finally decided to do was piss in a corner of the tent. This might occasion some embarrassing questions in the morning, but the hell with that. I'd be intact.

I was never more glad to see the light. I understood the birds, why their songs are so sweet in the dawn. Survival! They'd made it through the night.

I peeked out of my tent, and there was little black Francis running up with hot water as if he'd been waiting up all night for me.

When Jim appeared, it was in style. The zipper of his tent's front fold slid up, and there he was, taking his first steps of the day with that lordly vagueness he might have affected in his own home, where he, of course, was. Around his body he wore a midthigh-length robe of paisley cloth. He smiled at me in the manner of the host of a country estate and asked the ritual questions. I answered that I'd slept very well thank you, but he wasn't listening. It was much too early to listen.

Francis came running with the same little white pitcher, refilled with steaming water. Jim stirred his first cup of Nescafé while he issued his first orders of the morning.

"Mizzouri, bwana," Francis assented, then, "Mizzouri, Mizzouri," as he trotted off in the direction of the kitchen.

I heard him passing on the master's wishes, had a glimpse of him as he ran across the opening of the kitchen path, disappeared behind the bushes, reappeared at the canvas stall shower in the hollow where the wild fig leaves were heaviest.

"Forgive me," Jim turned in my direction, still balmy, still waking in his own time while servants scurried. "I've ordered a shower prepared." He sipped some of the Nescafé. "Of course it's for you. They'll have it ready in precisely the time it will take you to drop out of your clothes. You'll find the water quite hot and very refreshing."

Francis had lowered a canvas drum which had been suspended over the shower stall, and he and Kimani were filling it from one of the large fire pots. I could see the steam swirling up as they poured the water.

"I'll wait till tonight, Jim."

I don't know why I refused, perhaps out of deference.

"As you wish." Jim nodded pleasantly and had another sip of the Nescafé. "It'll be ready for you when we get back this afternoon."

Francis ran up with a large bath towel, stood at the ready while Jim emptied his cup. Of course Jim did not hurry. When he finally got up he smiled at all present, not in apology but in the sharing of pleasure, at me waiting for him to turn on my day, at Francis waiting with his towel, at Kimani waiting at attention beside the shower stall. Then he took the towel, said "Thank you, Francis," and strolled off, holding his robe closed in front, a crown prince of the days of empire who did not expose to gentry the royal organ which would continue the line.

There was nothing to do while he was gone but pretend to like Nescafé.

Fifteen minutes later he reappeared, rather more alert.

"Did I inquire," he said, "how you slept?"

"To tell you the truth, only pretty well."

"The lion can be a bother till one learns to ignore his histrionics. By the way, they finally made a kill about five or six miles down range. Would you like to have a look?"

"Oh, yes, yes."

Something about the way I responded made him smile.

"What amuses you?"

"People from the States are always so eager to witness a kill," he said.

"How did you know there'd been one? Where it was and how far off?"

"See those birds circling?"

He indicated the top of the long slope above our camp and past.

"No."

"Then I'm afraid you'll have to take my word. I've asked Kimani to pack us a picnic lunch, and we'll have a look at our noisy neighbors. Shall we?"

"Zebra," he announced. He'd stopped the Toyota and pulled a pair of Swiss field glasses out of his glove compartment. "They got a zebra."

Through the heat haze, I could barely make out a large herd of some kind, a couple of miles off.

He handed me the glasses, and it was what he said.

"These lenses," I said, "pull everything together. The lions seem to be eating the zebra right in the middle of the herd."

We rolled up slowly, making the least possible disturbance. The rain of the night before had left reflecting pools of water in which I could see the white clouds moving. Other places there was a skim of green over the water which made it shine. The whole country was emerald fresh.

It was the least likely setting for what we saw.

The survivors, about two hundred of them, were grazing not a hundred feet from where one of their number was being devoured by a small pride of lions.

Jim stopped the Toyota. "She was with foal," he said, giving me the glasses.

One of the lions had his head up into the somatic cavity of the dead animal. The front quarters of the mare and its head were still intact. I asked about that.

"They always go in the back. They love the vitals, the heart and the testicles, the liver, the sweetbreads—and the unborn young."

"Can we get closer?" I asked.

"Well, maybe, a little. I don't like to disturb them. This is their place, you know."

I was annoyed, controlled it. "What is?" I asked.

"This whole place. We're guests here."

He turned the motor over, slipped the Toyota into low, and began to creep forward as slowly as the vehicle would move until we were within twenty feet of the lions and their meal. One of the predators, a beautiful animal, looked up, its muzzle blood-soaked. Then, unconcerned, went back to feeding.

"See the little fellow's feet," Jim whispered.

They were delicately turned and very small.

"I imagine they're still soft, the hooves," Jim said.

"Horrible."

"There are men, gourmets, who consider unborn pig one of the great delicacies."

'The picture I'd like to get is the zebra's head, which is intact and rather peaceful-looking, as if it had no idea what was happening below, and the lions gorging into the rest of her."

Jim circled, slowly and carefully, then stopped.

"This is as close as we'll go," he said.

I took my picture but wasn't satisfied.

"Got it?" Jim asked.

"Yes, but it's not really what I wanted."

"I'm sure you'll have a very nice picture."

"Can't we get a little—?"

"Sorry, this is as close as we go."

We sat and watched.

There was no sound except slobbering as the lions pulled loose and gulped down the hunks of warm, moist meat. Occasionally there'd be a quick, angry snarl within the family circle, but there was enough there for the whole pride, so no cause for quarrel.

"How much can one of them eat?"

"Full grown, a tidy forty pounds, thank you very much. I've seen them after a meal when they couldn't run if they had to."

A lioness suddenly pulled away from the zebra and dashed at a hyena who'd come too close. She didn't catch the slope-backed animal. He cut off at a sharp angle, and she did not follow. The hyena came back to precisely where he'd been and waited.

Now I noticed the others waiting in circles of privilege, four other hyenas, barely able to contain themselves, trotting back and forth like kids who had to pee. They were next. Behind them were three light-foot jackals with lovely gold pelts and delicately pointed noses in contrast with the snouts of the hyenas. But they were there for the same purpose. Since they had longer to wait, they were more patient. On the ground and absolutely still was a college of carrion-eating birds, naked-necked vultures with feverish red eyes. They knew they were to be last and had no choice except to accept their place at the bottom of the brotherhood.

"These lions won't eat again till perhaps the day after tomorrow," Jim said, "more likely the day after that."

"And the zebras know?"

"Look at them."

Just thirty yards away they were cropping grass as fast as they found it. Occasionally one of them would look up at the lions devouring his comrade, but the look was brief and unconcerned and he'd return immediately to the food at his feet.

"Do animals have feelings?"

"Same ones we do, fear, hunger, sexual desire, competitiveness, anger—"

"Guilt?"

"Not guilt. If a zebra felt sorrow and guilt every time one of his herd went down, he'd crack up, life would be impossible."

"You mean to tell me the fate of their comrade does not interest them?"

"Oh, it interests them very much."

"How?"

"As a cause for rejoicing."

"Rejoicing?"

"In the animal world a survivor celebrates. When a lion dashes into a herd, what do they do? They get as far away from their weaker brother as possible, they particularly leave the incapacitated, in this case a very pregnant mare. Take her, they say to the lion, don't take me."

"So each day's ease is bought by the life of a brother or sister?"

"Did you hear them last night, barking, how restless they were?"

"I thought that was dogs, wild dogs."

"Zebra bark. They were barking on and off all night. They knew it was time for their pride to eat."

"*Their* pride?"

"Certainly. It's a very close bond, predator and victim."

"So the kill relieved them?"

"Obviously."

"Now you're going to tell me that they wanted the lions to—"

"Well, perhaps they did want to get it over with, one way or another. The proof is that if they kept still, and quiet, they'd escape notice completely. At night their disguise is perfect, and the lion is really a boob. But the zebra never stops barking and switching his tail, and the lion hears one and tracks it down till he sees the others and there you are. What do you want to do now?"

"Could we possibly watch a little longer?"

"Of course, of course. For how long? I ask only because I'm concerned."

"About what?"

"I saw you brought a white golfing cap along. Better put it on. The big heat of the day is about to come down."

"I was in the South Pacific during the war," I said. "I know all about the sun."

"I really wasn't trying to hurry you."

I put on my white cap.

"There's a great rock just off the road not far from here." Jim was pressing me. "It has overhanging trees, and there's a brook below. We can picnic in the shade, and then you may want to nap—"

"I want to watch until she's disappeared," I said quietly. "For some reason the dismemberment and consumption of this zebra fascinates me."

Jim burst out laughing. "Forgive me," he said, "but she'll be there, and the lions, too, a couple of hours from now. I really ought to insist we go, you are, after all, in my care, aren't you? Let's get into the shade and relieve your head of this heat."

"I'm perfectly all right."

"We're almost exactly on the equator, you know."

"I've been there before."

"But never, if I may say so, at sixty-five hundred feet. You are not feeling the sun, but it's pressing down just as hard."

"All right." I gave up. "let's go."

My wife, Ellie, would have warned Jim that when I give in to persistent hectoring, suddenly become agreeable and compliant, then I am at my most hostile and treacherous.

But once in the shade I enjoyed it. The picnic was delicious. Kimani had packed a cold bottle of Soave, and there were two remarkable salamis, one from Genoa, and the breast of a plump chicken and oranges from Spain and homemade bread and sweet British biscuits.

"I want to apologize to you," I said. "You were quite right about the heat. The only other time I've known it like this was in New Guinea during that other war, long ago. It was so hot then, I remember it felt much hotter than this, that it aroused the opposite sensation, a chill, a feeling of sudden cooling, like a fever does. Actually I had dengue fever in Manila in forty-four, and I remember how I shook with cold, then burned up—"

"I've heard of dengue. There's some down on the coast around Melindi. It comes back, doesn't it?"

"It did once. Anyway, the point is you were quite right, the shade is delicious and so was the picnic and I'm awfully glad to be here with you, O.K.?"

'Please don't ever feel you have to apologize,' Jim said. 'The heat makes everyone irritable, especially at first."

I liked him. A lot. He'd packed the remains of the lunch away and we were lying on our backs looking into the foliage as it moved to the breeze, and I thought I was lucky to be with him.

"I'm going to make a confession," I said. "I had to urinate—"

"Francis told me."

"I'll tip him extra."

"Not necessary."

"You see I was too frightened to—"

"Please don't mention it again. You're not the first to do that."

"Suppose I'd been courageous instead of a miserable coward, and waiting for me in the WC had been the lioness you told me about, remember her?"

"Very well."

"And forgetting your instruction to show a fearless front, I'd called for help. I was wondering would those boys come to help me?"

"Would you have gone to help them, in the same situation?"

"I don't think so."

"Well, don't feel guilty about it. It's not natural to risk your life."

"You mean I should stay in my tent and rejoice that it was Francis or Kimani who'd met the lady in the WC and that I was safe?"

"I didn't say should, I said natural. The way it is."

"Would you have come to my rescue?" I asked.

"Yes," he said.

"Why?"

"Honestly?"

"Of course."

"Because you pay me."

A breeze had come up, fluttering the leaves above us and washing the rock where we lay. The film of moisture evaporated from my body, and suddenly I was very cool. It was pleasant there, and I was at home with Jim.

"God, ain't it peaceful," I said.

"It is." Jim was short. He wanted me to sleep. And I was going fast.

"Two nights ago I woke in the middle of the night," I remembered for him, "and what woke me was sidearm fire. It wasn't very far off. There must have been twenty rounds pressed off."

"In New York?"

"In the capital of contemporary civilization. Not two blocks from where my wife and I were in bed. Two blocks. Twenty rounds. Rifle? Sidearms, I thought. In the well-lit streets of that goddamn city."

"Who was it?"

"I don't know. I never left my bed."

"Didn't rush to the rescue?"

"Rolled over on my stomach. And now, my friend, I believe I am going to nap."

"Pleasant dreams."

"There was nothing about it in the papers next morning. No one considered it unusual, I suppose. It was like another time I remember, in Manila. They were shooting all over the city that night, snipers, you know, and what was left of their army. They didn't know the city had fallen."

"No?" He was careful with my sleep.

"They're probably still shooting in the suburbs."

"Yes, of course, the suburbs," he murmured.

"Of Manila. They may still not know." I laughed, but I was asleep really.

"Manila," I heard Jim say.

"Great sport! We were celebrating in the center and in the sub-urbs they were still fighting. And tough? Better believe it! Those Japanese, I mean. I know I'm not making sense, it's O.K. O.K.?"

By then it was too much trouble to explain anything, it was all too involved, went too far back, before Jim was born, no doubt, mean-ingless now. What did it matter, that other war, that city's fall? The invasion money, that Great New Eastern Brotherhood League paper money, littered the streets like shredded carpeting. We'd scooped it up in handfuls and thrown it up in the air. It was our night to celebrate. Jim stuffed his pockets with it—

Jim? How the hell had Jim come into this? And perfectly in place? "I can only suppose," he said, "they haven't heard that their officers surrendered and that we've captured the Great Fat One."

On the way to the one street where everyone except General MacArthur was heading that night, the city dark because the Japs had blown up the power plant as they retreated, we passed the stockade. There we had lights on the prisoners, had our own genera-tors there. The Japanese soldiers watched us go by. Oh, they were tough! And good fighters, everyone said that, even Jim. "I regret having had to kill so many of them," he said. "I don't go on shooting safaris anymore."

How Manila unbuttoned for us that night! Outside the big house where we all went, there was a line more than a block long, and, inside, every crib was busy. After he was through Jim said he proposed to pay off in Japanese invasion money.

Well that Little Mother, she came screaming. "Madam," Gentleman Jim said, not using the word in the vernacular, "be reasonable. You've been taking it from the Japanese for three years, now I'm afraid you're going to have to take it from us."

Well, did she fuss and holler! Jim had to laugh, because she began to look good to him. "I find your cussing most agreeable, Madam Mother," he said, "so I'm going to do you, too. We rescued you from your Japanese oppressors, as you say, so now, at least for a night, we'll enjoy your gratitude. No charge. You won't have to pay me, dear old bag, or I you. It will simply be friendly intercourse."

It was all in fun till she yelled out and this strong-arm young Huk came running. He was dead and covered with a blanket before I got a good look at him. "Jim!" I shouted, and Jim turned and shot him. It was a reflex by then. Later someone said the boy was her son. While he kicked the boy to make sure he was dead, Little Mother got a shiv somewhere. We hollered so Jim saw it in time, let her pass, as Ellie had taught him, "Tai-saba-kee," then grabbed her wrist and twisted so the knife fell to the ground where the rest of us fought for it, a souvenir.

Meantime Jim had pulled her skirt up over her head and tied it off. The rest of her looked O.K., what you could see in the thin light. "Not too bad, actually," was how Jim put it. Then he let her go, "just to keep it all sporting." With the skirt bagged and bound over her, she looked like a hen running from the block where she'd left her head. Wherever she ran, we were there, turning her around. It was a game kids play. Jim was laughing so, he couldn't get it hard. Finally he did, and she gave up, lay on the ground, two legs, a belly and a bag. Jim did her in front of the rest of us. "Great sport!" he said and, as a mark of respect, wouldn't let anyone else at her though there were candidates. He cut her head free, formally thanked her, calling her "an exceptional person," and so adieu.

As we left, she screamed, "You're going to get sick, soldier. You're going to get what the Japanese gave me, because you're all the same, soldier. You're no damn good!"

But if she thought this would faze Jim, she was mistaken. "That's what I mean by sentimentality," he said. "All that justice crap. I ain't going to get no damn clap because you know why? Because I deserve it. Malaria neither," he said, reaching into the soup plate full of yellow pills that were on every table in our dining room to protect us from the fever.

I remember everybody was eating breast of turkey that night, and there was sweet rice wine to wash down the tender meat. I'll never get tired of breast of turkey. It's really for victors.

"Did you ever get the clap she promised you?" I asked, sitting up. "Jim?"

There was no one on the rock but me. The light breeze moved without a sound, and it was cooling. I lay down again.

It wasn't quinine, I remembered, it was atabrine, made you just as yellow though. Maybe it was good for malaria, but it was no good for what hit me, because two nights later, when we were done with the Manila celebration and getting ready to move north, General Gill commanding, onto the Villa Verde trail, where our spies and spotter planes told us the Japs had massed to defend their capital, Baguio, well then, just then, I came down with the dengue. Damn thing probably saved my life, because we lost one thousand and eighty men on the Villa Verde trail. That was the last fuck, that night in Manila, for many of our guys. I was left behind when they saw me crawling around the backyard on all fours like an animal, the conqueror of Manila puking prime breast of turkey, all white meat, I can never get enough of that!

I could still taste it, now in Africa, retching in my sleep. I must have fallen off again, because I heard myself saying, "Who the hell do you think you are, Jim, to shoot that young Huk and leave him with a whorehouse blanket covering him while you tie his mother's skirt over her head and fuck her in the chicken-yard dirt before the entire 32nd Regiment, Jim, who the hell do you think—?"

I'd thought it funny at the time.

It wasn't Jim, of course. Why now had I made it Jim? What was I doing making a villain of that very decent man who was taking care of me, even against my will, forcing me to protect my balding head from the heavy sun? Jesus, how unfair!

Jim came into sight over the edge of the rock. Behind him the green fields were glazed with heat. He'd made a little sack of his handkerchief, and it was full of freshwater crayfish.

"We'll have them tonight with our drinks," he said. "How did you sleep? You seemed to be having pleasant dreams when I left."

"My dreams? . . . were terrible!"

"Safaris do that. Want to go back to the kill, see what's left?"

On the way we encountered an old male lion, walking the middle of a buffalo path, his head down, his belly slung like a hammock and swaying from side to side.

"Now, there's a fellow who'll sleep well," Jim said.

Most of the lions had left. Two cubs were playing tug of war with a foreleg. Their mother was cracking vertebrae, the sound of hard candy. In a few minutes she stood, looked at the cubs, must have communicated something, because when she moved off they followed.

She wasn't fifteen feet away when the hyenas were all over the skeleton, rushing off with legs and pieces of the rib cage, all in different directions. Then the birds came down and at the same time the jackals dashed in. One against one, they were evenly matched, but the vultures were a flock and soon covered all that was left of the mare. The three little jackals were lucky to get what they got and be free of the loathsome mass of feathers, gristle, beak, and claw.

"I'll take that shower," I said.

It was waiting, the canvas drum filled with very hot water. When I was through, Kimani was waiting with a towel. Jim, having detected my anxiety, had told Kimani to stand by during my whole adventure with that canvas shower stall.

I'd have to find a way to apologize to that man for what I'd dreamed about him.

After the Scotch, we ate the boiled crayfish, husking them with our front teeth, then dipping the soft little bodies in butter and English mustard. We were happy and as silent as friends can be.

As I finished my Sanka, the spotter walked into sight at the head of the kitchen path, carrying a small bag.

"Obowatti is leaving us," Jim said. "I'm going to drive him back to the lodge, where he can pick up a ride home."

Jim waved a hand to indicate he was not ready to leave, and the spotter walked back out of sight.

'I was wondering what happened to him " I said.

"Not been himself," Jim said. "Now. About tomorrow, I thought I might take you to that private game preserve. remember?"

"I want to see the wildebeest migration."

"Oh, right right. We ll certainly do that.

There was the sound of a ruckus from behind the bushes.

"Kimani!" Jim called in his full voice of command. The silence was immediate. Jim turned to me. "Obowatti's got a wife who's sharing her nights with Obowatti's brother."

"Oh, no wonder—"

"Obowatti's determined to kill his brother. I offered him money enough, it was Kimani's suggestion, to buy another wife. But apparently he's going to carry out his plan. I must say it seems to me that one woman, especially when she's quite plain and that black, is just like another. Too much religion, don't you know. These people were so much better off without civilization. Now they're becoming as neurotic as the whites."

Kimani came up, looking apologetic, and said something in Swahili.

"He said, 'What's the difference,' which is what I'd like to know. Let him do what he wants, Kimani."

"How long will you be gone?" I asked as Jim got up.

"An hour. I may bring back some company," he said. "Just overnight."

"A girl?"

"Oh, God, no!" he laughed. "Fine dinner, Kimani," he called as he drove away.

I decided to go to bed early. Francis lit the Gaz and provided the little pitcher of water for brushing my teeth. He'd placed an empty biscuit tin on the floor in a corner of my tent.

I couldn't sleep till the Toyota returned. There was a strange voice, then Jim's answering. As soon as I heard him, I fell asleep and, to my surprise, slept through the night. The lions of the area, I suppose, were sleeping too.

When I woke next morning, Jim and his guest were in earnest conversation, leaning toward each other over their coffee. The visitor's back was to me, and he didn't look around when Jim waved good morning, simply waited till he had Jim's attention again, then went on with what he'd been saying.

Francis came running with a table and chair and set them up in front of my tent. I was to have breakfast apart.

I sat with my back toward them, so I didn't get a good look at the new face in camp till later when Jim came to see how I was getting along and I turned and saw the man walking slowly toward the jeep with his head down. Then he stretched his neck in a compulsive and strained gesture, looking off through the trees to the field on the sunny side of our camp.

Jim's guest was an East Indian.

He was well dressed, in the clothes of a trader, gave the impression that he never took off his suit coat in public, put it on in his private chamber every morning, took it off in the same place at the end of the day.

Jim was extremely apologetic. "His car," he said, "is no good through open country. I'll have to take him back to the main road where we left it last night. Only be a few minutes."

I indicated the Indian. "Is everything O.K.?"

"Oh, that? Just a personal matter, trivial, so silly."

I looked at the Indian gentleman, and he was looking at me. Whatever their meeting had been about, it had not been trivial to him.

When Jim came back he had another Nescafé, seemed troubled and in no hurry to set forth. Then he noticed me looking at him, jumped up, and called out, "Let's go, let's go!" and walked quickly to the Toyota.

He didn't say a word about his visitor and I didn't ask. I was curious, of course. It was the first indication I'd seen that Jim had a personal life.

We headed in a new direction. Even heavier rains had fallen here. It was like riding a road of water-filled sponges. Then we began to climb, up a hill, then another, then over a ridge, and looking down, we saw the migration.

To say there were thousands of beasts in line would be untrue. "In line" would not be accurate, and "thousands" quite inadequate to describe the horde which spanned the horizons.

Leaderless, without guides or marshals, they seemed to be following instructions in an old memory. Their movement suggested a great crowd leaving the locus of a disaster and moving to a place where they'd been told they'd find safety.

Along the skirts of their path we saw piles of fresh-cleaned bones. Carrion birds circled, their cries the final rites.

To get a better look, I climbed up on the hood of the Toyota—we were down on the flat now—then jumped off and walked toward the herd. Jim had usually discouraged my going off alone, and I expected he would now. When he didn't, I asked, "O.K. if I go closer?"

"What lion would be interested in you?" he said with a smile.

I looked back after twenty steps. Jim was sitting on one of the mudguards reading a letter written on blue note paper.

I got closer to the herd. They did not notice me till I was twenty feet away then all together, at a signal I couldn't see or hear, they hobbled off in their lumbering stoop-backed trot just fast enough to keep a minimal distance between us. Heads bowed, without a sign of pleasure or hope, they were like the human masses of the Middle Ages.

I walked back to Jim, who was still on the jeep, cross-legged, reading. When he saw me, he stared at me for an instant, holding the letter in his hand as if he was debating giving it to me. Then he put it away and, with an effort, found another subject.

"You were asking me yesterday," he said, "what I wasn't indifferent to?"

"Since we're alike in so many ways, I did wonder."

"You know what a free fall is?"

"Yes. No. Not really."

"You fall out of a small plane and for sixty seconds you're free of everything."

"Say it again."

"You fall backward out of a plane, which is immediately not backward, because directions are the same in space. And for—"

"Sixty seconds. That seems a very long time."

"It is. At first you find it impossible to keep from pulling the cord even for three seconds. Then, it takes months and months to develop the control you need, you do twenty, thirty, forty seconds. One day you're doing sixty, and those sixty seconds seem like the only pieces of your life worth living, the only time you're entirely free."

"I don't think I could ever do that."

"It's a matter of control. You could do it, you're like me that way. But I've only found one woman who was able to do sixty seconds—"

"So you fell in love and—"

"Just the opposite. I couldn't stand her. She began to be competitive and make demands. She changed personality, and so I—"

"You left town, went out on safari."

"How did you know?"

"It's what I would have done."

"When I got back from one trip, she was married. She's pregnant now, but I hear she still goes up, against doctor's orders, of course. She really does it only to annoy me, but I have no time for that. Well, look, I think we have something going over there."

He pulled his Swiss field glasses out of the glove compartment.

"Wild dogs," he said, handing me his glasses. "We're in luck today."

I could see seven or eight mottled animals loping along the skirt of another part of the migration.

"What are they doing?"

"You'll see."

"They're just standing around. No, a couple of them are running. They don't seem very eager, whatever they're doing."

"They don't have to be eager."

"Now those two have stopped. Two others have taken it up."

I kept the glasses up as we moved closer. Now I could see that their casualness was confidence. They were skillfully cutting one of the wildebeests out of the herd. It didn't surprise me when I saw this animal's brothers and sisters and cousins edge away from him. What had horrified me only the day before, I was now taking for granted.

The Toyota stopped. I lowered the glasses. "Let's drive closer," I said.

"Wait till after the kill." He took the glasses from me.

"Are you sure there'll be one?"

"Wild dogs? They never miss."

"You admire them."

"Oh, yes. No hysteria, no eccentricities, absolutely efficient. And even though they eat their victims while they're still living, they are also the least cruel citizens of this world."

Jim gave me the glasses. "Look! Quick, or you'll miss it."

What I saw was one of the pursuers making a quick grab at the rear ankle of the chosen, at which the heavy animal spilled over. The pack was on him precisely as he hit the ground.

"It's just a matter of getting them off their feet," Jim said. "Then they're finished."

"You mean they're eating him now?"

"He'll be partly gone by the time we get there."

Jim stopped at a decent distance as he always did, but the glasses put me into the flurry of feeding. The dogs raised their heads and wagged their tails, then went back to their meal.

"That animal is still living," I said. "This is terrible."

"He's in a state of shock," Jim said, "not feeling much, really."

"Awful," I said.

"I'd like to die like that," Jim said, "heart beating fast, blood running. Now your lions, they grab the muzzle or the neck of their prey, clamp shut, then hold on—five minutes, more—till the animal suffocates. If you want to know the picture I have of civilization, that is it, slow death by suffocation."

There were nine dogs feeding and three pups, all tearing great mouthfuls off the wildebeest's rack, wagging their tails as they did, and the wildebeest still kicking his feet.

"Want to get closer?"

"I can see fine."

"You'll get used to it. You're used to a lot worse."

"Am I?"

"We all are. The higher up one goes in the order of beasts, the crueler they are. Man, of course, surpasses all. And women."

There was a strange sound, a sort of whirring and slapping. The vultures were coming down. I saw the hyenas arriving and the jackals. They all paid the dogs as much respect as they had the lions, even though these good fellows never stopped wagging their tails as they ate.

"They seem so friendly," I said.

"Why shouldn't they? They have nothing against the wildebeest."

One of the dogs suddenly turned and chased a hyena, nipping at his anus, as if for the sport of it.

"Would they have eaten the hyena if he'd pulled it down?"

"No," Jim said, "the hyenas would have eaten the hyena."

Suddenly I'd had enough of the spectacle, the wagging tails and the way Jim took it.

"Let's go," I said.

"They're not through yet."

Was he teasing me? His face was perfectly composed, deadly calm. I couldn't make out what he was feeling. "I've had it, Jim, thanks. Let's go on," I repeated. He nodded and started the motor.

When we caught up with the main body of the migration, Jim asked, "Still interested in this?"

"I imagine I've seen what there is to see. Tell me, is the grass greener and more plentiful where they're going?"

"It used to be. At one time it was thigh-high, very rich and very beautiful. But that's gone now."

"Then why do they go? Why does that animal go along that path to that place?"

"Because there's a lion waiting for him there."

"Oh, come on, Jim."

"True. They know how they're supposed to die, and they don't know a better way. Do you?"

"I'd turn around."

"And disappoint the lion? You wouldn't want to do that, would you?"

"Yes. I'd find a better way."

"You really believe there is one?"

"There has to be."

"Why? You don't even know why you're here. You told me so."

"Here on earth? Or here in East Africa?"

"Here in East Africa for a start. Sorry. No offense meant. I'm a little upset about—a personal matter."

"I know I'd rather be here than where I was."

"Well, that's something. And how about here on earth? Oh, of course, your career. You've found a meaning."

"To what?"

"Footprints on the sands of time, all that rubbish. Back in the Bush we know better. Tomorrow it will rain, and where will those footsteps be? Where do the bones go? The ants don't differentiate between saints and sinners, successes and failures, predators and victims. Who of this herd remembers the beast he walked alongside of yesterday? What male remembers the female he topped the day before? He forgot her as he got off her back. Oh, look!"

He pointed to a wildebeest calf toddling along, looking like a lost child.

"Where's its mother?" I asked. "Devoured?"

"I doubt it. The cat would take the calf first, much more tender."

"Then where the hell is her mother?"

"You don't see her looking for her calf, do you?"

"She should be."

"Should is a word to forget. It goes with hope and charity and love and all the rest of it, fidelity—forget them all."

"What's eating you, Jim?"

"I'm not myself. Please forgive me. I certainly don't want to intrude my personal—"

He stopped. Neither of us could find anything to say.

"What will happen to that calf?" I said finally.

"You will go out there, presently, and pick it up, and we'll put it into the back of the Toyota and take it back to camp, find us a baby bottle, fill it with cow's milk, feed it, continue to take care of it till it grows up, which means, for you, taking it back to the States. Wouldn't you like to do that?"

"Why would I?"

"Because you're precisely that kind of sentimentalist."

"Don't talk to me that way, Jim. I don't like it."

"No offense was intended. Just a confrontation with facts, which you seemed to want. Very well. You abhor my view of universal indifference. So tell me, where do you stop being responsible for your fellow man? Tell me that. That's what Mr. Gargi, the Indian chap, came to see me about this morning. Here. Look at this."

He pulled up hard on the hand brake, and the Toyota stopped. Jim reached into his pocket and pulled out the blue letter he'd been reading and handed it to me.

"See if you don't think this pretty damn cheeky," he said.

At the top of the blue note paper, embossed in white letters, was the word ANDREA.

"Who is Andrea?"

"Read the letter first. It's written to Marge, the girl I was with the other night. The girl you were with got the same letter. Frightened both girls a bit, let me tell you."

I didn't reach for the letter. He put it in my hand.

'Go on, read it. Only remember I did nothing to lead her on, absolutely nothing. And I had nothing to do with her being pregnant."

He protests too much, I thought. Then I read Andrea's letter.

Dear Marge. Please don't see Jim again. He's incapable of loving anyone, you know that. His heart is as cold as a stone buried in the earth. That's his curse. An occasional go with him can't mean anything to you. Please don't hurt me for an instant's distraction. My happiness depends on him. I'm ashamed of that. But it's true. Even now after all he's done to me. Even though I don't respect him anymore. That's my curse.

I looked up.

"She's married to that Indian gentleman you saw this morning," Jim said. "Go on. Turn the page."

I have plans to reunite us. If anything goes wrong with that I will not want to live. Do you want to be part of what kills me? I can t believe you do.

I remember the night we met. Your eyes were soft and kind. I know you'll understand me. Read between the lines. And help me. Before it's too late.

Andrea

"What do you think of that?" Jim demanded.

"Seems a terribly unfair letter," I said.

"Insane. absolutely insane. We agree."

I'd lied. Immediately, instinctively, I was on the girl's side. Why hadn't I said so?

"The Indian gentleman?" I asked, carefully folding the blue note paper precisely where Jim had unfolded it. "He's—"

"Married to her, and she's pregnant and still goes up to free fall."

"Oh, she's your friend who did sixty seconds?"

"She would have gone ninety if I'd said go ninety. 'Ask me anything, she used to say. 'My life belongs to you.' Well, I get along very nicely, thank you, without anyone's life in my hands."

"Is she the one you almost married? No, that was in Rhodesia."

"She followed me here. Then I couldn't get rid of her. When I went out with other girls she'd follow us. I'd come out in the middle of the night, and there she'd be, sitting in her car, smiling and waving. I finally decided to see her one more time and try to convince her the more she went on that way, the less chance there was of our ever getting together."

"But then, weren't you leading her on?"

"Most certainly not! I told her over and over again that we were finished. I left Nairobi, went on safari for weeks at a time, ignored her messages, didn't answer her letters. Now she writes these girls, threatening them."

"I didn't see any threat in her letter."

"Why do you keep taking her side?"

"Do I?"

"Yes. You do. Sorry. Well, then, I did what I hope is a kindness. When you see Andrea she looks ever so demure. I told Gargi about affairs she'd had before me that I knew about, all unhappy, all did not last. She's seen much action, as they say in naval communiqués. 'No need to feel responsible for her,' I said, 'she was that way long before either of us.' "

"Do you really think that helped?"

"Not at all. Made him feel for her even more. There are men like that, you know, saints in sackcloth, born to suffer. 'Walk away,' I told him. 'She'll get over it. People do.' "

"Always?"

"If they don't it's no one else's concern, is it? I resent when people try to put the full load of their lives on you. The least we can expect from each other is, 'I don't tax you, you don't tax me.' "

"I don't understand. Why did she marry him, the Indian?"

"To hurt me. But I wasn't hurt. As she found out. Still here he comes last night, clearly under her whip, to inform me she's pregnant and not by him. They're married, but she hasn't let him have her, he says. I find that a bit hard to believe, don't you?"

"As you say, I don't know her."

"You don't have to know her. It's ridiculous on the face of it. And what's the message this poor clod carries from Cassandra? She has made up her mind to wait for me. He will divorce her, he says, if I'll marry her. Isn't that outrageous?"

"True love. He must be terribly jealous of you."

"No, no, he's very fair, a perfect gentleman, no matter what those niggers in Nairobi say about him."

"Even a perfect gentleman has his breaking point."

"I had to tell him, 'Sorry, dear boy, but I'm not at all sure the child is mine and if by some chance it is, I advise you, and her, to abort at once and start over again.'"

"And what was his answer, poor clod?"

"It's against his religion to take a life, that sort of thing. So I said, 'Surely since you feel that way, it's your responsibility.'"

"How did he take that?"

"It's not a matter of how he took it. He said he understood how I felt and that he'd simply have to keep close watch to make sure she didn't swallow every pill in her collection, which is the largest in East Africa. Well, I'm certainly not going to be stampeded by that kind of emotionalism."

"Actually you are, just a little?"

"Not at all. By the way, what made you say that about a breaking point?"

"When he was in camp, he kept stretching his neck, like a heron. Remember? Then he shook his head as if it was a bottle and he was trying to shake something out of it."

"A crick in his neck, no doubt. No? Well, whatever it is, he brought it on himself. What astonishes me is how this very decent chap, educated, you know, quite civilized, I'd travel anywhere in his company, believe me, how he can tie up with a madwoman like Andrea."

"You did."

"I knew when to stop. You have to pull out of a situation like that when the moment comes."

"Do you really think you can just cut a person off? Cold?"

"To save yourself. Surely you must have been in that kind of stew. Everybody has."

I laughed.

"Are you laughing at me? Not that I blame you. All this fuss about a woman."

"Is she pretty?"

"I doubt very much you'd think so."

"She must have something. Beautiful eyes?"

"Eyes? Like Marge's, frantic. Make you uncomfortable all the time."

"Beautiful hair?"

"A scruff of the stuff you pull out of a carpet sweeper after it's been over an old rug."

"Then what the hell attracted you?"

"I cannot imagine. Chicken-breasted. The bones coming through the skin. A rocky ride, let me tell you."

"May I see her picture?"

"How did you know I had one?"

"Let me see it."

He reached into his back pocket and pulled out a worn lionskin wallet.

"You won't get anything from this," he said. "She's all covered up."

It was an old snapshot, cracked over its surface and frayed at the corners. Andrea wore a swagger suit lashed at the ankles over hard-nose boots. There was a pack on her back, the parachute, and on her head, unbuckled, an aerialist's helmet. Draped over her shoulder was an animal.

"What's the cat?" I asked.

"The cat is Andrea. The kitten is an ocelot. She had animals all over her place, even snakes." He laughed. "They'd leap on us at the most inopportune moments."

Andrea's eyes shot out a light that fired her face. The angle of the cigarette in her mouth defied the world.

"She's terrific," I said. "She's really something!"

"There've been days when I thought so."

"Her eyes? What's that light?"

"My father had a word for it, when he met her. Apocalyptic."

There was a tiny cry, and we looked around. The wildebeest calf was standing as if he'd been waiting for us. Then he began to trot.

"That little fellow will be dead by morning," Jim said.

"Let's take it back to camp."

"Now, really!"

"I know I'm behaving like a silly American, but I can't leave it here helpless. I mean, I can but—would it be all right?"

Jim smiled at me affectionately. "Of course," he said.

The little fellow was a born broken-field runner. We had great sport catching him. Jim finally brought him down, bound all four feet with one knot, threw him in the back of the Toyota, and told me to sit on him. As we rode home, the little wonder released a pungent yellow fluid all over me which made Jim laugh. "Excuse me," he said laughing, "do excuse me but—"

The tension was gone, but when I got back to camp my head

ached. "I think I'll take a nap before dinner," I said, touching my head.

"You left your hat off again," Jim said. "Take some aspirin immediately." I looked at the calf, and Jim said, "Don't worry about him. Lie down."

"I don't think he appreciates that we saved his life."

"They never do. Want some turkey broth?"

He brought it himself.

"I had a difficult time prevailing on Kimani not to butcher your ward," he said. "When I told him we wanted some sort of nursing device for the little fellow, he thought we were insane. Feeling better?"

"Oh, I'll be fine."

"I warned you that sun is treacherous. By the way, I'm fearfully embarrassed."

"By what?"

"By the way I—by what happened out there this afternoon."

"Oh, please don't be."

"Well, I am. Making you put up with all that, her letter, and—oh Lord! The only excuse for my behavior is that we seem to have become friends."

"We have."

Suddenly he reached for my hand and shook it. "Thank you," he said, "thank you very much." After he left, I thought that an intimacy.

Neither of us woke for dinner.

Jim had warned me the little calf's presence in camp would be quickly nosed out, but the lions I heard seemed to be far off, so did not disturb my sleep.

Then there was a sound which did, something between the one a rotary saw makes when it hits a knot in an oak plank and the scream of a child through the barred windows of a home for the deranged. It was answered from the opposite side of camp.

This conversation went on for a time. Then there was silence.

My head was banging. I got up, fumbled in the dark for the aspirin, swallowed four, fell asleep, woke, slept, not on and off, but drifting half between.

I was in that kind of a doze when there was a sudden commotion, terrible and swift. I thought I heard a tiny cry. Then I saw Jim's light go on, heard him curse. The flap zipper of his tent went up. Jim was walking out into what I never would have. I heard his voice, could not make out what he was saying to the boys. Then there was, most surprisingly, some laughter, more talk, more laughter.

In the morning my headache was mostly gone. I felt unsteady, a little testy, the natural result, I thought, of a bad night. I took two more aspirin.

"What was all the laughter about last night?" I asked Jim when he appeared for breakfast.

"You've been relieved of your responsibility," he said.

"The calf? How?"

"Leopard, I think. He's gone."

"Didn't they stake him down?"

"The practice here is to enclose a walking meat supply in a fence of thorn, a *boma*, very effective usually."

"Apparently it wasn't. What happened?"

"The boys believe in the magic of the leopard. It's the animal they respect most, trust least, same thing, I suppose. What they say is that a leopard leaped into the enclosure, then leaped out again with the calf in his mouth."

"Could a leopard do that?"

"Not even a big male."

"What's your theory?"

"Rather romantic. The wildebeest calf, hearing the leopard calling—you did hear the leopard last night?"

"Those screams?"

"Yes. The little fellow felt very wanted. Who can resist being wanted except a fool human—by the way, what did you think of the letter on further reflection, Andrea's letter?"

"I felt sorry for her," I said, glad for the chance. "Very sympathetic."

His face clenched, but he didn't speak.

"So what do you think happened?" I said. "To the calf?"

"It went looking for—for whoever. It got through the thorn enclosure some way, jumped, perhaps. How can you possibly feel sorry for her? That is a totally unfair and impertinent letter."

"I suppose it is."

"Suppose! Forgive me, but I can see you've never had an experience with that kind of person. People like that can be terrible bullies. Have you any idea what emotional blackmail she was demanding? Excuse me for speaking to you this way, but I'm out of patience with her, really."

"I can see that—about being a bully."

"I will not be moved by it."

"I suppose you're right."

"I know damn well I'm right!" He was breathing very hard. "Forgive me, but I will not be blackmailed—"

I tried to help him. "And the laughter"—I changed the subject—"what was that about?"

He looked puzzled. "What laughter?"

"Why were they laughing, the boys? After the calf—"

"Oh, the boys. The laughter was Francis and Kimani's tribute to the surpassing cleverness of their friend, the leopard. You're aware that they had no sentimental feelings about the calf. They regarded it as fresh meat, simply that. They think you're an absolute fool, excuse me, for being sentimental over that damned calf."

We drove up the long slope which hung over our camp, then across some stubbled meadows.

Jim laughed. "I have just broken," he said, "every rule of the Society of White Hunters. Again. Oh, dear!"

"Which only proves you're human."

"Well, you'll never be bothered with my personal life again, I can assure you. I will remain impersonal as we're supposed to be. At all times, O.K.?"

"I don't mind," I said, "either way."

The damned ache in the bones of my head would not go away. The sun was pressing down. I put on my golf cap. I felt edgy and a little cold.

"Today," he said, in his professional voice, "I thought we might have a look at the private game park of Monsieur Oscar Jamet. Will you be agreeable to that?"

On a terrace at the side of their long, low settler's house, M. and Mme. Jamet were entertaining a guest for breakfast. He was presented to me and identified as the game warden of the district. A plump black, spending his middle years in sedentary postures, he used the interruption of our arrival to protest a busy morning ahead, thank Mme. Jamet for her hospitality, and take his leave.

M. Jamet, dissatisfied with the conclusion of their conversation, accompanied the game warden to his car, while pressing a last point. M. Jamet was a huge, pneumatic man of perhaps fifty-five—an Alsatian, Jim had said—sprouting strawberry-blond hair from every ruddy aperture. Santa Claus in summer, he spoke perfect English.

Mme. Jamet twinkled off to make her staff attentive to our arrival.

"Sit here in the shade," Jim said. "Keep your hat on. I will explain."

I changed seats. As I did I noticed an eight-foot pyramid of skulls and skins at the top of a flower garden.

"That's from the animals they've lost to poachers," Jim explained. "They drive the animals into the fence Oscar put up. Easy victims. Oscar is very exercised about it, and I must say I can hardly blame him."

Mme. Jamet was back, followed by a black servant in a short white butler's jacket who offered us a choice of fruit punch or a Bloody Mary that tasted odd.

"*Marie la Vierge,*" Mme. Jamet explained in her twangy French accent. "We do not allow alcohol on the place. The blacks smell it out, break in like mice, lose all control with a single drink. It is impossible here, a normal life."

A cloud moved and the sun touched her. She was older than her husband, a woman thin the way Jacques Cousteau is thin, a variety of chic. She made a virtue of her raillike body, wore tight boots of glove leather and whip cords. A broad belt dramatized her wasp waist, a sweater showed no irregularities in front to mar the flow of green vicuña. A lesson in how to make an asset of a physical disaster.

The game warden's driver opened the car door for his boss. We heard a few words as M. Jamet's voice was raised in outrage. "Must I create my own police force?"

"The poachers," Mme. Jamet explained. "This government does nothing." She looked at the warden's car. "*Merde!*" she said.

The driver closed the door and the game warden sank into his tonneau.

"Oscar had to cut out tobacco, too," Mme. Jamet said. "A problem of circulation. Suddenly his pressure goes up to one hundred and ninety. But he permits me these." She was smoking a Dutch cigarillo, held elegantly between shell-pink fingertips. "Will you try one?"

The game warden's driver, on instruction, started his motor. This act tripped something in M. Jamet. He erupted, and we heard every word.

"Well, then, tell me, can I ever expect any assistance from your government?"

I couldn't hear the game warden's reply but couldn't miss the ambivalence of his manner.

Then the car drove off.

"M. Jamet," I said to Jim, "has your authority voice."

This remark, intended as a social joke, nettled Jim. He turned to M. Jamet who was returning to us and said, "Oscar, can you find a moment to inform this representative of the greatest democracy on earth what techniques the fact of being a white man in East Africa makes necessary?"

M. Jamet expressed his disgust in sounds without words. Then he shook my hand and said, "It's so good to see an American face."

Our breakfast was brought to table, and I was served.

"Here, here." Oscar took my plate. "Come on, sir, ranch style. Let me put a piece of this impala steak under your eggs."

"No, thanks," I said. "I was up with a headache most of the night."

I'd felt the nausea again as soon as the meal was served. Perhaps it was the presence of all that meat. There was fat link sausage as well as the impala steak and hand-cut hog's bacon.

"I will have that last piece of toast," I said to the butler, who was carrying off the silver toast holder to have it refilled.

"Zoo-zoo!" Mme. Jamet trilled for his attention.

The butler kept a course for the kitchen door.

"Attention!" Oscar shouted. "Where are you going with that?" Then he added something in Swahili, an elaboration which made the butler recover from his start and laugh with relief.

Everyone joined in except me. I didn't know the joke.

Oscar noticed I wasn't smiling.

"My client," Jim explained, "doesn't like the way we talk to our blacks."

"I'm certainly on his side in that," Oscar said, "but there is no other way, as you must have observed, to get their attention, not their obedience, simply their attention."

During breakfast, Oscar Jamet told us of his efforts to preserve one tiny corner of East Africa as it was. "Do you think that is appreciated here? I give employment to more than thirty of these people, pay them better than they pay each other. Am I showered with gratitude? I no longer expect it. What I am concerned about is the animal life here, to preserve it. Come, let me show you what I've created."

Reaching out a huge hand, he pulled me out of my chair.

We went to the game preserve—the Jamet home was outside its cable-link fence—in two vehicles. Oscar asked me to go with him, and on the way he told me the story he must have told hundreds of times, his success story.

"In June of 1940, German tourists wearing helmets and riding tanks rolled into our country," he said. "Soon afterward, some of my friends were invited to join the Wehrmacht. They took me too, a mistake because I am a practical man and value my life. As soon as I found myself opposite an army known to take prisoners, I surrendered. To the Americans."

"At that time there were no sleeping facilities or dining accommodations for prisoners in France, at least not on the level of comfort you Americans choose to provide your guests. So your generals, excellent fellows, sent us to the States. There I found my ideal, particularly admired your business methods and your films. I worked behind the cigarette and candy counter of the prison camp's PX. There I learned English, polished it at the cinema. Now they tell me I speak rather like Bing Crosby. Also I read your magazines, discovered that many of your big men were born on the wrong side of the Atlantic. This taught me hope."

He was pushing his open Land Rover at nearly sixty miles an hour.

"When the day came for us to be returned to our motherland, I had my big idea. I opened a small plant to manufacture a confection, called it Bonne Nouvelle. You've seen it, no? An exact imitation of the most popular American candy bar. My only innovation was to use American methods of marketing and advertising—in France. I had learned what you have to teach. How you sell is more important than what you sell.

"Five years after the first Bonne Nouvelle appeared on the market, I sold my entire operation for twenty-two million francs, not French, Swiss."

The jouncing had me dizzy.

"Now I wanted the Garden of Eden with sanitary facilities," he laughed. "I found this place. I doubt Adam's preserve was any bigger."

I was about to beg him to drive a little slower, and a little more smoothly, when we came to a nine-foot fence surmounted by three strands of barbed wire set at an angle pointing out.

"I have sixteen thousand acres inside this nine-foot fence. I live here as if this is all there is to the world. I don't know who the president of the United States is now."

"It's—"

"Don't tell me. I don't care to know." He seemed to be very worked up, either in exhilaration or anger. I imagine nothing exhilarated him like his rages. "The wonder of it is," he said, "that all this comes from a bar of candy."

"I'd like to taste a Bonne Nouvelle."

"No, you wouldn't. Anyway, you can't. I don't allow it in the house."

We'd arrived in front of a large sportsman's lodge. Oscar stopped the car and jumped on the steps, taking a keyfold out of his back pocket.

His headquarters—a sign across the lintel of the front door so declared it—was on a corner of the preserve. On one side, I could look along what seemed to be miles of fence that went up a rise in a perfect line, out of sight over the top, then up and over the next rise of land.

"Come on in, friend," Oscar shouted. "Ah, it's so nice to see an American face again."

"What did this fence cost?" I said from the porch.

"Don't ask! An absurd expenditure. The fence was made in West Germany, excellent construction. You can imagine what I had to pay these Nazi bastards, but it gives me a completely controlled paradise in a world whose rapid disintegration I don't want even to hear about."

"Here you are God," I suggested.

He took this as a compliment.

"My only problem is a few poachers, but we're going to control them too, and pretty damn quick."

The walls of the room were weighed down with huge trophies, the biggest horned creatures still not extinct. A field telephone on the table screamed to be picked up.

"Oh, my God," Oscar said, "they found another poacher, at the other end of the—" He was out the door, moving like an elephant. "Come if you like, good way to see the place." I was running down the stairs, head banging inside. "Don't if you don't feel well, it might shake you up." I was in the jeep, and he'd started the engine. "Stay here and wait for Monique and Jim if you—" We were rolling.

Going up the incline we hugged the fence. Antelope looked through the mesh as if they wanted to join the animals on the liberty side. Oscar drove right through, scattering them.

It was a terrifying ride.

In the four or five years since he'd put up the fence, the strip of land along its base had sprouted acacia trees and thorn bushes, which Oscar simply rolled over, the young, resilient stems crashing along the steel underpan of the Land Rover, one after another, like heavy surf under a Boston Whaler.

"Hold on," Oscar shouted.

Suddenly I began to scream. At the top of my voice!

Everyone screams differently. I have no idea what mine sounds like. But for the first time since I was an infant I lost all control of my feelings, all caution about letting them be heard. I didn't give a damn how it would sound to the other fellow, what he'd think about me or say to others about me later.

The fact is Oscar seemed rather pleased. He gunned his Land Rover even faster.

We'd turned the crest of the hill, were heading down.

Later I found I'd been holding on so hard I had three breaks in the skin of my fingers around the nails.

I remember Oscar yelling, "Isn't this—? It's *formidable!*" as another tree and its heavily leafed top was swallowed under us.

There was a hammer inside my head, and it was trying to get out by beating a hole through the skull.

Once I almost fell out. We'd reached the corner, and as he turned he saw me going, grabbed me, and held on. He had a grip like a bear trap.

Then we stopped, and he jumped out of the Land Rover.

I would have puked, but I saw Oscar drawing a pistol out of a holster I hadn't noticed and advancing on a man a couple of his wardens in olive drab shorts and underwear tops were holding at gun-point.

It amazed me that blacks would turn in blacks. I had to ask Jim about that. How could they continue to live in that part of the country?

Oscar, giving orders in Swahili, held his pistol on the poacher as the pair of wardens bound the man's hands behind him.

"Come here, sir," Oscar said to me impatiently, "come here and look at this."

My head was throbbing like my heart's motor was in it.

The black kept his eyes to the ground, a captured animal.

Oscar was pointing to—it was a Grant's gazelle, the first time I'd been close to one, a perfect young animal, its throat cut. The wardens had come on the poacher as he was dismembering the animal. Its head was on one side, eyelids up, eyeballs looking straight at me. The two legs, cut free of the body, were tied together at the ankles. The animal had been skinned, and on the skin lay those cuts of meat the blacks liked best.

'They love the liver and the kidneys," Oscar explained, "just as the big cats do. They eat the heart raw." He turned and looked at the two wardens. "You can have all this," he said, indicating the meat on the skin, "but put the legs in my car." He turned to me, and I thought he winked. "We'll have them for dinner," he said.

The poacher was ordered into the back seat of the Land Rover, a warden on each side. Driving back to headquarters, I realized that running over small trees was not special to emergencies. Oscar ran over everything in front of him all the way back.

The area to the rear of the headquarters' lodge was a sort of hospital. Small cages and enclosures held animals, sick or wounded, which needed care. In one cage an ocelot ducked out of sight as soon as he saw us. In another cage, behind small mesh, a python was asleep.

Oscar ordered the door to one of the cages opened. Jim and Monique and some of the other wardens watched as the poacher was pushed into the enclosure and it was locked behind him.

"You all right?" Jim asked me.

"We had an exciting ride." Oscar laughed. "He almost fell out."

I couldn't take my eyes off the poacher. He was standing motionless in the middle of the enclosure, head down, waiting for whatever disposition Oscar would make of him.

"What are you thinking?" Oscar asked me.

"Nothing," I said, turning my head away.

The keeper of the little zoo came up with a small cage in the shape of a pail. In it were a dozen white mice. He saluted M. Jamet, then dropped a mouse into the enclosure where the python lay asleep.

"He ate yesterday," Monique said. "He may not today."

"Is something disturbing you?" Oscar asked.

I'd been looking at the poacher again.

"Nothing special," I said.

"That man," he said, pointing to the poacher in the cage, "is breaking every law, the law of the state, the law of humanity, the law of God, and he has no damn business taking my property. What would you do with this problem?"

"Oh, darling," Monique said, "they're just meat-starved. You have so much here, let them take a little."

The man in the cage lifted his head and looked at me. A new face? I looked away quickly.

The mouse in the python's cage was behaving in a way I hadn't anticipated. It was inspecting the eight-foot snake with its nose. The python opened its eyes without revealing the least interest in the small, clean rodent.

"What's he doing?" I asked. The mouse nosed around the python, who had again closed his eyes.

"Am I right, Oscar?" Jim said. "If the python doesn't eat the mouse, the mouse will eat the python."

"Eat the python? Where would he begin?" I laughed.

"Where he found the meat most tender. That's what he's determining now. Since the python doesn't show interest in any way, the mouse might even believe him dead, but dead or alive, he's meat."

The mouse's confidence was up. It was nosing the python's long body like a master chef inspecting a whole filet he might purchase for his kitchen.

Slowly the python woke, looked at the mouse, a fixed stare. He didn't move except his head. The mouse looked back at the snake, not the least bit intimidated.

"All right," Oscar exploded, "go ahead, let him out."

He did not wait for one of the wardens, went to the enclosure, opened the door, and, taking out his knife, cut the bonds around the poacher's wrists. "But for chrissake, this is the third time—" He was not addressing the poacher because he was not speaking in Swahili. He was addressing me. "So stop it. You're going to make a villain of me."

Oscar barked some orders in Swahili which the poacher understood. He ran and was gone.

Then I had this thought. I hope Ellie's safe.

The snake looked at the mouse with interest now. I was watching intently, or so I pretended.

"They're meat-starved, *chéri,*" Monique said.

"Well, then, why doesn't their goddamn government do something?"

"They're trying to get them to raise cattle but—"

"*Merde!* They're too lazy." Oscar was challenging me directly.

When the snake struck, it was a move so swift I couldn't follow it. He had the side of the mouse in his mouth, and before I could see what happened, it had happened. He'd coiled his body around the clean little animal, and there was nothing to see but the head of the tiny white predator who a moment before had been enjoying great dreams of consuming the choicest part of the python.

"You know what the game warden's advice to me was?" Oscar

yelled at me. "Kill the next one. That, he says, is the only warning they'll pay attention to. And that warden, you saw him, is a black man."

"Then why don't you do it, *chéri?*" Monique said coolly.

The hospital attendant kept dropping mice into the ocelot's cage. The cat charged out of its little box-shelter, grabbed a mouse, and was eating it as it crouched back into cover. One of its legs was badly twisted.

"What happened to its leg?" I asked.

"A hyena," Oscar said. "Wouldn't you say, Jim?"

The ocelot was out again, grabbed another mouse. The sound it made was similar to the one a man would make eating an Oh Henry! bar, the bones as they were chewed up made the sound the nuts make with the candy.

"What will you do with it?" I indicated the cat.

"If I let it free," Oscar answered, "it would be dead in a week. He's there for life."

"Who would kill it?"

"Its brothers," he glared at me. "Nature has no tolerance for cripples and weaklings." I did think he meant me.

The ocelot was eating another Oh Henry!

"That damned head warden advising me to kill one of them. What do you say to that?"

I shrugged, turned away.

But Oscar came after me, and I had to face him.

"You have no right to come here judging me," he said.

"I wasn't judging you."

"He wasn't doing that, Oscar. Now come off it," Jim said.

"He doesn't have to live here and face these problems. He has no right to be morally superior to me. I do my best."

"Of course," I said.

"This is their place. They are more than ninety-eight percent here. They have the government. We live by their tolerance. If I killed one, I'd be stood up in a trial where I'd have no chance of mercy. They wouldn't do what I just did, would they, let the man go?"

"I understand that," I said.

He sighed with disgust. Then he said, "So tell me what you're thinking."

"I'm wondering," I said, "why one of these blacks hasn't killed you a long, long time ago."

I turned from his gaping face and walked to the Toyota.

A half hour out of that controlled paradise, I asked Jim to stop while I threw up Oscar Jamet's breakfast. After which I felt so much better that I resented Jim putting his hand on my forehead, that hand with the message, "Now calm down, little boy."

"I'm all right," I said. "Take your hand away."

"You have a fever."

Was he pleased or was I paranoid?

"You should be in bed."

"I didn't come to East Africa to go to bed. Let's see the sights."

"What sights? It's four o'clock."

"Make a suggestion. What sights are there at four o'clock?"

Now, why did I begin to needle Jim? I don't know. I can tell what happened. I leave the explanation to you. One last mystery, I did what I did for Jim's sake. It was an act of friendship.

"What are you so edgy about again?" I started.

"I'm really quite the same as always, thank you."

"Always when? Yesterday afternoon or when you met my plane? You're not always the same, you haven't been the same since I expressed some sympathy for the author of the letter you insisted on showing me, sympathy I still feel. You've been pissed ever since I said I felt sorry for that poor bitch, what was her name? I asked what her name was, Jim?"

Sidney would enjoy this, I thought. "My boy, when am I going to see your Rave Act?" Well, man, now!

"Andrea."

Jim was good and mad. It was oozing out of his face.

"Andrea! That's a beautiful name, you know."

"Suppose you tell me what you'd like to do, sir, and I'll do my best to oblige."

"Sir?"

"What would you like to see?"

"Let's get into something, I mean, really into something."

"What do you mean, into something?"

"Into. Close. Let me touch this goddamn continent, not just look at it."

God, that felt good. My control had been my curse. Now, sick and feverish, I was coming out, mean, nasty, my honest-to-Christ self.

"What sort of thing would you like to get into?"

"Into some of the wildlife I've seen on your gay tourist postcards. The bastards who took those candy-colored cards must have been closer to the animals than you've ever allowed me to be. They must have got off with their lives."

I could see the cables he'd wound round and round himself tighten and strain. I had to cut those cables, for his sake.

"Well, let's see," he said and stopped, his eyebrows up and stiff.

The man was just like me. I'd never seen such control. I had to push him over the precipice. I had to help him fall into that disgraceful human morass where I was now wallowing.

"Well, let's see now," he said, looking around, the poor catatonic son of a bitch, "let's see now," for the third time, his neck so clutched in that chronic muscular spasm he could hardly look right or left, his profile so veddy clean-cut, like those members of Yale secret societies who meet in club rooms without windows. "Well, let's see now," teetering on the brink, still like one of those Kennedy boiler-room studs, somehow the elite, "Well, let's see now," talking through his goddamn nose, the sound vaulting through the chambers of that high bridge and coming forth so special.

Then he broke out of it. Control won again. "I believe there are buffalo over there"—he pointed—"on the hill opposite."

He handed me his glasses.

"Please do not offer me those glasses again. I want to get close."

Where he'd pointed there were black smudges in the green.

"Well, then, suppose we have a look."

"I've really seen enough buffalo," I said. "Buffalo, I must tell you, were the major disappointment of my first trip. They are all, male and female, nothing but spooky black cows, lumbering, heavy-footed, spiritless, with shit dripping from ass hole to ankle."

"You're quite mistaken, you know."

"I'm quite mistaken, I know, but about what?"

"The character of the buffalo." He sounded so starchy again. I had to break this man down.

"Well, if they're not docile and boring and cowardly," I said, "if they're what they're cracked up to be in your tourist propaganda, then for goodness sake help me experience these marvels. Or else this whole goddamn trip has been like watching a TV show in your living room on a rainy Sunday afternoon."

I gulped. Some sour nausea juice had risen to the back of my throat. I swallowed it.

Jim noticed and smiled. "I think you should be home in bed," he said. "You are not yourself."

"All right! Let's see the fucking buffalo."

"I think you are not being sensible but since you won't be, very well, we'll take a ride."

He threw the Toyota into gear, and we broke out over green cover.

"What is it the buffalo can't," I shouted, "see, hear, or smell?"

"They see, hear, and smell very well."

We hit some terrible holes. The bocci balls inside my head bounced and banged.

"Personally I think all their senses are dull," I shouted, making my head hurt worse. "Look." We were coming up the slope toward them. "They look so stupid, just staring at us."

"That's because they're uncertain about our intentions. Watch it." Another hole. "Wart hog!" Jim swerved.

I've seen Arabs in the Cairo market pounding copper plate. One of them had got into my skull.

"The fact is," Jim shouted, "they are very dangerous and completely unpredictable. You never know what they're going to do.

"When you know it's a milk cow!"

Many times at the seashore, when I was carrying a throbbing head, a quick jump into the surf had cured it. If you get the blood running fast it will carry off the tension, therewith the pain.

"It's a large herd," Jim said, "bigger than I thought."

No doctor, no analyst, no wise man, no scientific spiritualist, no swami, no friend, boy or girl, no mother no father had ever told me. "You have headaches only because you choke down what you feel."

"You get headaches?" I asked Jim.

"Never."

Another theory shot to hell.

"A very big herd " he said. "All through the Bush there. Here, take these glasses."

"No, thanks."

He stopped the Toyota. We were a hundred yards away.

I slyly felt my forehead in a gesture I hoped would pass for accidental. It was very hot.

"Let's get closer," I said.

"We might a bit," Jim said. He moved the Toyota twenty feet, pulled up the hand brake.

The animals stared at us. We stared at them.

"Nothing," I said.

"What do you mean?"

"Look at them."

"Very pretty."

Actually, they were, in a picture postcard sort of way, hundreds and hundreds of them, exactly alike, a mother couldn't have told which was her son. All had that same expression of undirected anxiety on their— 'If you call them faces," I said out loud. "All their stupid expressions are the same."

They didn't move and we didn't move.

"How about it?" I said.

The only sound, a wind and its song, quickened the silence. Occasionally the soft end of a branch moved against the soft end of the branch next to it. I closed my eyes. My head throbbed.

I concentrated on the silence. It didn't help. "Let's go," I said, eyes closed.

He moved the Toyota another twenty feet, pulled up the brake.

The animals looked at us fearfully. Jim turned off his motor. It didn't reassure them.

"All boxers," I observed, "in their most formidable photographs look frightened."

·'Don't know quite what you mean," Jim said.

"I mean that the stance of these black cow-asses may be aggressive, but their eyes are very, very scared."

"That's why they're dangerous," Jim said.

"Now will you move up a little, please?"

"I think this is as close as we should be."

"Well, I think we should be closer, so move it."

"It's really not advisable."

"Fuck what's advisable."

I was waiting for Jim to say "Fuck you!" but he couldn't make it, poor wretch.

"I'm asking you to move closer, man," I said.

"I'm sorry, sir, I must refuse."

"I don't think you're sorry, but if you are get over it and move. I cannot take a head shot from this distance."

"In that case I'm afraid you'll have to take what you can. Perhaps when you see them later, the snapshots, and remember the circumstances under which they were taken—"

"All I'll remember is that you refused. I'll give you one more chance, I ask you once—"

"By the rules of my organization, the Society of White Hunters, a decision of this kind is entirely mine."

"I came here to take pictures, and I will not take a single—"

"You should have brought a longer lens. Next time—"

"There will be no next time. I am formally asking you and for the last time—"

"Absolutely no."

"In that case I will have to complain to your superiors."

"They will maintain my position."

"Do you think I've been sounding like a typical ugly American?"

"I'd rather not say, sir."

I burst into laughter and he joined in. Then we stopped and stared at the buffalo and they at us. My stomach was souring again. I could taste it. My whole gut was beginning to go into spasm-cramps. I knew I mustn't let Jim see any of this or he'd go into his authority routine again and ride me back to camp.

Then he made conversation. "There's a cow," he said.

"So what?"

"She's got a calf. Look at the little fellow. Can't be more than three or four days old."

"Will you stop that old-maid's drool! 'Look at the little fellow.' It's revolting, really, stop it. Where is the little fellow?"

Jim pointed to a clump of very small trees, and in the thickly leafed center I could make out a black hulk.

"I see the cow," I said. "Where the hell is the calf?"

"If you'd use my glasses you'd see her plainly."

"But since I won't and I can't see the calf from here, will you move up, please?"

Jim dropped his head.

I had him going!

"What are you doing, thinking?"

Jim didn't answer.

I had him.

"Jim, will you please take me to where I'll be able to see what I came all the way from the United States of America at great expense to see?"

He looked at me and smiled. Nasty and very human. At last!

"All right, sir," he said. After another moment of staggering silence during which he seemed to be enjoying a joke of his own, he said, "I will do what you ask."

He turned the motor over, and when it caught on, he pulled a short lever near the floor. The Toyota was in four-wheel drive.

Slowly we moved toward the cow.

Jim didn't say a word. He held the Toyota in a dead line, straight for the cover where the beast and its calf were. His pace was slow, but it was even, and anyone would know, even a dumb buff, that Jim was not going to stop, that he was putting it up to the other fellow.

In the clump, nothing moved.

"Hold on," Jim said, his voice calm, nearly casual.

I took hold of the side of the Toyota's frame.

"Not there," Jim said. "Here."

Lightly, with one of his long fingers he touched the handle directly in front of me, over the glove compartment. "Both hands, please," he said.

Foot by foot, we moved forward.

There was a ravine on one side, and as we moved it got deeper. Jim was sizing it up, three feet deep, going on four, on five, on six. Now, there was no way out, not to that side. Jim looked in the other direction, straining up in his seat. Satisfied there was no obstacle there, he settled in again.

The cow, when it came, came out of the silence and through the cover like an explosion. She headed straight for us, looking bigger with every gallop.

Jim spun the Toyota, jerked it around. "Hold on!" he yelled. I held on with both hands, watched that big black cow coming for me with nothing between us except a little space and some steel made in Japan.

It was too late to avoid a collision, but the way Jim handled the Toyota, the animal's huge skull and horns caught us only a glancing blow. She slid off, scraping along the body of the Toyota, rocking it.

She'd hit right where my hand would have been if Jim hadn't moved it.

The cow, turning on dancer's feet, came at us from the other side. Her momentum was like that of a great boulder falling off a cliff, then bouncing down a long incline, throwing off mud and pebbles and smaller rocks and the sparks of its ferocity.

Again she caught us a glancing blow. Jim had seen to that.

She turned, at us before we were ready, coming from the other side, so our only escape was the ravine.

She was not to be denied this time. Charging with all her weight off balance, forward, she was going to destroy us this time, put our back on the ground, our four rubber feet in the air. She was going to turn us over so our soft, vulnerable parts would be open for her to horn, penetrate, rip, and destroy, sending our jangled junk flying in all directions. She was going to finish us with her horns and her great boned head.

No, this woman wasn't like Mrs. Rhino with calf we'd teased the day before. That housewife was only too glad to turn and waddle off, her child following. It was kill or lose her calf, the way this big black girl played it.

She hit us head on, cracked us low, cracked us hard, catching a place with her horn down and under our side, lifting the ton of Japanese metal off the ground on one side, straining, pushing with her hooves, making mud of the ground under her, wrestling, twisting to get her horns deeper up and in, again under, then deeper, under, deeper, lifting each time till we were on an angle, the last angle, I was sure, before she'd have us turned over.

When she gave her last heave, I would have fallen out except that Jim caught me. His grip wasn't gentle. I know from its feel that he thought I was getting what I deserved.

Having saved me, he headed straight for the ravine, our only way out, at a speed that would get us away from the buffalo, perhaps, but which might very well break the axle pin or that vulnerable place where the steering mechanism breaks into joints.

Just as we reached the ravine, just as we started down the incline at top speed, he slammed on the—

There were no brakes.

We hit that side a terrible galump, the chassis slamming down on the two ankles. Then we straightened up and out, turned, and started up the other side, and since we were headed straight for the lineup of buffalo which were till then watching, but would spook and come at us if they felt threatened, Jim turned the wheel sharply away, and it was then I fell over the side.

I was still holding the handle. Jim grabbed me by the top of my jacket and collar. He couldn't slow down, that had to happen by wheel friction, nor could he let the wheel go. He had to keep the Toyota going away from the buffalo. So I was dragged a dozen yards, my feet scraping ground, then a dozen more before he could pull me into place. He slammed me into my seat.

The buffalo cow wheeled in place—how beautifully she turned! —and trotted back to where her calf was waiting.

Jim kept his path, running over bushes and small trees like the mad Alsatian Oscar Jamet.

I looked at his face. It was angry but it was also pleased. I'd behaved like a prime number one U.S. prick, and I deserved what I got.

Jim down-shifted. Finding a little upgrade, he was able to bring the Toyota to a stop.

He was out of it in a second, found a buffalo skull, put it under a back wheel. Then he got on his back and took a long look under the car.

"We have no brakes," he said.

He got back into the Toyota, took out a butt-edge, shorthorn briar pipe I hadn't seen before, filled it with some scraps from the bottom of his pocket, lit it.

"Kimani is a good bush mechanic," he said. "If he can't patch us up, he can at least get us to the lodge at Keekorock where we'll get another vehicle."

"What happened?" I asked.

"She ripped up the brake rods on one side. We'll have to zigzag back to camp and try to avoid any steep downgrades. We may have some difficulty. How's your head?"

"Forget it."

He smoked.

"Sorry," I said.

He did not accept my apology.

We made very slow progress. There were places where I had to get out and put a tree bole under the wheels. We found we could brake the wheels with a rope around a tree and let the car down a grade. On upgrades we were O.K.

"I'm really sorry," I said.

He nodded.

"I was quite frightened, you know."

He had no comment.

Later when he saw me putting my fingertips to my eyes and pressing in, he asked, "How's your head?"

"Not too good."

My eyeballs were burning.

After we'd negotiated another long, difficult downgrade, he said, "I'm the one that needs to apologize. I should never have let you egg me into that foolishness. I know better."

"I sort of enjoyed it—"

"I doubt it," he said.

"I was scared, but I did enjoy it."

"I could get thrown out of the association," he said.

"Blame me."

"We are very strict. That kind of excuse is not accepted."

"The client is always right."

"The client is generally a fool. It is our responsibility to protect the client from himself."

At the top of the long incline into camp he hollered, and Kimani and Francis came running, and I got out, and we held back the Toyota as he let it downhill in low gear, four-wheel drive.

He dropped me in front of my tent. I said, "I'm not feeling too well, Jim, but I'd appreciate it if you'd proceed as if I was in perfect shape, which I am not, O.K.?"

He nodded. I thought about the expression on his face when I was lying on my cot. He was ashamed of himself. Poor soul.

Almost immediately I was in a kind of sleep, my body covered with dew. I was shivering, then shaking, then perspiring. I put my arms around myself and embraced my body. Hard.

There was a blizzard over the east coast of the North American continent. I wondered where Sidney was. I turned on my face, arched my back, trying to relieve that slugging in my skull. I pushed my forehead down on the cot cover. I pressed my eyeballs into my head with the heels of my hands.

There was no way to turn aside what was coming. I hoped only to get through dinner, then, zipped in my tent, let come what may.

New York City had eight inches. I could hear the sirens of the police cars, muffled by the heavy fall of flakes. Then everything was silent, as it is in a blizzard at night, and I heard the frantic bark of zebras. I knew what that meant. Where was Sidney now? Where was he sleeping? How was he making out? Probably blaming it all on me, the record heat, his mean, sweltering room in Harlem. Still, would I prefer to be Sidney's understudy again?

I only had a few minutes before dinner. I couldn't show Jim the least weakness. He'd stop the safari.

I got down off the cot and onto all fours. I swayed from side to side, crawled a few steps, rocked again. It was great to be on all fours. It had been my only relief that night in Manila, when the dengue hit me, to crawl around the rain-soaked yard of the hut on stilts where we were quartered. It was a relief to be an animal then, and now.

Jim pulled up alongside, signaled me to pull over with a jerk of his head, then pushed his motorbike off the throughway and turned off its motor. Slowly, deliberately, he dismounted, pulling a heavy leather-covered pad out of his back pocket. What was he trying to do, set a new world's record for how long it could take a cop to get off a motorbike? He was like a man free-falling through space. "You're going to have to turn in your license.' he said in his biggest voice. "This trip is over."

I heard light, quick footsteps. Francis was holding the basin of warm water he provided me before each meal. "Dinner," he said, putting the water carefully on the little table outside my tent.

The warm water cooled my face. When I reached for the towel, Jim handed it to me.

'Those zebras are giving themselves away again " I said.

But Jim had gone. He was sitting at the dinner table. sipping his whisky and staring into the fire. He was not looking at me in a disapproving or superior way. I was grateful for his good manners.

"You look better " he lied when I joined him.

"I had a nap." I said. That usually helps.'

"May we get you a drink?"

'Whisky and hot water, yes, thank you.'

"Francis!" Now he sounded like a cop again. "Bwana," then some sharp Swahili, then, 'Whisky, hot water.'

"What I said to your friend with the fence,' I said. 'I regret that.'

'Oh, well, I suppose that's the kind of thing one thinks but doesn't necessarily say."

We dropped the subject.

They brought the meat, an animal's leg garnished with a mint sauce and flanked with greens cooked Chinese-style, crisp and unnaturally green. I was seeing the safari for its poetry, the sudden astonishing brotherhood of human creatures who would not otherwise have been together. There was a sweet murmur among us, Francis serving the table, Kimani in the kitchen, Jim talking. Then the blending aromas, the meat in its crisp-flaked skin, the delicate but insistent mint sauce, and the heavy, all-pervading odor of the rotting Bush. But above all there was my own fevered sensibility, distorting everything, the heat pumping through me, followed by the cool of evaporating perspiration, all making me open to feeling and wonder.

"I still don't see how they do it," I said, "prepare a meal like this in the Bush, particularly when it's raining."

"You O.K.? More or less?"

"For instance, the roast. Is that lamb?"

'Impala."

"Well, that needs an oven. The bread, another oven. The mint sauce, a slow burner, no? How do they manage it? The hot water for my whisky, a trifle, but it needs a burner too. Kimani must have, at the end of the lane through the Bush, at least eight adjustable burners."

"That is what he has, and as many more as he might need. And each burner is capable of infinite adjustments."

"Come on, Jim, stop being so mysterious."

"It's no mystery." he said. "They build a great fire, starting hours before so that by the time they're ready to cook, they have a huge heap of red embers, a flaming pile of jungle charcoal. The ovens are just pots. Are you listening?"

"Intently."

"They take shovelfuls of these embers and build any size and temperature and duration of heat source they wish. The ovens are the classic ovens of primitive peoples, earthenware—" He stopped.

"Go on."

"Air tight. The bread and the leg of impala are placed inside those pots, which are set on beds of embers. Then their lids are covered with shovelfuls of the red-hot coals. One shovelful will do under the small saucepan in which the mint sauce— Don't you really think we should get you back to Nairobi as quickly as possible?"

"No."

My head had nodded. I'd caught it at the last instant before it fell to the ground.

"Go on," I said. "I'm O.K."

"That's all there is to it."

He didn't know how to continue the pretense at conversation. There was a silence.

"By the way," he said, "Kimani's confident he can patch up the Toyota."

"I'm sorry I behaved like such a shit," I said.

"When?"

"Come on, Jim, don't tease me. This afternoon, all afternoon."

"Oh, don't concern yourself about that."

"Well, I do."

"You were simply not yourself. I've been aware throughout this trip—"

"Aware of what?" He'd stopped, hesitated.

"That you haven't been yourself."

"I was extra intolerable this afternoon, even for me. How did you stand me?"

"It is our profession to look after our clients, not to judge them."

"How could you be so controlled?"

"As soon as we get back to civilization and you've paid your bills, I will revert to my hairy-back self."

"I wouldn't blame you. You've been very patient with me."

"Because I was worried about you."

"No need. I've had this fever before. It comes suddenly, goes the same way."

"May I suggest once more—"

"That we cut this safari short? Forget it. I have engaged you and the boys and this little caravan of equipment for three weeks. Andrea will have to wait."

He laughed. "Oh, come now, it has nothing to do with Andrea. Andrea is nothing to me but a nuisance."

"If that were so, which it isn't, you would still have to— Imagine the conversation, if you have the courage, that must have taken place the evening of the return of the Indian chap. Can you hear the talk between that husband, no matter how mild, and his wife pregnant by another man who is white, a colonialist, a member of the master race, against whom the benedict doesn't even dare raise his voice, poor sod?"

I was raving again. The heat had come back, very hard.

"And this hero has nothing but scorn for the husband, scorn so deep that it has never occurred to him to fear the man's anger were it ever released, his revenge were it ever exercised. Scorn so great that he, the white master, can be polite and generous, drive him here, drive him back, share a meal, share a tent, conduct the whole episode with that well-bred smoothness, that stainless-steel control, the kind that he might show a well-hated brother back from overseas, instead of the husband of a woman whose life he has ruined."

"God," he said, "I thought that kind of romantic palaver had gone out with the ruffle."

"No. It's only that people since the last century have ceased opening their minds to the reality of torment when it's in another person. Someone like you, especially, has become so hardened to the pain of others, animal or human, that he pretends it does not exist. Christ! This goddamn head hurts."

Sweat was seeping from my hair roots into my eyes, stinging—

"You are getting yourself overwrought," Jim said. "And for nothing. You're right. I've lost the ability to have those feelings, but you have not. Congratulations."

"Why congratulations?"

"I wasn't angry at you this afternoon. I envied you. I think that is the best part of you, that ability to feel hurt. Are you really all right? I never met an actor before. I can't tell."

"Yes. What's for dessert?"

"Francis!" he called.

Francis came charging up the green chute, through the green bush, throwing off sprays of Swahili, frenzies of deference, fireworks of subservience, poor Francis, scrambling the dishes together onto a tray, rushing them through the bushes. He was gone, was back, was gone again.

Kimani brought the steam pudding himself. It was a perfect shape, a lactating breast, a soft bomb. He poured brandy over it, detonated it with a match. As the flames subsided, he sprinkled the confection, using both hands, confectioners' sugar from a large blue enamel shaker, cinnamon from its red mate.

The scent of of cinnamon filled the air.

"Cinnamon, Kimani!" I said.

"Mizzouri, bwana." Kimani was proud of his presentation.

Jim gave the delicacy the respect it deserved, cut into it slowly and carefully so it wouldn't crumble.

"We cannot undo the hurt we've done, said the prophet."

"What prophet is that?" Jim asked.

"So don't try. That's your stand, right?"

"More or less," he said. "We do our best. But I don't think we can be responsible for the pain we cause others. In the end it's every man for himself."

"Oh, fuck that," I said.

"Fuck what?"

"Fuck you, you arrogant, pseudocolonialist, master-prick!"

He cut the pudding into several slices. We only needed two, one for him, one for me, but he kept cutting it. God, so gently, not crumbling it, so exercised he was, yet so controlled.

"We are only two here," I said.

He gave me mine on a plate.

"Talk to me," I commanded. "Don't sulk."

No answer. He was pouring a white, creamy sauce the consistency of whipped marshmallow over my pudding. Again Kimani dusted it with cinnamon.

"I knew a girl once who smelled of cinnamon," I said.

"How fortunate for you! Her breath?"

"Not her breath, her being, her body, her most private parts, they smelled of cinnamon."

"How wonderful! Where is she now?"

"Lost in the herd."

"Too bad."

"I think I'll lie down."

"Do. Sleep will help you."

"I think I won't."

"Why in the world are you so miserable?"

"For the same reason you are. I betrayed a friend, I think."

"Oh."

"A close friend."

"Perhaps he deserved it."

"He did, but does that make a difference?"

I closed my eyes. I was dizzy.

Suddenly, to my surprise, I was telling him the entire story, in detail, slogging through the mud of memory with the last nits of my energy, pushing that great stone out of the swamp in which it had become mired.

After I'd finished, he said, "You're much too generous. You are nowhere at fault in this."

"Is that your only reaction?"

"Put him out of your mind forever."

'I haven't been able to."

'You haven't tried."

"All right then. I don't want to."

"Man is not, as the politicians and the priests, the prophets and the poets would have us believe, cruel to his fellow man. He is, as you are, generally too kind."

"You can't seriously believe that."

"And because of that false kindness, that destructive compassion, we have now filled our society with freaks and psychos, criminal assassins, all feeling they are justified for their crimes, all screaming as they wield a knife or point a pistol, 'What else could I do? Can't you see I'm really a saint? Pity me, forgive me, protect me.' "

"Instead of—what should we do?"

"Don't offer help. Don't save them. Let them die off. Because if you don't, the victim will not be them. He will be you. So you—stop."

"Stop what?"

'Stop feeling guilty about this Sidney."

'I am not."

"Then why are you crying?"

"Not about him."

"Then?"

"I was remembering the girl who smelled of cinnamon."

"Oh, that's different, that's all right."

"Except for one thing."

"Which is?"

"She's dead. And she was Sidney's wife."

"When? His wife?"

"Her name was Roberta."

"You believe in the sanctity of marriage?"

"No."

"She was probably leaving him, wasn't she? She'd probably been with others before?"

"Many, very many."

"The day before?"

"And the day after."

"So, you do believe in the sanctity of marriage."

"What I believe in is the sanctity of pain. We must respect pain. We must not cause it. That's what I did, and that's what I am ashamed of. That's why I wish so often that I was someone else."

"But we can't help giving each other pain, especially if we like each other."

He was still talking when I keeled over. The last things I remember were his mouth moving without sound and the taste of that steam pudding with its warm aroma of cinnamon.

Jim must have lugged me to my tent, undressed me and covered me, turned off that hissing air-sucker, the Gaz, lest I set myself alight, zipped fast the single seam opening of my envelope of synthetic cloth, left me entombed, thank God for small favors.

Now I let myself enjoy my fever. I was grateful for its heat.

I felt what Jim had described. I was falling free. I spoke a conjuration to drive out of my body and up into that flickering light those old ghosts who'd chewed my spleen, summoned before me the characters to deny whose threats I'd sculpted my stone mask. My eyes looked unblinking at the citizens of my hitherto secret state.

Particularly that preposterous one with the snap-brim black Borsalino hat. How absurd he seemed now.

But not as absurd as my obsession with him.

About what followed that night—I can't tell how much of it

happened, how much I imagined. I'm not going to try to convince you, for instance, that later that night I talked to an old male lion outside my tent. I remember thinking he looked like Bert Lahr and that I'd seen him at Equity meetings. I remember remarking to myself that the eyes of old animals, like those of old people, get smaller. They begin to peer. I remember how that old lion smelled. I can still smell him. No, not cinnamon, you fool. They mark their territory with piss.

I remember these details, so possibly it all actually happened. But I am not going to bother convincing you. Make of it what you will.

It started when I fell asleep, which was immediately, and the dream was there. It had been lying in wait behind a bush of the mind, or in a WC like Jim's lioness, and came busting out.

I was in the dining room outside the Polo Lounge in Beverly Hills, that favorite spa of talent brokers with its tables scattered through the trees in back of that old rambling luxury hotel. The foliage was not as heavy as in the East African hollow where I was going through all this. Still it was tropical, semi. I was feeling sort of feverish too, that day long ago, very wrought up, so the dengue fitted. This agent comes rushing up, late as ever, to "take me to lunch," and after the BS about how was my trip out, which I'm sure he didn't care about, he says something he means.

"I think something good is happening for us," he says, us being him and his client, me.

"That'll be nice," I said.

"I'm going to take you out to the studio to meet the director," he said, checking his wristwatch and throwing the waiter a "get moving!" look.

"Will Sidney be there? Mr. Schlossberg? Castleman?"

"Oh, sure."

"Because he doesn't know I'm in California."

"I told him."

"What did he say?"

"He said, quote, 'I'm glad you're trying to do something for the boy.' "

I snorted. He snorted.

Yeah, Sidney deserved everything I did to him that day.

When we got out to the studio, he was sitting in the director's office as if it was his. They were playing gin. When Sidney loses at cards, he makes it seem he is losing on purpose, a gift from on high to the poor clod behind the other hand.

"Well, look who's here," he said, "the mechanical rabbit."

Everybody laughed though they didn't know what Sidney meant. I did. He meant I was the kind of actor who went precisely the same route in a performance every night while he, impelled by that unpredictable thing, his genius, would take different courses depending on how he felt.

I was glad he lost the game. The director accepted his check.

An assistant of some kind came for him, looking rather resentful. Seemed Sidney was supposed to have been at wardrobe an hour ago. There was a camera crew waiting to test his clothes for the part.

"What the hell do I need another test for?" Sidney demanded.

"Just part of our routine out here," the assistant said.

"What was wrong with what I wore on stage?"

"They looked stagey, Sidney," the director talking.

I noticed there was an edge to the director's voice and it was sharp.

Sidney took no notice. "You should have brought my tailor out like I suggested and had him make my clothes. Your hack has made too many suits for gangster parts."

Sidney jumped up, hooked his arm through that of the assistant in a democratic gesture, and made an exit like the one he had in his last play, very gay, very gallant, very indomitable, waving his hand. You know! As he went past where I sat he mussed my hair and exited to general laughter.

Which stopped as soon as the door closed.

"If Mr. Sid Castleman would work at it," the director sighed, "he could develop into quite a pain in the ass. Even if he didn't work at it."

The director was looking forward to ten weeks of Sidney, and not with pleasure.

Sidney came back into the room. He always stretched his exits. "Meet me in the Polo Lounge at five thirty," he ordered. "We'll have a drink. Roberta is here. She'll be glad to see you, or at least she'll pretend." Then he turned to the director. "Now you find this boy something in our film, Eddie," he said. "His mother put him in my charge when she died."

He left again. The director sighed again. The thing about Sidney in these days was that he was always sure he overwhelmed people with his charm, when actually the opposite had happened.

The young agent who was shepherding me caught my eye.

The director was looking at me, carefully.

"He's quite an actor," the director said, jerking his head toward the door.

"Sidney's great," I said, "on stage. Of course I don't know anything about this medium."

"This medium is the most honest one in the world. The camera is a microscope. It reveals anything phony. If you're a goddamn ham," I thought he looked at the door, "that's what comes over. If you're a prick, you can't hide it from the camera."

He kept looking at me.

"Stand up," he ordered.

I stood up.

"Turn around."

I turned around.

"Take him to see Mort," he said to the agent.

We were out of the room without a wasted word. "He likes you," the agent said as he hustled me down the hall.

Mort Benesch was the producer on the picture. Sidney was in his office, too. I could hear him from the anteroom. He was complaining about the director, and the costumes.

"They make me look older than I am," he was shouting. "The idea of a costume, it's supposed to make you look younger. Your director, Mort, should know that. It's basic."

The secretary was an older woman and very experienced in her field, which was Mort Benesch. "I don't think he'd mind being interrupted," she said and called her boss on the intercom.

"Bring him in," Mort shouted, not using the intercom.

Sidney came up and threw an arm around me as I entered. "This boy has some talent," he declared. "Under the right direction he can be quite effective. Mort, I expect you to do everything you can for him."

Mort sighed. Sidney was causing a sigh epidemic.

Then Mort looked at me. Hard. "We're going to try," he said.

The young agent looked at me to say, "Did you hear that?"

Sidney finally left. His last words were, "I'll do the fitting in the morning. I'm going down to take a steam. Call down there for me, will you, Mort? Tell them I want the Turk, not your Swedish faggot. I don't like his hands."

Mr. Mort Benesch was exhausted when Sidney left.

Oh, yes, Sidney deserved all that happened to him that day. But, looking back, I prefer him to the men who were unloading him.

"I didn't realize he was that Jewish," said Jew Benesch to my agent.

My agent made a gesture meaning, "He's what you see."

"Or that hammy," Mort Benesch said in his chopped-liver accent.

He looked at me again, a long time. I felt I was expected to say something.

"I'm absolutely sure," I said, coming to Sidney's defense, "that a strong director can hold down Sidney's tendency to ham." If you call that coming to Sidney's defense.

"I don't know we got a director that strong," Mort Benesch said. "You want a schnapps?"

"No thanks," I said. "He's always that way at first, till he settles in."

"If he settles in any further, he'll take the studio over," Mort Benesch said. He yelled for a drink.

"He's really a great old man," I said.

"Yeah, he's too old," Mort Benesch said. "What the hell is your goddamn agency trying to sell us?"

The agent looked at me.

The secretary came in with a drink. "Mr. Benesch," she said, "they can hear you out in the hall."

Mort Benesch waved her off. "Get me Burt Allentuck," he said to her, "and don't criticize me."

"Yes, sir," the secretary said. "Mr. Castleman asked for a limo to take him back to his hotel as soon as he gets through in the steam room. Will that be all right? I've only got your car. The rest of the drivers are out on that Malibu location."

"Let him get his own car. Why the hell doesn't your agency provide your client with transportation?" he said to my agent.

"We did," the young agent said, "but he found fault with it."

"What?"

"Said the driver was insufficiently respectful."

My agent was a murderer. Too.

Mort Benesch kept looking at me as he talked to Burt Allentuck. He bawled Mr. Allentuck out as much as he dared. Mr. Allentuck was one of the important agents in town. No one trifled with him. Mort scolded, then complained, then softened altogether, looked at me and said, "He's in here now." He kept studying me and listening to the phone, and then he said to my shepherd, "Take him back to Eddie Diamond's office."

By then I had an idea what the score was, so I wasn't surprised when I got back to the director's office and found Head of Wardrobe there with a tape measure and his assistant to write down my sizes.

"How did it go?" Sidney asked when I walked up to his table in the Polo Lounge.

"O.K., I guess," I said, bending over and kissing his wife, Roberta, on the cheek she offered. "They took my measurements."

"Which part?"

"I don't know," I lied.

"They don't know what they want," Sidney said.

"Get up, Sidney dear, so he can sit between us."

I kept Sidney between us.

Even fully clothed in her light silk dress, Roberta gave off the fragrance of cinnamon. Most women smell of seafood mama, especially when they're caught unprepared. But I was never with Roberta when she didn't smell of cinnamon, not only between her legs, but wherever those particular glands are, under her arms, in the roots of her hair, her skin. Each time I was with her and long after she'd gone, I could smell it on my fingers and in the air where I moved.

Roberta had been an actress, too, and while Sidney's career had prospered, hers faded. She quite correctly felt that Sidney didn't give a damn about the career of another person even if she was his wife. Actors are more honest than other people.

The difficult part for Roberta was that when she and Sidney had come together it was she who seemed to have the big career ahead. She had a natural sexiness about her, something uncalculated, animal and innocent. She was absolutely open about enjoying her power to attract me, played the game of Changing Partners as if it was the only game that mattered.

"Are you going to be in the film, too?" she asked.

"They're going to give him a part, or I'm going home," Sidney said.

"Why don't you come live with us? We rented this Spanish mansion for six months. It's got a pool in back, heated and perfumed, and more bedrooms than I've seen yet."

"No thanks."

"I get it," she said. "You'll be having visitors. Well, we got a garage, and there's a lovely little apartment over it. It's supposed to be for the chauffeur, but we don't have one—"

"We haven't worked that out yet," Sidney interrupted. "The agency promised to get me a chauffeur. It's in the contract."

Sidney did not drive a car.

"If they don't, then Burt Allentuck's got to pay for it."

"Oh, Sidney—"

"I'm seeing him for supper tonight. I'll straighten the whole thing out."

"Will you take me to supper?" Roberta said to me, snuggling against Sidney. "Sidney won't!"

"It's not I won't take you. Burt Allentuck said we had some business to talk."

"Will you?" To me.

"No thanks."

"Why not?"

"Ellie's going to call. I've got to stay in my room."

"You mean it's that serious with the young lady—what's her name?—"

"Ellie."

"That you can't have dinner with the wife of your oldest and best friend?"

"I was up all night in the plane. I'm bushed."

The headwaiter, a man who looked like he played the violin, came up and said there was a phone call for me, I could take it in the booth just outside the Polo Lounge.

"Bring the phone here," Sidney ordered. "What's the matter with us? Everybody else got a phone at their table."

The headwaiter gave me a funny smile, shrugged, and left.

While I waited for the phone, I took in Roberta. She was sitting snuggled against her husband, kissing the side of his neck from time to time, which Sidney took as perfectly natural obeisance. She agreed passionately when Sidney called the director, whom she was later to bed, a knucklehead, joined Sidney in all the Broadway versus Hollywood snob humor current at that time—it's the other way around now—said what she had to say, which was plenty, about how stupid and corny and insensitive the people of this place were—"They've never offered her a job," I thought—and was making Sidney feel just fine with her body's pressure and her sharp wit.

While all the time, she was working me. I'd had premonitions in New York, heard she wasn't always faithful to Sidney. But this was the first time she'd come on that strong. When she reached up and tucked the fall of Sidney's side hair behind his ear and kissed his lobe, for instance, she looked straight at me without blinking.

I couldn't have said then if Sidney was unobservant or indifferent. It didn't occur to me that he was naïve, till now.

Finally they got the phone connected and in my hand. It was the young agent. He knew where I was and who I was with so he was careful not to require any answer much longer than a syllable. He said that things looked good, they wanted me to read some of the shit for them tomorrow, and not to worry about hurting Sidney Castleman because, even if it wasn't me, it wasn't going to be him. They'd had Sidney.

"O.K.," I said, "O.K. Yeah. Tomorrow. Any time."

"What are they bothering?" Sidney asked when I hung up. "I told them to find you something. Now that agent will take the ten percent for doing nothing. I'll tell Allentuck tonight that I should have the commission. Which part did he say they're giving you?"

"He didn't say. They just want me to come in tomorrow."

He believed it.

The phone rang again. I picked up. It was the young agent again. "Where will you be tonight, in case they want to see you, or talk to you?"

Roberta was looking at me again.

"I'll be in my room all night, 427, here, in this hotel, 427."

I remembered I said it twice, four twenty-seven, once for the agent, the other time for the wife of my friend.

I can still remember her face watching me through that phone conversation, a perfect mask. She was not innocent like Sidney, not good-but-foolish like Sidney. She knew all about betrayal, expected it, dealt it. Betrayal was her field.

"What did he really say?" she asked after I'd hung up the second time.

I was flustered. When I stalled, she said, "Sidney doesn't suck up, so people like that get sore at him. They think no one has the right to be arrogant except them."

She had a good idea what was going on. The thing that made her suspicious, she told me later that night, was that none of the wives had called her. When you're really in that society, the wives want to socialize. Roberta hadn't received a single call from a wife.

After I hung up, she kept looking at me with that mocking smile. Finally I said, "Sidney, ask your wife to stop staring at me."

"I can't control her," Sidney said.

"Sidney tells me you devote a lot of your time and energy to fucking the wives of your friends," Roberta said.

"Is that right?" I said, which is to say, nothing.

"Who is it tonight?"

"Do I look like the type who'd do that?"

"No, that's why I suspect Sidney is right."

Sidney's date with Burt Allentuck was at six thirty, the time at the end of the day Mr. Allentuck preferred for that kind of conference. If anything unpleasant happened, it would happen gracefully over drinks, or, as in this case, he would take Sidney to Romanoff's. Even Sidney wouldn't throw a scene in Romanoff's.

Roberta took her husband to the agency in a yellow cab, then herself back to the hotel and quick like a bunny into room 427, as if we'd made the date.

I pretended we hadn't, acted surprised.

She said I must not think because she'd come there she didn't love Sidney. Sidney doesn't have time for anyone else in his life, she said, "But I do love him, only him. I love him a lot."

She'd guessed everything. "I knew it when they kept making wardrobe and makeup tests," she said. "You don't keep pissing money away on stuff like that if you're sure. They're not asking you to do a lot of wardrobe tests, are they?"

"What do you mean?"

"Oh, come on, I'm not going to fuck you unless you're straight with me. I know why they brought you out here. Naturally, they have no imagination so they hear about his understudy, that he has a short nose that turns up. You know these rich Jews here. They're the biggest anti-Semites."

She was undressing all the time. How careless women are with their clothes when they decide to take them off! I had, I remember, folded my pants along the crease and laid them carefully over the back of the armchair, hung my coat on a hanger, my shirt too, spread my underwear, carefully, pulled my socks inside out so they'd cool and dry. I was controlled even at a moment like this.

But Roberta just dropped her clothes where she'd pulled them off, some on the chair, some on the floor, the dress in wrinkles, her underpants in a ball, the hose rolled and wrinkled.

"I don't like to do this to Sidney," I said.

"Christ, you're a hypocrite!" she said.

When she came to bed, she carried herself as though her disproportionately large breasts were not an awkward burden, as so many heavy-breasted women feel. She came bearing gifts, crossing her forearm under them, supporting them as she moved slowly toward me. Then she kneeled by the side of the bed, and before she kissed me or anything like that, she laid the Bobbsey twins on my chest, carefully and gently, laid them there, as if to rest them for an instant. Then she stroked them—Roberta's sexuality included herself—following along with her hand over my chest and onto my stomach and so on. It all came back to me with the smell of cinnamon.

When Ellie called from New York, I was in Roberta. Roberta looked up and waited and listened to everything, didn't pretend not to. I had the impression she enjoyed the scene. Later when I knew her better I knew that she was anxious to prove to herself and to everyone else that the world was all double-x.

Talking to Ellie I didn't hide anything from Roberta, told Ellie there was an excellent chance I'd get the part. She should be prepared to come out. We could get married out there, I said. I'd have real money for a change, seventeen-fifty a week, the agent was talking, eight-week guarantee, probably run over. Eddie Diamond, the director, usually did.

All through this—I remember how delighted Ellie sounded —Roberta smiled faintly, not moving, still hosting me.

Then there were tears in her eyes.

By the time I hung up I'd gone soft.

But it didn't take long to get it up again. Roberta took it as soon as she could get it, like she was starved, fucked with her eyes closed— both of us did—as if what she was doing had less to do with me than with someone else, the man getting the bad news at that instant, the fool still pretending, no doubt, that he didn't feel the pain of the knife eviscerating him.

Something born of guilt was running wild in us both. The usual controls by which people try to be passingly decent to each other were relaxed. For who can enjoy being a perennial understudy? Who wife to a man as self-centered as Sidney? We were both working it off, getting back at him, clutching at each other, the press of our embrace squeezing the cinnamon out of her body and into the air.

That night it was Sidney who was the proud person and Roberta and I partners to the guys with the knives who'd been ripping our friend all that long day.

That's what I hadn't got over. That's one reason I still felt guilty so many years later in that East African encampment.

Sure I could see Sidney sloughing it off, that big phony, pretending it was something he'd expected all along, smiling that twisted half-smile. But some of his life's blood spilled that night all over the floor of Romanoff's Restaurant.

And in room 427.

He called me about eleven. Roberta and I were fucked out, lying across each other, almost asleep. I said yes, I was asleep, and yes,

Sidney had wakened me. I must have sounded quite annoyed. "How the hell do I know where she is?" I said. "I'm not your wife's keeper. She probably went to a movie."

It was then, as Roberta moved close to the phone to hear what her husband was saying, that Sidney told me he'd withdrawn from the movie, decided he couldn't ever get along with that knuckleheaded pretend-director and that he detested Hollywood, more as he got to know it better not less as everybody had promised. Sidney even suggested that I try for the part. They'd probably give it to me. It was that unimportant, I suppose he meant, and they that stupid. Perhaps it would solve my money problems, Sidney suggested. Besides I had more tolerance for vulgarity than he did, and much more control of my temperament. Actually Sidney thought I didn't have any temperament, I could live through any humiliation. He wasn't far wrong about that. Anyway, he said, to sum up, perhaps I needed the part. He sure as hell didn't.

"I'm asleep," I protested.

But Sidney went on and on, making fun of the director, then turning his venom on Burt Allentuck the agent—what a phony he was, Sidney, laughing uproariously at his own jokes—then suddenly, saying as if it was I, his understudy, who was keeping him on the phone, "Well, I've got to get some sleep," and abruptly hanging up on me. And Roberta. Without saying goodbye.

"Why did you talk so mean to him?" Roberta said.

I'd hardly said a word.

"A baby," she said, "just a baby," and again there were tears in her eyes.

She dressed slowly, doing her best to smooth out her rumpled clothing. I got off the bed, naked, to take her to the door. She touched my penis goodbye, running her fingers over it, brought it half up again, saying, "You've got a pretty cock."

It was then I asked the question, "You like me better than him?"

I knew it wasn't a question to ask someone as hip as Roberta, but I couldn't help it. I just couldn't prevent myself from asking. "Do you like me better than him?"

"Oh, that's what this is all about?" she said.

I was pretty embarrassed, but that is what I wanted to know more than anything else. I wanted his job, I wanted his woman, I wanted to be better at everything than he was. Success to me, in those days, was beating Sidney. He was the goal posts and the finish line. When I got past him, I'd scored, I'd won.

Roberta, of course, didn't answer my question. All she said was, "You've got a very pretty cock."

I knew his from the Luxor Baths. It was long and spindly and freckled all over. I thought it ugly.

But I wanted her to say it.

I stood naked at the door of my room and asked her just before she began to walk down the hall, "When will I see you again?"

"I never plan ahead," she said.

Then she walked away, and I watched her go, standing bare-ass naked in the empty hall on the top floor of the Beverly Hills Hotel in the middle of the night, still without the answer to my question.

When Sidney abandoned town with Roberta the next morning, he left it to his agent to sublet the Spanish mansion. The agent, in an act of expediency, rented it to me.

A few days later I wrote Sidney a note telling him I'd been offered the part, "just as you said they would." I said I hoped he wouldn't be offended and then, butter for his ego, that they were rewriting the script according to some suggestions he'd made.

I had a telegram back. "Not offended in the least. It's a mediocre part. Know you'll do what you can with it. As for rewriting that script, it's like rearranging deck chairs on the *Titanic*. Call me when you get back. Sidney."

I loved Sidney when I read that wire—the big phony! In fact when I read it I began to cry with relief, but with love, too.

And that's what woke me that night years later. I was crying in my sleep. I wasn't even in bed. I was standing in my tent crying.

The fever was really boiling up.

I had to get on all fours again.

Then I was outside my tent that way, like an animal on the ground.

The wind, a whisper, stirred the fig leaves. The waning moon threw their shadows, a host of huge moths, onto the tops of our tents.

I was suffocating. I kept trying to fill my lungs.

My entrails were writhing like a snake on a gig.

My head was one of Kimani's little ovens, cooking my brain. My eyes were being pushed out of their sockets by the heat.

On all fours, swaying back and forth, I hit my head again, then again on the damp earth.

Oh the sounds! I had to control the sounds I made or Jim would hear me and the safari would be over.

In another minute I was going to vomit. The impala's leg, the Chinese-cooked greens, the cinnamon steam pudding were all going to come up. There was no way to make that silent.

Was there a breeze? My body shivered with cold.

I crawled to what was left of the fire. I could see better than I expected. I understood how animals get around in the dark, why they're more comfortable then.

My body began to burn again.

The sound of the brook led me toward cool water. Moving through the bushes on all fours, I found myself before a small tent. I could tell by the smell the boys were in there. A soft cry in Swahili, then some murmuring from inside. Laughter. Silence.

They thought I was an animal. Perhaps they were right. I'd known them by their smell. I'd frozen when I heard the sounds my enemy makes.

I didn't have much time. When it all came up, I didn't want to be near that tent. They'd hear and call Jim.

Lifting each paw carefully, laying it down softly, I didn't make a sound.

At the edge of the stream I circled in place. I'd seen insects do this when their guts had been squashed out and plastered to a spot.

The stuff still wouldn't come up. If I could have been assured at that moment that it would be painless and quick, I would have chosen to die.

Then it came up, a churning below, exploding up.

Usually vomit is a reassurance, I'm getting rid of what ails me. But on this night when I threw up there was no relief. I just kept sweating, then shivering, then burning again. My stomach did not settle. It kept trying to come up, the bag to follow its contents.

The final heaves brutalized me. When they were done, I had no strength left. Exhausted, like any common beast, I waited, head down, for a saving bit of strength to come back. Till that happened I was completely helpless, completely vulnerable.

Finally I had just enough strength to lift my head.

I was looking into the eyes of an animal.

He was an old lion, a male with a scruffy mane, some of it pulled out and worn away, moth-eaten in my frame of reference, quite shabby, surely over the hill.

His odor was heavy, it was ripe. You could see he'd been through a lot. An old male alone, Jim had taught me, has generally been driven out of the pride by younger rivals.

He snarled at me, still seemed anything but aggressive.

"Lions have nothing against humans at night," meant "Fear equals hate." This old fellow had no reason to fear me, so how could he hate me?

He'd obviously gorged. His belly hung like an old sack. When he took a step in my direction, his load swung from side to side.

This silly, squint-eyed old glutton was friendly, despite another snarl or two, and very curious. I guess he'd never seen an animal with so little hair. He kept looking at me, cocking his head to this side, then that. He had the kind of friendliness I've seen in very old dogs. When I swayed back and forth on all fours, he did too, playing the mirror game with me. Then he crouched on all fours like a kitten and watched me, his tail switching.

I knew I was helpless, but I didn't care. I believed he would not harm me. If he thought it necessary to harm me, that was all right too.

I was ready to pay for my past.

For a long time neither of us moved. The very end of his tail switched a few more times. I tried to remember whether Jim had said this was a friendly sign or hostile. Then the tail relaxed, disappeared from sight, and I knew.

I let him see, with my own body language, that I didn't feel well, shaking my head from side to side. I was careful not to make any sudden, frightening moves, for my own sake too. My head ached like a dying tooth.

I believe the old boy saw I was sick and helpless, perhaps even that I was offering myself for his mercy, petitioning his generosity.

His old face was an enigma, like prehistoric sculpted stone. He was a judge. Anyone can be who keeps looking at you and listening, yet shows no reaction.

"Why do you blame me?" I protested softly. "I got you jobs, didn't I? I kept your head above water. I kept you alive."

The old beast lifted his head in a proud gesture. Apparently he'd understood the spirit of my words, appreciated their intent. But he had no intention of thanking me.

The lion felt his superiority. Suddenly he looked vain and just a little pompous and more than a little patronizing and quite arrogant. He was equally foolish, equally absurd, equally lovable.

I spoke his name now, softly and in apology. "Sidney," I said. "Sidney, my old friend."

He didn't answer, of course, but he was listening.

I spoke his name again, now in the tone of confession.

Then it followed, I was telling the beast secrets I'd told no one else, not even myself.

I was confessing in a rush that I'd victimized him, not helped him, that I'd enjoyed his downfall. The pleasure I'd derived from helping him was the final evidence I needed for my superiority. Every good deed, every favor, every kindness I'd performed in his behalf was a punishment for his once having been superior to me. Every job, every understudy I'd sought for him, every recommendation, every twenty-dollar bill I'd ever slipped him were ways of asserting my superiority, of keeping him dependent and at my mercy.

That he'd had my mother, I'd never forgive him that.

I confessed all this to the lion.

He sat looking at me, patiently, making his judgments.

I hoped I was impressing him with my sincerity. I wanted him to trust me again. I wanted to be his friend for old times' sake.

Now I paused. I had a final confession, but it was hard for me to voice it because I really didn't quite understand it.

So I was silent.

The old animal lifted his head again and snarled at me. I thought it a gentle sound by then, an encouraging one. He was allowing me to go on.

Then something I didn't, still don't, understand happened.

I knew or felt or admitted that I was Sidney Schlossberg.

The lion had united us. We were one and the same.

I remembered in that instant certain dreams I've had where I changed my name to his, where I'd taken his talent, appropriated it, stolen it. I'd even had dreams where, along with the name and the gift, I'd seized the power and acclaim he used to have. I remembered those dreams, and in those dreams, finally, I'd become him.

I might as well confess it all. I've had dreams where I'd killed this man, then pulled out of his body all of him that I envied, the reasons I'd killed him.

And with him dead, I assumed his identity.

This is what I wanted to confess to the old lion and couldn't. It was this hatred, born of envy and self-scorn, that I wanted to admit and ask forgiveness for.

Here it is, plainer. For years I turned to the obit page of *The New York Times*, first thing every morning, looking for the name of my closest and oldest friend.

With him gone, I could be him.

The old lion cocked his head at me curiously. His look was steady.

He did not blink. He studied me, encouraged me, waited to see if I had anything more to say, gave me every chance to say it. He seemed to understand the difficulty I was having. His kindness and patience, God love him, made me frantic to express, somehow, that one final guilt.

But I never got it out, not that night.

Someone was calling from the camp. I could hear footsteps from the grove of fig trees above and behind me. There was the leaf-filtered light of a lantern.

Jim was looking for me. He'd found my tent empty.

I turned violently in place. "Let me alone," I shouted. "Go away. Don't come down here."

When I turned back, the lion had gone.

Then what I'd expected happened. I heard the camp being struck, and I woke in my bed.

The day before I'd been anxious that Jim not break off the safari, but now I couldn't have cared less. I'd finished with that place. I'd had that trip.

If Jim was surprised when he came in and said, "Guess we can start now," and I made no objection, he did not show it.

I dressed and walked out of the tent as if I'd agreed to the abrupt termination of the trip.

The boys had repacked the trailer, leaving niches for themselves in among the supplies and equipment. A bed had been made for me in the back of the Toyota. By the time we'd crossed the open country and hit the gravel road, I was asleep.

I still had the fever, but without the alternating cold spells. My head ached but did not throb. Jim took the bumps slowly. The motion must have been soothing. I slept through it all.

What woke me was that we'd stopped. I had no idea why, how long we'd been going, or how far.

Since I was lying on my back, the first thing I saw was a circus of birds overhead.

The kill was fifteen feet from where we'd stopped. Three cheetah, they were the mother and the two young we'd seen days before, Jim said, had consumed the rear quarters of a Thomson's gazelle. Satisfied, they were at play, totally indifferent to our presence. Even when they looked right at us they didn't see us.

"Can you sit?" Jim asked.

I did, with a hand up.

"Because this is as close to cheetah as you're ever going to get. It's the closest I've ever been."

It was an idyllic scene. The two young were playing kitten games while the mother, stretched on the ground, watched. They would pounce on each other, cuffing and slapping, then running, cutting tight corners, coming back to attack again. After a bit of this, they'd be still, staring into space as cats do. Suddenly, for no visible reason, they'd be up again, attacking their mother, practicing war on her. She'd strike back, repulsing them, but somehow also encouraging them to attack again. Through all this they never lost their mien of high seriousness, the King's Companion.

Even the boys were smiling with delight at the elegant cats.

"Cheetah are not big eaters," Jim said in a low voice. "They depend on their speed, so they don't load up their bellies like lion will. By the way, you were lucky last night. The boys told me they found the pug marks of a large lion around the edge of the stream, exactly where I found you."

Minutes before, in my half sleep, I'd concluded that I'd imagined my encounter with that old male.

I was too weak and hot to say anything to Jim more than, "I know. I was talking to him."

Not a flicker of reaction from my man.

Abruptly the mother cheetah stopped play and stood erect, her attention fixed. Her face, so deeply graven that no expression except an unwavering seriousness seemed possible, now showed a slight modification, a kind of regal amazement tinged with disfavor.

Jim nodded in the direction she was looking.

With his fellow lying on the ground, half-eaten, a little Tommy was trotting up to the cheetah, prancing, knees high in little steps, closer than he should have. He'd stop and look at the cat, his tail whisking nervously. Then, when she didn't come after him, he'd take another series of tiny steps toward her.

"What the hell is the little bastard doing?" I asked Jim.

"Watch."

"Frighten him off."

Jim didn't answer.

"He's going too close, isn't he?"

Jim looked scornful. "Yes, he is," he said.

I reached for the horn button, but Jim caught my hand.

"Don't do that," he said, his voice very unfriendly.

Now the little gazelle was hopping on all four feet, each hop taking him a tiny bit closer. As he did he shook his head and horns, challenging the cat to take after him.

The cheetah did not move. Her young were watching.

The Tommy bounded on all fours again, up off his feet, then down, straight up in the air, each foot equidistant from the ground, then down again, an inch or two closer with each hop, each inch doubling the danger.

"Jim!"

He didn't look around, but he was very much on guard against any move I might make. "Kindly mind your business," he said. "This is his."

It was then the cheetah bolted. The Tommy turned too late. The cat was almost on him when the Tommy swerved at right angles, then cut again, doubling back the other way. Scampering low over the ground, he stretched his body and his legs as far as they'd reach.

But the cheetah's legs were longer, so she kept gaining on him. Just as she seemed to have him, it was only a matter of another second, she stopped and walked away, stiff-legged, proud. She'd made a decision not to take the absurd little animal.

"Why did he do that?" I asked.

"It's a she, the cheetah's a mother," Jim said, "and if she were hungry she would have had him, easily."

"I meant the Tommy. Why did he challenge the cheetah that way? Why did he take that risk?"

"I don't know," Jim said. "You saw it. Why do you think?"

"I don't believe what I saw."

"Out of boredom maybe," Jim said.

"Did you see that little bastard hopping up and down on all fours that way? Wasn't he gallant, Jim?"

"You better lie down again. Oh, look at him now!"

The Tommy was prancing among his own, his foolish little tail twirling like a toy, his feet dancing those same tiny steps.

"Beautiful!" I said.

"They know just how close they can come," Jim said, "but that time he came too close."

"Why did he do that, Jim?"

"Better than waiting for it to come to you."

"It?"

"Those cheetah have probably been following that little herd for days, taking one of them whenever they were hungry. Perhaps this was like getting it over with, one way or another."

"It was worth the whole safari, Jim. It was beautiful."

"You got to do that once in a while, especially when you're feeling bad."

"Yes," I said, "yes." I fell back on the bed.

"Better than waiting for a lorry to run you down."

"I know what that little fellow was saying, Jim."

"Better be quiet and rest."

"It's like you doing sixty seconds. No, you're too fucking cool. It's like the friend you abandoned, Andrea, the first time she did it."

Jim didn't answer.

"Why did you turn against her?"

"Stop picking at me, will you please?"

"Those are the people, Jim. They are the people!"

"This is the last really rough part of the road," he said.

"That little Tommy was talking to me, Jim. They're all talking to me now."

"Lie down. We got another six hours to go."

"I'm O.K. Stop pretending to worry about me. Here's the thing. By defying it, you win a victory over it. It's the only victory you can win."

"But it doesn't work," Jim said.

"Nothing works, but it's the only thing that does for a while. Did you see how great that Tommy felt afterward, how big he felt? He was Muhammad Ali, the little bastard! It's worth risking your life for that!"

Then I was asleep.

Dreams, said the old Viennese male supremacist, are wishes trying to come true. For the duration of that long ride back to Nairobi I was in and out, not of a dream, for I did not sleep, but of a wish played out. I was the man I'd most wanted to be most of my adult life. The fever was a blessing. I could never have made it without that fever.

What a sense of power and pleasure I had through those hours! At last I was living as I'd always wished I could. I was Sidney Castleman at his summit.

Boston, the show a flop, the company of actors knew it was all over when the closing notice, which had been put up "provisionally" as soon as we moved into the theater for dress rehearsals, was not taken down before Thursday night's performance, an indication that our producers really did mean to close on Saturday.

But the star of the effort, I, Sidney Castleman, knew it opening night, halfway through the second act. I told my dresser and my understudy, who was always hanging around my dressing room with that hero-worshiping gape. "Boys," I said—it was a hospital play—"we're working on a stiff."

Unfortunately, this bon mot got around. When our playwright heard it, his feelings, already shredded by the cruel notices and the bewildered public reception, were crushed. He wasn't to be seen at the final curtain.

What rankled me wasn't only that a promising playwright was being profoundly discouraged and possibly alienated for good from the theater but that the actors, whose natural leader I was, would slink away from the engagement like a dog who'd shit on the living-room rug. After all, they'd done their best. They should leave the show and Boston proudly. I could not stomach the shame I saw on the faces around me that Thursday night.

There was another reason why our playwright, whom we'd nick-named the Pink Porpoise—he was terribly plump for a revolutionary intellectual—was very low. He'd been rejected in love by our leading lady, Peggy. What the enamored young man did not know was that she was, for the time, my consort. I'd hooked up with her only to make her road trip more enjoyable and give her a little more confidence in the love scenes. Anything for the good of the show!

The Pink Porpoise was a hard tryer, and when he was not re-sponded to by Peggy, his reaction was suicidal. I'd known from the first time I'd observed him watching us rehearse that he was going to want to mount her. I warned Peggy not to lead him on. But have you ever seen a young actress, just coming into her good looks and her first big chance, who could resist leading a promising playwright on "just a little"? Even if she was otherwise occupied, as Peggy was by me.

I also knew from sudden darknesses in our playwright's manner and certain internal evidences in his script that the man had suicidal tendencies.

So when we learned that our show had only three more perfor-mances to live, I resolved to save that promising playwright for the theater and my actors from shame.

I believed in the idea that was already old-fashioned, the leading man is the godhead of a production, responsible for all.

The party I threw was not really a week long. It started on Thursday night after the show, and it went on without a break until after the show on Saturday. It was a good party and a necessary party, but not the only one of its kind in the annals of the profession, as some of my young actors boasted. They just hadn't been around very long.

I was living in privilege, not at the Ritz, the preferred hotel where even the sheets had sheets and room service was performed by members of aristocratic Boston families, but at the Touraine. It was Olympian to be Sidney Castleman in those days, and the Hotel Touraine was at my disposal. That old place, now torn down, naturally, had a largeness of spirit. Anything went. All was forgiven. The evening sins were sent to the laundry every morning. All night through you could hear secret movements up and down the stairs, doors opening, doors closing, locked, unlocked. The telephone operators knew all and knew me well enough so they'd tell me, each dawn, the news of the night. In an emergency they'd been known to help a famous guest make intimate arrangements, knowing as they did who was in the hotel and who needed companionship.

Certainly "Mr. Sidney's" every need had to be taken care of. I could get anything I wanted any time, day or night, at the old Touraine. The entire staff served under my flag. The bellboys were my Mercuries.

I had the Presidential Suite. I don't know why it was called that. I can't imagine any president staying there. It would have stained his reputation beyond redemption. My suite, for instance, had four entrances-exits, facilitating a variety of moves under stress. There were also two kitchen-spas. It was a perfect place for a party.

The first thing that made it a memorable party was that I invited the critics. I didn't tell them the whole cast was going to be there. When they arrived, they found themselves facing a jury of their victims. They finally had to answer for their ignorance and their spite. I chose various members of the cast, each as I thought suitable, to read the notices out loud to resounding applause from the cast members. The parts dealing with the "grotesque overacting" in my own performance—I was already being faulted for this—I had read twice.

As for my chill-hearted, piss-pumping understudy, the only one in the cast to get good notices for that lousy five-minute bit I suggested be put in for him, I made that prim little bastard apologize to the entire cast for being out of step with their efforts.

Well, most of the critics got into the spirit of the thing, drinking and demeaning their profession, as what sensible person wouldn't. Only one seemed resentful. I, Sidney Castleman, champion of intellectual liberty, encouraged the man to express his mind. I knew full well what would happen. We were all too happy to let that pass. The orderlies from the last-act operation scene, well-oiled by now, took off this Aristotle's robes, threw them out of the sixth-story window and the naked man into the Touraine's corridors. This critic was as well hated in Boston as I was loved in the Touraine, so he had a tough time getting anyone, bellboy or maid, to help him. He must have reached home all right because he wrote his follow-up piece. It was characterized by caution. He didn't dare complain or bring charges against us. He knew that would make him the town joke.

The next thing that made it a great party—oh, you were great in the soul when you were Sidney Castleman in those years!—was that it found the sweet core of victory in the rotten fruit of defeat. The last performances of that play, instead of being disasters from which disillusioned and disheartened actors slinked away, were celebrations of the human spirit. Or the fact that we were still alive and well, that we had survived.

Riding in the jolly Toyota I was laughing in my sleep.

How trivial the failure of a single play seemed to us all that night in Boston! At first only I, Sidney Castleman, saw it in perspective, but by the end of that celebration, they all knew that so passing an episode must not ever be allowed to sour a life, or even a minute.

I had everyone flying so high that we carried our playwright with us, which was the first purpose of the party, remember? I was not going to have the symbol of our collective effort humbled. There was only one unanticipated problem. Because of this man's inverted psychology, at the peak of his exuberance, when he felt most loved, when he was so happy he couldn't stand it, what did he do but try to throw himself out of my front window, six stories over Tremont Street?

Now this plump soul weighed what you'd expect a man to weigh who wakes up at three o'clock in the morning muttering, "I've got to have some," and means ice cream. He was all pouter pigeon meat, slipped down a bit. When he went for the window, his charge had momentum difficult to block.

But I, Sidney Castleman, brought him down. People who saw my tackle said too bad it hadn't taken place in Yankee Stadium as thousands cheered. That tackle, long to be remembered, was so strong it almost carried my candle-flesh playwright out the window in the blessed company of the greatest actor of his day, a fulfillment the playwright, at that moment, would apparently have welcomed, because he kept scrambling for the open window's ledge, indeed had to be held down by the entire company.

This done, he reversed, became miserable, apologetic, and most unheroic. He began to whimper and cry for his leading lady, my girl Peg.

His grief was so profound and self-destructive, I had to step in. I whispered promises that he'd have her, and I meant to fuck, the very next night. Please, I said, be patient, leave it to me.

This quieted him immediately. A hopeful light made his eyes glow. He sat down, pulled a small pad out of his pocket, and began to make some notes.

When I gave that promise, I must confess, I had no idea how I might carry it out.

I began by the obvious, talking to Peggy. I told her I could not understand, since she had after all led him on, why she now objected so vehemently. The plump scribbler was physically repulsive, she said. I knew for a fact, I told her, that she had entertained less palatable flesh when it suited her purpose. None of this shook her. Finally I tried my last best tactic. I told her if she didn't help me now, I would not see her when we got back to the Big City.

This brought her to her senses. She got on the phone to her roommate in New York, a girl named Hilda, and asked her to come to Boston immediately. Hilda, apparently, was finding New York a sexual desert. She badly needed to get laid. So she agreed immediately. The friendly faggot who lived on the same floor would drive her up. "She'll be here in the morning," Peggy chirped as she hung up.

Of course this wasn't what the Pink Porpoise wanted, but it was at least something to work from. I began to exercise my mind.

The party swelled into the dawn. By the time Hilda arrived I had my plan.

She turned out to be a warm-hearted girl, one quickly affected by the eloquence of a Sidney Castleman. I poured it on, every word golden syrup. I had only one anxiety, that her first glimpse of the playwright's corpus might send her back to New York, lickety-split, in the car of her faithful faggot.

To get her through that trial, I decided to first show her the playwright from a distance, meantime telling her stories about his potency, already famous in theatrical circles, I said, its sublimation the true source of his protean gifts.

Finally she agreed. She wavered a little, on and off all afternoon, but I never left her side. I was taking no chances with her cooperation. The only thing that worried me was that she was showing signs of attachment to me.

Every tree I shook dropped its fruit in those halcyon days.

It took me most of Friday afternoon, a snow job without letup, one in which I persevered through the time I was making up, then leapfrogged into the first intermission, then the second. I had my dresser and my understudy guarding her while I was on stage, keeping her occupied with conversation and carefully spaced drinks while I played the play.

Thinking about it blew my fuse as we bumped back to Nairobi.

It was without a doubt the greatest performance our fated play would ever have, which isn't saying much of course. That Friday night our audience sensed a unique event of the spirit. At the final curtain it stood up and cheered.

I don't know what made them cheer. Perhaps it was that bit of perverse kindness which exists in every human spirit and comes with sympathy to a mangled victim.

My understudy, that mechanical rabbit, said that the real reason the performance was great—he admitted that—was that I was un-concentrated. Get that? "When you don't try too hard," he said, "is when you're good." Well fuck you, Br'er Rabbit.

Actually that closet Jesuit had evidence of why I was so relaxed. He came into my dressing room between acts two and three and found me adjusting my makeup while Peggy's friend, Hilda, was in the one position women's liberation finds the most demeaning. I'd decided it was necessary for my purpose. So I was pretty damned relaxed for act three.

Yes, that whole Friday night's performance was devoted to my leading lady's friend, Hilda, keeping her willing and available for the ordeal ahead. It would take a full-hearted effort, I could see by that time, to turn her from me to our suffering playwright. Finally I had to accommodate her, which I did the instant I came in from the final curtain call, locked the door and did her. But before I granted her that favor, I made her promise on her father's grave that she'd follow my every least instruction for the rest of that night, no matter how unusual she might find what I'd ask.

She must devote herself—"Swear!"—to making our Pink Porpoise forget his artistic disaster. She must grow garlands of triumph in the rubble of his catastrophe. I actually said something like that. Hilda, I'd discovered, was affected by purple.

She was as good as her word, a fine woman, that Hilda, once she was brought to see the light.

How I could turn people on and off in those days! What a guide I was for the souls of others in their journey through this dark vale!

What I did, in the company of my minions, was to lead true dear Hilda to a room at the end of my warren of rooms. I always took an extra bedroom in those years in case I had two visitors at the same time. There we ensconced the temporarily exhausted young woman, suggesting that she take a restorative nap, from which she would be wakened by a kiss. A drink of her favorite, Southern Comfort, sealed the understanding.

Then we sought our playwright, found him asleep in the last row of the dark, empty theater. The previous night's celebration had cost this man. Before we took him to Hilda we must find a way of restoring his energy, a shower would help, and raising his confidence to its greatest tumescence. Otherwise he might have another defeat as damaging to his tattered ego as the failure of his play.

While he was cleaning up, I, Sidney Castleman, got an actor from another show playing Boston, asked him to pretend he wrote profiles for a leading New York daily's Sunday supplement and had come all the way to Boston to interview our genius. We arranged this encounter. "She's waiting for you impatiently," we told the Pink Porpoise, "but she will understand why this is necessary. Be sure to mention her performance."

Tête-à-tête across a table in the Touraine bar, our conscript interviewer told the P.P. that he'd seen the audience rise to its feet that night, heard their ovation, considered it his duty to make sure the whole world had the privilege of seeing his play. At a table close by we watched the spirits and energies of our man rise. Ego first, cock will follow, an old rule and a good one.

Our interviewer told our genius, for a climax, that the tide of time would refloat his play off the cruel rocks of the Boston critics' spite. I gave him that line.

From our sideline we kept sending in drinks, keeping ourselves up at the same time. Every time our boy looked the least uncertain, we'd give him the full mouth of teeth and remind him by certain obscene gestures what he had to look forward to.

Oh, it was earth-shaking to be Sidney Castleman in those days!

The interview done, we informed our man, now bursting his skin with desire, that his dream was about to come true. In the dark corridor of the Touraine's sixth floor, we indicated the door to the room where his love waited, ardent if awake, supple if asleep. Just before he started for her, we laid down certain conditions, call them restrictions. He must not, we informed him, put on the lights, any light. His lady, after all, was married. Furthermore, he would have to surrender his glasses. I took them off the bridge of his nose and rubbed the place where they'd rested. Finally he must not talk throughout their romantic interlude in consideration of her profound and abiding shyness. He must communicate with her in only one way, the tactile. She would entertain him to the limits of his desire that night, but after he was done he must never speak of his happiness or ask for another meeting. Her husband, I made clear, was given to violent physical outbursts. So he must be careful never to hint by look, by gesture, by innuendo that anything had taken place between them. What she was doing, she was doing for only one reason, to thank him for giving her that great role in his play and as a token of her hope that he might someday write her another.

He passionately agreed to each and every condition. He had to be a true artist to be as naïve as he was. Furthermore, he complied with the conditions faithfully. Love, as well as the loss of his glasses, had made him blind.

Outside I blessed their union, dedicated the mass they were performing to St. Jude, the Saint of the Impossible.

When he came out of the darkened bedroom, the company at the other end of the hall cheered. It had been eighteen minutes by our watches. Apparently that was all he was capable of for the time being. Perhaps the liquor had dulled his point. But on his face I saw my reward, the glow of triumph, all confidence restored. Here was a completely rehabilitated man, full of that particular verve the critics had tried to crush forever.

"This has been the happiest moment of my life," he whispered to me. "So far! Thank you, dear Mr. Castleman. You have made it all worthwhile."

I returned his glasses.

Now we really opened that night's festivities. I had caused a piano to be moved—what people would do at my bidding in those days! —into my suite. That rational rabbit, my understudy, had told me, of course, that it couldn't be done, it was against the regulations of the hotel. "Regulations, since they are made by man, are broken by man," I said. The damned prig also warned me that the playwright would immediately recognize the redoubtable Hilda if she came into the party.

"With all that liquor in him?" I cried as I struck him over his tucked-under haunches with my gold-headed cane.

Oh, the delight of being Sidney Castleman, in those days! Everything was sheer, spontaneous pleasure, something that my understudy, that toy cop, would never know. He calculates every move, that miserable man.

So starting about three that morning, following the happy descent from heaven of our great-hearted author, the full company joined in singing all the good old ones, "Green Grow the Lilacs" and "Manhattan" and "Give My Regards to Broadway" and "Going Down the Road Feeling Bad" and "Show Me the Way to Go Home." All that Mazola!

Even my understudy joined in.

Hearing our voices in song, great-hearted Hilda came out of her room, beloved by all, our Saint of Charity. Damned if she didn't show that along with her more spiritual virtues, she had the best singing voice of us all.

Despite the dire predictions of my understudy, that tight-ass prude, our great-souled playwright did not recognize Hilda. In fact under our ever-wondering eyes they proceeded to become true friends and fast. He was so charged with newfound confidence from having fucked her before, so inflated in his ego from the love pouring down on him from everybody in the room—he was lying on the sofa, Hilda crouched on the floor at his side—that in short order he seduced twice-seduced Hilda, and they departed the party, this time using my other bedroom. There, as he later told me, he had her again, though he thought it was only for the first time, which was better for his ego so I let it lay. Hilda told me later he'd paid her a true compliment, told her she was a much better lay than her friend Peggy.

Oh, the joy of being Sidney Castleman! It spread on those around him, it reached everywhere, liberated everyone, a true miracle. Those were happy days and now they are gone. Oh, Sidney, oh, Schlossberg! Bring them back!

No one else in the party took a break. Everyone kept going. A poker game developed in one room, a strip poker party among the younger folks in another. The bedroom, now known as Hilda's Rest, was the scene of much social fucking and the civilized exchange of partners. Some lifelong friendships started that night and, if rumors are to be believed, two fine children were conceived in Hilda's Rest.

When our playwright came back from his second bedroom scene, he told me he'd forgotten all about Peg. She was rather inhibited, he said, but Hilda! He stood before the entire company with his arm around Heavenly Hilda's waist and made the announcement. No, you fool, not that, not that they were to be married on the morrow, but that he had been possessed, while he was in Hilda's arms, by an idea for a great new play. He would get working on it immediately, he promised us. "Thanks to you all, but especially to you, Sidney. You saved my life."

Hilda was equally proud and grateful for her own reasons.

The revived genius considered this an announcement of general interest. I, Sidney, said it was magnificent news, and that we'd all long remember that night when the new play was born. Actually, it was another flop, more miserable than the first, but who knew that then, and if they had, who would have cared?

It was the hour for dreams.

So it went through the second night.

The next day, I'd agreed to attend a lunch in my honor at Big Crimson, just to break the monotony for the boys and keep their hands out of their pants for a couple of hours. I called them and declared I'd go only if I could bring my friends. The entire cast showed up—over the objections of guess who? "It isn't fair, Sidney!" Imagine! Fair! The Harvard boys showed their class, splitting their Salisbury steaks and chipping in for the blown-up booze bill.

Oh, the largess I scattered everywhere in those days. I made everyone around me generous-hearted!

Except? Who do you think?

Before we left the hallowed ivy, I called a pep rally of my people. I commanded that no one take so much as a cat's nap till the party was over. This was it, the hard part. They were to go through the two performances as they were, in style, the last two experiences they'd have together, their last two contributions to this work of art. "Let's keep going. Let's not blow it now." Everybody cheered.

Except who would you say, offhand?

No one sneaked off to take a nap.

Except? You guessed it.

That rabbit!

Drinks were served between shows, a gesture of the playwright to show us his everlasting gratitude. He invited everyone to his room where he and Hilda received the company in bed. When the hors d'oeuvre were trucked on in, I, Sidney, forbade them to all except the happy lovers, who filled their naked skins with pigs in blankets and pimento cheese spreads. My command, "Don't eat. It will make you sleepy," was observed by all.

Except? Right. He was in his room, again, so missed the occasion, the tassled cap of our triumph.

I understand he also sneaked a hamburger.

Despite all this, that Saturday night's performance was the worst performance, not of that week, but of the history of the theater, pure garble, back to forward, scenes transposed, desperate improvisations to cover lapses in memory and play for time. Fortunately the author was in the arms of his ever-loving. He wasn't there to hear the audience hiss and the leading man, I, the great Sidney Castleman, keeping my face straight at all times, always "in it," always "up," hiss back. I put them in their place!

And what Actors Equity company deputy would you guess, if you had to guess, had the temerity to come into dressing room number one and scold his leading man? I cursed the day I'd bedded his mother.

No, even then I was gracious, even under that kind of provocation I was patient with my frozen-hearted understudy.

I only hit him once.

Much less than he deserved, wasn't it?

That was the end of the party, that blow struck between acts two and three marked the formal close of our celebration. Everybody knew it immediately.

I had my dresser commission a taxi to stand by at the stage door. I entered that vehicle in full costume, without taking off my makeup. On the New York sleeper I engaged an upper and a lower, since there was no bedroom or compartment available. And so to a deeply deserved sleep! What is more exhausting than triumph?

And who do you think lingered in Boston through that night to make a futile pass at the real Peggy? The next week in New York, when Peggy met me for the first of a series of "one-last-time" rendezvous, we had some good laughs over what that scared little poopoo tried to do with his trembling little do-do.

But did I put him down for that? Sidney Castleman is never small. What I said to my understudy over the phone when I finally found time to talk to him was rather beautiful. "As you can see, my boy, the trick is not to survive, but to survive undiminished. And we did, did we not? We did not accept other people's evaluations of ourselves or our work. We did not tuck our tails between our legs and run. Those actors! It was the greatest week of their lives! They will never forget that week with Sidney Castleman and his friends in Boston, Mass."

And now, entering the outskirts of Nairobi, I had to admit it, after apologizing for causing him to hit me, I had to admit that I too would never forget that week with Sidney Castleman in Boston, Mass.

By which time I'd accepted that I was not the person I'd once most wished to be. I was a fellow with a fever and a touch of diarrhea and a number of other problems, riding in the company of two little black tribesmen and one normal-looking but terribly fucked-up Wasp, and so arriving in Nairobi City.

What a letdown! To be me again.

Still, as I found out the next morning, something of what came to be known within me as the *Spirit of Boston* did survive.

"Oh, you're awake," Jim said, pulling up the hand brake, "just in time. You know you were singing in your sleep?"

"Ah, but I was not asleep."

"That's a very good sign indeed. I mean your singing."

" 'Show Me the Way to Go Home'?"

"I believe that was one of them. You're going to be O.K. in the morning."

I didn't even see them bring in my luggage.

When I woke next morning I was well, not better, well, raring to go. I had an appetite and a hard on. I wanted the first plane home, called the airline, booked for the midafternoon.

At breakfast in bed, I had a visitor, Bennett Wells, the general manager of the safari outfit, a young man with pink cheeks who presented me a bill scribed in old-fashioned calligraphy, flourishes and all. "I trust you'll find this in order," he said.

"It's very pretty."

He reached me my folder of traveler's checks, which he'd guarded while I was away, and a pen. "If you do and so wish—" he said.

"My fever has left me exceptionally vulnerable to bills done in longhand," I waved my hand in a grand gesture, what Sidney might have said and done.

"Yes, yes, delighted you find it acceptable. By the way, Jim and I looked it up, just curious, don't you know? *D-e-n-g-u-e,* is that right, dengue fever?"

"That's the bugger." I signed in sweeps, trying my best to match his calligraphy.

"There is such a fever, but it does not recur."

"Mine did. I want to tip the boys. How about one of these?"

"No. The book was quite clear on that point. Dengue does not recur. Oh, twenty dollars. More than generous, more than generous."

"Not twenty, twenty apiece. We Americans, you know. Now, Jim. Will he accept a tip? So then, do tell me, what did I have?"

"Haven't the foggiest. Jim? I imagine he would, very gratefully."

"What does Jim say I had? He saw it. Fifty O.K.?"

"More than generous."

Sidney would certainly have given Jim a hundred. "A hundred," I said.

"My God, more than generous, yes, yes. Jim? What he said? 'Psychosomatic.' That's Jim for you!"

"If my fever was psychosomatic—here—I'd hate to have the actual thing."

"Thank you. Well, you know a little about Jim now, he can be quite a pill. Great in the Bush, but once he gets off safari he is quite impossible."

"I'd hoped to see him before I left. We never got to say goodbye."

"Probably just as well, don't you know."

What would Sidney have done? I'll tell you what Sidney would have done. He would have taken the man to dinner. Dinner, hell, he'd have thrown a goddamn party. How long do we live?

"I couldn't possibly leave without saying goodbye to Jim."

"Actually he did drop that he hoped to see you too, very much, but I rather discouraged it."

"What the hell did you do that for?"

"He's very black this morning, not himself, his mood, very scratchy!"

"Why?"

"One's never quite sure. He says you didn't have a very good time, and he blames himself but—"

"It's I who didn't give Jim a very happy experience."

"On the contrary, he enjoyed you enormously, said he'd never met anyone quite like you."

"You're aware that remark is open to more than one interpretation?"

"Oh, yes, yes. Well, I'll see to it that he's sober. The first day or two he's back, Jim, the city, our civilization, and so forth, it hits him pretty hard, and he drinks and becomes belligerent, talks about—well, this is the best of it—leaving the firm, going to Rhodesia, Australia, America."

I got on the phone, canceled the reservation I'd made, booked another on a plane that left at the easy hour of 2:40 A.M.

I knew I'd never see Jim again. I couldn't leave him that way, locked in his hell. In the spirit of Boston, I had to give him a last word of thanks, not one hundred cold dollars.

I spent the day shopping, bought Ellie a pair of turquoise earrings to startle her red hair and Little Arthur a lionskin wallet and belt like Jim's.

He came for me in a vintage Cadillac, a long black '62, the kind of car undertakers use. He'd been drinking and was definitely not himself.

Marge was crouched in the back seat, dressed in purple. Her eyes glowed malevolently. They weren't talking. I couldn't understand them as a couple. Obviously he resented her. Still here he was with her again.

Jim suggested the Indian restaurant. "Round things out " he said. There he chose the last back table. He had a sore on his lower lip that hadn't been there the day before. He kept pulling at it with his upper teeth.

I summoned the waiter and ordered drinks. "This is my party," I said, "and it's going to be a happy one. So why don't you two make up?"

Marge was sitting at an angle to the table, her legs crossed like a man's, ankle over knee, an attitude which seemed chosen to affront Jim. She displayed a pair of very long, very sharp heels, the kind Betty Grable used to wear.

"Marge," I joshed, "what's with those spikes?"

"She's looking for a short man to intimidate," Jim said.

"And what's eating you tonight?" I asked Jim.

"I can't take this city anymore," he said, "or anyone in it. I make the mistake of coming back here. Then I can't wait to get back into the Bush. Can we have a drink?"

"They're coming," I said. "Well, you'll be back in the Bush when?"

"I have to stay here ten days."

"Who you taking out?"

"Twenty-four of your tribe. Students. Longhairs, no doubt. Bi-sexed, I imagine."

He pulled the lionskin wallet out of his back pocket and found my check. "Thank you very much," he said, putting it on the table next to my knife and spoon. "I don't take tips from friends."

"It was meant as a token of appreciation," I said.

"That is a phrase used when letting servants go."

The waiter came with the drinks. Before he'd set them down, Jim ordered another round. Then he noticed I hadn't touched the check. "Will you please put that in your pocket?" he said.

"Bennett seemed to think that you'd accept—"

"Never mind what Bennett thought. Put your money away." He looked at me till I did. "I'm leaving Bennett's company," he said.

"What happened?"

"I'm leaving Kenya."

"Where you going?"

"I have a plan. I'll tell you later."

Marge made a mocking sound.

"Bennett told me this morning that you thought I didn't enjoy our trip," I said.

"You didn't."

"And that you blame yourself."

"I've reconsidered that," Jim said. "I don't believe I could have done anything more for you than I did."

"You're right. You did everything for me anyone could."

"I don't think you have a talent for enjoying things."

"Perhaps enjoy is not the right word, but I want to tell you our trip was a turning point in my life."

This seemed to intrigue him. "How?"

"I don't know exactly. But I feel so much more—I don't know."

"You had something on your mind through the whole safari," he said. "What was it?"

"I told you."

"Oh, I don't believe that. The man you described is not worth anyone's bother. Imagine how long he'd last if you dropped him into the Bush without a weapon or food."

"Do you judge people that way?"

"It's a damned good way."

"All people? Men and women?"

"Men and women," Marge said, mostly to herself. "And you, too."

The waiter came by with the second round. Jim took his off the tray, ordered a third round. I shook my head at the waiter, but Jim made a sign for him to ignore my refusal.

"When you go back to the States," Jim said, "put a pistol behind your friend's ear. It would be a kindness."

I reached across and shook his thick-muscled forearm gently. "Jim," I said, "we're all freaks and cripples and cowards and fools. We all need understanding. Be kind, Jim, be tolerant of those not like you."

He turned his head away.

"I'm sorry," I said. "I know that must have sounded terribly patronizing."

"It certainly did," he said.

"That's what's happened to me on this trip. What I've seen and the fever and certain things I've never let myself remember before, I've been softened—weakened, you'd call it."

Jim turned to me. "What makes you think I don't like all kinds of people?"

"Because you don't," Marge said.

For an instant I thought Jim would hit her. Then he bit his lower lip, finished his drink, looked for the waiter.

"You like yourself," Marge said.

"Don't we all?" I said.

They were silent behind their fortifications. Then, without turning his head, Jim said to her, "That man is looking up your skirt."

"Goddamn if I'll take this," I said. "Now come on, what's the matter? Marge? Jim, what's the matter with her tonight?"

"She's depressed," he said.

"No kidding. What about?"

"She had an offer of marriage. Oh, not from me. From a very decent—"

"What's wrong with that?"

Now Marge turned on me. "Do you think I'm that hard up? Don't you think I can get laid any time I want?"

Jim laughed. "I'm sure you can," he said.

"I'm going to eat somewhere else," I said, getting up.

"Marge!" Jim cracked out. "Go home. Now."

She looked at him a long time with her wounded eyes. Then she snatched at her purse and stood.

"Why do you treat me that way?" She was standing in front of Jim, breaking apart. "What have I ever done to you?"

"Oh, well, then sit down," Jim said.

"Fuck you, you sadist."

As she reached the street door, she passed a man coming in whom it took me a moment to recognize. He looked around, spotted us, then walked slowly down the center aisle of the place. When he came to the table next to ours, he sat. It was the Indian, Mr. Gargi. He nodded at Jim and me, then carefully composed himself in a chair, his ankles crossed, his palms on his thighs.

Jim had not seen the man. As Marge left, he'd dropped his head, ashamed and full of regret.

"Why do I do that to her?" he said, leaning toward me.

"Because every time you're with her, you blame her that you're not with someone else."

Aware of the man at the table next to ours, I didn't say the name.

"But I didn't ask her to follow me around. She's just a neurotic."

"So are you, Jim."

"I go mad in this city."

"So do they all. Have pity."

"I must ask you not to patronize me again," he said, his eyes like agates. "We're no longer on safari. I am no longer your employee. What do you know of what I've been through with Andrea? What I've taken from Andrea?"

The second time he said the name—perhaps my eyes shifted—he spun around in his chair and said, "Mr. Gargi, would you do me the courtesy of not listening to our conversation?"

"I'm not, sir," the Indian said.

"You chose to sit as close to us as you could in order to listen to every word we say, and I resent it."

"I've come to have a few words with you."

"We had a few words the other day. I haven't the time or the inclination to go into that matter with you again."

Jim turned back to me, rigid as steel.

"I didn't think you saw him come in," I whispered.

"I recognized his body's odor," Jim said audibly.

"Why don't you talk to him, Jim? I'd like to invite him to our table."

"Be very careful," Jim said. "I really hate that man. I can control it in the Bush, but here— You see, that's what I mean. You are full of false sentiment. Have you any idea what he does?"

"You told me, leather goods, shoes, skins."

"That's his father, though this one helps with the skins. He buys from poachers. He's listening? Good. I happen to know that you deal with poachers, Mr. Gargi," he said, not turning his head.

"That is a false accusation, sir."

"Where do you think all those skins come from?" Jim said to him. Then he continued to me in full voice. "But that's only his sideline. Gargi and his Heinie partner run the G-R Minibus Service. You saw them all over the Serengeti, those zebra-striped VWs. Remember? Full of sausage-fat Germans. He and this man in Frankfurt get all the Deutsche mark tourist trade here."

"Now I remember."

"Every time there's a kill, half a dozen of those ugly boxes swoop down and surround the poor beasts with krauts sticking their shaved heads through retractable tops and obese fraus shooting Leicas out of every window. The bloody lions can't even fornicate in peace."

He'd raised his voice. Everyone in the restaurant could hear him.

" 'Siehst Du wie often zat lion does it, Heinrich?' 'Already I count zweiundzwanzig, Bertha!' 'So, so!' 'Ja, ja!' It's people like this man listening behind me who are killing this place and driving me out. The animals can't live in peace so they disappear, die off. No one who could stop it cares. The African politicians are paid off. Pretty soon there won't be any animals or any parks, they'll have bloody well finished off the place. So don't ask me to talk to him. Besides, I want to talk to you."

Having delivered his diatribe, he leaned forward and spoke in confidence.

"I'm not myself today, just as you weren't yourself in the Bush. But I want you to believe me when I say that, despite everything, I like you. Because of you, in a curious way, our safari was a turning point in my life too."

He hesitated, worrying his lip.

"Will you forgive me for what I'm about to say, in advance?" he said.

"Of course I will."

"We'll see. Observing you as I did, I placed a new evaluation on myself. May I be absolutely candid?"

I nodded.

"I think I'm a better man than you. You are not nearly as capable as I am or as strong or as resourceful or finally as intelligent. Do you mind my saying that?"

"No."

"You're lying of course. You have no courage either. Forgive me, but these judgments are too serious to be trifled with. Again I must use you for contrast. If you can do well in the States, why can't I?"

"I see."

"That is what I want."

"I don't understand."

"You see there's no future for me here. That is one reason I dread marriage or any kind of permanent connection. At the same time, I want it. It's what my father and mother had before me and my grandparents on both sides before them, farms, substantial, permanent locations, and families. There is no reason why I shouldn't have a place and a family and a future, is there?"

"No reason."

"So I've made a decision. I admire your country, at least the reality under the pretense. Perhaps I admire it more than you do."

"Well, sure." I said, "I'll give you my address and when you get there—"

"I want you to help me get there."

He reached into his pocket and produced some government print. "You may consider what I'm going to ask dishonest," he said, "but I assure you it's done every day of the year."

"What is?"

"This is your government's application form for a work permit. It is granted only when aliens have an offer of employment in the States."

"You don't have, do you?"

"I want you to say I do."

"From me?"

"Yes."

"What would you do there? We don't have safaris."

"Don't patronize me," Jim said. "I know your country very well, I have read many books. I read *Time* magazine every week."

"Jim, what makes you think you'd be happier there?"

"Because I—" He wrenched away. "Never mind," he said. "Forget it."

He folded the form, not looking at me now, and put it back in his pocket. Then he finished his drink and looked for the waiter. "I didn't expect you to help me," he said.

"I didn't say I wouldn't, but I don't employ people."

"I made a mistake."

"I work as an employee of various producers "

"No need to explain."

"So you see there is nothing I can honestly say that I—"

"Please don't feel obliged to—"

"Well, you seem upset."

"Not at all."

He was looking around for the waiter, his face clenched as a fist. The anger inside him was trying to shake loose, but he was still able to control it.

"Waiter!" he called, half rising from his seat. "Waiter! Here!" There was a thick husk over his voice.

"The waiter is coming," I said.

"What makes me think I'd be happy there? Because I was born to be. I've seen your big ones here. I've taken them out. I didn't have to give them the lessons I gave you."

"What lessons?"

"Get 'em off their feet and they're helpless. Grab 'em by the muzzle and hold on till they suffocate. Eat 'em while they're still kicking. Everything that horrified you, they knew by instinct. None of that flood of Christian mush you spill every time you open your mouth—"

"Don't talk to me that way, Jim. I don't like it."

"You asked for it. Why will I be happy there? Up the strong! They survive for a reason. Down with the weak. Don't protect them, eliminate them. Up the two-party system. Winners and losers! Democracy? Bloody nonsense. An elite of muscle. Your lions are your industrialists. They don't look it. That's their cunning. They have tooth, claw, and clout. They know the place in the neck to go for. They learned it with their mother's milk."

"Don't go by those people, Jim."

He looked away and said, "Let's talk about something impersonal."

The waiter put down two drinks, caught Jim's eye ordering more, left.

I looked at Mr. Gargi. The Indian's heavy brown eyes were lowered, but I could see that he was listening to us.

"Why do you keep looking at him?" Jim asked. Then, as if to himself, he added, "Same species."

"What did you say?"

"I apologize. You are somewhat better. Actually I hold nothing against you despite the fact that you've spent the better part of a week patronizing me and insulting me and shaming me in front of my boys. Don't you think I've been very patient with you?"

"Yes, I do. Very."

"What do you think their impression of you was?"

"The boys? I have no idea."

"They see everything, you know. Did you notice that neither of them said a pleasant goodbye to you yesterday?"

"I was out on my feet when we got back to the hotel."

"Just as well. As for me, despite the fact that you've refused to help me, I will hold my true feelings in check. After all, we live by our reticences, you and I, don't we?"

"Oh, for chrissake, Jim, say anything you want to. Who gives a shit?"

He smiled at me. "I wouldn't be you for anything," he said.

He finished his drink.

"Does that offend you?"

"No."

"A man who leaves his wife unprotected in the situation you described then melts his heart over a miserable wildebeest calf!"

"Jim, I can't pretend to have employment for you when I don't."

"Waiter!" he called.

"I realize how disappointed you must feel."

"Not at all. Waiter!"

"And angry."

"Waiter! Here! I'm not angry."

"Of course you are. You're furious."

"I'm not. There'd be no point to that, so I am not. Goddamn it where is that—?"

It was then that he began to go, shaking like a motor out of phase, his face clenching and flushing with his last efforts to deny what he was feeling.

Behind him, Mr. Gargi discreetly cleared his throat.

Jim wheeled in place, the feet on his chair screeching on the tile floor.

"Goddamn it, Gargi," he said, "didn't I tell you to stop listening to us?"

Mr. Gargi winced and drew back into a posture of defense. "I'm truly not," he pleaded pathetically. "But if you like I will—"

"You promised that before," Jim shouted, "but here you still are listening to every goddamn word—"

Mr. Gargi got up in panic.

"I'll go to another table," he said.

"Go to another restaurant."

"Please. I came here to talk to you."

"You're not going to."

Jim, now in an uncontrollable fury, began to move toward the miserable Indian. I tried to take his arm, but he pulled it free. I got up and stood between them.

"Jim," I begged. "Please, Jim, please."

He was raving over my shoulder. "I don't want to talk to you, Mr. Gargi. That matter is concluded. Now, get out of my sight! Go on! Go!"

Gargi fled.

I pulled Jim down. He sat trembling, stunned by the force of his rage.

Gently I pulled him around to make him listen. "Jim," I whispered, "Jim."

When he turned his face to me, there were tears in his eyes.

Mr. Gargi was standing at the other end of the room, waiting still.

"I couldn't sleep last night," Jim said. "Having that man's child! Look at him. I don't know why I'm living. My father, Ronnie, he's a cold man. My mother is dead. My stepmother resents me coming into her house, though she has excellent manners and thinks I can't see what she feels. This country, as soon as old man Jomo dies, it's not going to tolerate us whites. We'd be clever indeed not to be here the next day. I've got to go somewhere. Where?"

I felt ashamed that I'd refused him help.

"Jim," I pleaded. "Listen to me."

"I'm trying."

"When I get back to the States, I'll look around and see if there isn't—"

"Oh! Will you?"

"See if I can't find some real offer of employment—"

"Oh, will you?"

"No matter how temporary."

"Just let me get in there once."

"I'll do my best."

The waiter was standing over us.

"Now don't have another drink, Jim."

"All right." He waved the waiter off.

"Did you really mean that?" he said to me. "Will you do it?"

"I promise. I want to."

"Christ, that's funny."

"What's funny?"

"You'll have another—what's that man's name, the sponge?"

"Schlossberg."

"You'll have another Mr. Schlossberg on your hands. But I thank you. I will never ask you another thing."

"Now you do me a favor," I said. "Go to that miserable, frightened Indian. Maybe you can't help him but give him some sympathy. Imagine how he feels, Jim, and pity him. He's in terrible pain. Please, Jim."

"O.K.," he said. "If you want me to, I will."

He stood on his feet, rigid as a drill master. In his voice of command he called out, "Mr. Gargi! You will proceed to the corner table, the one behind the telephone compartment. In a moment or two I will come to you and hear what you have to say. You look so worried," Jim laughed. "What did she do? Kill herself? Leave you for a large male baboon?"

He turned to me, smiling now. "Wait for me here," he said.

"I will."

"Promise?"

"I will be here when you're through."

Jim turned and watched Gargi walk to the table he'd indicated. This maneuver performed to his satisfaction, he finished his drink, still standing.

"Order me a Scotch," he called out to Gargi. Then he turned to me. "Did I do O.K.?" he asked.

"You were magnificent," I said. "Thanks."

"I thank you. Of course, it's the only decent thing to do. Not for him, for her."

"There's one other thing you should do. Talk to Andrea herself. Tell her what you told me. She may very well understand the way you feel, and when she does it will make things easier for you. And for her."

"Christ, you're a bloody fucking saint!"

"Will you do that?"

"Yes. Yes, I will. I don't think Andrea could possibly respect him, do you? How could anyone respect a person that weak, constantly whining and complaining? I know her. It must drive her mad."

He reached for his drink, but the glass was empty.

"Waiter," he called, "we'll order dinner now."

"I'm really not hungry," I said. "I'm not going to eat."

"Oh, yes, you are, you must. You promised me a party. Let me order for you. Waiter! Ah, yes, here. We want a curry of lamb, and we want it mild, not hot." He turned to me. "These bloody Indians got into the habit of covering their meat with hot curry because they had no refrigeration at home and their meat was often in distressing condition. But this place is all right. I guarantee it. The curry will warm your belly and make you brave so your wife will be glad she's with you tomorrow night."

Suddenly he threw his arms around my neck and embraced me fiercely and lovingly. He was fantastically strong. Then he looked at the Indian sitting at the corner table, ankles crossed, palms on thighs, composed and waiting.

"I'm going to talk to that man only because of you," Jim said. "He's going to whine and complain but I will conceal my impatience, for her sake. I really like her, you know. I have no time for any women, but if I did it would be her. I mean if she were normal and in control of herself, which she is most certainly not, the bitch!"

He straightened up. "Here I go." He looked toward the Indian. "Offal," he said, audibly. Then he leaned over me and said, "I want to tell you something. I really do admire Andrea. She has more courage than anyone I've ever known. She is worth a thousand sane people."

"Those are the people, Jim."

"At one time I thought she was my only hope. I told her that. You see I did lead her on. I made her believe that someday—"

"That you loved her."

"No. I loathe that word. You Americans have spoiled that word. I admire her. That I can truly say, and that is enough."

But his face did not lie. If he had ever loved anyone, if he ever could, it was Andrea.

"Yes," he said, in correspondence with my thoughts, "she is my weakness."

He walked over to the table where the Indian was waiting for him. Halfway he looked back with a smile and said, "Don't forget what you promised."

He had the twisted smile of a doubting boy.

They had what seemed to be a civilized and reasonable conversation, even a pleasant one. They seemed to be in agreement, and I thought Jim was actually glad to be talking to the man.

Then the Indian told Jim something that I could see affected him deeply because he dropped his head and let it hang like that of a condemned man. There was a silence for a few seconds. Neither talked. Then Mr. Gargi drew a small pistol out of his pocket and shot Jim in the forehead.

For a second or two I could see Jim fighting it. Then he collapsed. That was the end. He slid off his chair and fell to the floor, rolled on his back, and stretched out dead.

The Indian stared into space.

No one in the restaurant dared move. Mr. Gargi still held the pistol.

On Jim's face was the trace of his smile.

When Jim was quite still, Mr. Gargi gently laid his weapon on the table in front of him. Then he crossed his ankles and rested his hands on his thighs, again composing himself to wait.

Now people rushed to the body. There was nothing to be done.

Mr. Gargi was quite calm through what followed. When the police arrived, he went with them as if he'd sent for them himself.

The plane out of Johannesburg was nine hours late, so I saw the morning paper. It told of Andrea's suicide and the shooting of Jim. Motive was not mentioned. Mr. Gargi was being questioned, the paper said.

III

FLYING WEST, I was sitting at a window in the posture of Mr. Gargi, ankles crossed, limp hands on composed thighs, looking into a void, black as the road to the moon.

My attitude toward Jim and Mr. Gargi confused me. I felt badly about them both. Equally. That ambivalence, part of my softening, denied the basic rule of the theater in which I'd been schooled, the villain kicks the dog, the hero picks up the marbles. Neither man was one or the other. I'd not run to catch Jim as he fell. I'd waved a sympathetic goodbye to the killer as the police led him away, a friendly gesture Mr. Gargi returned. I would have put my arms around either man, if I could have, embraced them both.

The plane tipped and turned and I saw the Acropolis glowing in the last dark before dawn. We were circling that old marker, putting down to refuel.

Those ruins had no heartening message. They were cold, those stones, white as the bones on the Serengeti, asking to be neither pitied nor remembered. They were simply the most beautiful remains on the savannas of man's memory.

But the air in Athens—a delay had been announced, compass trouble—that breeze was a balm. Sucking it in, I recalled the fields above Delphi. I'd been there long ago, Easter vacation of my senior year at Yale, when I still believed I'd never die. Temples had crumbled there too, almost as gracefully, but what was I recalling? The poppies in the fields above the dead monuments and the quiver of silver off the sea of olive trees in the long valley behind Itea.

Despite the hour, a girl was meeting passengers as they came up the ramp and into the new "touristic" airport. Her young face was lovely, tinted pink like those colored postcards the Italians sell. She had a basket over one arm, and as each passenger passed, she gave him a bag of raisins with the compliments of—the Greek spirit?

How simple a culture can be! Olives, fish, raisins, wine. Goats for cheese, sheep for flesh. As much wheat as can be grown on the ruffles of man-made terraces. That is all.

Why couldn't I live that way, without the sweat of season-after-season competition, free of the anxiety that went with it?

Well, by the time you're fifty-four, there's no eraser left on your pencil's end. You're condemned to those choices you made before you knew they were choices. All you can do is pay for the trip you've taken.

Was it really that late for me?

What makes an actor an actor when he's not on stage?

Only this: he says so.

Ridiculous, isn't it? He has no identity till by a series of accidents beyond his control he's on a stage performing. And only for those few hours. That's why when he's lucky enough to be in a hit he goes backstage to the cubbyhole where the doorman sits to see if he might have a letter or a telegram, congratulating him or denouncing him, it doesn't matter which, just some proof that he exists. That is why, on other days, he will go into that cavern where the only light is a single seventy-five in a metal cage fixed to a stand and send his voice out over the empty seats to hear it bounce back, proof that he is there. That is why he keeps the newspaper clippings written by people he does not respect even when they're not cheering. That is why he goes to see his agent as often as he does. That is why he takes lessons when he can afford them, for that single hour's attention. That is why he goes to Equity meetings to encounter the reassurance of others in the same predicament. I am not alone, therefore I am.

He has no ID card, no proof of profession, no tangible testimony of his worth, no canvas of daubings, no carving into palpable stone, no sheaf of papers covered with his scribble, no demo tape of song, no high building to point to with pride, no calendar of intentions or purpose.

I'd worked all my life and had—what?

The hope that I'd get by one more time.

I was going back to that?

Then I did something I've always wanted to do. I got off the plane that was taking me home—haven't you, sometime or other, almost done that?—parked my bags in a corner of the airport bar, sat on a stool, and drank the waters of Lethe. They make you forget the past.

Hours later I was walking along the ticket counters to check out where everyone was going, and at one of them I bought a ticket to Vienna, for no reason. I had no friends there, no business or program in that city.

Was that the reason?

Wien! I stayed in a small hotel, a room without a bath, the bowl behind a tapestry screen. When I went out I found what I'd hoped, that I didn't understand a word anyone spoke and that it wasn't absolutely necessary to know. I selected food by pointing to what someone near me was eating. I walked the "Ring," up one side down the other. I visited old castles, stood before their defeated majesties (oh Sidney, oh Schlossberg!). Everywhere in that tired city I found the abandoned splendors of another day, the baroque facades sculpted in age-softened stone. Beethoven had lived here. Now these living places were occupied by mercantile offices.

At night, a movie dubbed in a language that was incomprehensible, providing the film with some of the mystery its makers had worked so hard to eliminate. Then, in the busiest of the pastry shops, I'd point to a *sacher torte*, enjoy the shock of its excessive sweetness, the dark chocolate shell, the raspberry jam filling. I purged my taste with bitter aromatic coffee. I had no trouble sleeping.

I stayed five days walking, eating, resting, a visit a show a shop, a sweet, then to sleep, mending my weariness. I didn't read a book, didn't once pick up the Paris edition of the *Herald Tribune*. The men of the city were strangers, the women went their way. With nothing to divert me, I made the acquaintance of myself.

God, I thought, I'm going to get out of my miserable profession. Sidney can't get out of it, but I can.

On the sixth morning, for no reason I know, I came out the other side of convalescence, bundled my possessions and went to the airport, without a reservation. The plane home was waiting for me.

At Kennedy, while I was waiting for my baggage to come through the little cat's door and make its hopeful trip around the moving rubber road, I called Myron Castle.

"What do you want?" he said. His voice was not friendly.

"Is he O.K.?"

"Who?"

"I got to worrying about him. Sidney."

"Don't worry about him. He's eating better than you. Last time I saw him, and I mean the last, he was putting on a belly from brisket of beef and potato latkes and driving everybody meshuga like he owned the place."

"I didn't know they had that kind of menu at the Old Actors'—"

"What kind of Old Actors? He left there."

"How come?"

"They asked him to sign a paper declaring he was without funds. He wouldn't do it."

"Oh my God! Where is he now?"

"In Queens. Mr. and Mrs. Isaac Gillenson's Queenshaven. 'Fit for a king,' that's their motto. Very nice neighborhood. Three old mansions strung together. Strictly kosher kitchen. Delightful. Music in the halls. The trees in front hide the cemetery. I'd move there myself next time my wife turns against me except for me it's too expensive. But by Brother Sidney it's my privilege to pay his bills. Except I'm not. You are."

"I am what?"

"He's off my back, partner, I warned you. 'I'm not a broken-down performer,' he says. 'The theater is broken down. I'm at the top of my form, never better!' 'So if you're so good,' I said, 'why don't you get yourself a job?' 'I will not support Broadway,' he said. 'It's contemptible.' And so on and on and on, that's the way he talks. Son of a bitch hasn't got a quarter! Well, now he's over there in this place for rich Jews their rich children don't want, running up a bill, and if you want to pay for it, that's your business. Count me out."

He gave me the address. "Don't call me back," he said and hung up.

Then, because I'm such a conscientious fellow, I called Sol Bender, my producer, and because it was Saturday, I called him at his apartment.

He and his wife Ida got on the phone simultaneously.

"I've been leaving messages for you all over the place," Sol complained with that whining energy producers develop. "Get off the line, will you, Ida?"

"Did you leave a message for me at the border guard compound on the Tanzania road below Keekorock Lodge?"

"You sick or something?"

"No, I'm fine."

"Because I got to see you right away."

"What's right away?"

"What's right away? Now."

"I haven't seen my wife yet."

"I'll explain to her, straighten everything out."

"You really provide a complete service for your actors, don't you?"

"Come on. Ida will fix you some lunch. Ida, you still there?"

"Thanks very much. I'll come by in the morning."

"No, no, not tomorrow, now, come here now, I got to make a decision today."

"What about?"

"I'll tell you when you get here. Grab a cab. If you'd had the brains to wire your arrival, I'd have sent a limo."

"Look," I said, "I'll drive home and—"

"Sol," Ida came in, "it's only human."

"Ida, will you get the hell off this line!"

"I'll just say hello to Ellie—"

"Well, just say hello once and come over here. I'll get young Garshman, and Bennie, my manager. We got to make a decision which I could have made without you but—come on! Ida will get you something. Ida!"

"You like sturgeon?" Ida asked. "With eggs?"

I didn't know how badly I wanted Ellie not to leave home until I looked at the mailbox in the hallway of our building. It was empty, and I was relieved. If she'd flown down to daddy, the box would have been packed—with bills.

Walking from the elevator to our door, I heard a piano. Was it a piano or TV? If it was a piano and Ellie playing, she'd sure lost her touch. She sounded like a beginner.

She was. Seated at a grand which had muscled most every other stick of furniture out of our sitting room was a girl of some nine years, playing a piece I later discovered to be "How to Construct Diminished Triads." At her side, looking trim and true, the perfect teacher in her white linen blouse and pleated navy skirt, her fine red hair bunned at the nape of her neck, was my wife.

Our three dining-room table straight chairs had been placed at the entrance to the room, and on one of them sat a restless young man whose sweatshirt's legend proclaimed him "Joe Namath."

"I'm next," he warned me when he caught my eye. He looked at his wristwatch, moved to the chair nearest the entrance.

I put my bags down. Ellie had turned her head only and was smiling at me. "Hi!" she said.

I started toward her to kiss her, but she shook her head vigorously and put her finger to her lips, never losing the rhythm she was demanding for the "Diminished Triads."

I tiptoed toward our bedroom, passed the door to Little Arthur's room, stopped, pushed it open a little. The boy was lying on his bed reading, the open book hiding his face. He raised it enough so he could sight me from under. I saw his eyes, then he dropped the book that inch or two, went back to his reading.

In our bedroom, the two long windows which looked out over the row of backyard gardens, the best feature of the room, were now barricaded by the kind of accordion gate I'd seen across store fronts on One Hundred and Twenty-fifth Street. They were secured by heavy brass padlocks, formidable hardware. Little Arthur's window, I now recalled, had the same protection. And our living room?

I'd stayed away two weeks, come back to a war zone.

On my dresser was a stack of bills to pay for these improvements. They were heavy, these accounts due, coming to just about what my African vacation had cost, a comparison of values I was sure would be made.

Mixed in with the demands for money was a scream for attention.

Traitor! [Sidney had written] Why did you leave the country without notifying me? No address! Not even a phone number! At a time when I'm in the final crisis of my life! My brother has joined the conspiracy against me. I expected nothing from him. I did from you. I cannot imagine what you consider important enough to abandon me this way. I am considering suicide. That's confidential of course. The next two weeks will decide my fate. At the moment I am in Elba. It's called "Queenshaven." Do not give this information to the drama desks. I am incognito here, preparing my return. Destroy this letter at once, then come here. Immediately! The address is in the phone book. Every minute counts. Written in my heart's blood. By this hand. Schlossberg.

I took a shower, stinging hot, shaved, anointed myself with Sidney's favorite, Eau de Lilac Végétal.

At the side of my dresser's mirror was a photograph of a lion I'd taken on my first trip. The animal was looking straight at me. Lions do not blink.

I decided to pay Sidney an immediate call. Ida's sturgeon, Sol's crisis would have to wait.

I could hear the strains of a piece that I remembered from a play.
"The Little Tarantelle." I peeked out. It was being rendered by "Joe
Namath." He gathered momentum with five or six notes hit off by his
right hand, then just as an imaginary dancer with a tambourine
tossed her head and flipped her train, just when the hem of her gown
began to whirl—freeze action! Silence. What happened? "Joe," I
saw, was organizing a chord, finding the notes, making sure he had
them right, which took time. Then he struck. Ellie nodded approval.
Another few notes from the right hand, again some momentum
gathered, the dancer twirled and—stop! Another chord to be col-
lected while Ellie hung in there.

She was so patient, so devoted, so gallant.

I decided to put on my Sunday suit, one I'd never worn.

By now you know I'm possessed by as many eccentricities as the
rest of the herd. One of my silliest dillies has to do with Sunday suits.
That, of course, is what my generation used to call the blue serge suits
our mothers bought us every fall to be worn on Sundays only. The rest
of the week the garment hung in the closet, on a hanger not a hook,
the only suit so honored. Each year's model differed from that of the
year before only with respect to size. Mine always came from Rogers
Peet, that fine old store which, before the thaw in men's styles, dealt
only in identical classics.

This habit of buying a new Sunday suit every fall was one I could
not break. As I grew older and in some other ways more sensible I
kept buying these Sunday suits, one a year and hanging them in the
mothproof bags Ellie provided. I never wore any of them except when
I dressed for a special occasion, a party a night club. After I got
married and stopped chasing, these outings became less and less
frequent. Also as I got older I didn't change size every year so the suits
accumulated. At the time of this tale, I had five in mothproof bags,
blue or oxford gray, some plain, others with pin stripes, variations
which made them no less interchangeable. Of the five I'd worn one a
few times, the other four never. Ellie had dismissed it all as madness.

Why did these five unused, perfect, spotless garments in my closet
make me feel by the fact that they were there more secure that
everything in my life was under control?

Don't ask me. I still do it.

I'd bought the last of these suits about a year ago. It was a creamy
vicuña, cost four hundred and fifty dollars, and I had never till the
day I'm speaking of worn it.

When I tiptoed out Joe Namath" had disappeared, and in his

place was a child whom nature was preparing for motherhood, her new-grown bulk spilling over the sides of the piano stool, completely concealing it.

Ellie didn't look around. She was completely professional, her neck straight as her back. How clean her lines were! How generous her attention to that fumbling student.

I noticed our three floor-to-ceiling sitting-room windows. They were unguarded, but at each side were the furled gates, ready to protect us from the terrors of the night.

I'd wanted to tell her that I'd allowed myself to consider changing professions. It would be, I hoped, a reach in her direction, a tender of good heart, a way of saying "I understand what's happening with these lessons and these One Hundred and Twenty-fifth Street gates." For an instant I thought this important enough to interrupt her.

But then the doorbell rang, and Ellie scooted past me without a word, unlocked the door to let in still another pupil. "You're awfully early," Ellie said as she rebolted the door.

In front of me, she fluttered in midflight. "Surprise!" she said, smiled, and bustled back to duty.

I decided to tell her what I'd been thinking later.

But I never felt that clear or that sympathetic again. That's the history of good intentions, isn't it, short?

Myron had exaggerated. It was obvious he'd never been to the Haven, because his description, "three big mansions strung together," may have applied when these structures were put up fifty years earlier, but now the compliment was undeserved.

When I leaned over and put my face in the little glass window of the receptionist's office, I could see past her into the waiting room behind. Seated there was a familiar figure, Paul Prince, bending close over some odd-sized pieces of paper held by a large photographer's clip to a bound script, Prometheus gripping a pencil stub and rewriting *Titan*, what else? When he heard my voice asking for Sidney, he looked up without raising his head, did not acknowledge my nod.

The nurse-receptionist got Sidney on the house phone. From somewhere in the upper regions of the place, I could hear him over the wire shouting at her as if she was his personal secretary and he had a swarming calendar which it was her job to juggle.

How had this man in less than two weeks been able to make that Haven into his office and trained this *zoftig* nurse-creature stuffed in professional starch to be his confidential, personal secretary?

"Send him up in ten minutes," I could hear him command. Then he hung up, and she was left holding a dead phone. Apparently accustomed to this, she turned to me with the glassy look David Merrick's secretary might put on me if I dared interrupt that very big man on one of his very busy days.

"You can go back in there and sit down," she said, indicating the little waiting room where Paul Prince was writing. "Mr. Schlossberg is going to see you."

"Thanks," I said, controlling my temper. "When?"

"When he's ready," she said, turning her back to me and beginning to unwrap the frosted paper from around an egg-salad sandwich.

I sat alongside Paul Prince. He gave me a quick look without lifting his head. I didn't see how he could not have known me, I was thigh to thigh with him, but he didn't give the least sign of recognition, kept writing. I watched him finish, then, opening the bound manuscript across his lap, compare what he'd written with what he'd rewritten, all the time totally ignoring the fact that I was looking over his shoulder.

The place smelled of age and antiseptic. The magazines on the little table at my knees were no doubt the donation of some charity-oriented law office, old copies of *Forbes*, *Fortune*, and *Business Week*, still promising a continuing upturn in a market that had already collapsed. What possible comfort could the men in this place find in those magazines? Yet there is very little those who have not made it find more fascinating than the faces and descriptions of those who have.

"Do you want to play the part in my new play?" Paul Prince asked someone. I didn't understand immediately that he meant me. He hadn't looked up at me. But I saw there was no one else in the room.

"Who? Me? Hello, Paul. How are you?"

"At the end of my rope," he said. "This is positively the last rewrite I'll do." He seemed to be threatening me, as though it was I who'd forced him for four years to rewrite the same play. "Not because my interest in the subject has diminished," he went on. "I simply can't stand the sight of your friend Schlossberg."

"Then why are you here?" I didn't say that, I thought it. What I said was, "He can be very trying, I know. But may I say this in his behalf? He is completely devoted to your play, has had nothing else on his mind, or schedule, for the past five years, passed up everything—"

"Nobody offered him nothing," Paul said. "Furthermore, I am no longer convinced he's the right person to play the Prometheus I am now calling Paul Prince. He's aged, you know, your Sidney, and while aging has become not more chastened, but more arrogant."

Then I did ask, "So why are you here?"

"Because he has given me his word that out of the blue there has come forward a totally new source of financing. Private money. But so far I haven't seen any action, just Sidney's usual, talk! That's why I am asking, why don't you take it over? My play is incontestably a masterpiece. Everyone who's read it has said so. I'm ready to put it in your hands."

"Why me?"

"Because your last two shows were hits, and money goes where money's been."

"I know you don't think much of me as an actor."

"I don't remember a performance of yours I liked, but an actor can't do better than the roles he plays. You have allowed yourself to be seen in some slimy projects. Still somewhere, I believe, there is an ember of talent glowing. I want to blow off the ashes and make it burn again. I understand why you have commercialized your talents. You have a wife and a family, which is to say, bills. A really dedicated artist, of course, never marries. I, for instance, have never allowed myself to be trapped that way. I know if I did I'd be forced, like you've been forced, to do work I despised just to pay the—"

"Paul, I don't despise the plays I've—"

"That's your defense speaking. I'll tell you what I'm going to do for you—"

"Paul, let me say this, your play is not my—"

"Of course. My play is far beyond the range of what you've done till now. But I am going to coach you, personally. I will also show you how to move properly, not in that Odets-Miller manner, but in the heroic mold. I promise you you will do well, despite the fact that you have had, as far as I know, no training in classical diction, in the rhythms, physical and vocal, of dramatic poetry."

"None whatever," I said, glad I could say so convincingly.

"Don't worry. You will learn my play as you would an opera, one where you don't know the meaning of a single word, learn it phonetically and mimetically. I will act the part. All you have to do is imitate me."

"I don't know if that is my way, Paul."

"I'll be at your side through every rehearsal."

"Look, Paul, at this particular time I—"

"I know, I know, you've signed for another miserable comedy. I've read it. It's not very funny, bound to be a flop. But eager as I am to get my play on the boards immediately, I'll tell you what I'm going to do for you. I will wait till that piece of filth folds, O.K.? Just so long as you now give me your word that when—"

"What makes you so damn sure it's a piece of shit, Paul?"

"I was at a party the other night. Adam Garshman was there, and he said that—"

"Then why is he doing the play?"

"Same reason you are, the grocer and the landlord. He did allow, to be perfectly fair, that he might be able to do something with the thing, get it by, you know."

I could have killed that young squirt. I could have castrated him with a butter knife. "Why don't you get Adam Garshman to direct your play?" I asked.

"That sixty-day wonder! He's had one filthy success, now everybody wants him. He used to sleep on the floor of my kitchen, your Adam Garshman. He used to borrow the shirt off my back when he had a date and bring it back with his stinking come all over the shirttails. Now he's being interviewed by *After Dark* magazine, the new Mike Nichols, for chrissake. Don't you think my sense of values is sounder than that?"

He stopped, looked around, edged closer, and put his lips into my ear. I could feel the moisture as he hissed, "Give me your soul, friend. I will return it to you replenished. How many works like *Titan* do you find in a lifetime? How many have been offered you to play? When you're dead, they'll say, 'He played *Titan*.' Give yourself this gift, my colleague, because I promise you this play"—he pounded the script with his fist again and again—"is flawless! Every page will be quoted. I'm sure Aeschylus offered an actor, one who is now long forgotten, a part in the *Oresteia*. If you pass my play by, I warn you, the rest of your life will be spent in regret. Don't turn away now. I may not be as generous tomorrow. Are you listening?"

"Paul," I pleaded, "I just can't do that to my friend, Sidney." It was the only ground he had left me for refusal.

"If this were an ordinary play, perhaps I could understand that kind of petty loyalty. But this play makes all considerations of conventional morality irrelevant. Considerations of commerce, too, I know they particularly concern you—"

"It has nothing to do with money, Paul. Sidney is my—"

"This play will support you for the rest of—" He stopped, suddenly took another tack. "Suppose Sidney played it and you directed?"

"No, Paul."

"You could do it in four weeks."

"No."

He didn't speak for a long moment. Then he said, "I know you're afraid of my play, and I can well understand why."

He turned his body away from me, bowed his head, and began to write with his snub-nose pencil. He didn't speak to me again.

The receptionist's phone rang, and I could hear Sidney from upstairs. "I've changed my mind," he announced to the nurse-creature, "I'd prefer to see him down there. Tell him to find a seat in the little room behind you. Is the other man still there, Mr. Prince?"

"Yes, Mr. Schlossberg."

"And he's going to stay here," Paul Prince murmured without lifting his head.

"Get rid of him," Sidney shouted. "I want privacy when I come down."

"I don't think he wants to—"

"I don't care what he wants, get rid of him, immediately."

The phone upstairs was dropped into its cradle.

Paul Prince began to shiver with rage. When he lifted his head, his eyes were bloodshot.

The nurse looked at him and decided not to take him on. She bit into the soft heart of her egg-salad sandwich.

Schlossberg stormed into the room, carrying odd-sized sheets of manuscript which, in a third-act gesture, he flung in the general direction of Paul Prince's lap.

"This scene is not as good as what we had," he said.

"Then why the hell did you make me do it over?" Paul came back, his head still bent low.

"One can always hope for a miracle," Sidney said. "That's the kind of fool I am."

"What you are is a son of a bitch sadist!"

"Please don't raise your voice," Sidney said. "Remember you're in a rest home."

"I am through with you, you poet-killer! You talent-murderer!" He turned to me. "For five years he's had me working on this." He waved his script and loose pages fell in all directions. "I've had—oh God!" He noticed the pages flying and bent to pick them up.

I helped.

"Fuck you," he said to Sidney, who hadn't bent his back to help. Then he looked at me. "You had your chance," he said, "so fuck you, too!"

"Dr. Mittelman is coming in the door," the nurse-secretary creature whispered, "sh, sh, sh."

Paul Prince was on his knees, reaching under the sofa to retrieve the last bits of his precious play. "Oh God, God," he murmured, "the paper's becoming brittle." He sat on the floor and began to insert the loose pages carefully, each in its proper place.

A heavy, Germanic man came in and looked in the receptionist's window. The nurse-creature gave him some messages.

He looked at Paul Prince, then at the nurse. "What have we here?" he asked. She shrugged and Dr. Mittelman spoke to Paul Prince. "Get up," he said. "What are you doing on the floor? Also, do you belong in this building?"

"Don't speak to my friend that way," Sidney said, approaching the doctor, eyebrows raised, lips taut.

"I'm Dr. Mittelman."

"I don't care who you are. This man is my guest here and under my protection!"

"Why is he on the floor?"

"For a very good reason. Now go on about your business."

"I will report this."

"I suggest you don't. I have friends who will make your personal safety a dubious—"

Paul Prince had his manuscript together by then. He walked up to the good doctor, said, "Fuck you, too," passed Sidney, and said, "This is the end."

Paul left, the doctor was glad to depart, and Sidney and I were alone.

"Why are you standing? There is a comfortable chair. Sit."

"Why do you torture that man?"

"Paul? How else can I keep him on the hook? He'll be back. He likes punishment."

"It's a wonder he hasn't turned against you."

"He would have long ago if he had somewhere else to go."

"He asked me to do his play."

"When the time comes to select a director I will choose the man I consider most qualified, and I doubt if it will be you."

"No, he wanted me to play the part."

Sidney burst out laughing. I could discover no quiver of uncertainty in his laugh. He was genuinely amused at the thought of me as the incarnation of the heroic spirit.

"What's so funny, Sidney?"

"The poor man is certainly desperate, isn't he?" he said. "Now, Sonny, I need a favor from you."

"What about the amenities, Sidney? How are you feeling?"

"How would I feel? Here? Alone? Abandoned by my friends? Well, I don't consider you one of that company anymore."

"Why not?"

"How dare you quit this country without even leaving a phone number where I could get you in an emergency?"

"Sidney, there are no telephones on safari."

"Suppose when you first came to New York with that letter from your dear betrayed mother, an invisible letter, I didn't need to have anything in writing, still, a letter asking me to help you, which I was delighted to do only because of her—what would you have thought if I'd decided at that critical juncture in your life to go on a vacation, disappear for a couple of months—?"

"Sidney, I was away exactly fifteen days."

"Those were the crucial weeks. By the way, what did your safari cost?"

"I can't tell you."

"Ashamed, of course, guilty. Don't ever deny me money again. Come on, how much did it cost?"

"It's the only money I've spent on myself in—"

"I'm not asking for an apology, and I'm not interested in your personal finances."

"What was the favor you asked?"

"I didn't ask it, and now I'm not sure I will. I am profoundly angry with you."

"I thought about you a lot in Africa."

"Thank you very much."

"You look well. You've gotten heavier." I looked at his abdomen.

"What you see below my belt is from enforced physical indolence."

"It's quite a pot, Sidney. How are you *really?*"

"In a prison. But it's not that I haven't other accommodations offered me. My presence here is part of a large design which I will tell you about at the proper time. But first let me return the compliment. You're looking well."

"Like the suit?"

"It's too big for you."

"I lost weight on the trip."

"Like *my* suit?"

Sidney was wearing an old pair of trousers and a coarse gray sweater, buttoned as high up his neck as possible to conceal, I suppose, the disintegration of that part of his body.

"No answer?" Sidney said.

"Where's the suit you had on last time I saw you?"

"My brother who is no longer my brother confiscated that suit as well as the rest of my presentable wardrobe with the help of certain treacherous members of the staff of this place. It's his technique to keep me here, make it impossible for me to leave."

"Come on, Sidney, tell the truth. You hocked your clothes."

"That too, that too, but I did keep one suit and shirt, and it did disappear. Now let's get down to business."

"I'm sorry about—"

"I don't accept your apology. You will have to reestablish your loyalty-credit with me by some actions. That is what I want to talk to you about. By the way, not since Jack Kennedy has anyone buttoned both buttons of a two-button suit. That coat is supposed to be worn like— Take it off, let me show you."

I never wore that coat again, not as my own!

He put it on, nodding as he felt the fabric, buttoned the top of two buttons. He couldn't have buttoned the other because it spread over his belly, which had swelled for sure.

A glance in the mirror over the fireplace. Sidney liked what he saw. Then, not taking off the coat, he made his announcement: "I am on the verge," he said, "of getting *Titan* financed."

"Wonderful. But really?"

"Have you ever known me to exaggerate?"

"As much as anyone I've ever known."

"Hyperbole is the door to poetry. In fact it is poetry."

"Is your new source of financing Frank Scott?"

I'd dropped my voice when I said that name, and he joined me down a few decibels when he answered.

"That schwartzuh!" he said scornfully. "It turned out he didn't have the kind of money I need. He's a small-time operator, a goniff with perhaps a little style, but only skin-deep. No, I wish I could trust you—"

"Sidney, if you can't trust me, whom can you?"

"Nobody. I expect no good from anyone. I'll tell you this much. Through Frank I've made a friendship with another man, a superior type, white for one thing, but also a gentleman, surprisingly cultured—"

"And he has promised you?"

"Not so fast, my friend, not so fast. We've only had two meetings, but what I plan to do when I come back from my research trip to Greece—"

"What research trip to where?"

"Greece. I am there now inspecting the great rock above Delphus where the legend has it Prometheus was bound."

"Oh, I see, that is what you tell people."

"Paul Prince is the only man who knows where I am—"

"And Myron and me and probably—"

"There is no one of you I can trust, but there is no one of you I can't call a liar. I am in the Peloponnesus of Greece above Delphus. In fact I have gone, yesterday this was, on the back of an ass, with a single daring guide, a local alpinist, to the top of that mountain and found the place where Prometheus was fettered. There I saw the eagles of Jove still circling, still waiting for me."

"When are you getting back?"

"Only a mediocre man would ask such a question."

"I don't understand."

"I will return at the right moment for me to return. When I get back the first thing I'll do is put gentle pressure on my benefactor-to-be—"

"Does he have any idea what you have in mind?"

"Not yet. I will make him suggest participating. That is where I need your help. My man is presently in the Bahamas, where he has lucrative interests. This person, I may reveal, carries enough money in his pockets on an idle Tuesday—he banks on Monday—enough cash loose in his pocket to back my production, so don't give me that unbelieving look."

"I wasn't—"

"Do you believe what I've been telling you?"

"If you say so, Sidney, yes, I suppose so."

"It is necessary that you believe what I have said before I can go on to the next step."

He sat in silence, looking at me with his arms folded, a judge measuring a suppliant.

After a long wait I said, "What's happened?"

"I'm waiting for you to speak. I want you to say that you—"

"I believe you—"

"Not that, who cares if you believe me or not? God, you're a fool! Success has addled your brain. Your wife hasn't helped, nor those plays you've been in. What I want from you is an assurance that you'll help me."

"I will if I can."

"Oh, you can, all right. Don't worry about that."

"I wasn't worried about that."

"Don't you think you'd better find out what I want before you give me your assurance?"

"Yes, I'd like to know. What am I in for?"

Suddenly he got to his feet. "Forget it," he said.

"Come on, Sidney, cut it out. Have you lost your sense of humor?"

"It's hard to laugh in the eye of danger. I believe Napoleon said that."

"I'm sorry," I said. "Now sit down."

"There's no need to apologize. You keep apologizing."

"I wasn't apologizing."

"You should have. What I want from you—" he sighed profoundly, drawing in air.

"Yes, what?"

"My next encounter with my benefactor—this man is stage struck you know. I recited ten Shakespeare sonnets to him the other night, and there were tears in his eyes. He is no ordinary hoodlum. He has the deepest aspirations—"

"I'd like to meet him."

"That, of course, is impossible. When I come back from Greece, which will be to the day coincidental with when he comes back from the Bahamas, I want to entertain him at an afternoon affair, a discreet, intimate cocktail party. I have the girls from the top floor of your last play ready. They will do the superficial entertaining, bring their own special perfume, give him the feeling that he and I are equally adored—"

"So what do you want from me?"

"I want you to hire a suite at the Plaza, my old space, you remember, for a couple of days, one of which will be used for this affair, the other for whatever may follow with the young ladies and my new friend. I also need something I can only get from you at the moment, I'm sorry to say. I need to be properly dressed. This suit will do."

"Wait a minute. Sidney."

"Wait for what a minute?"

"This is the first time I've worn that suit, I have some others that perhaps—"

'Do you think one of your discards will help me when I have the promotion party for this man?"

"They'll have to."

"I don't want one of your hand-me-downs."

"That suit you have on is too small for you—"

"It's too big for you," said Sidney.

"Only temporarily. Because of my diarrhea—"

"Please, don't be distasteful. It fits me perfectly. Look." He turned in place, modeling it. It did fit him well, except at the abdomen. Sidney has always been a clothes horse.

"Answer honestly, if you can. Doesn't it fit me perfectly? Where did you buy it? Barney's?" He looked inside the coat. "Knize's! Good."

"I meant the pants. The pants won't fit you."

"Take them off. We'll see."

"Sidney, I can't give you that suit. Now, stop it."

"You may or may not know this," he went on, as if he hadn't heard me. "When you go for money, the first principle is to look and behave as if you don't need it. Now do you understand? All my friend has to do is feel this cloth—what is it, camel?"

"Vicuña."

"Perfect. Take the pants off."

"Sidney, I am not going to—"

"Yes you are. At the risk of losing my friendship forever, you bloody well are. Now take the pants off. Immediately."

"Goddamn it, Sidney," I grabbed at him and began to pull the coat off his back.

'Stop it," he shouted.

The nurse added hers. "Stop that immediately," she scolded, "or I'll have to ask you to leave. Mr. Schlossberg, shall I call an attendant?"

'It won't be necessary," he said.

Then I saw he had tears in his eyes. He walked away from me and over to the fireplace with its imitation logs fed by gas. There he sat, silently looking into the fire that wasn't, a forlorn figure at the corner of the room with his back to me.

'Sidney," I said, approaching him.

He didn't look at me. Sitting in his chair, he took off the coat and held it out for me to take. "I don't want your suit," he said. "I don't want anything from you. I have new friends I can turn to. Goodbye."

"Oh, Sidney, cut the shit."

"There's the door. Get out." He was on his feet again. "You and Myron! You are no different—a trader, a bourgeois. This 'home' is your disposal plant. Why don't you line me up with all the others upstairs and shoot us? That would be the truly convenient thing, wouldn't it? Be honest, if you still can. Wouldn't that relieve you? To be rid of me forever? Go ahead. Out the door. There is no reason for you to again be aware of my existence. You won't have to hear the cries of agony, the last frustrations, the final shame."

"Oh, Sidney, come on, this isn't one of your corny old melodramas—"

"There is no need to insult me. We have nothing more to say to each other. I don't want you here anymore. Miss Englehart, call an attendant. There's the door. Go through it and forget me."

He was breathing hard. His face was red.

"You," he said, "and these are my last words, are part of the general conspiracy. You will have to accept the general guilt."

"Come on, Sidney, what conspiracy?"

"The conspiracy of mediocrity against talent. You have always been a mediocrity, you will always be one. You never deserved my help. You don't merit my friendship now."

"Sidney—"

"There is no need to apologize."

"I wasn't apologizing. Did you hear what I said? You are not a victim, and there is no conspiracy—"

"There is a conspiracy in this nation to humble people of talent and spirit, to bring them down to the level of our ruling class of businessmen. You have all kinds of clothes, have you not?"

"Yes, I do."

"Still you cling and clutch and—what's a suit?"

"This is the first day I'm wearing this suit."

"That is why it was perfect for what I needed. Oh, forget it. I wouldn't take it now if you begged me. Miss Englehart, where is the goddamn attendant I asked for?"

"He's at lunch."

"What conspiracy? he asks. The conspiracy to deprive people of their souls. What else does this place do? It is a continuation of the Broadway theater. Deprive people of their pride, then they die abandoned and alone and not caring to live. That is what kills them. Yes, I accuse you. You are among the men who think only of the dollar, who've forgotten the things of the spirit, even when they go to church and slip those big bills to fat cardinals and bishops. I despise them, those thirty-day geniuses like your new director, Adam Garshman. Did I hear right, that errand boy is now a director? That squirrel! And your new producer, the one who is going to do me a favor and offer me a job understudying, what's his name?"

"Sol. Sol Bender."

"Ah, yes. Sol Bender. He is doing me a favor and giving me, only at your insistence, no doubt, an understudy? What is that except a way of depriving me of my pride, of killing me before I die."

He stood up now as straight as if he was playing the third-act climax of a play by Arthur Miller, and he leveled his whole accusing body at me, pointing with his long forefinger and unloading. "Tell me this, tell me truthfully, if you can, do you think I can understudy without losing my pride? Do you think that is how I should be swept under the carpet, a man who has played Peer Gynt, Richard Second and Third, who played Vershinin in Paris, the artist who took *Death of a Salesman* to the great cities of the Australian continent and left behind him there the only bit of culture those aborigines have ever known, I who brought back *An Enemy of the People?* Why, man, in Europe theaters would have been named after me! Streets! Parks! I have been called unforgettable, historical. So now, at the end of my career, what do I get? Not from the oafs abroad in this country of merchants but from a man whom I sheltered under my wing, helped with his first steps, what do I get from my understudy?'

He imitated me in a baby's voice. "Give me back my coat."

His face was flushed with his heart's blood. "All right," he shouted as he pulled on his gray sweater, "since this is what you want, this is what you'll get. My death is on your hands."

He turned toward Miss Englehart and thrust his hand through her window opening. "Forget the attendant," he said. "I'm going for a walk." He was not asking her permission, simply informing her, as Merrick might have on his way out of his office.

She put something in the palm of his hand, but I couldn't see what it was. With this, he walked out.

Miss Englehart resumed eating the egg-salad sandwich, which she had put aside because of the excitement.

I put on my coat. It was too big for me.

"You know," Miss Englehart said, "you shouldn't get him all excited that way. It's not good for him. He's a pretty sick man."

"I didn't mean to. What's the matter with him?"

"I don't know exactly, but Dr. Mittelman seems worried about his throat. Didn't you hear his voice? How hoarse it was? And it's getting worse."

"Does he—is he worried about it?"

"You can't tell with Mr. Schlossberg. He's awful proud, you know."

"What was that you gave him as he left?"

"A sedative. Dr. Mittelman's orders."

I had to run to catch up with him. He was blowing down the street like the wind off the Hudson in winter. He'd been furious when he walked away from me, but when I caught up with him he put his arm through mine the way he used to long ago. I remembered how much that had meant to me the autumn I first came down to New York from New Haven. He'd done that then in front of the Music Box Theatre, saying, "You're with me now, kid." I remembered that moment. He'd skipped to get in step with me and now he did it again, skipped a step and pulled me up against him so we were walking together, side by side. He was smiling in a strange way, not angry, a sober, thoughtful smile it was. Everything of the ham and the clown seemed to have dropped off him.

"Why are you smiling?" I asked.

"I want to tell you a story," he said.

"You can have this fucking suit," I said.

He didn't bite. "The night before I came out here," he said, "I wanted to celebrate, don't ask me what, that I was still alive, I suppose. So I got hold of one of the girls from the top-floor dressing room—remember Polly, the plump one?—and I asked her if she wanted to go see Lou Masters' new play with me. I'd heard it was a piece of shit but had a perfect part for me, which, of course, was not offered me so I shed no tears when it got roasted. You remember Lou Masters, the author?"

"Well. A pretty nice fellow."

"I hadn't made arrangements beforehand," he went on, "figured I didn't need to because the company manager was still Otto Brand, remember him?"

"A nice guy too."

"He'd been on the play I'd done for Masters, oh, when was it?

Seventeen years ago? So this kid, Polly, she got all dolled up, and I had on my last suit. You were right about that. I hocked them one by one, my cane too, for tobacco money. They were not in good shape anyway, all I got was a deuce apiece. So I walked up to this company manager, Otto the groaner we used to call him, remember? And I says, 'Otto, I'd like to catch the show tonight.' And he says, 'I can't take care of you, Sid.' At least he remembered my name. 'Why can't you?' I says. 'It's our policy,' he says. 'No paper on this show. Lou Masters' orders.'

"So I took him aside. He kept looking around nervously, not really listening, you know. I pointed out that I had a young lady with me, she'd dressed up for the event, and he shouldn't embarrass me in front of her. Furthermore it was natural, my request, wasn't it, since I'd once played a lead in a Lou Masters play, not too long ago, did he remember?

" 'Oh, yeah,' he says, like that, 'oh, yeah.' So then I put a pretty good pitch on the groaner. But in the middle of it, he says, 'No can do, Sid,' and again he starts to walk away, the son of a bitch.

"Well, I pushed him into a corner and reminded him of that night in Philly when Lou Masters' play looked hopeless. The audience was not coming back for the third act, and Lou was ready to give up.

"But I wasn't. I sat up all night with the man, and we got into one of those drunks where inspiration comes. I analyzed his problems for him, and by morning when I pointed out for the fifth time that he'd left out the scene for which he'd written the play in the first place, he was beginning to see what I meant. I acted that scene out for him, I remember, twice. I was brilliant. And then, suddenly, it was clear to him, like it had been all along to me. Hope came back, the feeling he could do something after all, that he wasn't licked, not yet. He's a tense, cold author, always stands sideways even when he kisses his wife, but that night he hugged me and he kissed me. Maybe it was just the booze.

"I talked very straight to him. I told him to get his ass up to Manchester, Vermont, where he pretends to be a working farmer and there write us one hell of a new second act, starting from scratch and aiming right for that scene I'd acted out for him. 'Remember that, Otto,' I said, 'remember that, when Lou Masters suddenly disappeared for a week while we were in Philly and I told you not to worry, it was the best thing he could do for the show?'

"I could see it was all coming back to the groaner. He wasn't fidgeting anymore. I reminded him, then, of how Lou had come down from the big snow country and he had a new second act with him and the big scene was there. When he read it to the cast, how they applauded, mostly from relief, but also because he'd shown some courage, Lou. 'Remember his face that night, Otto,' I said, 'when they were cheering him?' "

"I remember it," I said.

"That's right, you were still my understudy in those days. Well, Otto said yes, he remembered it all, it was all coming back to him. By now he'd stopped looking around and his face had softened. Can you imagine his face softening? He goes into the box office, and when he comes back out, he has two tickets with him, and what do you suppose they were for?"

"Fifth row center?"

"The balcony. And he stands there waiting for me to thank him. 'Otto,' I said, 'I got a young lady with me.'

"Well, he begins to groan and whine, 'What do you waaaant from me?' Remember how his voice slid up into that whine, like everything was too much for him? 'What do you waaaaaant from me?'

" 'I'll tell you what I want from you,' I said, 'I waaaaant you to go down to E101 and 102 and tell the people in those seats that you've made a terrible mistake and ask them to move back somewhere. Then I want you to come back here and bow real low to my bride of the night and escort her and myself to those seats. That is what I want.'

"Well, then he began to laugh in that very nervous way he has and again he starts to walk away. But I held on to him. 'Wait a minute, Otto,' I said—I could see he was beginning to get the call-the-cops look—'because there is something else I want from you. I'd like you to take these two walkup ducats, coat them with vaseline, drop your drawers right here in the lobby, and shove them up your ass! Will you do that for me, Otto?' "

Sidney was in a paroxysm of laughter.

When he recovered he went on. "Then I took Polly to Fallaci's Italian Garden, the last restaurant in town where I still have credit, thanks to Mario, the headwaiter, whom I slip a buck every time I walk in. Like I say, when you need money, act like you don't. That night I gave Mario my entire bankroll, two bucks, right as I walked in, and he treated us like he used to treat me in the old days, bringing us the dishes himself and hanging over our table until we'd tested each one and nodded our approval. I ordered hot stuffed clams and garlic soup and that was their osso bucco night of the week, which they still make good at Fallaci's, and with it we had Chianti, but imported, you understand. The food and the jokes were good so we had to go for another bottle of the vino. Then at the end Mario brought out a beautiful Persian melon he'd been saving for Little Father Fanelli, who always eats there, and in that priest's honor we had a glassful of the Tears of Christ with our espresso.

"Polly was so happy she took me home. Little plump Polly, her tits have that old-fashioned feel, and she held me all night, and in the morning she told me she didn't have anybody just then so why didn't I move in. Imagine, an old man like me! So you see I don't have to worry about a place to stay now. I couldn't stand the schwartzuh's place, Frank Scott's. It smelled from pig meat and the sweat of too many people. So I told Polly my problems, and she said not to worry because the girls from the top-floor dressing room would never forget me, they'd raise money among themselves for the suit and get their boy friends to put up for my old rooms in the Plaza. But I told her I couldn't take it from them, because those girls are on the balls of their ass, just getting by, and if they have to fuck old men, it should be old rich men who leave presents, not deadbeats like me. So I refused her offer of a roof, with many, many thanks. But Polly said it was O.K., she liked me to fuck her, and her friends, the other girls, would like to see my play get on. I'd read parts of it many times to them upstairs while they waited for their scenes. Again I said no, but I promised if I ever got desperate I'd call them up, my army of irregulars. I'd remember they were ready to serve, and I'd call them to arms."

He hooked his arm through mine.

"Anyway, about you, I understand. You have bills and obligations, and you're trying to make sure to keep enough money together so what happened to me won't happen to you. But don't worry, everything will turn out bad. The only people who'll die with a balance in the bank are the bankers. And their lawyers. People like us end up like me. I never thought it would happen to me, but it did, and you don't think it will happen to you, but it will. So you're right. Don't give me any money. Save it all. I started you, and I want to see you come out of it better than I did, understand, better not worse, even though I don't think it can possibly happen."

"Sidney," I said, "you can have the suit, and I'll get you the room at the Plaza."

"Two rooms, my old suite—"

"Whatever it is, you don't have to go to the girls in the top-floor dressing room—"

"I don't want it from you," he said.

"Please, Sidney, forget the way I was before. Forgive me, Sidney, will you, forgive me?"

I said it. "Forgive me."

I was thinking of that old lion I'd confronted on my knees outside my tent a few nights ago. Maybe because when Sidney smiled that particular way, he looked like Bert Lahr, Mr. Lahr at the end of his life. A lot of old men get that dazed smile just before they die. What do you call it, sardonic? That's not really it either. What that smile means is that the person doesn't expect anything good to happen anymore in his life, understand? We smile that way so we don't do something else, something that will humiliate us, whimper and pity ourselves, you know?

I had an idea what Sidney was feeling. I was beginning to feel it myself.

"Sidney," I said, "your old place in the Plaza, you got it."

"You're losing your grip, kid," he laughed. "I meant what I said. I don't want it from you. What I want from you is a cup of coffee. There's a Dunkin' Donuts around the corner. I want a frosted cruller and coffee."

"Look," he said after the comfort, "I know I'm ludicrous. I'm a dirty old man, a broken-down goat that can hardly get it up, a shameful person. I'm sick, and I'm twisted, and what's worse I'm a fool who still speaks in the ridiculous phrases of last century's theater and even then doesn't make sense. I know I always exaggerate. In fact, I always lie a little or a lot. What I say is not to be trusted, it is always in my favor. I have much more pity for myself than for anybody else, and despite all that I am very vain. In short, I am nuts. But why do you—not you, the world—why do you discard me? Why do you wish me dead?"

"Sidney, I don't wish you dead."

"Sure you do. I'm an embarrassment to you, a burden. You don't like the company I keep and—"

"There you're right, but it's for your sake—"

"Look at it from my point of view. The only men I've met who appreciate me are those outlaws, those scoundrels, those petty thieves, and now my new friends, the classier type goniffs. Let me tell you something, those men have grace. Can you imagine them refusing me a pair to a show by a man for whom I'd played a lead? In a theater where I'd starred? Why, I'm afraid to admire the necktie that little schwartzuh Frank Scott wears, because he'll pull it off and give it to me. Those outlaws, they have generosity, the old-fashioned kind.

They have soul, they understand friendship. They are the nearest thing around to the world of Shakespeare. The other night I was with this one man I'm telling you about—he's white, Polish, I think—and I recited some bits of Shakespeare for him, and you should have seen his face. 'There is a man like me,' he says. Richard, he was talking about. You know the scene where Richard stops the funeral and takes Lady Anne? My friend liked Richard. Most people pretend, call Richard a villain when the fact is they wish they had his balls. Even you. I have often wondered what it is, that respectability you are protecting? What does a suit mean to you, that you try to pull it off my back?"

"I really don't know."

"You see, I am sympathetic to you. But I am also telling you when it comes to size in a man—well, like now I need—you can't call it an investment—it's a romantic gesture. So where do I turn? Imagine a Sol Bender putting money up for a play which Paul Prince wrote and in which I am to star? Ridiculous, isn't it? But I know a man who I think will do it if only to spite the income tax people. What do I care what his reasons are?"

"They're not the only people like that, Sidney."

"Show me another. Just before, I mentioned Otto Brand and I mentioned Lou Masters. What do you come back with? 'He's a pretty nice guy.' What does that mean?"

"What I meant was—"

"I know what you meant. But let me tell you something. These new friends of mine, they scare you, and you are right to be scared of them, because they live on anger. A man is either their friend and they'll kill for him or he is their enemy and they'll kill him. That is what I meant like Shakespeare. You know, anger is a talent. It's a gift, like sex. When you let it go too long without using it, it shrinks, and you become incapable, incapable of anger I'm talking about, you understand? Everybody now sees everybody else's side of everything, so they are incapable of holding a position, you see? We're too nice, too understanding. Most of the time when you don't get angry, you should. When you take and take humiliation, you are betraying yourself. When you let people cross you and don't say anything, want nothing but to keep the harmony going, you're a traitor to yourself. That is what's happened to you. I'm not going to say anything about your wife, but I have an opinion. It's none of my business. But about you, I got to say this. You lost your fight somewhere along the way, old friend. That is why you never became a real star. O.K.?"

I knew and he knew that what he'd said was true, and he knew that I knew, so what the hell was there to say?

"Walk me back to the place," he said.

As we walked along, he said, "You know this is it for me. So I'm trying to be practical. I don't want to do this play on Broadway. Even if somebody was fool enough to put up for it. There's no audience for it there, is there?"

"I don't think so."

"It would be like pissing into the wind. Where I want to do the play is—there's a theater on the Lower East Side in my old neighborhood, Second Avenue just down the street from where the Café Royal used to be and across from where I used to play with Maurice Schwartz, his Yiddish Art Theatre. I was seventeen then, too young to play fathers, but grandfathers I could play. Well that theater is gone, but there is this other one across the street, and it's named after a shikseh, believe it or not. She was a fine lady, this Phyllis Anderson, an agent, yes, believe me, and somebody down there had the good sense to name a theater in a Jewish neighborhood after her. I met her a couple of times and, oh, my God, was she a square! She believed everybody had some talent in them somewhere and it was her mission in life to find it, that little bit of something good where nobody else would even look for it. And she did, she brought it out. That theater down there is like a candle lit in her memory. Well, I'd like to get that theater for just one week, four days' rehearsal, two performances Saturday and two Sunday. Four performances, that is all I want. Maybe there are still people who want to be reminded that twenty-five hundred years ago there was a man who stood up against the power gods of his day. That's what it's about, you know, about the one man who did not back down. Maybe a small audience still exists for that."

"Well, Sidney, if it goes down there, you can move it—"

"It ain't going to go nowhere," he said. "I am not a fool, I just act like one. But you can see, can't you, why I need some kind of freak to back it, why I keep the company I keep?"

"I can see," I said.

In front of the Haven now, we faced each other. He took the slack of my cheek between the knuckles of the first and second fingers of his right hand, pulled and twisted it. It hurt a bit, but it was affectionate and ultimately forgiving, and beyond that it made me a little ashamed and pretty sad and very loving. In fact, to tell you the truth, it brought tears to my eyes.

"I'll be back in the afternoon with your suit," I said.

He didn't answer.

"Let me do that for you, Sidney."

"O.K. " he said, "if you really want to."

"I do," I said.

I knew he had something else to say, and finally he came out with it. "You've noticed my voice?"

"It's sort of hoarse," I said. "You got a cold?"

"It started three weeks ago, and every day, maybe just my imagination, it seems to get a little worse. A drink or two loosens it up, but then—"

"What's the doctor say?"

"I didn't go to a doctor."

"Sidney, you've got to go to a doctor."

"What's he going to say? Don't use it for a while, give it a rest? That would be a laugh, wouldn't it? I've been resting it for ten years." He laughed. "Save it, he'll say. Right. I'm saving it for four days of rehearsal where I'll not talk above a whisper and four performances where I'll break the chandeliers."

"Sidney, Equity has—"

"I've worn out the free doctors. The Equity man hides when he hears I'm in the building."

"I'm going to take you to a specialist."

"Get me the suite at the Plaza for three days if you want to help my voice," he said, "because it's a psychic thing, no doubt. Notice I've gone up a day."

"Sidney, it could be serious."

"Suppose it is, what's he going to tell me? You haven't much time, Mr. Schlossberg? That is what he'll say, if he's got the balls. If he's like everybody else, he'll bullshit me, and I don't want to hear either one. I'll tell you this. I'll die only when something happens to my soul. That's the only place I can get hurt. If I ever get licked there, I'll die because I'll want to! I will not live in humiliation and die after months of complaining and generally making a pest of myself. Look, there's Paul Prince. See him in there? Back of the glass door? The son of a bitch. You got to like a man who's that desperate. Don't you?"

"You're very late," Ida whispered as she let me through the door. "They're in Sol's den." She indicated the direction, then held on to me. "Please, I got to remind you. Sol had a couple of—" She touched the valley between her breasts. "So try to keep everything, you know, halfway, you know?" She smiled at me, a swell old girl—she'd been in vaudeville, famous for her imitations and her great head of golden hair. "I'll make you sturgeon with eggs, no onions. I understand about your wife, believe me!"

The men were stunned by the long wait. Sol was flat on his red leather sofa, moist pads of something soothing on his eyes. The young director was standing at the window, staring for no purpose at the back of the Great Northern Hotel. Only Bennie, the general manager, was improving the hour with *Screw*. As I entered, they all looked at a timepiece, two wristwatches and a ship's clock salvaged from the cabin cruiser Sol had in the days when he boasted three big hits on the Street and owned the road.

No one reprimanded me, which was wise because I was in no mood for guff.

The decision was to cancel the four-week out-of-town tryout, yes or no, maybe substitute a week of previews in New York.

"You know this is sort of a comedy we're doing?" I threw this in the direction of Adam Garshman, hoping to get him on my side.

"I know that very well." He replied as if I'd been challenging him.

"And the road," I said, "for a comedy is—"

"Look, I'd rather spend four weeks out too but—" He looked at Sol, who was now sitting behind the fortification of his desk, playing Silent Solomon the King.

"No can do," Bennie said, putting down *Screw*.

I ignored him. "That," I announced to the others, "is where I shape and refine my performance, that is where I really do my rehearsing, especially for a comedy, with a regular audience that laughs—"

"I don't have anything in the budget for out-of-town losses," the general manager said.

"Well, personally, I don't work that way," young Adam answered me. "Personally, I like to really rehearse."

"But you know what I mean," I said, giving the boy this last chance to get on the right side.

"Not really," he said, shrugging and walking to the window where he turned his back.

That finished him with me. I took a moment to decide what size I'd cut him down to and how long it would take. "About a week of rehearsal," I said to myself, then turned to Bennie. "What makes you think we're necessarily going to lose money on the road?" I asked.

Bennie smiled at me, his answer, then looked at the producer. There was a silence. Then Solomon spoke.

"I'm sorry," he said and sighed.

"We just can't do it, boss," Bennie said, picking up *Screw*.

"Bennie, put that filthy sheet down," Sol said, showing his steel. Then he turned on me with all the force of his unflappable patience, my master, and said, "I just can't take the chance. You see, here in New York we can sell a week of parties, maybe a couple nights more but—"

"We'd die on the road," Bennie said.

"What makes you so goddamn sure of that?" I asked.

Bennie didn't see fit to answer me. He turned to the young director. "Since this show is a one-lunger, maybe you could chop off a couple of days' rehearsal and I could sell maybe three, four, more parties here. That would give you—" He turned to me with a lupine smile.

"You know," I said, "the road's been good. Bennie, I'm talking to you."

"For established hits," Bennie disagreed, "last year's established hits. Am I right, Mr. Bender?"

"He's right, Bennie," Sol said, agreeing with me. "It's been better than New York," then not agreeing with me, "but for the big stars."

I got the point of the meeting. "And I'm not?" I said.

God, was my master's smile benign! "Almost nobody is anymore," he said. "Perhaps"—oh, was he gentle!—"this play will do it for you."

"They're not crowding me for parties," Bennie said.

"Bennie, would you mind going to the corner and buying me a cigar, three for a dollar," said Sol Bender. "Take half an hour."

"I got one right here," Bennie offered it to him.

The producer's look—if only an actor could act that good!

"The point is," Bennie said, lighting his boss's cigar, "I think we should be realistic about what we got and what we don't."

"What do you think?" I turned to the young director.

"You know you're not a big star," he said.

"He will be after this play," my producer repeated.

"Oh, yeah, sure, maybe, but right now"—the young director, was he ever a truth-teller!—"he hasn't quite made it, have you?" This last to me.

"So who's a big star?" I said, picking a fight.

"Playwrights," the young director said, "that's who. Neil Simon."

"The only one," Bennie said, "the main man."

"Arthur Miller," young Adam said.

Bennie smiled and shrugged. "At one time," he said.

"Tennessee Williams," the producer said wistfully, stroking the lapels of his blazer.

"Not him," Bennie said, "please."

"He's finished," young Adam agreed.

I revised my time allowance on cutting the young director down to size. I went after him now. "Bennie," I said, "shrugged off Arthur Miller. Do you agree?"

"Well"—the young man did a peculiar little duck with his shoulder as if avoiding a big block being thrown at him—"he's on the side of the angels, but he's sure old-fashioned!"

"Whom do you admire, may I ask? Inge?"

"Inge?"

"William Inge. He won a Pulitzer Prize."

"Oh, I know the name all right. I'd say he died ten years too late."

"I don't want to work with this son of a bitch," I said, turning to my producer.

Sol Bender took it without flinching.

"What about Albee?" Bennie said. I could only suppose he hadn't heard my announcement.

"Oh, Albee," young Adam was reminded. "Yeah." He thought for a minute, then gave his verdict. "The jury is still out on him. That absurdist period is over, but he may have one more playable play in him. We'll have to see." Then Adam turned to me and said, "You don't have to work with me."

I didn't understand whether he was resigning or suggesting that I do. I looked at my producer who gave me a little smile and nod. I didn't know what the hell that meant either. I was frustrated. I didn't seem to be able to arouse any concern anywhere. The brilliant young director, the *Voice* critic had so identified him, was really insulting. He went right on talking to Bennie as if nothing of consequence had happened. "Of course, now there is the director. Nichols!"

"Now you're talking!" Bennie said. "He takes a play out on the road, you're a sure four-week sell-out!"

"Of course I don't like his work," the young director said, "but—"

"Fosse!" Bennie exploded. "Now that he's straightened out his personal life. Fosse! Dynamite!"

"Did you hear what I said before?" I asked the producer.

He nodded and waved his hand, ducking the issue.

I decided to show my class. I turned to the young director. "I want to ask you a question which, now that we're not going to work together, maybe you can answer frankly—"

"Oh, I would anyway," he smiled. Nothing I'd said had fazed him.

"Why have I never become a big star?"

"It's a good question," Adam complimented me. "I'll answer it in the spirit which you asked it. I know it must disturb you so—"

"You *have* seen me on stage?"

"Oh, yes, twice. Had to, you know, in case, you know, this job."

"So?"

"Well, since you ask me I'd say it's because your performances are mechanically excellent. I mean timing, reading, general stage deportment. But there are never any surprises in your work. Have you read the works of Abraham Maslow?"

"No," I said.

"You can get it in paperback. *The Farther Reaches of Human Nature.* I'll give you a copy. See, it's a matter of empathy. The human in the audience should look at the actor on stage and see his own turbulent and erratic humanity revealed, not just an entertainment machine. You show them a perfect front but no soul."

I didn't say anything. It had occurred to me that the young man might have a point. Certainly something had not gone right with my career. Maybe he knew what.

"That's why you've never made it big in films," the young man said. "Film is the greatest of the performing arts because it is the most human. Alice Faye was not Duse, she was better. She was all soul."

I had to admire the little bastard's courage.

"I'm sorry you don't think we can work together," he continued, "because I think I could help you."

The fact that the young director had said things that might be true—I knew because they hurt—made me more defensive. So I ignored again the first law of show-business intercourse, which is *never say never,* and I turned to the producer and despite the fact that I knew as well as anybody that an ultimatum in this world of compromise and adjustment is always weak, I said, "So, you can tear up my contract."

Sol was wise and Sol was gentle and he made me feel like a fool. "Now baby," he said, "what the hell kind of a way is that to talk?"

"I told you he'd be upset," Bennie said.

"I'm not upset about canceling the road booking."

"By the way, what was Inge," the young director said, "a particular friend of yours or something?"

"Yes," I said, then, "No. I mean yes, but not personally."

"O.K. I don't know what all that means, but O.K." Adam shrugged and laughed. "You know we boys from downtown, you have to forgive us a certain provincialism." He grinned at me and showed his teeth, which looked sharp.

"Come on," the producer said to me, "have a drink. Sit down. Calm yourself. Where the hell is Ida with your eggs? Bennie, get him a drink. You like bourbon, I remember you like— Ida!" Sol left the room.

"I don't want a fucking drink." But Bennie was already at the bar. "Scotch, Bennie." I sat down. I was really in a fool's spot. I looked at the young director, and again he showed me his sharp front teeth. It was at that moment, I decided later, that I began to have the obsession that this young man was born to kill me, that I had to fight him for my life.

Sol came back. "Your eggs are on the fire," he said. "Feel better?"

"No, I don't," I said. "Let me level. It's no secret," I pointed to the young man across the room, "that he wanted Jason Robards for this part and not me. Didn't you?" I put Adam on the spot.

"Yes," he said, getting off it, "I did."

"Or Hal Holbrook."

"Not him, but Jason, yes. But look, Jason has his problems too."

"Anyway, you didn't want me."

"I didn't know you, personally, but now that I—"

"You don't know me now. But I'm going to tell you a few things, then maybe you will. I think you are some kind of little shit. You have yet to say anything about anybody that showed the least compassion. Or kindness, did you ever think of anybody with that? Kindness! Or grace? It's all a rat fight to you, and the problem is to survive by killing others. Bill Inge had ten times the talent you'll ever have. When you criticize a line of Tennessee Williams you have the impudence of a child that should be spanked because he's too young to be shot. A drop of his piss is better than your heart's blood. And Miller, you patronize Arthur Miller! He's old-fashioned! That's your final judgment on a man who's contributed what he's contributed to the history of our theater? Why you shallow, arrogant, uneducated asshole! I'd like to take your head off—"

I was shouting. Everybody in the building could hear me. "You squirt, you piddling prick! To have those opinions! You got to earn those opinions, I mean earn!"

I'd come up to the producer's desk as I said this last and slammed my fist down on its glass top. It split, a beautifully curved line.

"Tell me," I said, standing over the young man, "what the hell your confidence is based on? Two shows downtown which maybe looked good there where anything is excused? But what else? Nothing. Am I wrong about that? Sol?" I shouted at my producer who was looking at his destroyed desk top, "Sol!"

Ida came running in, a tray, eggs, toast, coffee, prune cookies.

"What are you shouting? Boys, stop shouting. Mrs. Frost upstairs, she'll—"

"I saw one of those shows," I interrupted her, "and I don't think he did a goddamn thing! A lot of actors walking around, what they call improvising. What the hell is that? Sol, am I wrong? Say something, Sol. I'm talking to you!"

I noticed Ida behind her husband. She'd put the tray down and was making signs to me that Sol didn't see, touching her chest, begging me to ease up.

"All right!" I turned from Sol, who was still shaking his head dolefully over his ruptured glass top, and went for the young director. "If I were your best friend, which I'm the opposite, what I'd hope for you is defeat! Destruction! Rejection! Disaster! To be torn down! Ripped apart! To be taught humility. Some grace. A shred of kindness for other people. That is the only thing that will make a human being of you, that's the only hope you have. Maybe if you know enough pain and trouble, something human will finally emerge out of that bitch-faggot, style-oriented, Yale Drama School—"

"A faggot I'm not," the young director said. "The rest you're right about."

Now what the hell could you say to that?

I allowed Ida to push me into a chair behind the eggs, and I drank my Scotch.

Then the little son of a bitch said the most arrogant thing of all. "I too believe," he said, "that a setback or two may be just what I need most."

"But not this time out, huh?" Bennie said.

I had to laugh, and when I did, I gave up.

"Ida dear," I said, "I can't eat these eggs."

"I'll eat 'em," Adam said.

He sat down, looked at the dish, nodded his approval, used the pepper mill.

"I'm going home," I said.

"May I say one more thing?" Adam said as he relished my eggs. "We really never met before today, but what you've just done has convinced me like nothing else could that you can be superb in this part. I mean, excuse me if this sounds patronizing, I didn't think you had it in you! These eggs are great, Ida. I didn't think you could break through that plate-glass front. But you sure as hell did, didn't he, Sol?" He chuckled, pleased with himself. "So I got to say it. Sol, you were right. He's talented. You know that? Talented."

"Come on," Sol said to me. "I'll walk you a few blocks, get the papers."

A soft spring afternoon was fading. We had a nice stroll up Central Park South, and he was covering for Adam.

"I think I got a great combination here," he said, "the new and the—"

"Say it, Sol, say it."

"That's not what I meant. Experienced. But we all need to be shaken up. For instance me. Every once in a while I feel I'm over the hill, old-fashioned. I need a hit, baby! Just for my confidence! I'm beginning to wonder, maybe I lost the knack. Now this kid—Ida's got an instinct. She likes him and—"

All this time I was giving side thought to that sheaf of new bills on my dresser, and I decided to allow Sol the pleasure of talking me back into the fold. Which he did:

"I only wish he had some compassion," I said. "All right, I can smell his talent. He's quick as a weasel but—"

"That comes later," Sol said. "Heart and all that, later."

"Did you see him eat my eggs?"

"Weren't you a snotty kid once?"

"I suppose so. But I can't be that mean anymore. That's why I'm thinking of quitting."

"Quitting? Now, baby, come on—"

"Not your show. I'm signed for that. The whole thing. The profession."

"All actors feel that way in the spring."

"Every year I'm back at the start mark. I got to prove it all over again. You said it yourself. 'I got to have a hit, just for my confidence,' you said. 'Maybe I lost the knack,' you said. After all these years, Sol, still so anxious?"

"Where else can you make a living doing what you like?"

"Save that for the screen version," I said. "Personally, I never liked it that much."

There was no one home. On the little bulletin board by the phone, pinned next to the karate schedule, I found the announcement of a block meeting. The agenda: NEW STREET LIGHTS. TWENTY-FOUR-HOUR STREET PATROL. COMMITTEE TO PLANT NEW TREES. The hour? Now. That's where they were.

On my dresser, a little pack of money was under my hairbrush, the fare and a half to Sarasota that Ellie had demanded the day I left for Africa.

And this note,

Dear—I'd rather not take this from you. I didn't like the grudging way you gave it. But I understand how you felt. Agreed, you shouldn't have to pay for our travel, if and when. Or if you should, I don't want you to if you don't. I'm making sure now that I have enough to pay my way—if it gets to that. I want to be independent that way—and in other ways—and that seems to depend on having ready cash, doesn't it? Money gives strength! Who said that? Another gem from the puritan work ethic?

I'd like to stay on here and try to work things out, O.K.? Events, I'm sure, will make any decision simple. They usually do. Let's see what happens. As a friend of mine said, "It's a whole new deal. Clear the decks." And maybe it will be fun.

Eleanor

Under this letter I found an item from the obit page of *The New York Times*. It was headed "Lewis Vincent Doyle" and informed anyone interested that the dead man had had one marriage, one divorce, one son, and, all his life long, one employment.

While I digested that—poor Lace Curtain Louie!—I didn't waste a minute. Into a shopping bag I stuffed my four-hundred-and-fifty-dollar Knize suit, three of my best white shirts, two of my most confidence-inspiring striped ties—I noticed Big Arthur's picture had disappeared from above the bed—a pair of black shoes with a high polish, two pairs of close-ribbed black socks, cuff links to harmonize, and a pearl stickpin for flash.

The last thing I did was put the fare and a half in my pocket. Money gives strength.

On my way out, in a flash of intuition, I recognized the piano. I'd never seen it before, but there was the true owner, his picture presiding over a plateau of perfectly polished mahogany.

Arthur was back. In style.

This time Sidney let me come upstairs with my delivery. "I think they're working," the night girl cautioned me in a key of total respect. The big man had got to her, too.

Sidney had space with four others, the room jammed with five cots no wider than a body. The other men had that waxy look the dying develop, their mouths drooped open, their eyebrows arched anxiously and frozen there. Two had Parkinson's tremble.

I walked to the cot where Sidney was lying. Apparently his scene with me earlier had exhausted him. One arm was bent under his head, his neck rested on his elbow. He didn't look around at me when I spoke but made a sign to Paul Prince, who was sitting in a chair alongside his bed, writing what appeared to be the same sentence over and over. Paul got up and sat on the floor with his back to the cot.

"We were working," Sidney said, "or else I wouldn't have subjected you to this." He indicated the other men in the room, who were all breathing through their mouths and looking at me as if I was an executioner come to select his next victim.

Sidney accepted my gifts without an expression of thanks. As if by radar, he found the twenty-dollar bill I'd put in the inside coat pocket of the vicuña, unfolded it to see if it had a mate. Then he said, "Where's my breast pocket handkerchief?"

"I forgot it," I said.

He nodded his head. I'd confirmed what he'd expected, that I'd forget something essential. "I'll be in touch with you when I need you again," he dismissed me.

"I see what you mean," I whispered, indicating the roomful.

"Isn't old age loathsome?" Sidney said in a voice loud enough for everyone in the room to hear. "Not sad, not dignified, not wise, but boring, tedious, stupid, shameful, despicable."

I expected the other old men might resent what he'd said, but one of them began to laugh, and two others joined in. The one who didn't was deaf.

"I resent it when I can't remember a name," Sidney went on, "or a phone number I've known all my life, or a few lines of a poem I love. I resent it when I puff out on ten stairs. I resent it when I look into the mirror and see my hair coming out, not white, but grave yellow, fluffy and feeble, like Prince's here. I resent being in with these loathsome creatures." He turned on them scornfully. 'I'm not one of you,' he declaimed.

Those who'd laughed, laughed again. The deaf man tried to find out from his neighbors what Sidney was saying.

"What are you laughing at, you crepuscular ghosts?"

They shuffled and squirmed, giggled and whispered, making sure that each knew exactly what Sidney had said this time.

What's so funny?" Sidney demanded of me.

The old men had me laughing, too. 'Nothing,' I said.

"Nothing. You'll find out. You're in the same hole. Please leave now. You see I'm working. I'll be in touch with you when I need you next. The rest of you premature cadavers be absolutely quiet."

It was during the trip home that I made up my mind.

I was going to see Sidney through it the suite at the Plaza, the party for his newfound angel the production of *Titan*, Paul Prince's quirks. Sidney's romantic criminals the whole insane trip.

If he was Hieronymus Bosch's madman in a box so was I. If he was Dali's burning giraffe and no extinguisher within reach, what else was I? If he was the Godfather's setup, pinned against a bar and waiting for the garrote to tighten, turn by turn, well, tell me, how many turns were left for him and how many for me?

At home everyone was asleep. When I put on the light, Ellie moved over to her side and pulled the sheet over her head.

I unpacked, which caused some bustle and stir, perhaps more than was absolutely necessary. I was hoping to wake her.

The last thing I did was roll the lion belt around the lion wallet and put them at the foot of Little Arthur's door.

Then I undressed and got into bed.

She was awake by then, and I asked her about Lace Curtain Louie.

"These window gates were his idea, of course, the last thing he did. He thought they'd relieve my worry, which they did, though they're shockingly ugly, aren't they?"

"I wish he'd paid for them, since they were his idea."

"He didn't have the money. In fact he was deep in debt."

"Are you talking about the Lewis Doyle I knew?"

"He was an excellent counselor for his clients, conservative, meticulous, worried about their portfolios, taking the swings of the market personally, feeling betrayed when it went down. But after he died we found out that with his own money he was an absolute adventurer."

"Our Lewis Doyle?"

"It was his duty, he once explained to me, to make the future safe for Little Arthur by putting together a packet of stocks, bonds, and real estate so carefully chosen, so safe— 'That boy is all I have, he'd say. 'I'll happily spend the rest of my life so he'll never have to worry about money. All he'll have to do is live.' "

"I wish someone would do that for me."

"To accumulate these securities, Lewis conceived a great speculation to acquire an enormous capital gain. As I understand it, and I was never sure I did, his plan was to buy with a large sum of borrowed money, the interest on this loan being tax deductible, certain triple A bonds which he'd hold till maturity. In order to be able to meet his interest payments, he lived in a tiny room, was tight with food and drink spent nothing on himself, wore identical dark gray suits, you remember?"

"Always looked like he was fronting for a funeral home."

"And as far as I know never saw another woman. He worked like a desperado to meet the payments, sweating out three years, four years, before his capital gain could be reaped."

"I've never understood all that."

"And when he couldn't meet the payments, Lewis began to borrow money from the accounts in his custody, always intending to pay it back, but he fell more and more behind—"

"All this for Little Arthur's future safety?"

"That's it. Then one day, he couldn't go any further without being caught, saw his whole structure collapsing—"

"So he killed himself?"

"He always slept on his back, arms folded over his chest, like a Pope laid out for the public to see, and that is how they found him, dead of a massive hemorrhage, windows locked shut, eyes wide open. When his landlord and neighbors burst through his door they tripped a gigantic alarm system Lewis had installed, and this great bell roused the whole neighborhood."

I reached to give her comfort.

Ellie and I had slept naked from the first day. Now she wore pajamas. When I touched her, she said, "Don't do that, please," and edged away.

Silence.

When the baby shark raised his head, I woke.

Ellie, a coincidence? was propped on one elbow, studying me.

"When you left me," she said, "I was furious. I had nightmares, against you."

Shark-baby had had nine hard days in the African Bush and five days of ascetic privation in old Vienna. He wanted attention, not explanations.

"The man who came to install Lewis's gates," she said, "he was a clumsy, careless fellow. He pushed my geranium pots off the window ledge."

"We'll get some more," I said.

"When the gates were in, I felt more frightened. So I got Arthur's piano out of storage and from the instant it was here I felt safe."

"It's certainly a very handsome instrument." I shifted closer, trying to be fair, at the same time make her aware of my condition.

"I began to give lessons," she went on. "And I practiced. Regular hours. Every day."

"I think all that is terrific," I said.

"I found I liked being alone. Every morning I played the *Appassionata*. At night the *Nocturnes* or the piano of the *Kreutzer*. I sang the violin part. I heard myself singing. My own voice again! For ten years I'd let the best part of me go deaf and dumb. Now I can't wait for the day to begin."

I was glad to get the good news but would have preferred it at another time.

"And I stopped being angry with you."

A kind of cue? Perhaps. I took her hand and put it where I wanted it to be. In the past this had had gratifying results.

"I thought about you a lot," she said, holding me. "It was unfair of me to expect you to solve my problems. You can't solve your own."

That pulled the plug. The blood in my system began to return to a more even distribution.

"I'm not sore at you now," she said. "You can see that, can't you?"

"Yes," I said.

She gave her neglected old friend a little pat, kissed me, a touch of her lips, said, "Goodnight," and turned away. Quickly, she was asleep.

What she'd said was true. She was a stranger again.

Next morning—I looked, it was six thirty—an alarm rang. Ellie got out of bed and disappeared. Sometime later I heard Arthur's piano. She was practicing, playing the same bit over and over.

Then, a period of silence. Little Arthur was being given his breakfast, I guessed.

Right. Dressed for school, he stood by the bed, on my side, pulling on the lionskin belt.

"This for me?" He seemed terribly surprised.

"Yeah."

"Oh, thanks." He cinched the belt.

"Fit good?"

"Yeah. Look. What's this?" He was into the wallet.

"A shilling note. That's their money. Kenya."

"Oh, and this?" He'd found the stone.

"Good magic. It'll keep off the evil eye."

"Oh, neat."

He still seemed a little suspicious and surprised. It was the first off-holiday gift I'd ever given him.

"Thanks," he said again. "Really." And he left.

I heard the door slam and the bite of the bolt. The practicing resumed.

I gave up trying to sleep. It was almost nine.

"There's coffee," she called from the piano.

But she went right on playing, the same piece, over and over. A clear enough message, "Get your own breakfast, please."

All right, I did.

I had to say this, she was good. In all the time I'd known her, I'd never heard her play. She'd packed it in with Arthur's death and never played again. But I could see where she might once have had a legitimate hope for the concert stage.

First, it was Chopin. She played the Prelude cool and crisp, not stretching it, no false romantics, no inner weeping.

Then she turned to Bach, did him like he was a wild romantic. I'd never heard the old Teuton done that way.

Then she turned to a sonata—Aaron Copland, she told me later —all glass and steel slivers, as tough and confirmed as the girl herself.

Again I got the message. She wasn't going to be trifled with. Or was it this: She was arming herself for a long war. If that's what it was going to be, she was prepared.

I sat over the coffee listening to her. If I resented her a little, I also felt for her.

Then she stopped. It was ten of ten.

"You want some coffee?" I asked.

"Yes, thanks." She looked at her wristwatch. "My first lesson is at ten."

I went to get her a cup of coffee, the first time I'd ever done that.

She smiled her thanks with that straight-on look she has.

She seemed thinner, strained, even drawn, but there was something I had to admire. I mean, what the hell did it matter who got whose breakfast?

"I like the way you play," I said.

"Do you? I'm awful rusty."

"Sounds great to me."

"I don't want you to think that I'm taking you for granted," she said, "but this is my profession now, and I'm going to pursue it just as you do yours. That means I've got to give lessons, Sundays too. I've got to accumulate money, since that seems to be the secret of independence. I got an awful lot of pupils from one of Arthur's old teachers at the Mannes School. He gave me those they couldn't take."

"What do they pay?"

"Twelve dollars an hour."

"That's pretty good."

"Well, yes. Then there's my practicing. Maybe you can't stand it. Then I'll have to move, or get a studio. But I hope you'll get used to it. Just like I did when you were making that movie in New York and getting up at six every morning to go to makeup. I couldn't go back to sleep then either. Do you understand?"

"Yes, I do."

"You do?"

"Yes. I think so. It's pretty clear."

"And it's all right with you?"

"I'll get ear plugs."

"That's an idea."

"Besides, I begin rehearsals next week."

"That's right. You won't be around much."

"Well, what about the rest of it?"

"What rest of it?"

"You and me."

"I was going to say, about last night. I can't do it unless I'm feeling right. That's the way I am."

"I understand."

"Like you said before you left, it's a whole new deal."

"Clear the decks?"

"That's it. Because what we had before—"

"Wasn't going anywhere."

"Right. Now, if something develops—"

The doorbell rang.

"—it'll be much better. I hope."

"Who can tell?"

"Right. Is that O.K. with you?"

"Yes. It really is."

The doorbell rang again.

"Thanks," she said, 'for understanding."

She seemed surprised by my acceptance of the situation. She looked at the wristwatch I'd given her the Christmas before.

"That's Wilhelmina," she said, 'Wilhelmina Jackson."

She still hesitated.

"Better let her in," I said.

That's all we said that day. We had a truce. She didn't ask me about my trip.

The following day I had an endless conference with Adam and his costume designer. I was delighted to have a message to call Myron, an excuse to get away from our sixty-day wonder.

Myron was furious. "Sidney escaped," he said. "I had a call this morning from Mrs. Isaac Gillenson at Queenshaven."

"What do you mean, he escaped?"

"Disappeared in the middle of the night."

I wasn't surprised. I told Myron about my day with his brother.

"So it's your fault!" he shouted. I make sure he doesn't have the clothes or the *gelt* to leave that place, and you give him a suit and a twenty! What the hell did you do that for?"

"How far can he go on twenty bucks?"

"That maniac is probably bombed out of his mind this very minute. I wash my hands of the man. He's your responsibility."

"O.K.," I said, "he's my responsibility. But Myron, listen—"

He'd hung up. That goddamn family had a thing about hanging up before you did.

I figured I'd be seeing Sidney as soon as he'd blown the twenty. Maybe in a day or two. Twenty dollars wouldn't take him far in the traffic he was riding.

A week passed and I didn't hear from him so I supposed the Plaza party was one of those schemes Sidney dreamed up and forgot before anyone else did.

I had another problem, a serious one.

I don't mean my hot-shot director. I handled him all right. I've learned, as with a horse, so with a director, it's important to get the upper hand immediately.

Adam kept trying to suck me into a "little chat about the text." "Let's take a nice long walk in the park," he'd say, "and rap about the text."

"You mean the script? What the hell for?"

"So you'll know how I see it."

'I'll know how you see it after the first morning's rehearsal. What's so complicated? My part, it's a piece of cake."

"There's a lot more to it than appears on the surface."

"Adam, look. Your old shirt-lender, Paul Prince, told me what you really think of this play, so don't con me. I've played the exact same part five times on Broadway and twenty times in stock."

"I thought we might develop certain values a little more deeply."

"Isn't there a danger in that? We might make it heavy. It's only a matter of finding where the laughs are, and we can't do that till we have an audience."

Adam blew. "So what the hell are we rehearsing for?"

I'd found the weakness to cultivate, his temper. It would give me a definite advantage later on, him liable to go through the roof any minute, I the veteran cool-head, always controlled, always making sense.

"You tell me," I answered his question. "Why do we rehearse?"

Adam didn't give up. Next morning he called me again. "Why don't we take a nice long walk along Riverside Drive," he said. That's where the apartment of the man I was to play is located. "It's going to be a beautiful day."

"Is it?" I said. "Good. I'll go out to the track and walk there. I'll walk from the bar to the paddock to the window to the enclosure, then, I hope, back to the window. You can come along if you promise not to mention that play whose name I've forgotten."

So went the professional side of my week before rehearsals. I won every engagement. But I wasn't so up top elsewhere. Good intentions are one thing, day-to-day facts another.

The second morning after our truce, the alarm woke me again. Ellie slid out of bed. Then, the piano. I lay alone, awake when I didn't want to be. Despite my good will, I was furious.

But I put down that feeling. It wasn't fair to her. I understood what she was trying to do. I wanted her to succeed. I still thought her gallant.

So I made my breakfast and ate it slowly as I listened. I admired how she went over and over each piece, perfecting it, never satisfied, it seemed. She's a true pro, I told myself.

If she was aware, or disturbed, by my sitting there, listening but never commenting, acting as if what was happening was a perfectly reasonable and normal way to be, I living inside her music box, she didn't show that either.

I finished my breakfast and left.

The days passed. A conference, a meeting, an interview. Then I'd hit Sardi's Little Bar and join the other refugees. Then home. She'd be at the piano. If she wasn't, they'd be at the karate institute, learning to defend themselves.

Drink would raise my appetite, but there'd be nothing I wanted in the icebox.

One afternoon I got sort of loaded. I came home. Nobody. I saw that dinner was to be frankfurters and cole slaw from the deli. I went to a Chinese restaurant. I punished her. Lobster Cantonese, beef with oyster sauce. When I got home, she had three places at the table. I informed her I'd eaten. Well. No reaction. From the bedroom I heard them buzzing about their Sensei. Between them was my unused place.

She was showing me what I was showing her, that we could get along without each other. It was becoming a competition of indifference. In a few days, all talk stopped.

We were living on islands, the bridge between was burning, and no one was trying to put out the fire.

I began to hate Chopin, and Bach, and a particular piece by Gustav Mahler, that prophet of doom, and Debussy. I still detest Debussy.

The only way I could figure to keep something going was by staying away.

Well, when I thought about it. how else do the middle-class palefaces hang together? The wife and husband don't see each other. Nothing kills a marriage like social intercourse. The man goes to work in the morning, comes home as late as he can, exhausted, disgruntled, and loaded with every excuse for not making any contact but the most elementary.

Imagine what would happen, I thought, if the husband stayed home all day.

Even in our good days I hadn't dared try that.

At night we were in the same bed but didn't touch. This was driving me up the wall.

She slept behind the protection of her back, offered me her vertebrae. Even in her sleep, I could feel her tensed against me.

I, lying in bed, pretending to sleep when I wasn't, listened to the police sirens and, every so often, the love groans of the couple above us.

When I slept I heard lions.

I was keeping a countdown of days till the first rehearsal. I've always been confident that once I start work, all my problems fall into place, that place being the bottom of a long black velvet sack called forgetfulness. Work is my drug. When I'm in trouble, I reach for a job instead of a pill or a bottle.

But rehearsals started, and the drug didn't work.

"What am I trying to preserve?" I'd mumble to myself in the middle of one of Adam's long-winded explanations of the obvious. "Isn't it simply that there has been such an accumulation of furniture and cooking utensils, sheets and towels, books and records, bank accounts and charge plates that it's a bore beyond contemplation to break the place up? Isn't it only that you're too goddamn lazy to move out, that and nothing more?"

The morning of the third day of rehearsal, she broke her silence.

"I need some money," she announced.

"For what?"

"To buy Arthur some clothes. Summer is coming."

"What's wrong with what he wore last summer?"

"He's been growing. Didn't you notice? He had a birthday while you were away. Say something to him about it, maybe."

"What about all the money you've been—?"

"I'd rather not use that."

"Why the hell not?"

"I figure as long as we're living here, he's your responsibility."

"How much money you asking for?"

She had trouble bringing herself to name a number. I knew it must be humiliating for her, but I insisted she name an amount. Then I chiseled her down.

"I'm only getting rehearsal pay now," I said.

"I thought you drew an advance."

"I paid for your goddamn sliding gates with that."

"Forget it," she said. "I don't want it from you."

"O.K.," I said and left the house.

Those fleeting lines, the tracks on which we moved, had seemed till this moment separate but parallel. Now they began to diverge.

On the fourth day of rehearsal, Adam asked me, "What are you mumbling about all the time?"

"That's the way I work," I said.

"And what are you thinking about when you pretend you're thinking about your part?"

A pretty snotty remark, but I was too tired to take a shot at him.

"I have a little personal problem," I said, "but I'm getting rid of it."

"Do that," he said. "Soon."

Work hadn't helped, so I tried the other drug. The whole go took under an hour and all I remembered the next day is how messy her bed was, littered with the *Enquirer* and *Show Business*, with unanswered phone messages and used tissues, discarded panties, and cookie crumbs. After, I had to be polite to her. I was relieved a week later when Sol and Adam decided to recast the bit. I hear she blames me. A mess.

Well, it had to come to a climax, and it did when it generally does, the day of the first run-through of the first act. This rehearsal is often disappointing, but ours was a disaster. I knew it, no one had to tell me. And I thought I knew why.

I had no peace of mind at home. I'd come to work each morning more tired and flat than when I'd left the day before.

It was time to take steps to protect myself. After all I couldn't afford to look inept. I had to keep my pro status intact.

So I made up my mind to do what I'd done before, get a hotel room. I simply could not face the arctic cold of that double bed again.

It was at this rehearsal, with the cast assembled to hear Adam's scold, that I got the message. Ellie had called backstage. Since she hadn't really spoken to me for three days, I figured something serious must have happened, a fire, a robbery, a leak in the plumbing?

"I just wanted to tell you"—Ellie sounded very high—"in case you hear something, you don't have to rush home."

"What happened?"

"I got mugged."

"Where are you?"

"The police precinct."

"I'm coming right up."

"I don't want you to come right up. I have to go to the hospital now."

"Ellie, tell me what happened?"

"I got a broken finger or two, it seems like."

"Are you in pain?"

"Only when I talk on the phone. Goodbye. I'll tell you about it later."

"Tell me now. Tell me what to do."

"Do like you always do when there's a problem, rehearse."

"Listen, I got a friend who's a cop."

"I had enough of your friends. By the way, do you know where he is?"

"Who?"

"Mr. Sidney Schlossberg."

"What's he got to do with—?"

"He was there. You know where he lives?"

"No."

"You probably do. You got rehearsal tonight?"

"I'm supposed to have, yeah."

"What time will you be getting home?"

"I can be home any time you say. Why?"

"The police want to talk to you."

"About Sidney?"

"Yes. How about eight o'clock?"

"I can't get out of rehearsal by then."

"Then what did you mean you can get home any time I say?"

"Can't it wait till tomorrow?"

"I thought you wanted to rush to my side?"

"Well, sure, but—"

"But when it involves Sidney you're less anxious?"

"Ellie, cut it out."

"I'll see you later."

She hung up.

When I got home my key wouldn't work the lock. I had to ring the bell. She opened the door on a chain, then let me in.

"I thought I better change the lock," she said.

"This time of night?"

"They have twenty-four-hour service on locks now. You pay extra."

Ellie was in her little quilted bathrobe and seemed under control.

"Why? Nobody's got a key."

"Evelyn has, and you have."

Evelyn was our twice-a-week cleaning woman, a black.

"Christ, Ellie, Evelyn's been with us since—"

"I know how long she's been with us, and I trust her too, but—one of her friends might have gone through her purse. Why take a chance? Or your pockets, one of your friend's friends."

Pistol shots! Little Arthur was watching "The Rookies."

"Let's see your insurance claim," I said.

She held up her right hand. There were splints on two of her fingers.

"Broken?"

"Torn ligaments." She was a kid proudly holding up a football injury. "They don't hurt now."

"You seem all right," I said.

"All right!"

"Except, sure, you won't be able to practice."

"Three weeks at least, the doctor said."

"I'm sorry, Ellie. Well, now tell me what happened."

"I was in front of the house talking to your friend Sidney—"

She waited to see if I'd pick up on "your friend Sidney." I didn't.

"Then I noticed these two men—"

"Black?"

"I'll say! They were pretending there was something wrong with the tire of a car at the curb. Another pair of spades were inside the car, acting too innocent for words, just laying back, you know."

"What was wrong with their car?"

"Not a damn thing, because one of them suddenly comes at me. He grabbed my purse, pulled me to him, and when I was close, put a pistol against my head."

"A pistol?"

"You know, you've seen them on TV. Not against my temple, here, across my neck. Look, see that red mark?"

"And Sidney?"

"Scuttling like a crab! Flash! He'd disappeared."

"How come?"

"I guess he'd done his part."

Again I didn't pick up.

"Then?" I said. "Then what?"

" 'Don't make a sound,' this big black booger says, 'or I'll blow your brains out.' That's when I wet my britches."

"For a fact?"

"For a fact."

"Jesus! When was all this?"

"Right after dark. The lights were on up and down the block. I was just coming home from my jujitsu class."

"And Arthur?"

"He had a cold so I'd fed him and left him with the TV. I'll never do that again."

"What?"

"Leave him in the house alone."

"He said he'd blow your brains out?"

"If I made a sound. So I began to holler at the top of my voice."

"What did you do that for? He might have—"

"Because I wanted help. Because I am not going to be bullied and terrorized. I'd rather die."

"Why the hell didn't you just give him your purse?"

"I had two hundred and twenty dollars in it."

"Oh, my God, and that's—?"

"Gone! Every penny I earned in there." She looked at her silent piano. "And my license and my credit cards and my charge plates. You know the amount of nonsense you have to go through to get another driver's license?"

"He pulled the purse out of your hand?"

"He twisted it by the leather strap and began to drag me—"

"And still nobody came to help you?"

"—this big ugly buck dragging me up the street. He was quite good-looking, actually—"

"Then you could identify him?"

"You're damn right. He's the one who's stooped over, holding his balls."

"He is what?"

"I kicked him, caught him right where daddy showed me! You should have heard him yell. It was beautiful!"

'Then he let go?"

'No, the other one grabbed hold, too, and they both gave a big yank, and that's when the ligaments snapped."

"Where were the members of your block association all this time? And that jujitsu didn't do you any—"

"We haven't come to the part about how to handle a man with a pistol yet."

"I'll tell you how. Give him everything you've got, quick!"

"That's you all over, give the black man everything. Well I don't have that kind of guilt. I really believe in equality. I kicked that son of a bitch right in his very black, very equal balls, just like I would a white man. And if I ever get another chance, I'm going to put a bullet right through his very equal eyes."

'You're going to do what?'

I'm buying a pistol. Daddy, before we got married, gave me one, remember, a little one with a white handle? For my bedside table. But I was so full of that liberal hypocrisy, like you shoot a white, but never a black. No matter what they do, it has to be excused because of social conditions and all that applesauce. Well, no more, not after tonight. I'm goddamn sore, and I'm going to stay that way. I'm going to fire Evelyn, for a start. I won't have any of them around the house—"

"Ellie, that is the most completely foolish thing I've ever heard you say."

"I don't care if it is. And when I next see your dear friend, Schlossberg, he's going to have an experience he won't ever forget. You tell him for me!"

"What was he doing there in the first place?"

"To see you, is what he said. But I believe he was there to make sure that you weren't around and I was unprotected so his black buddies could—"

"Ellie, you're really hysterical."

"I'll bet part of my two hundred and twenty dollars is in his pants pocket this very minute."

"Ellie, come on now, Sidney is erratic, and he's foolish, but he is not a mugger's accomplice."

"Your pants pocket! He had your suit on. When did he steal that?"

"I gave it to him."

"If he's not a criminal, tell me why he scuttled down the street like a rat, instead of helping his friend's wife who was being brutalized—"

Ellie was beginning to cry bitterly.

"Brutalized! Brutalized—"

"I'm sorry," I said.

"I hate that man. I can't stand that phony voice. I can't stand the way he smells. And his teeth, they're so filthy! And the way his ass moves under your pants. What did you give him your suit for?"

"Because he needed it, and he's my friend."

"You call him a friend! When he abandons me—?"

"I'll ask him about that—"

"Don't bother. I don't care anymore. When?"

"When what?"

"When will you ask him?"

"When I see him next."

"Which will be when?"

"Whenever. I don't know."

I'd given her a tissue, which she used.

Then she said, "Tomorrow, first thing, I want you to come to the precinct with me and tell the police where they can find him."

"I don't know where he lives."

"You're lying."

"No I'm not, and what good would that do anyway?"

"Through Sidney they'll find out who—who—whose side are you on, anyway?"

"I can't tell them where Sidney is if I don't know."

"Answer my question."

"I'm on yours."

"Prove it."

"It's not a matter of sides—"

"A few days ago, you took him the only suit of yours I've ever liked—"

"That was a week ago. He was in a rest home then."

"Where is he now?"

"I don't know."

She looked at me a long time.

"I won't ever forget that on this night you lied to me. I won't ever forgive you for that."

In the bathroom, Little Arthur was toweling off.

"I was listening," he said. "Why don't you help her?"

"But, kid, she wanted me to turn a friend of mine over to the police."

He picked his pants off the seat, pulled my belt through the loops, dropped it on the floor, and left.

When I got through I could hear Ellie on the bedroom phone.

"I'm sorry to tell you, officer," she was saying, "he doesn't want to come down there."

"I didn't say that!" I yelled loud enough for every cop in the precinct to hear. I took the phone. "I don't know where Sidney Castleman lives now and that's the truth." I gave her back the phone. "Now you tell that man I don't lie, tell him I'm not afraid to talk to him."

"I think he's saying he will come down," Ellie said quietly. "What? I'll ask him."

She looked at me, in complete command of herself again.

"I'd like to know the precise time when you'll go down to the precinct station tomorrow morning," she said, "so I can coordinate this."

"I got a rehearsal at—"

"When?"

"Stop acting like a cop, Ellie."

"When?"

"Eleven, the rehearsal is at eleven."

"So what about, say, nine?"

"Ellie, stop acting like a cop."

"Is nine all right, yes or no?"

"I might make it at nine."

"He says nine," she said into the phone. "Nine all right with you?" She listened, then answered, "I certainly will be. I wouldn't miss it for the world."

"You can go and fuck yourself," I whispered.

She covered the mouthpiece. "That is one thing," she said, in her most ladylike tone, "I have never had to do for myself." Then she spoke into the phone. "To put it plainly," she said, "I believe my husband is lying to protect an old friend, and I want you to make him tell the truth."

"Don't hang up."

I pulled the phone out of her good hand.

"I'm not coming down there," I said to the cops. "If you want to talk to me, you come here."

The voice of the man was soft and rather high-pitched. "All right, sir," he said. "We didn't ask you to come down here, did we now?"

"No," I admitted.

"It's entirely up to you and the missus."

'Not the missus, just me," I said. And hung up.

I was in the tub when she came in to brush her teeth. She behaved as if I wasn't there. From where I was watching her she looked more like her father than ever. Look at that jaw, I thought. Ten years together and I'd never noticed the command in that jaw.

"I'm sorry I yelled at you," I said, "and I'm sorry about your hand."

She gargled, wiped her mouth, and said, "You're not sorry enough to do the one thing that would make me feel safe."

When I got into bed, she wasn't there. With Arthur, I supposed.

I was asleep when she got into bed, her arms pulling me to her.

"What happened to you, baby?" she said. "What happened to you in Africa?"

Her cheeks were moist. She'd been crying.

' You were always so good-natured, so sweet. Now the least thing, you yell at the police, you yell at me."

'What happened to you while I was away?" I said.

She held me with all her might, close as she could get. "A lot," she said, 'but none of it was against you. Don't you see I'm still here?"

'Why did you call me a liar to the police?"

'That was inexcusable. I'm ashamed I did that."

She clutched me closer, pressed up against me.

'Don't say anything now," she said.

'You were asking me to turn my oldest friend over to the police."

I know. I'm sorry. I even think there's something gallant about the way you stick up for that louse. It's so goddamn illogical. Why do you? Oh, I don't care."

She was kissing me now with all of her mouth.

'Maybe when I look at him, I see what's going to happen to me, how I'll finish."

"Baby, that's not going to happen to you. You? Like Sidney Schlossberg? Never! I won't let it. I'm not going to even let you die, baby. Baby!"

I didn't need what she was doing to turn me on. It was the first time since I'd been back that she'd faced me in bed, the first time she'd come to bed without her goddamn pajamas on.

So then I moved.

I was surprised to find her so open.

Ellie is a house with two doors. The first opens quickly. Then there is another portal, set some distance back, and this opens only when her heart unclenches. When that happens—

"I'd forgotten," she said. "I'd forgotten how it is."

"Me too," I said.

"Oh, thank you," she said afterward. "Thank you."

"Baby, I thank you."

We held each other like two people who'd survived a shipwreck, clinging together in the driving sea.

Then I fainted. That is, I slept suddenly. It was like a faint.

I'm like old Jim. After love, I sleep.

And I needed it. I was well worn down.

It was the best five minutes' sleep I'd had in a hell of a time.

Then something woke me. Ellie was wide awake, looking at me like a worried mother.

"Let's never fight again," she said, kissing me.

"I don't want to remember longer than ten minutes ago," I said.

"It's this city," she said. "This city is killing us."

"I suppose, I suppose."

I put my head on her chest between her father's chin and her breast, closed my eyes, and tightened my arms.

"Have you forgiven me?" she said.

"Oh, sure."

"Then go ahead, go to sleep."

"I am."

"But, tomorrow, baby, let's think about moving out of this terrible city."

"Move where?"

"Not Florida. I know that's impossible for you. I was so scared that day, I was hysterical. You know, after I got mugged the strangest thing happened. I got less scared, not more. Isn't that extraordinary?"

"You peed your britches." I laughed. She peed her britches.

"If we lived in the country, you and I, we'd always be like we are right now. Wouldn't that be beautiful?"

"Yes, yes."

"Remember that drive we took? I love New England. Near Hartford there are some beautiful little towns. Remember? Or Kent? Kent, Connecticut, is so beautiful. Sharon too. Have you ever been to Sharon?"

"Sharon. It sounds pretty."

"Or by the sea. Westhampton, East Hampton, Bridgehampton, Quogue."

"Let's sleep now. We'll talk in the morning."

"All right, but I'm afraid it won't be like this in the morning."

"It's so complicated, you know. I've got to be around, close to what's happening. When it gets down to it, we live by what I bring in—"

"Yes, of course, but—"

"I don't want to talk about it tonight. Let's sleep tonight."

"Go ahead, love. Sleep."

She held me. "I'm not going to let anything kill us," she whispered.

"Goodnight, baby."

"It's just that I get so anxious—"

"I know you think I should find another line of work, but I'm fifty-four, and—"

"You're a young man."

"I can't start all over again."

"But it might just come to that."

"Tomorrow, tomorrow."

"Because I love you, and because I love you I want to feel—settled, don't you know?"

"Love you, too."

I was almost asleep again.

"If I was in command of my daddy's old squadron," I heard her say, "for just one day, I'd give them this order. Level that city." She was laughing softly. "Leave nothing standing!"

Then I swear I heard her father's jaw lock into place. I was asleep, I guess, and I heard his voice.

"I don't care what the concentration of ack-ack over that harbor is," he said. "We are going to hit it. We are going to hit it every day. We are going to hit it till there's nothing left standing!"

"I'm against it," I said.

"We'll come in low," he said. "Direct reckoning."

"Fuck you, you misreckoning son of a bitch," I said. "A lot of my buddies got killed by your direct reckoning. I haven't forgiven you for that, you brass-balled son of a bitch."

"What? What did you say?" Ellie asked.

"We can afford losses up to fifty percent," her father said.

"Fifty percent is me," I said.

"It's worth it," her father said.

"Not to me," I answered. "The human factor comes first."

"What else do you think I'm talking about?" I heard Ellie say.

"What comes first," her father said, "is the next generation."

"Arthur," Ellie said. "He's the important one now."

"I'm selfish," I said.

"No, you're not," Ellie said. "Not when it comes down to it."

"I really am selfish."

"All right then," she said, "we'll go where you suggested, Stamford."

"To tell you the truth, I want to stay here."

"Stamford is exactly fifty-five minutes from Grand Central."

"And you're asking me to—twice a day?"

"Think of Arthur," her father said, "and you can do it."

"All right, about Arthur," I answered him. "There's as much drugs and crime and sex—"

"My grandson," her father said, "does not go in for indiscriminate, off-limits fucking!"

"What I mean is—" I made a supreme effort to wake up and meet the developing emergency. "What I mean is—"

"What you really mean is you won't do anything to protect me from being mugged right in front of my own house," I heard Ellie saying.

"Not true." Now I was awake.

"Well, tell me what you'll do."

"I'll go to the block association meetings!"

"Big deal. Many thanks. All right, I'll put it to you straight. If you really do care about me, help put those four blacks in prison, then I'll stay in your goddamn city with you. Do that and I'll believe you."

"Which means now you don't?"

"How can I?"

I pulled away from her.

"I don't have to prove anything," I said. "You talk as if I have to prove something."

"You do."

"I do not know where Sidney lives."

"I don't believe you."

"I'm telling you the truth."

She sat up, trembling now, her chest all goose flesh.

Then she took the big step.

"What if you did know?" she asked.

"I don't think I'd tell the police."
She got out of bed and left the room.

The piano woke me. Damn if she wasn't practicing, left hand only!

It was seven forty-five. What the hell is she doing, I wondered —that left mitt sounded awful determined—breaking me in for suburban life? Seven forty-five is probably the time I'd have to get up in Stamford to get to New York for a ten o'clock rehearsal.

In the shower I put my head under the nozzle. Ellie hates my hair slicked down, especially now that it's almost gone.

Little Arthur, dressed for school, put his head between the plastic curtains, which were covered with daffodils.

"Mummy wants you to come to breakfast," he said.

She stopped playing when I walked in.

My eggs were on the dining-room table, waiting. She poured my coffee. Standing a little behind me, she watched as I ate.

"I see you're wearing my belt again," I said to Arthur.

"Mummy gave me hell," he said.

"What about?"

"Said you had enough trouble without any guff from me."

"Oh, that's O.K. Forget it."

"Everybody in school is trying to trade for this belt," he said. "Thanks a lot!"

As I was putting marmalade on my second piece of toast, she spoke.

"Are you ready to go?"

"Go where?"

"To the precinct. I told them I'd bring you at nine, remember?"

I stopped eating.

"You've got some goddamn nerve," I said.

I finished my coffee and left the house.

Adam, our leader, kicked off that day by giving the cast his reactions to the last rehearsal. Style was mentioned. The new wave in the American theater was extolled. References to my work were neither favorable nor indirect. Finally a note of conciliation, Adam said he wanted to forget yesterday, there would be a general amnesty. Could we now, he wondered, perform in decent style what he'd asked for yesterday?

A scolding, no matter how pompous and ill-humored, always

shakes up a cast. The run-through was going much better until there was an interruption.

At first it was only an uneasy shifting of the eyes of those working toward off-stage right. From there came sounds of levity and a general hustling toward the door leading to the street. Then in his own time and at his own pace—enter Sidney Schlossberg. What was happening on stage collapsed. We were suddenly supernumeraries.

Like a great kabuki star he was accompanied by his attendants, Paul Prince, of course, and Rudy the doorman, and at a respectful but attentive distance, some of our small-part actors, old men who'd been in the wings waiting for their scene. The critics and the public may have forgotten Sidney but not Rudy, not our old professionals. Rudy still blessed those halcyon days when each Friday after the performance, Sidney would pass by the little box which was his office and drop off a double x. No one since had been that majestic.

Sidney wasn't trying to disrupt the rehearsal. He simply did. He was telling, as near as I could make out by a quick look off, an anecdote the old actors particularly enjoyed. You could hear his voice, even his whisper rumbled, and you could hear him leading the laughter, the cackling and sniggering of the old players, the boffo of Rudy, and Paul Prince whistling like a tea kettle.

Having thrown his favors, Sidney proceeded along a sweeping path—all Sidney's approaches were curved—toward the fire door between the stage house and the auditorium. He did not look at what was happening on stage. We looked at him. Royalty was paying us a visit.

"What the hell is going on up there?" Adam yelled from his seat in the house.

We heard the heavy chain which holds the fire door's counterweight rattle in its pulley, the metal hinges creak disrespect-fully, then Sidney and Paul disappeared from our sight. Repri-manded, we resumed rehearsal.

What was so strikingly different about Sidney this morning was his air of affluence, created not so much by the suit I'd given him as by a new sweep-brim hat of black velour and a new ebony cane—that accounted for the tap-tapping sound I'd heard. Even Paul Prince looked amazingly improved, dressed in a new suit and hat, a black homburg. Compared to these two our working cast seemed shabby.

As we resumed playing I could see Sidney sidle across the fifth row to the center aisle, followed by Paul Prince, in the row behind. Sidney, ever a believer in courtesy, waved at Adam, who did not wave back. Our young leader couldn't believe what he was seeing.

As Sidney composed himself in his aisle seat, he threw a hostile look at the thousand-watt bulb, the sole source of illumination, then pulled down the broad brim of his new hat to shade his eyes. Putting his cane between his legs, he rested his heavy hands on its crest, his chin on his hands, prepared to judge the proceedings.

Was he trying to make clear to the management and the young director that he wouldn't have accepted the understudy in their miserable comedy if a run-of-the-play contract had been offered him on a piece of Mr. David Belasco's personal silverware by a pompadoured servant on his knees and even if that contract stipulated a salary higher than the one being paid the leading man, myself?

Now, as we continued, was he asleep? His eyes seemed to be closed. No. Paul quickly leaned forward in his seat. Everyone in the building could hear Sidney's cello, "Paul, I want to give him a few notes. He needs help here." Paul Prince sent his hands scurrying inside his clothing for pencil and paper, positioned himself to put down whatever notes the Jewish King might see fit to drop.

Where the hell had he found the money to buy himself an expensive cane, a very special hat, as well as a complete wardrobe for his author, Mr. Paul Prince, including, I now noticed, a pair of pince-nez glasses with gold fittings?

Arrogant and disrespectful as I thought him, I began, without willing it, to play for his laughs. But the lines I was speaking sounded vulgar, badly phrased, unfunny. If they weren't good for laughs, what merit did they have? I was ashamed of myself.

Adam must have been feeling something similar. Even after he exercised his anger by sending his secretary darting up the aisle for managerial help, he would laugh at some of the "goodies" in the scene, then turn and look at Sidney to see if we'd provoked some amusement there.

Not a flicker. Sidney did turn his head once to look at Adam, but it was a look of wonder. What had passed him by, the expression on his face said, that the young director found so funny? Sidney leaned back and asked Paul Prince's help in determining this. Prince shrugged.

After one bit which Adam, and I, too, let me confess, found absolutely hilarious, Sidney looked over his shoulder at Paul Prince and gave him a long, detailed note, which Paul carefully transcribed. I wondered what it was. Then, thinking back as I played on, I understood exactly what he was criticizing. I should have given myself that note long ago. I was, at that moment, imitating another comedian, Sam Levene in this case, relying on comedic techniques which were as personal to Levene as they were inappropriate to me. I was giving a poor imitation of a better performer.

You see, Sidney's taste was unchallengeable, except when it came to himself.

Sol Bender hustled down the aisle, Adam's secretary following frantically. There was a whispered consultation, Sol throwing one quick look toward Sidney, whose composure and concentration did not waver. Then Adam stopped the rehearsal.

At this Sidney slowly got up, slid majestically along the aisle to where Sol and Adam waited anxiously for his verdict. Greetings and general laughter. Sidney introduced Paul Prince as if he was Eugene O'Neill. More strained cordiality. Adam and Sol were ill at ease. Sidney certainly was not.

"I want to talk to the cast," Adam suddenly yelled to his stage manager. He was going to take his anger out on us.

We could hear Sidney say to Adam, "I've given Mr. Prince some reactions your leading man may find useful. Shall I simply pass them along to him?"

"Of course, of course," Adam said, the coward.

The cast was assembling center stage. Sidney waved the back of his palm to them in a gesture reminiscent of Vittorio de Sica. Then he shook hands with Sol, less ardently with Adam, wishing them all good fortune—"It's a time for trivial comedy, isn't it?"—and slid back along the aisle toward the fire door. In a moment I again heard the rasp of the metal chain that suspended the counterweight as it ran over its pulley. I hurried to meet my old friend.

Now I saw what it was about Paul Prince. He'd given himself the benefit of a heroic new wig, jet black. Where had the money come from?

Sidney shook my hand, saying, "Paul has some notes for you." Then, noticing my look of absolute wonder at Prince's reincarnation, he added, "He hit a number." Prince smiled confidently. "He made me a present of this hat, generous of him, wasn't it? Prince, give me twenty dollars, will you?"

The gambler reached into his pocket, pulled out a rat's nest of paper currency, and freed a twenty. Sidney took it and after giving it a flash and a wave handed it to me. "We're even," he said.

Then Sidney passed his arm through my elbow's hook and pulled me toward the door to the street. The cast was coming together, but they were watching us. Adam leaped up on stage on the other side and clapped his hands impatiently. "Let's go, let's go," he called.

"Sidney, I have to—" I indicated the gathering on stage.

"He's certainly not going to start without you, is he?" Sidney led me into the little dark hall and asked Rudy the doorman if he would excuse us for a moment. Rudy jumped, said, "Oh, yes, Mr. Castleman, any time, Mr. Castleman," and disappeared.

There was no one in sight now except Paul Prince, who still seemed to be transcribing notes on my performance, apparently adding some of his own. In a dark corner, Sidney gave me one of those odd-size envelopes bookies use to make cash payments. It had seen much service, was marked and tattered, clasp broken and presently sealed with a piece of Scotch tape.

"This should improve your life at home," Sidney said. Then with a bow and that ambivalent half smile, he turned away, pulling down his sweep-brim black velour, and left.

"I want to talk to you," I called after him.

But he'd disappeared. Paul Prince thrust some sheets into my hands. Old laundry lists they turned out to be, the backs covered with Paul's hand, which was indecipherable. Then he ran after his hope on earth.

On the street I found Sidney getting into a taxi. "I've got to speak to you," I called out. As I tried to lean into the car, Paul Prince slammed the door.

But Sidney turned the window down and said to me, "I haven't time to talk to you now. I'll be in touch with you in a couple of days."

The cab drove off.

Later, while the young director was making a speech on style which sounded exactly like the speech on style I'd heard at the Yale Drama School thirty years earlier, I opened the envelope Sidney had given me. It contained Ellie's license, her charge plates, and all the rest of her nontransferable assets, the ones she said she would most miss.

No sign of her hard-earned two hundred and twenty.

I didn't give our young director the total attention he wanted that day. He seemed terribly worried every time he looked at me, and I didn't blame him. I tried to comfort him with that old bearded one, "Don't worry. When I get in front of an audience, I'll come through."

When I got home we had visitors.

I don't try to hold on to names at a first introduction, but I liked Officer Boruff immediately and had his name from the beginning. His partner, also in plainclothes, was a black. No matter how I faced, he was behind me.

Ellie had served them coffee and a Sara Lee product.

Boruff, it seemed, had had Ellie's father as a C.O. in Korea and was telling flattering anecdotes.

"He was our kind of people," he said, picking up the conversation I'd interrupted. "I mean he was gung ho and all like that, and the men usually resent officers who—you know? But he flew point, led us to the target area. See what I mean?" He turned to me.

My memory of her father's career was less flattering. He was the C.O. of the squadron which had dropped a string of five hundreds on our front positions in Leyte, a staff miscalculation. The official apology brought no one back to life.

"I know what you mean," I said.

The black policeman was watching me except when I turned and looked at him. Then he shifted his eyes. I was so aware of the man I didn't hear much of what went on between Ellie and the white cop.

"Come on," I broke in, "what's this all about?"

"Well," Boruff said, looking at Ellie.

"I told them I was pretty wrought up the other day," she said, "and I guess I didn't behave very well. I'm sorry."

"Perfectly natural," Boruff said, "under the circumstances."

"I'm sorry, too," I said, "yelling at you over the phone."

"Oh, we're used to that," Boruff said. "Everybody's teeing off on us now."

He laughed. The black cop didn't join in.

"I don't know where the man lives," I said. "Schlossberg."

"If you did know," Ellie said, "it would help."

"I don't," I said.

Little Arthur came into the room, hurried to his mother, and whispered.

"Oh, darling," she said, taking his hand and walking him to our bedroom. At the door she turned and said, "I can't help believing my husband must have some idea where this man can be found, and I know when he sees what's involved here, he'll want to help you."

Mother and son disappeared into the bedroom.

"She said you'd taken some clothes, a suit, to him just the other day," the black cop said.

"I did," I said. "He was in Queenshaven, an old folks' home, but he's moved."

"Where?" the black cop asked.

"I told you, I don't know."

"Oh, come on, baby," Ellie called from the bedroom. Then, in the tone of a joke, she called to the cops, "Make him tell you."

"I don't know quite how we'd go about that," Boruff said, smiling that uncertain way he had.

"Maybe thumb screws," I said.

Coming back into the room, Ellie said, "Poor kid's had a headache ever since that happened. I just gave him numbers five and six for today, aspirin."

She took the chair facing me. They were all waiting for me to say something. Arthur too, he'd come in and was looking at me.

"Incidentally," I said, "here are your cards and charge plates, and your driver's license."

"Oh, good," said Ellie, opening the envelope. "How did you get these?"

"They were in the mailbox downstairs," I lied.

"What about the two hundred and twenty dollars?"

"I guess it's not there."

The black policeman reached toward Ellie's lap, took the now empty envelope. He turned it over in his hand, caught a look from Boruff, replied with a body sign.

"He's asking," Boruff explained, "if he can have the envelope."

Ellie nodded. That's all the black cop needed. He slipped out the door of the apartment, and I could hear him dropping down the stairs two at a time.

"Do they usually return things like this?" I asked Boruff.

"They usually return nothing," he said.

"They must have admired the way she fought back," I said.

"I don't care what they admired," Ellie said. "I want those men taken in and punished."

"So do we," Boruff said. "Suppose we find Mr.—?" Boruff shifted his ground.

"Schlossberg," Ellie provided.

"Would he be able to tell us who the assailants were?"

"No," I said.

"He absolutely would," Ellie said. "The way they looked at each other! He left at a signal from them. He didn't come to help me as any decent person would, ran off like a coward, or worse. Much worse."

On her feet now, she was addressing Boruff as a public servant. "You are aware," she said, "that the police in this city have a reputation for incompetence."

"We do our best." Boruff controlled himself.

"It's not good enough," Ellie said. "I am not going to be roughed up on the street in front of my own house."

· 256 ·

"We're sort of fed up, too, ma'am," Boruff said. "No one helps us. What have you given us to work with?"

The black cop walked in.

I knew where the son of a bitch had been. He'd gone to see if that envelope would pass through the slot of our mailbox. It would not.

"Well?" Boruff asked his partner.

The black made no sign that I saw.

Boruff studied his wristwatch. "We'll be leaving," he said.

"Without doing anything?" Ellie looked at me.

They were moving toward the door.

"Well, damn," Ellie said, "I'm going to speak to your superiors."

For the first time the black reacted. He smiled.

"Patrolman, may I ask what the hell amuses you?" Ellie said.

"Lady, we have ways of finding this male, Schlossberg. When we want them, we find them. And if there's anything you want to report about me, I am not a patrolman. I am Detective Alvin Bird, shield number 2022, Public Morals Division, Organized Crime Control Bureau, Control Investigation Section."

He went out the door.

Boruff showed me a slip of paper. "Have I got the name right?" he asked.

I looked at the name of my friend. "He uses two *s*'s, Schloss, two *s*'s, berg."

"Thank you, and here," he gave me a number. "Now, if you change your mind, call me, and I'll be glad to come to wherever you work, or here."

Then he turned back to Ellie, a well-brought-up Catholic lad he was, and said, "Thanks for the coffee and cake, ma'am."

At the door he had an afterthought. "By the way," he said, "when does the postman bring your mail?"

"First thing in the morning," Ellie said.

"Has anyone else got a key to the mailboxes downstairs?"

"No," she said, "no one else."

"Thank you," he said and left.

Ellie looked at me a long time.

I poured the dregs of the coffee into my cup. Then Ellie went into our bedroom. She came through, carrying sheets and a blanket, and went into Arthur's room.

I ate cake.

Ellie came back. "I've fixed you something to sleep on in Arthur's room," she said.

She went into our bedroom and closed the door.

"Those cops," Little Arthur said, "they're not like on TV. Are they really cops?"

"Oh, yes."

"That one who did the talking, he seemed stupid."

"Cops are human, too."

"What did he mean, 'Now, if you change your mind, call me.' "

"When did he say that?"

"Just before he left. Doesn't he believe you?"

Later, as I undressed, he said, "You tired?"

'Rehearsal all day,' I said. "Then this."

I stretched out on the sofa bed. We could hear Ellie through the bedroom wall crying.

"Why did you marry Mummy?" Arthur said.

"Once we liked each other a lot."

Another thoughtful pause. College roommates talking in the night.

I wish I was someone else," he said. ' I'd marry Mummy."

"Isn't there a girl in your class that you like?'

"Mummy is more beautiful than any of them. Sometimes I come into your bedroom, after you're gone, I mean, and I just watch her. Did she ever tell you?"

"No."

"I sit and watch her take her bath and fix her face and dress and tidy her room, little things like that. She's so beautiful. Why don't you like her anymore?"

"I do, but— I don't know what happened."

"Maybe it's because she doesn't like you as much as she used to. Maybe you're angry at her about that."

"Maybe."

"You don't have to stay together on account of me, you know."

"Where did you get that idea?"

"Kids in school, they say their parents are doing that. Is that what you're doing?"

"I don't think so."

"You don't have to."

That was all we said that night.

An eleven-year-old boy snores, too, but so gently. And sometimes I could hear him murmuring in his sleep.

I got to worrying that the police, for all their cool talk, might have a pickup out for Sidney. He should at least be warned, I thought.

After an hour of not sleeping, I got up as quietly as I could, dressed, and left the apartment. Coming down the stairs, my heart was beating hard, as it might in a jailbreak. There was the same panic and that final relief when I was free.

The block committee had used its accumulation of dues. New lights had been installed from Central Park West to Broadway. They shed a lemon light, the kind of illumination thrown by flares over the battlefields of World War One. While ambush had been made more difficult, an atmosphere of terror had been created, like that last silent instant before a bayonet charge.

In the middle car of the five-unit subway train there was a policeman under whose protection white passengers rode in silence. The other cars were sparsely occupied, mostly by people of some color who because of disposition or muscle were unafraid. Some even joked and laughed as they joggled downtown.

The Fourth Street station is on three levels and it is six blocks long. Even at rush hours it is too big for its service. Now at past midnight, it suggested that the city had finally been, on Frank Lloyd Wright's advice, abandoned.

Eighth Street was hustling. The ice cream cone place was being rushed. The book store at the corner of Waverly offered remainders. In the doorway of a souvenir store little Japanese mobiles of glass tinkled. Along the way, lesbians clamped to their catches. The gay liberated cruised.

On the other side of Fifth Avenue my money arm was pulled every few yards. "Can you help me out with carfare, mister?" became, as I walked east, "Got any spare change, fellow?" then as the street darkened, 'Come on, give me a quarter.' That block had become a beach for beggars, unexpectedly arrogant, unnaturally proud.

It had begun to drizzle, bright drops of cheap jewels.

Under the wings of the abstract metal sculpture that a future-proud citizen had placed on the island in Lafayette Square, there huddled some hippies, the fragmented and demoralized survivors of a once victorious army.

On the north brick wall of the Publix Theatre, Shakespeare was extolled.

Then, St. Mark's Place, where it was early, not late. On both sides, the street front and the stoops were jammed with living creatures, like on those mysterious atolls in the mid-Pacific where birds of passage land by instinct, huddle for their season's business, then leave.

How in this company to find Sidney?

Socked into the side of the Valencia Hotel was the Two Saints Bar. I had a drink. There was no one there who might know Sidney.

Across the street was PAUL MCGREGOR'S UNISEX HAIRCUTTER, closed for the day, its entry packed with the nameless starlings of the night.

Ahead I could see the DOM where, clustered like bees, was some of the human debris of the sixties. You could smell defeat there. These sour citizens watched the tourists entering the ELECTRIC CIRCUS in the building above without their old-time scorn. History had moved on.

Here I found two actors whom I knew. Even stoned, they looked more affluent than I remembered them. I asked if they knew where Sidney Castleman was living now and one of them broke silence.

"Been looking for him myself," he said. "There's a job he can pick up."

"In a play?"

"What kind of play, man? This is a commercial."

"I don't think he—"

"Perfect for old Sidney. A bum too proud to go on relief."

"Who's it for? The Republican National Committee?"

"One of those big corporations, some of their public service shit. If you find him tell him. He got me a job once. I didn't forget."

"How do you like working those commercials?"

"They suck," he said.

THE GRIZZLY FURS, THE HINKERKUSH TRADERS, THE BOWL AND BOARD, THE HAIR POWER COMPANY, THE DIVINE SALES, and finally on the corner, THE GEM SPA, where "creams" are served to nonalcoholics while outside other men, some with fresh cuts and bruises around their eyes and mouths, drink from bottles still in brown paper bags.

Here someone grabbed my arm roughly, and when I turned to defend myself, it was Ralph "Andy" Andrews, an actor who twenty-five years ago was the most sought-after juvenile in the trade, now long gone and far down the hill.

I never got to ask him anything, for instance, how he was, which I could see, shot, because he was all over me with his spiel.

"Brando!" he said, squeezing my biceps and giving me the worst of his breath and the heat of both eyes. "Have you heard from Brother Marlon?"

"Hello, Ralph," I said. "What's with that brother shit?"

"He used to call me that. Brother. 'You're my brother,' he'd say. As thousands cheered."

Ralph was in terrible shape. He leaned hard against me, then pushed back almost falling, so that he had to snatch at my arm to stay on his feet. Finally he achieved a precarious balance for an instant and took advantage of this equilibrium to wipe his tongue on his sleeve.

"You heard from him?" I asked.

"Not since when he was calling me in the middle of the night when—when was he making *Julius Caesar,* you remember?"

"Long time ago," I said.

" 'Member? When Gielgud and those other West End voice-placement boys were set to run all over him, it was then. Mr. Brando suddenly remembered his brother—"

"Look out."

He had started to fall again, righted himself, fumbled into the brown paper bag, found the nipple of the bottle, and pulled at it. Then he grabbed my arm, but with the wrong hand so the bottle fell and cracked on the pavement. Ralph didn't notice this tragedy.

"Brother!" he went on. "The night Brando remembered! You know we used to read Shakespeare together?"

"No."

"Many times. Mostly me reading and him listening. You can see how that would be, right?"

"Sure, Ralph, sure."

"Because he hadn't ever done Shakespeare, and everyone said, 'Don't try it,' including that director he used to have who said, 'Stick to your mumbling, kid. You're doing great.' But I told Marlon, 'You can do anything' "—Ralph poked my chest with a hard finger—" 'if you really work at it!'

"I gave him the confidence," he went on. "We used to read together for hours, all night, all the great plays, *Hamlet.* He would have been epoch-making. I saw Barrymore, and Brando, goddamn it, he would have been—you know. Now look. Hah! Porno and lobster tails. Money, money, money." Ralph was beginning to cry.

"What happened he called you that night, Ralph, come on, Ralph, tell me."

"He remembered how I'd handled a certain line in that speech—I can't remember the exact line. Goddamn it, I was just saying it, I was saying that line all morning. Now I can't remember it. I'm too mad to remember. Wait! Don't go away. I'll remember it. Wait, I want to tell you this—"

"I'm not going anywhere."

"It was in the 'Friends, Romans, countrymen' bit. He remembered how I said it, my reading, my phrasing, something I'd done. Oh, I know, it was how I always picked up the ends of lines. 'Don't drop the ends of your lines,' I told him. 'Respect the pentameter. It's not fucking prose.' God, what a mess he was when he first came to me, hopeless. That's why he called me on the phone. He knew I was the only one who could help him. 'Get on a plane' he shouted. 'I'll give you the fare when you get out here.' Did it occur to the son of a bitch I might not have cash to buy a plane ticket? 'Come out here,' he shouted. I want to know how you read that speech.' He was going to put me up in the house he'd rented. 'I want you to live with me, like a brother' that's when he said it."

"And you wouldn't go out?"

Ralph sobered. "No, I wanted to. There's where I made the mistake."

"What mistake?"

"I read it for him over the phone."

"I see."

"Not once, ten times. Made him repeat it. Insisted on the pentameter, drilled the rhythm into him. I gave him hell. 'Never mind those Actors Studio phonies,' I shouted. 'This is poetry. Don't reduce it to prose. Now again, do it after me, again.' Still on the phone. 'Friends! Romans! Countrymen! Lend me your ears. Lift "ears." Don't drop that last word.' Oh, yes, I made him do it again and again, and finally he had it, and then I made this other bad mistake. Changed my life. Where's that fucking bottle?"

It took him a minute to discover the purple flowing on the asphalt. "Oh well," he said. "Oh, well, his loss, right? I could have made him great. I could have been his soul's companion, I could have—"

"Did he ever invite you out again?"

"No. He'd call me on the phone. It was cheaper that way. I made a mistake."

'Well, if you wanted to go to California, you sure did."

"I mean a worse mistake. One night when he calls me, he's giving me that 'you're the only one I trust' shit, and I said to him, 'How come if I'm your brother, how come I haven't got a part in your movie? How come if I'm so brilliant with Shakespeare as you tell me every night, how come I'm not playing one of those scenes in the film with you?' Guess what his answer was?"

'What?"

' 'You know how this director, Mankiewicz, is.' That was his answer. 'Bullshit,' I said. 'All you had to do is ask.' Well, then Brother Brando, he laughed in that nervous, high-pitched way of his, and he said something about Mankiewicz again, and I said, 'Yeah, yeah, I know how Mankiewicz is, and I know how you are. You're no brother to me. So don't call me anymore. I charge for coaching beginners,' I said, 'even if they get their names in the paper.' "

"I see."

"I think that was a mistake."

"Yeah, probably."

"After that he didn't call me."

"Poor Brando."

At this Ralph got furious. He grabbed my neck and began to squeeze it, and I had a hell of a time getting loose. Then suddenly he softened and apologized. "I feel sorry for him, too," he said. "It's his loss. Right?"

I was rubbing my Adam's apple. "You're still pretty strong," I said.

"Oh, sure," he said. "I could be in shape in two weeks. But what the hell for?" Then he leaned forward. "I still hear from him," he said.

"He still calls you?"

"No. Not that. But every once in a while some chicken-shit agent calls me, says there's a little part for me in a Brando film. Well, I know what went on behind those scenes. There's nothing like guilt to jiggle the memory, is there?"

"Nothing like."

"But still, it wasn't necessary for me to say that, was it? 'Charge for coaching beginners.' Those four words, they ruined my life."

He would have fallen except I caught him.

Around the corner, standing in front of M. SCHACHT'S DELI, SMOKED FISH A SPECIALTY and looking through the window over the sacks of dried cherries, peaches, and apples, dried apricots and pears, over the prunes, sweet and sour, the crystallized ginger and the shelled nuts, I saw at the counter the girl, Polly. She was buying a smoked whitefish, homemade horseradish on the side.

I knew who that was for.

She was glad to see me. "Oh, yes," she said. "He's there all right."

I didn't have to ask her if I could go to her place with her. She invited me. But first she said she had to stop at the all-night drugstore.

"You're up late," I said to her.

"I was asleep," she said. "He woke me. 'I want a whitefish,' he

says, 'a smoked whitefish.' 'Now?' I said. 'What are you, pregnant? I'll
get you one tomorrow.' 'Tomorrow I won't want it,' he says. That's
the way he is. I have the greatest respect for Mr. Schlossberg, but I
really wish he'd find another place to stay. He says everything will be
different after this party you're throwing for him day after tomorrow
but—"

"Day after—?"

"I thought you knew."

"No."

"He sent Mr. Prince to tell you."

"I didn't see Prince."

"Oh, will he catch hell! They're insane, aren't they?"

"Sort of."

"That's why I was glad to see you. I want you to come home with
me. Maybe you can talk to him. I don't want to be unkind or
inconsiderate. He's such a fine man, but he's beginning to get to me.
He's got Mr. Prince there with him, and I can't tell you what they talk
about, but if I make a human sound they shush me. Then he can't
sleep, and he plays the TV all night. He won't go out for his meals,
sends me out, to a Chinese restaurant, to Lüchow's, to the Balkan. He
acts like the whole city is his to choose from. He never gives me any
money, says he'll take care of it later. But my father only sends me a
hundred dollars a month, and now that's gone and most everything
I've saved. I don't begrudge Mr. Schlossberg anything I've saved. I
don't begrudge Mr. Schlossberg anything, you understand, as long as
I have it, but pretty soon I won't anymore. Now he's got me doing his
laundry. I mean he has mental nobility, but personally he doesn't
clean himself after, can I be frank, after going to the bathroom.
There's something else, can I be frank? He keeps trying to make it
with me, and sometimes, you know, he's sort of old, and he can't get it
up. Then there's this terrible scene. He blames me, says I did
something that stopped him, and I don't want to hurt his feelings, but
really, he's got me praying that he makes it, even though I'm not
attracted to him physically. You know he doesn't look in good shape
when he takes off his clothes. His skin, it's like that rubber cement
Dustin Hoffman had on his face when he was supposed to be a
hundred and five years old in that film, except Mr. Schlossberg has
some of that all over. I don't mind once in a while. I want to be good
to him every way I can. He's having a bad period, and maybe the
world owes him. You agree?"

"I think you're very kind."

"So will you talk to him?"

"I'll try. You're an awful nice girl—"

"I'm not so damn nice. I wish he'd get out of my place. He's been there over two weeks now and—may I?"

"Tell me everything."

"What it is is, I think I've finally got this one boy interested in me. You know how slippery boys are. You think you've got them, then they disappear. But I really think I got this one. Maybe. And you see if Mr. Schlossberg weren't there I—"

"Would invite the boy to your place."

"Exactly. That's it. May I be—?"

"Aren't you being? Frank?"

"Not quite, not yet. What I can't understand is since you're his best friend, his only real friend Mr. Schlossberg says, why don't you take him to live with you?"

"My wife can't stand him."

"Why not?"

"All the things you said."

"Well, I can't stand him anymore either. Suddenly I'm going to start screaming and never stop."

She looked at me from the edge of the precipice. Then she bit her lip and smiled and said, "O.K., I'm sorry. I'll go back. I'll give him his fish. Then after you go maybe he'll make it with me, I pray, and we'll get it over with, and he'll fall asleep. It's the only thing that gets him asleep at night. I've thought of running away, moving in with one of my girl friends and leaving the place to him, but I can't. Here. I'll only be in here a minute."

We were in front of an all-night drugstore.

"Now don't you run away," she said. "You are going home with me, aren't you?"

"Yes, don't worry."

"Maybe you better come in with me, just to be on the safe side."

Inside she asked for Demerol. In this place no prescription was necessary.

"Let me pay for that," I suggested. She was fumbling around in her purse and not finding much.

"That would help," she said. "I'm forced to accept, as they say. I was also going to buy some—"

"Get anything you need."

"Some Arrid for Mr. Schlossberg and some Glade for the room. When he and Mr. Prince get in there together, the room—I've only got one window."

I paid for the Demerol and the Arrid and the Glade and I bought her a small bottle of perfume, a gift which broke her up.

Outside I asked her, "What's the Demerol for?"

"You know he has something wrong with him, don't you?"

"You mean aside from everything else?"

"That's one reason he can't sleep. He wakes up with these terrible pains and shouts for Demerol."

"I saw him this morning. He was in rare form."

"Mr. Schlossberg, you know, is a great actor. This Demerol, he really needs it!"

"What's wrong with him?"

"Didn't you see his belly?"

"I've only seen him dressed—"

"You'll see it now."

"But I did notice it was getting sort of big."

"Swollen. You'll see. About Mr. Prince, I don't mind taking a certain amount of shit from Mr. Schlossberg because I really respect him. But when Mr. Prince told me yesterday, 'It's either them cats or me,' I said, 'It's you, get out, now, out. I mean I was going to kill him."

"What was that—cats?"

"I got cats, three of them. I love my cats. They're my only friends. They're so nice and affectionate and clean. But Mr. Prince, he says he's allergic to cats, can't stand them, and they hate him, and I don't want to make it harder for them, the cats I mean. It's tough enough for them having Mr. Schlossberg living with us, but Mr. Prince, he hits at them with a rolled-up *Voice,* and finally yesterday, one of the cats is not housebroken yet, she's only a kitten, and Mr. Prince stepped in it, and he got like crazy, took off after Teenie, that's the kitten, with this rolled-up *Voice,* and I had to hold him down. Boy, does he smell! And that's when he said, 'It's either those cats or me.' Well that was the limit, don't you think?"

"I'm not fond of Mr. Prince," I said, "but he means a lot to Mr. Schlossberg, especially right now."

"Well then you take him home, take both of them home." She was crying again. "Mr. Prince comes in at ten every morning, something like that, and Mr. Schlossberg says to me, go out and don't come back till five or six, or whenever. He gives me a time when I can come back.

To my own house! Then he tells me what kind of meal to bring when I do come back. But I'm not supposed to show up as long as Mr. Prince is there because he can't work, he says, with me in the room. I don t know what they do there together. but I doubt they do very much work. I think they just sit around and read Mr. Prince's play and fight. I had to come back one day, and there was Mr. Schlossberg fast asleep. He can sleep O.K. when Mr. Prince is in the room. He hadn't slept all night the night before, but there he was now, and Mr. Prince had the TV turned way up to cover the sound Mr. Schlossberg makes. He snores terrible you know. 'It's not time for you to come back yet ' Mr. Prince says to me. 'Go fuck yourself,' I said. I was going to throw the man out, physically I mean. He's nothing, physically, you know, nothing. Did you see his wig? But then Mr. Schlossberg woke up and decided he wanted some shrimps with lobster sauce, and he sent me out. So there's this problem about the cats. I don't dare leave the place because I'm afraid that little bastard will kill my cats. I told that to Mr. Schlossberg, and he promised to watch out. 'But you fall asleep as soon as Mr. Prince gets here, I said—"

We'd arrived. Polly lived in a walkup on Avenue B and Seventh Street. It was supposed to be one of the meanest neighborhoods in the city. but actually this particular block was rather nice. There was a park there—an open place is such a blessing in a city—and across the street from where Polly lived was the University of the Streets with its lights still on and a lot of black kids outside who seemed peaceful and kind of jolly. We could hear them laughing.

We climbed the stairs, which were lit by twenty-watt bulbs and creaked. Four flights up Polly stopped at a door and knocked.

There was a sound of grumbling and cursing and after a long time Sidney opened the door.

"About time," he said when he saw me.

"What do you mean about time?"

Sidney was wearing a peignoir of pink chenille, one which fitted him because its owner, Polly, was a very ample girl. But I could see his belly protrude, and it was swollen, and as soon as I saw it. I knew what Sidney had.

"I have sent you message after message."

"How? Where?"

"I told Prince to go where you live and get you. Didn't you receive my message?"

"No."

"I don't believe you, but let it pass."

He got back into bed, taking the deli bag from Polly, ripping it open.

"Knife, fork, and a plate, Polly, please," he said. Then he looked at me. "I told you to be alert. I told you the time was coming soon. Well, I can't trust anyone anymore. I have to do everything myself."

He turned the whitefish over and found it good. Polly gave him a plate and opened the carton of grated horseradish and put it on the side of the plate.

"You forgot the lemon," he said, testing the onion roll with his nose. "How do you expect a person to eat smoked fish without a lemon?"

"I'm sorry," she said.

"Go get a lemon," he said.

"Oh, Sidney, eat the fucking fish without the lemon," I said.

He looked at me for an instant as if he was going to send me out for a lemon. Then he decided not to make waves, began slowly and deftly, with the most delicate moves of his knife and fork, to strip the fish of its paper-thin brown skin. He was pretty angry but needed me right then, so swallowed his rage. The fish helped. It pleased him.

Polly's place had only one window, and it was closed, the glass protected by iron bars. The bottom of the window was covered by a poster which advertised the appearance of an Eastern religious personality. Under this prophet's picture was the promise, "Everybody's going to be blessed out."

There was a terrible smell in the room. My mother's brother had died of cancer, and he'd smelled the same way.

The room was overflowing with Polly's belongings. Her two suitcases had been placed one on top of the other and served as a coffee table. The bed Sidney occupied was a convertible of uncertain age. I suppose the original idea had been to close it during the day, allowing room to walk around. Now it looked permanently opened and badly sprung. The only way to get to the window side of the room was to step on the bed and land in the tiny aisle under the outside wall, which was also jammed with possessions. The TV was on a metal milk box at the foot of the bed. It was covered with a blanket under which three cats cowered. I could see them ready to leap for a safer place if I turned out to be another Paul Prince.

Along the side of the bed, a pallet had been made on the floor, obviously where Polly slept. Her blanket was a greatcoat which she'd inherited from Leo Tolstoi, so it appeared, a massive black garment of the coarsest wool.

But what finally filled the room beyond the possibility of normal human movement was Sidney's papers, his scripts, his notes, his clippings, his illustrations, and his old theatrical bags of odd hats and character shoes. Everything Sidney owned in the world was there, none of it worth anything to anyone but him.

He paid me no mind as he ate the fish, chewed the seeded onion roll.

"You see the condition you've left me in," he said as he drank his black coffee. "At the mercy of this good girl. I've disrupted the poor thing's life, but I promised her that the time was almost here when I'd set her free. Now, compose yourself, we have to have a serious talk."

"Before that," I said, "I've got something to tell you."

I told him what had happened with Ellie and the police, that they might be looking for him.

"I haven't time to worry about anything like that now," he said. "Of course I know where those fellows can be found. Frank can find them. As you know, he did. But do you imagine I'd tell the police? Anything? Remember Prometheus. When have they done anything for me except bind me to this rock? Do you imagine I'd tell you? I don't trust you, as you well know, for the single simple reason that you are so much under the influence of your wife. What the hell is she so hot and bothered about anyway? She got her damn papers, didn't she?"

"There were two hundred and twenty dollars in her bag she didn't get back."

"Those black kids need it more than she does."

"Oh, Sidney—"

"Anyway, the money's spent. Those fellows are users, and the two hundred and twenty dollars have passed on. Money is not meant to stay in one person's possession."

"She is furious at you because you ran away."

"Oh, her standards are very romantic, aren't they, very cavalier! I suppose she wanted me to stand there and defend her."

"I think she did."

"Did it ever occur to Miss Law and Order that—"

"Nothing occurred to her, Sidney, except she was being attacked."

"Why do you think I ran, and where?"

"How would I know?"

"What would your guess be?"

"I say, I don't know."

"O ye of little faith! I went for the police."

"The police didn't say anything about you—"

"Not your police, their police. She got her cards back very quickly, didn't she? Does she think your police could have retrieved her possessions? Why don't you educate that foolish woman? Polly I want some more coffee, and don't make it so weak. I don't want a kind of tea. I want stand-a-spoon-up coffee." Then he turned back on me. "Does your wife really believe that Sidney Castleman is a coward?"

"Well, she was being roughed up and—"

"How would I know she'd be foolish enough to resist?"

"They tore the ligaments in two fingers."

"Let that be a lesson to her. Now sit down. We have serious business."

He shifted his weight and sat up. It wasn't easy for him.

"Polly," he shouted.

She turned, saw what it was, brought him the Demerol.

"What's the matter with you, Sidney?"

"What do you mean?"

"What are those for?"

"Quiet my nerves."

"Oh, Sidney, come on."

"These little white ones make it possible for me to face my present humiliation. Now don't ask any more foolish questions. Make yourself comfortable. Do you want coffee?"

"No."

"Polly, I'm waiting."

"Coming," Polly said.

Sidney now looked at me fondly. "You're a good boy," he said. "Despite everything you've done and not done, I think I can still rely on you. Be worthy of my faith."

"Sidney, come on, cut the shit."

Just then there were shots fired from Jimmy Cagney's pistol.

"You can turn off the TV," Sidney said. "Jim Cagney is underrated," he added. "Bogart overrated, and that will be the judgment of history. Now, are you comfortable?"

"Yes, fine."

"How did you prevail on your wife to let you out tonight?"

"I escaped."

"About time. May it be permanent!"

"I will have some coffee, Polly, if you—"

"Polly, another coffee for our guest." Then he turned to me. "I have warned you repeatedly about that woman. I have told you that if you stay with her you will come to a bad end. She is a quiet hysteric who has no world view and is a born castrator. What state is she from?"

"Connecticut. Hartford."

"All women from the city of Hartford are castrators!"

"O.K., Sidney, O.K., lay off Ellie."

"You lay off her. That's my final advice. Now, some good news. My new friend is coming back to town. The day after tomorrow. I am now able to reveal his name. You have heard of Bernie Kasko, of course?"

'No."

"Don't you read the papers, for chrissake?"

"I guess I have heard of him, vaguely."

"There is no one but no one as ignorant as a working actor. Well, you will hear more about Mr. Bernie Kasko, a lot more."

"Is he the one who—?"

"He's my benefactor-designate. Now I don't know what you heard about the man, but if you heard he's a hoodlum, you are dangerously misinformed."

"He's white?"

"Have you ever heard of a black man named Bernie Kasko? He's a Pole. He was born there, came to this country at the age of four. His earliest memory is of the ghetto of Warsaw where all his people were killed. He survived like her cats survive, by living in a hole. The Nazis simply found him not worth the price of a bullet. Ditto the Russki hordes. 'We were getting it from both sides,' he said to me. That was his education. He took the planes and tanks as a part of normal living. When peace came, a man from Wilna, who'd lost his wife and family, adopted him, took him along when he escaped to Vienna. This man was a great musician and immediately found a place in the Oper Haus orchestra, but he had his sights set higher. In time he made his way to this country, little Bernie with him. Here he put the boy in school, but Bernie was already a graduate of the University of Survival, and he knew the only important knowledge is to expect no mercy from anyone, so hit before you're hit. His defender soon found a job, and Bernie remembers sitting in Lewisohn Stadium on summer nights listening to *Les Préludes* of Franz Liszt. He has a tremendous love of culture, is of the highest order, morally, and there is no way to frighten him. He is ruthless, of course, but absolutely fair. He administers justice as if he was a king, which is what he is. He is capable of an act of quixotic generosity, and I believe he will make possible the fulfillment of my last wish on earth. It is for him that we are going to throw a party."

"But, Sidney, be realistic. What makes you think he will provide you with—"

"Because I have ferreted out his secret guilt. His benefactor, the man that brought him to this country, died in an accident where Bernie was driving the car. Bernie, in the caverns of his soul, is looking for a way to pay that dead man back. I have provided him with a solution to that problem. Convinced?"

I didn't answer.

"It doesn't matter. It's only important that you do precisely what I tell you."

Then he proceeded to describe to me what he wanted done in his old Plaza rooms, and how. I could see it was going to be a lot more expensive than I'd anticipated.

It was dawn when he got through. Polly slept comfortably through it all on her pallet. I agreed to carry out all of Sidney's absurd plans, precisely as he put them to me.

I knew, from his belly, this was going to be his last stand.

It was quarter of six when I sneaked into our place. I don't think Ellie even knew I'd gone out.

When I woke she'd left, and the house was quiet. While I ate six sausages and three eggs, I called the Plaza and told an assistant manager what I needed, giving my name, which he recognized or pretended to, and the room number of Sidney's old quarters. That space, the man told me, was occupied, but there was the same space available two floors down. I told him to hold it, I'd come around in the early afternoon to have a look.

The party, Sidney had instructed me, would take place sometime within the next three days, whenever was best for Bernie. But I would have to move Sidney into the place immediately to give him a chance to set up there and the girls a chance to make it seem as if he'd lived in that luxury for a long time.

Then I went to rehearsal.

I've never been worse on the stage than I was that morning. I sleepwalked through that first act. I was thinking of how I might make the suite look lived in, where to rent a record player, where to borrow stacks of records. I mustn't forget *Les Préludes* of Liszt, must remember to tell the girls to bring all kinds of magazines and books—the man was impressed by culture—must purchase a big basket of fruit from Charles and Company and a board of assorted cheeses from Cheese Unlimited, and a Polish ham. No, that was going too far, but candy, yes, lots of candy. Hoods often have sweet tooths.

All that was going through my mind as I played act one. So when it was over, I wasn't surprised that Adam asked for a private talk.

"This is the first decent run-through you've given me," he said as the dressing-room door closed. "What happened? I can't tell you how hopeful you've made me. You must have had a great night's sleep last night—"

"How did you know?"

"Oh, I knew it, because now I think this show is going to work, kid. I'm sure it will. So what do you say, let's go after act two?"

"O.K., fine," I said, "but first I really got to get some lunch. I didn't have breakfast."

"Maybe that was it. Maybe that's why you were so goddamn good, you were hungry."

"Maybe that's it. I must remember that. Ten hours' sleep, no breakfast before an important run-through. Now give me just an hour, Adam, and I promise I'll be even better this afternoon."

"Take an hour," he turned and shouted to the company.

At the Plaza I O.K.'d a cream-colored suite on the seventeenth floor, a duplicate of Sidney's old place, right down to the sofa under the window where Ellie and I used to tangle.

What happened to all that heat? Oh, fuck it, forget it!

When I got back to the theater, Polly was waiting at the stage door. A green Chevy at the curb, driven by a red-headed young man, was full of the "college-now-girls" from the last play, all ready to go to work. I gave Polly the key, waved to the others, and dashed into the theater. Adam was on stage, waiting with a fond smile and a sincere compliment.

To this day I don't know exactly what happened at "my" party. I was in at the beginning for a couple of hours, returned after rehearsal when most of the guests had left, and stayed another half hour. In all that time Bernie Kasko didn't leave the bedroom of the suite. Behind that connecting door was a chamber of power. There was decided who would be favored with an audience and for how long. The only sounds which reached those waiting in the parlor were Sidney's low rumble followed by a retort of coarse laughter ending in a nicotine cough.

Waiting my turn to be presented, I did as the others. Every time there was a change of audience, I lifted my eyes to the mirror attached to the bedroom door and there caught reflected a glimpse of two beds and on them, seated in identical postures of relaxation, two men. The stranger, in his middle-time, was short, thick through, otherwise unexceptional except for his clothes. Sidney's benefactor-designate was dressed in a sports jacket of camel's hair over a boldly patterned shirt open at the neck to show a crucifix. Both men were garlanded with girls from the top-floor dressing room.

At about seven fifteen Frank Scott and three of his bloods strutted in. Frank was dressed to pass, a businessman with a large black attaché case and, tonight, a very worried look. The men with him defied our time. One sported a high-belted floor-length Lincoln coat and white high-heel shoes. Another a brown leather coat trimmed with fur at the neck, wrists, and hem, and cut knee-length to reveal high-heeled boots of red glove leather. A third, the most striking of all, was dressed in great green shoes, a coat of white lamb's wool, and the whole topped by a purple hat with a sweeping brim, banded in white leather pierced in little wheel designs. All these men wore jewelry that filled the room with jangle. It was a scene from *The Merchant of Venice*. These were the bully boys of our Rialto.

"Charlie, tell him I'm here, will you?" Frank said to the guardian of the mirrored door when he'd sized up the situation.

Charlie opened the door just enough so he could slide into the bedroom and disappear. There came more rumble, then laughter ending in a nicotine cough.

Out swept Sidney. "Hello there, Frank," he said, passing him by. "I believe Bernie's going to see you in a very few minutes."

Then Sidney came to me. "Why didn't you tell me you were out here?" he demanded. "We wouldn't have kept you waiting."

Was it a deliberate snub of Frank Scott? There was no other way to read it.

"I'm only going to be a couple of minutes," I said to Frank, softening the insult as I passed him by.

Frank nodded. His supporters looked displeased.

At the door Sidney whispered, "He's going to ask you some questions."

I'd never seen Sidney uncertain before. His hand on my shoulder trembled.

Les Préludes was coming to its climax. The girls from the top-floor dressing room were all over the furniture. In a corner by the door and looking neglected was a centerfold blonde dressed and coifed in the tradition of the paid companion, Bernie Kasko's date, no doubt.

Bernie didn't get up from the bed, didn't ease his back off the headrest as he offered me his hand.

"Bernie, this is my oldest friend," Sidney presented me.

"Heard a lot about you," Bernie Kasko said. He began to prove that he knew who I was professionally, which wasn't necessary, particularly because he really didn't and it was all the same to me that he didn't. I saw that he was very impressed with me for whatever reason and that this was important for Sidney.

I was struck by his eyes. Set inside a great head of meat, over a jut of a chin and a hard-drawn mouth, his eyes were anomalous, small and bright and soft and full of some kind of longing. His hair, tight-curled and sleeked back, did not conceal a long scar across one temple.

"What would you like to hear now, Bernie?" Sidney said. *Les Préludes* was done.

"Play the Chopin again." He put a cigarette in his mouth, immediately took it out and threw it away. "I didn't know till to-night," he said to me, "that Chopin had written a piano concerto." Was he trying to impress me? "This kid brought me the record."

He smiled at one of Bennington College's gifts to Broadway.

"I want you to have it," the girl said, "so you'll remember me."

Then she looked at Bernie's date.

'I'll remember you, all right," Bernie said. "You're the first pretty girl I met who isn't stupid."

Again Bennington looked at the centerfold, who apparently was not offended by Bernie's remark.

"You must come home with me later," Bernie said. "I got a lot of great stuff. This is my passion, hi-fi."

"I'd like to," Bennington said, "if it's all right with—" She looked at Bernie's date, who was composed in patience.

Sidney beamed. His little brigade was meeting the test.

Polly put a drink in my hands, then leaned over and kissed me on the forehead.

Euphoria everywhere.

"Frank Scott's out there," Charlie said from the door.

Sidney looked at Bernie, then, turning to Charlie, said, "Let him wait. Won't hurt him, will it, Bernie?"

'I want to talk to you," Bernie said. He meant me. "Here." He moved over on the bed, making a place for me. "Sit here."

Sidney waltzed up with a tray of cheese puffs. He was jittering like a thief.

"You read this play, right?" Bernie asked.

I heard a sound like the whistle of a distant tea kettle, found Paul Prince against the wall on the floor, drunk as any freeloader, glowering at everyone, but particularly me, his mouth twisted into a sneer which, translated, said, "What the hell makes you think his opinion of my play is worth listening to?"

"Yes," I said, "I have."

Sidney was behind me, his hand on my shoulder. I could feel it trembling, then clenching to hold still.

"What do you think of it?" Bernie asked.

"I liked it."

"He doesn't understand it," Paul Prince said. The jet-black wig was slightly askew, and his own gray hair, grown out and frayed, showed around the edges.

"I've never read it all," Bernie said.

"Well—" I said and shrugged, meaning, "Read it."

"You see," Bernie said, "I got no experience in this field. I've always been careful not to invest in anything I don't know a lot about, and"—he shrugged—"this is way out of my line."

"Would we let you do the wrong thing, Bernie?" Sidney, from over my shoulder.

Bernie looked up at Sidney, and you could tell he loved the old man. "See, I don't like to be taken," he said to me, "even for—what? A few thousand? It's a matter of pride, you know? I'd rather give Sidney the money as a present. See how I am?"

"I know how you feel," I said, "but his play—"

"Don't worry," Sidney rode over me, "you're with me now, kid."

"Bless you, baby," Bernie said, "that's why I'm here."

"We're going to take a whole weekend," Sidney said. "I'm going to Bernie's house in Jersey, and I'm going to play it for him. Not just read it, perform it, the whole play."

"Maybe this weekend," Bernie said, "depending on, well, a lot of shit, you know. Anyway, sometime soon." He turned to me, and you could see the hardness there. He didn't have the affection for me that he had for the old man, and the international tough showed through. "If it's so goddamn good," he said, "why do it downtown? I like to go first class."

"He's right," Paul Prince said from the floor. "It must be done uptown. I insist. It's the only way I'll let it be—"

"Why don't you stick to writing?" Sidney was barely controlling himself.

"Don't take liberties with me," Paul Prince said. He got up and went to where the booze was and poured himself reinforcement.

I quickly intervened. "Sidney's idea, Bernie, and it's a good one, done a lot these days, a play is tried out inexpensively down in the Village, East or West. There it's reviewed by the critics much more favorably. When these reviews are good—"

"Think they will be?" Bernie asked.

"Bernie," I said and took the time to lay this on him good, "Sidney will be another case of Brando, a giant forgotten, now risen again. He will waste them."

Sidney's hand squeezed my shoulder.

"That's what I think," Bernie said, "but I don't know anything."

"Oh, you know, you know," Sidney said. "Look at those eyes," he said to me. "God meant Bernie to be an artist. His sensitivity, it's so deep, his feelings are so full, so close to the surface. This man has known pain. Right, Bernie?"

Bernie didn't think the compliments clumsy, he trusted Sidney. "Yeah, I really been through a lot," he said to me. "Maybe someday I'll tell you."

"What an actor he would have made!" Sidney's hand on my shoulder was shaking. He dropped it behind my back so no one would notice.

"A musician," Bernie said, "a violinist, that would be my wish."

Paul Prince whistled like a tea kettle.

"I'm glad you confirm my opinion," Bernie said, "about the play."

"My play is a masterpiece," Paul Prince said. "It will make any actor who plays it. Like *Death of a Salesman.* Any actor can play Willy Loman."

"You know what I miss most?" Bernie asked us all, his family. "What I crave? Not more money, not even love," he looked up at the girl from Bennington, who'd moved over and was sitting behind him on the bed. "Not even a family, though Christ, I'd like a son. You'll never guess what I—?"

"You miss talk," Sidney said. "Intelligent talk."

"How did you guess?" Bernie asked. "Oh, I told you. That's right. Like we're having now." He looked up at the girl from Bennington. "I have never been with a woman who interested me conversationally."

"Your experience," the girl said, "seems to have been extremely circumscribed." Again she looked at the neglected date, who didn't understand what was happening or didn't care or—was she encouraging her rival?

"For instance, 'circumscribed.' I don't know what that is, but I love the sound of the word. I love words. I love poetry, even when I don't know what it means. But the way Sidney says poetry I understand what it means, even Shakespeare. It's simple when Sidney—say that one, Sidney."

" 'When to the sessions of sweet silent thought,' " Sidney began, " 'I summon up remembrance of things past, I sigh the lack of many a thing I sought, and with old woes—' "

"We had a great night that night," Bernie said. "Didn't we, Sidney? It takes a little explaining for me to understand what these poets are trying to get over, but Sidney tells me they had the same feelings I have, that it's universal what I have, these violent feelings I have—"

"I'll explain poetry to you," Paul Prince said, "starting with my own. I'm free most afternoons after two o'clock, but don't bother me mornings. I work in the morning, and I cannot give you my phone number."

"You strike me as a phony, Mr. Prince," Bernie said.

"He's just a poet," Sidney said. "You're not used to poets."

"If a guy talked to me like he just did in my business, I'd wipe him out."

"Bernie, all sensitive people have a ludicrous aspect. I mean, take him as funny, see?"

"Yeah, yeah, I see, Sidney."

"He's just a poet, Bernie," I said.

Polly was trying to get Paul Prince to leave the room, but he'd folded back on the floor.

Bernie turned to me. The conversation had lit up his eyes. "I'm very happy sitting here with all of you," he looked up and smiled at the girl from Bennington, who had her arm around his neck now. "Sidney tells me you may be able to direct *Titan.*"

"I would do anything Sidney asked me," I said, "that's how much I respect him. At the moment I happen to be in a witless comedy that will probably be a big hit, but within the limits of my time, I am at Sidney's disposal, and yours."

The look Sidney gave me was worth the whole cost of the party.

"Why are you in it, that play, if it's—what was that word?"

Sidney danced over to the hors d'oeuvre trays.

"Witless. Same reason you're in—whatever you're in."

"You know what I am?" Bernie asked, his eyes pleading for my esteem.

"Rich," Paul Prince said. He was terribly drunk now, flung over the floor and talking to himself.

"I don't know if I'm rich or bankrupt, maybe both," Bernie said. "I meant what line of enterprise?"

"He doesn't read the papers, Bernie," Sidney said, gliding back with smoked oysters.

"In this country," Bernie said, "it's no distance between the top and the bottom." He looked up at the Bennington girl. "I'll tell you something. I've been rich and I've been poor. Rich is better. But even when I was, you know, loaded, I never felt sure I wouldn't be on my ass again any minute. That's why I got these little bank accounts all over the world. Case one country goes, there's always another. You might say I'm a permanent refugee. My cash I keep in traveler's checks. Like, I keep buying stuff for my deep freeze. I got food enough for a year in Jersey. Cans, bottles, a closetful! I'll show you later. I have no confidence in anything, you see?"

Bennington leaned over and kissed him on his temple where the long red scar showed. This time she didn't bother to look at his date.

Bernie finished his drink in a gulp. "I've never done what my mother wanted me," he said. "Oh, Sidney, I wish you'd known her. She was a saint. But strong! I'd be nothing except for her. Be careful, she said, what you set out to be, because you may make it. Get the trust there? Try to do something you'll be proud of, son, she said, something excellent that will make the world better. You see what I mean, what I am now, how far from that?"

"But, Bernie," Sidney said, "you got so many years ahead."

"You think so?" He put a cigarette in his mouth.

"I'm sure of it."

"I hope so." He threw the cigarette away. "I've always wanted that"—he looked up at Bennington—"to live more than one life. I mean I've had this one, what I am now, so—you know?"

"You're still a young man," she said. "You can do anything."

Bernie believed her.

Polly darted back with another drink for him.

As he leaned forward to accept the replacement from Polly, Bennington dropped her arm so Bernie sat back into her embrace.

"See, I had a bad start," he said, "a very bad start. Has Sidney told you?" He looked around at his new family.

"Yes," I said, "of course. But I admired your guts for overcoming it. That's how it made me feel, your story."

"Did you feel that way, really?"

"Yes. It's not too late for Sidney, and it's not too late for you."

"Age is a matter of spirit," Sidney said.

"I'm very disappointed with my own life," I said.

"But I saw your name in *The New York Times*, their theater section," Bernie said. "What's the matter with you, you're disappointed? You know what I'd give to have my name in there?"

His eyes gouged mine. I thought, "You'd kill to get in there."

"What?" I said.

"Name it. Why is everyone who's worth a shit so dissatisfied?" he asked. "Notice? Why is that?"

"It's the times," I said.

"Anyone who's adjusted to what's out there"—Sidney indicated the window—"is insane."

"Right," Bernie said. "Sidney, you just said something."

"That's what this play is about, Bernie," I said.

"I haven't read it all yet," Bernie said, "but you're so right what you said about out there. It's so crooked, so rotten, no honesty, no honor, no trust, no true friendship—"

"Jesus Christ!" Paul Prince exclaimed, but no one knew what he meant.

"Sidney is the only man I've met whom I trust."

I had to get Prince out of there before he loused everything up.

"Frank's waiting outside," I said to Bernie, standing up.

"Fuck Frank." Bernie pulled me down. "Let's talk. Let's talk truth and philosophy and ideas. I never got enough talk in my life. Those mutts who work for me, yeah, you, Charlie, you—"

The appointments secretary at the door grinned, shamefaced.

"You're ignorant, you know that, Charlie?"

"I know it, boss—"

"Charlie, for chrissake, will you tell them to shut up out there? We're trying to do a very simple but a very difficult thing, have a conversation."

Charlie disappeared.

"Don't bring up his name again," Sidney whispered to me. "Frank."

"I have to go to rehearsal," I said.

"What's your play called?" Bernie wanted to know.

"*The Last Nail in His Coffin.* It's sort of a comedy-mystery. Something awful!"

"He's embarrassed to talk about it," Sidney said.

"It pays the bills," I said. "I mean I hope it will."

"You family man?" Bernie asked.

"I have a wife and one kid."

"A boy, I hope?"

"Yeah."

"That's great," Bernie sighed. "Really great. You love him, don't you?" He wanted me to, badly.

"He's a beautiful little person."

Bernie sighed. "Great," he said. "And he lives with you?"

"Where else, sure. Now, how about you?"

"I was married once, respectable, but I fucked my way out of that. No children, not from that. I got a couple of kids outside, but I don't see them. One, I don't even know where or who. The other I dropped in Mexico years ago. I had some interests down there and, at night you know, when you feel like"—he clenched his fists and shook them to show me what he meant—"like this, at night, you got to do something, drink or fuck or fight. Something! The mother, though, she was a damn whore, it turned out, the expensive kind. I don't even know if it's my kid. Just on the chance, I give her pesos every month. But it's a girl. I told her, when I was with her, 'Give me a son and I'll marry you.' That's natural, isn't it?" He looked over his shoulder at the girl from Bennington, "No offense meant."

"None taken," the girl said.

"It's nothing derogatory you're a girl," he said.

"I'd like a son, too," she said. When he looked up at her, she leaned over and damn if she didn't kiss him on the mouth. She really liked him. She wasn't doing it to help Sidney, not anymore. She dug Bernie's pain. "Everyone wants a son," she said. "It's natural."

"I've had so many dreams about girls like you," Bernie said, his voice suddenly private and soft. He sighed. Then he decided something, made a gesture toward the centerfold.

She got up, made sure the back of her dress was down, and walked over to where he was holding out the money, two fifties off a roll of fifties.

"I won't be bothering you tonight, Gretchen," Bernie said.

"Oh, Bernie!" Gretchen said.

"She said that to me once, 'Are you going to bother me tonight?' I tease her. Gimme a kiss, Gretch? Kiss, kiss."

She did. "Oh, Bernie," she said. Then she looked at her replacement. "Goodbye, dear," she smiled. "Be sure to call my service now, Bernie," she said to him as she left.

"You're coming back, aren't you?" Bernie said. He was talking to me.

I'd looked at my wristwatch, and he'd caught it.

"After rehearsal, of course. What do you think?"

"I want to talk to you some more."

"Don't worry." I was amazed how impressed he was with me for whatever reason, perhaps because my name was in *The New York Times*. "I'll be back as soon as rehearsal's over."

"That's the trouble with my line of work. It's all numbers and double talk and contracts and lies, you know?"

"I don't know what your line of work is," I said.

"Just as well," Bernie said. "O.K., go ahead. Go to rehearsal. Charlie."

Charlie slid in the door.

'Get Frank Scott in here. Without his buffaloes."

Bernie offered me his hand to shake. It was heavy, very meaty, but the grip was surprisingly light and soft. "I'm expecting you back here," he said, his gold wristlet jingling. 'Don't disappoint me."

"I'll be here," I promised.

"You girls will have to step out awhile. But none of you go away. I want to see every one of you back here in ten minutes. You too, Mr. Prince. Excuse me what I said before I'm not used to poets. Sidney, you stay. And you"—he looked at the Bennington girl—"I want you to see the kind of shit I go through. My life is—" He couldn't find the word, made a gesture of disgust put a cigarette in his mouth, took it out, and threw it on the floor. Make me stop smoking, will you?" he said to his newfound love.

Prince and I went through the door together. As we were going out, Charlie ushered Frank in, then turned and said to everyone in the parlor, "Keep it down in here. Bernie don't like a lot of noise at a party when he's talking business."

After that no one in the room dared talk. Except Prince. He pulled me into a corner, his face fiercely intent. 'What arrogance!" he said.

"Shsh," I whispered to him. "Be careful. I think Sidney's got your money."

"Not my money," Paul Prince hissed. "I'm not satisfied with my deal, not a damn bit."

I was sorry I'd spoken to him. "Look," I said, "I haven't time now. I got a rehearsal."

"I'm not going to let him do the play unless he sweetens my deal," Paul insisted.

"For chrissake, Paul—"

"I want expense money. I've had expenses for five years, secretaries, research, books, new script copies. Who's going to pay for all that?"

'Paul, just be happy your play is finally going to be done."

"Downtown! That piece of shit I saw you rehearsing the other day gets a theater on Forty-fifth Street, but my play—"

"Paul, that's the way it is now."

"You better tell your friend Sidney I'm going to pull my play right out from under him. I mean I'm not going to kiss some crummy hoodlum's—"

'Shshsh!"

"—ass even if he does wear a camel's hair coat. Not for a few measly hundred dollars I'm not, no sir."

"Paul, keep your voice down or—"

"The play's the thing, and I want my play respected."

'You, poet. Keep it down," Charlie said from the door.

Paul was quiet but he held my arm and shook it in a kind of code, continuing his protest. "Let's go out in the hall," he hissed.

Before we got up there were sounds from the throne room. Frank Scott's voice could be heard, not his words. Then Bernie's words. "You are going to be fair, Frank, because I am going to make you be fair, because if you don't you will be taking a chance you don't want to take."

Then there was some more from Frank, then Bernie's "Because that's the way it's got to be, Frank."

Then there was a long silence, in both rooms, and we heard Chopin.

Then Frank's voice, and this time we heard his words. "I've only got three places, Bernie, I got one on Hundred and Three, I got one on Hundred and Six, and I got the big one, Hundred Sixteen. That's all I got."

Bernie's laugh with Chopin.

Then Frank's, "That's the best I can do."

And Bernie's, "Frank, you can do better, believe me."

Then Frank, pleading, but no words.

Then Bernie's, "Frank, I'm trying to be a nice guy."

Then there was another silence, a long one. I assumed whatever differences they had were resolved. Then I heard Bernie, and his tone was most affable and relaxed. "Bless you, baby, you won't be unhappy with me."

That's that, I thought, and looked at my watch. I was late for rehearsal. Pulling my arm out of Paul's grip, I got up and started toward the hall door.

Suddenly the bedroom door opened, and Frank came through followed by Charlie. Charlie suddenly whirled Frank around and, I thought, embraced him. But then I saw him slap Frank's body several times in a way the English call "smartly," under his arms, in the small of his back, between his legs. Satisfied, the frisk over before Frank knew what it was, Charlie went back into the bedroom and closed the door.

Charlie had found out what he wanted to know.

Now Frank wanted to get out of that room as quickly as he could. I was at the hall door and as I went through, Frank followed.

Furious, he hurried down the hall with his attaché case swinging. His men followed a few yards, then stopped and turned to face the door to Sidney's suite. No one, it seemed, was to be allowed to follow Frank.

Except myself.

Halfway to the elevator, a man came out of a service hall and cut in, joining Frank. They didn't speak, but I knew they were together. This man had a huge soft Afro, but like Frank he was dressed to pass, unexceptional.

We waited, the three of us, for the elevator. Although neither man looked at the other, I could feel the vibes. They anxiously watched the door to Sidney's suite then looked up at the elevator indicator.

The elevator arrived, and they entered. I hesitated. Frank reached out and pulled me in as the door closed.

The instant the door was closed, the man with the soft Afro reached down into the crotch of his trousers and, after some fumbling, pulled out a small reel of magnetic tape. He gave this to Frank, who was watching me. I pretended not to notice anything unusual.

The elevator stopped at the seventh floor. A pair of old-marrieds got in. The man with the soft Afro got out.

The elevator stopped again at five. Four Frenchmen were saying goodbye to someone who didn't want to leave. Several times they prevented the door from closing.

The delay aggravated Frank. He made his displeasure known. Then he looked at me, seemed to be considering something that involved me.

"Nice party, Frank," I said, for want of something better. "Sorry I have to go to rehearsal."

Frank didn't answer. He took his eyes off me, apparently he'd made up his mind. He slid along the side of the elevator well to its gate, just as we reached the ground floor.

As the doors opened, Frank looked out and around, blocking the exit passage for an instant. Then with a whispered apology, he stepped back and allowed the other passengers to leave.

Which they did. Frank thrust his hand into his pocket, saying, "Where's your rehearsal?"

"The Helen Hayes," I replied quickly, picking up his pace, his anxiety.

"I'll be there in an hour to get this."

He thrust the reel of magnetic tape into the side pocket of my coat and left the elevator.

I walked out slowly, watching Frank hurry through the lobby. I felt the reel through the cloth of my coat, then quickly pulled my hand away. I didn't want to give anything away. I was part of the conspiracy.

Turning in place, I saw a man leave the house phone and run out the front door of the hotel to where Frank was getting into a cab. He jumped in with him.

I decided not to go out that door. There was another entrance on Fifth Avenue.

As I turned, the other elevator door opened, and the man with the soft Afro got out. As he went through the front door, I couldn't swear to it, but I had the impression someone was following him, too, and getting into the cab he took.

All through rehearsal, I kept looking anxiously toward the stage door, expecting Frank.

Adam's notes were endless that night, most of them for me. He was no fool. "Tonight," he said, "you seemed to be working under a long distance mood of anxiety totally unrelated to this play. What we're performing here is comedy. It cannot be played as if the Tupamaros are going to enter any minute from stage right."

I promised to do better the next day.

When I called Suite 1707–8, Sidney answered.

"How's everything?" I asked.

"Great," he whispered. "What do you think Bernie's just given me? One thousand dollars in traveler's checks. Two five hundreds.

Seed money. Thank you for what you did for me tonight. I'll never forget it. Now come over, quick, hurry."

"What's the big rush?"

"You got to sign the checks for liquor and room service."

The waiters were waiting for my signature. Sidney had written in the tips, and they were a royal twenty percent. But it was no time to fuss. I signed.

Bernie was still in the bedroom with the girls, happy drunk and having the time of his life. He was telling the story of his respectable marriage, in complete detail.

"She was so respectable," he said, "when she went down on me, she held her nose."

Everybody roared with laughter. Bennington was on the bed with him, enjoying his vulgarity. This is a new era of kicks for girls. They're going for the kind of man who would have scared them to death in my day.

Bernie greeted me as an old and good friend. Whatever had happened between him and Frank hadn't left him any the worse for tension. It was simply part of his workday.

I was soon on the other bed feeling no pain. It was pretty crowded there, Sidney and Polly and a couple of other top-floor girls. I was the hero of the hour.

"You're really a terrific guy," one of the kids said to me. "I mean I played in that superstinker with you for a whole year, and this is the first time I noticed you were human." A few minutes later she asked me to come home with her.

I was considering her proposal when Charlie came in with a man who was unexceptional except for one thing.

He was carrying Frank's black attaché case and was, I saw, the one who'd run from the house phone and entered Frank's cab.

I couldn't tell whether Bernie noticed his arrival, but a moment or so after this person entered, Charlie said, "Boss, maybe we better break it up for now. You got a big day tomorrow."

"Yeah," Bernie said. "Come on, we go," he said to the Bennington girl carrying the Chopin LP. She got up quietly.

"Wait for him outside," Charlie instructed her, meaning the parlor.

I shook hands all around and left. Going down the hall I realized I'd left my script behind so I went back to the suite to pick it up. The parlor was occupied by the girl from Bennington and by Polly. As I entered, the door to the bedroom swung partly open and a man came through carrying my script. He was headed for the elevator to give it to me.

As I took it, I had a glimpse in the mirror of Bernie on the bed, ravishing Frank Scott's black attaché case, examining its contents, then ripping out the lining with a knife.

As I got into a cab downstairs, I felt for the little reel of tape. It was still in my coat pocket.

Where was Sidney? Only then, in the cab going home, did I remember I'd also seen Sidney in the mirror. My old friend had been on the other bed, fast asleep, one of his fine old hands on his swollen belly.

Too damn early the next morning, Ellie came in and threw something on my bed. "Show this to your friend," she said.

It was a copy of the *Daily News*. On the front page was a blowup of Frank Scott and another picture of his body as found in a vacant lot in the South Bronx, shot through the head with a single bullet. The piece on page four described the scene. Frank, after his murder, had been pulled apart, his possessions scattered all over, his pants ripped open. On his thighs were bits of medical tape left where they'd been cut with a knife, also marks where other bits of the medical tape had been pulled clean off the skin, hair and all.

There was a kind of innocence about Frank's expression.

I stayed in bed till I heard Ellie and Little Arthur leaving. Apparently she was taking him to school herself.

Then I dressed, finished the coffee, and left the house.

Adam started rehearsal by saying he'd decided to work with me in much greater detail, hoped I wouldn't mind. I said, "Work any way you like," but when it began to happen, it did feel odd. Adam was treating me like an amateur. He was on stage with me, sometimes at my side, sometimes just behind me, pointing out where my concentration should be, instant by instant, reminding me what the difference was between what I was saying and what I actually meant. It was the way you direct beginners. Everyone in the cast was a little shocked at a kid director treating an established performer this way, but it was the only way I could have done that morning.

At the lunch break, I rushed out for a *Post*. They had the picture of another dead man on their front page. He was flopped on his face under the structure of the Harlem River Drive among the broken bottles, pigeon droppings, cans, and wastepaper. He wore a huge soft Afro, one I'd last seen whizzing through the lobby of the Plaza Hotel.

He too had been ripped open with a knife, he too had medical tape marks on the inner flanks of his thighs.

Whatever had been taped to these men's thighs, the *Post* revealed, had been taken.

I decided not to go to a restaurant. I still had the reel of magnetic tape in my pocket, so I gave Rudy the doorman five bucks to get me a club sandwich and a quart of milk to ease the clench in my stomach.

After I ate the sandwich and drank the milk, I did a thing peculiar to me. Fear quickens others. I sleep.

It was Adam who woke me, finding me stretched out on an old four-fold at the back of the stage house. "I thought we decided you had to get a full night's sleep every night in order to rehearse well," he reprimanded.

I didn't say anything. What the hell, I sympathized with him now. I'd even begun to admire his patience.

Waiting for my entrance in the wings, I read the *Post* carefully. What the police had found on the legs of both men was identical, the medical tape, where placed, even the suggestion of what the tape had been used for, to hold some sort of bugging equipment, the *Post* said. Then the writer speculated. The men had been killed, he wrote, to get a tiny quarter-watt transmitter and a receiver, the kind anyone could purchase at his neighborhood do-it-yourself bugging center.

The police particularly wished to find the magnetic tape. It had not been on the body of the second man when he was killed. They were "scouring" the city for this reel. The grand jury investigating corruption in the police department would value that tape. There were hints that Frank Scott had been in with the cops, been paying them off, other rumors that Frank might have turned informer, obtaining immunity for his own crimes by revealing the crimes of others.

It was with all this on my mind that I finally stepped out on the stage.

A miserable comedy like *The Last Nail in His Coffin* is shameful under any circumstance, but when it's not played with full Rex Harrison vanity-plus-arrogance zip in its leading performer, it is indescribably flat. This is not an aesthetic judgment. It is the beginning of a speech Adam was to start that afternoon but never finish.

A phone call from Ellie interrupted him, Rudy frantically signaling me from the wings to run to the wall phone opposite his cubbyhole. "I'll be right back," I said as I hustled off. I knew Ellie wouldn't call now unless it was something important. I also knew I would not be right back. When I did return I had my hat on.

"What the hell is it now?" Adam groaned for all to hear.

"My son hasn't come back from school," I said.

I didn't wait to watch Adam's contortions. When I got home Little Arthur was there, and a locksmith was putting a new cylinder lock on our front door.

What had made the kid miss the bus from school was he'd lost his key to the house and had looked for it in every classroom he'd been in that day. Not finding it and the bus gone, he'd walked home through the park.

Ellie decided not to live in doubt. "Lost or stolen," she said, "I decided to change our lock. Again."

Ellie was beginning to crack up. What had made her more hysterical that day was a number of phone calls. Picking up the ringing receiver she'd said, "Hello? Hello? Hello?" and received no response except the sound of the phone being hung up on the other end. Finally, on about the fourth or fifth call, a girl's voice came on and left a cryptic message for me that Ellie had written down.

"What does this mean," she demanded, "and who is it from?"

The message was, "Titan seventh decamping."

"How should I know," I said, "unless it's a race track tout? That's what it sounds like."

Titan, you know. Polly's house was on Seventh Street. Decamping. Who would do anything that dramatic except my man Schlossberg?

"I know it's a message you understand," Ellie said, "and I know who it's from. Now tell me what it means?"

The doorbell rang, and the locksmith installing the new lock said, "The police are here!"

It was the same team, Boruff and the black one named Bird.

They wanted to speak to me alone, but Ellie wouldn't leave the room. She sat there like Wellington on the hill overlooking Waterloo.

These fellows had found out that the bills for the party where Frank Scott had last been seen bore my signature. They showed the Xeroxes for $331.50, to Ellie first, then to me.

"This is your signature, isn't it?" Bird asked.

"It most certainly is," Ellie said.

Of course I'd never intended Ellie to know anything about that goddamn party.

The detectives, this time, were not casual. They wanted to know what happened, who was there, and exactly what I'd witnessed. I had to pick my way carefully through a very broken field.

"Now tell us exactly what happened at that party?"

'It was very jolly," I said.

"They don't care about the mood." Ellie said.

"Who was there?" Bird asked.

"A lot of different people."

"Was Frank Scott there?"

"Yes, Frank was there."

"Was there a Bernie Kasko at the party?"

"The party was in his honor."

"Everything friendly between Kasko and Frank Scott?"

"As far as I could tell, very."

"When did Frank leave?"

"The same time I left."

"When was that?"

"When I had to go to rehearsal."

"Which was?"

"About a quarter to eight."

"Where is Kasko now?" Boruff asked.

"I don't know."

"Where is Mr. Schlossberg?"

"I don't know.

"He knows," Ellie was heard to murmur.

"Madam, do you mind going into the other room?" Bird was Ellie's equal—almost.

"I do mind, very much, but I will try to keep still.'

"Why was a party thrown for Bernie Kasko?" Bird went on.

"It was a gesture for an old friend," I said, "mine."

"That would be Mr. Schlossberg?" Boruff asked.

"That's right."

"Some gesture," Ellie said, "three hundred and thirty—"

"Please," Bird silenced her. Then he turned to me and asked, "What kind of a gesture?"

I just couldn't look at Ellie as I said this next. "He is trying to raise money for a theatrical production"—God, it sounded absurd—"and he's promoting Kasko."

"What's the play called?"

"*Titan.*" Did that ever sound silly said out loud to these men!

"Have you ever heard," Bird asked, "of Kasko backing a play in the theater?"

"Never."

"Don't you think it's odd that—"

· 290 ·

"No, there are always new angels. Most backers get burned and leave the theater for good after one production."

"Did Kasko go out after Frank left?" Bird asked.

"No."

"How do you know?"

"When I came back to the party he was still there."

"How much later was that?"

"Maybe two hours—and a half."

"He could have gone and come back," Ellie said. "Why don't you tell these men the truth?"

"I think," Bird said to his mate, "we better go somewhere—"

"I'll keep quiet," Ellie said. "I really will."

Boruff took over. "What did you come back to the party for?"

"To sign these liquor and room service bills."

"Did Frank Scott have a black attaché case with him?" Bird asked.

"I don't know," I lied.

"He knows," Ellie said. "That man always carried a black brief-case."

"Did he?" Bird asked. "Please try to remember. It's important."

"I think he did, yes, come to think of it. He had it when he came in anyway."

"And when he went out?"

"He had it, yes."

"Did you get into the same elevator with Frank?"

"Yes."

"Talk on the way down?"

"Yes."

"What did you say?"

"Nice party, wasn't it? That's all."

"Then when the elevator reached bottom?"

"He walked out and got into a cab."

"Alone?"

"Yes."

I'd never lied so continuously for so long a time in my life.

"When was this? You said just before rehearsal?"

"Five, ten of eight."

"The stage manager told us rehearsal was at seven thirty that night," Bird said.

"I got there late."

"You're lying again," Ellie said.

I got up. "Either she keeps quiet, or I won't say another goddamn thing," I said. "Not a word."

"She'll shut up," Bird said, "and you will answer our questions, either here or elsewhere."

"Your lock is in," the locksmith said, giving Ellie two keys. "If you want more keys you'll have to buy them. Only two come with the lock."

"We won't be needing any more," Ellie said.

"You know that lock is no good," the locksmith said.

"Then what the hell did you put it in for?" Ellie shouted. "Sorry," she said, "sorry, really. But tell me, why did you—I mean, what's the matter with it?"

The locksmith gave me his bill, forty-two dollars and ninety-eight cents.

"You should a got a police lock," he said.

"What's he mean?" I asked the two detectives.

"There's no way of keeping these kind of men out of any place they want to enter," Boruff said.

"That's comforting," I said. "What do you do in your house?"

"I got a police lock," Boruff said. "A sliding bar."

"They can get through that too," Bird said. "Nothing works."

"Ellie," I said, "I've only got thirty dollars. Have you got twenty somewhere?"

She disappeared into the bedroom.

"What do you have in your house?" I asked Bird.

"My father-in-law. He's crippled and retired, and he's got a gun permit. He stays home with the gun in his lap, hoping somebody will try to burglarize us, watching TV and hoping. I'm scared to go in there myself. He don't see too good, and he's dying to cut loose."

Ellie came out with some money and gave it to the locksmith. "Give him yours first," she said to me. The locksmith gave the change to Ellie and left.

"Now let's all sit down," Boruff said gently. "It's not always easy to answer truthfully when friends are involved," he said to me. "I'm not accusing you of lying. I'm only reminding you again that two men's lives have been taken."

He turned to Bird. "You see any reason why I shouldn't tell him?" he asked.

"It's been in the papers, most of it," Bird said.

"O.K.," Boruff said, turning to me. "Frank Scott," he started, "came to us a few months ago. He complained Kasko was subjecting him to extortion procedures, putting the muscle on him to make a new arrangement favorable to Kasko. Scott said if he agreed to what Kasko was demanding he couldn't make a decent living."

"What's he do?"

"Numbers. A policy man."

"And he complained to you, the police?"

"Yes. He knew we wanted to know more about Kasko and his operation. Scott said if we promised him immunity he'd testify before the grand jury."

"What is that? Immunity?"

"Immunity from any of his own crimes his testimony before the grand jury might reveal."

"He's going to testify before the grand jury?"

"Was! Willing to. He told us he'd obtain proof for us that Kasko was extorting or trying to. He told us about this bugging rig and how it would work, told us that at the first opportunity he'd get a tape which would be certain proof of Kasko's tactics and operations."

"So that's the reel you're looking for?" I said.

"How do you know there is such a?"

"The paper said so. The *Post*. This afternoon."

"Right. You see, Frank Scott didn't mind paying Kasko some protection money. All policy operators have those expenses, but Kasko was asking more and more, and Scott knew that if it went on he'd take Scott over. Big fish, little fish, one gulp."

"Why you telling me all this?" I asked.

"We are trying to impress on you its seriousness," Boruff said. "We got to get control of the underside of this city."

"If we can't get people like you to help us"—Bird was very earnest —"we're not going to be able to do it. This city will remain—"

"The most disgusting, the most corrupt, the most shameless city in the history of man."

That, of course, was Ellie, and this time the detectives didn't mind her extra little push.

"This is your chance," Boruff said, "to do your part. We're asking for your help."

"That's wonderful," Ellie said.

"I can't say to you," Boruff said in his soft city-street voice, "that I believe you've told us everything you know."

"That's a nice way to put it," Ellie said.

"If you know anything at all you haven't told us," Boruff said, "no matter how trivial it may seem to you, now is the time!"

"I've said everything I know," I lied.

The detectives looked at each other.

"O.K.," Boruff said, "we will have to recommend that you be called before the grand jury. They will put you under oath and—"

"What?" I asked.

"You will have to tell everything you know under considerable pressure. You will have to talk or else."

"What is it you want of me?" I asked. "Really?"

"That's for you to say," Boruff said. "I just have this instinct."

"Instinct!"

"An instinct," Boruff said, "is something it takes years to develop, but in the end it's pretty reliable. I rely on mine."

"What do you want?"

"Information that will lead us to that tape."

"Why don't you believe me?" I asked.

"It's hard to believe that a man as intelligent and analytical of human behavior as you could actually believe that Scott and Bernie Kasko were on cordial terms that night or any night."

"I can't help you," I said. "I can't even guess what you think I know. I'm tired of answering these—"

Bird stood up. "Let's go," he said, turning to Boruff.

We went downstairs together, I back to rehearsal.

On the elevator I asked Boruff, "Then Frank Scott was cooperating with the police?"

"Yes," Boruff was short with me.

"The equipment he was wearing, the police supplied?"

"No."

"But you knew he was wearing it that night?"

"He told us what he was going to do."

"Then he was an informer?"

"You could call him that."

"What would you call him?"

"An informer."

"Aren't all informers killed sooner or later? Don't they know they will be? Don't they expect it?"

"You mean in life or in the movies?"

"Both."

"In movies, they're always shot or knifed or garroted, whichever is most spectacular. In life they sometimes become prosperous. Sometimes they even work for a good cause."

"But anyway," I said, "Frank met an informer's death."

"You don't like informers." Bird asked, "do you?"

"No. Do you?"

"No, but sometimes I admire their courage. I don't know what the police would do without them, or governments, including our own. Right, Bill?"

"Right," Boruff said, "and they are very courageous. I've seen corpses where they've been tortured to death. You should see some of the corpses of informers I've known."

"One more question," I said at the corner of Central Park West. "Weren't you asking me, really, to become one?"

"One what?"

"An informer?"

"How can you be," Boruff said, "since you say you don't know anything?"

"That's right," I said and walked away.

During rehearsal that night, I looked over into the wings and there was Polly, waiting to catch my eye. When I looked at her, she made a quick sign, which I interpreted to mean, "Come downtown quick."

Then I heard, "Now what the hell is happening?" and Adam pounding down the aisle. He got to the pit, leaned over the orchestra rail, and looked off right. Perhaps he saw Polly disappearing, but I don't think so, because he would have used any grounds to complain to me now, and he didn't.

Actually I'd given up on that play and my performance in it. I expected to be fired any minute, so for the first time in a few days I was pretty good. Figure it out.

Adam said so in his first note. Everything was O.K. between us till I asked him if I could be excused from any more notes that night, could I get mine the next morning.

"They're all for you," Adam said. "Not all bad, but I think it's important for you to know when you do it right. Gives you something to hold on to."

I acted like the jeebies were coming on, scared the shit out of everybody. "Maybe I'm just tired," I said, "but I don't have any concentration left. I hear your voice, Adam, but I don't hear what you're saying. Your notes, I want very much to have them. But tomorrow, Adam, please, tomorrow."

He said he'd let me off if I promised to get ten hours' sleep and meet him an hour before rehearsal in the morning. I promised.

At eleven thirty I got to Polly's.

Sidney was packing to leave. Correction. Sidney was directing the packing. Polly was doing the work, then me.

All over what floor space there was, all over the bed, the table, the stove, the toilet lid were Sidney's papers and projects, his scripts and sides, his accumulation of clippings and ten thousand notes, his wigs, his odd shoes, his character hats, his hand props, watches, knives, jewelry—and the cartons and shopping bags which had contained them for all these years.

"I've decided to throw most of this away," Sidney announced. "After all, how many more parts am I going to play?"

That's what took the time, Sidney deciding what he was going to keep and what throw away. He was looking over each crumbling clipping, each dusty note, studying them, then making a difficult decision. He had stuff from forty years back, Roosevelt's inauguration, the first interviews with Clifford Odets after *Waiting for Lefty*, the first copy of *Life*, Hitler and Hindenburg, a project for him to play both parts, a picture of the ladder used to carry off Lindbergh's infant with a note in understanding of Hauptmann, Jacob Adler's obituary boxed in purple crayon.

"Sorry I can't help with this packing," Sidney said, "but the dust fills my sinuses and my resonance cavities. As it is I may have to go into the hospital soon—"

"You mean for—" I looked at his belly.

"Yes, for my throat. I have a couple of little nodules on my cords, I may decide to have nipped off, child's play for an able surgeon, especially with the new electric knife they have. Just a touch. Zip. Polly, look out, let me see those, lay them down carefully. You handle the historical stuff, Polly, and you"—he pointed to me—"the clippings about my career and so on. That's my Bismarck collection. I've always wanted to play Bismarck. And Henry Luce. Careful! I have an outline worked out on Luce. His life falls naturally into three acts, perfect dramatic structure. See, I've got it all laid out. I have over thirty plays here, ready to go, all they need is dialogue. The hard part—no, you can't throw that away, Polly!—I've done. I intend to do a whole series on the great men of my time. It would amount to a history in living drama of our era."

It became evident Sidney was not going to throw away anything.

"Sidney," I said, putting it cautiously, "this stuff is too precious to make a quick decision on late at night. You might, out of simple weariness—"

"I am not weary."

"—throw away something you'd later regret. This is a magnificent collection really and—"

He thought about it for a minute.

"Where are you going with it?" I asked.

"Bernie is sending his Eldorado for me at two in the morning. Our hours, you see, coincide perfectly." He looked up at the ceiling. "Hold everything," he said. "I think I'll take your advice. I'll keep the collection intact. Bernie might be interested in it."

"Where's he taking you?"

"To his house, somewhere in Jersey. He says he has a little apartment there I might enjoy. Private, of course. Don't worry, the production is definitely on, merely postponed. After all, what's the hurry?"

"Postponed till when?"

"Until certain business matters that Bernie has not found time to discuss with me are resolved. Didn't Bernie tell you all about it?"

"When?"

"On the phone. He asked me for your address and your phone number. Your apartment is 2F, right?"

"Right."

"By the way, he liked you, very much!"

"Good. Ellie did say she received some calls, but when they heard her voice, they hung up, whoever they were."

"Bernie doesn't talk to strange women."

We packed everything, threw away nothing. When we'd finished, I asked, "What do you think Bernie wanted to tell me?"

"He's worried about some kind of tape. That Frank Scott, he turned out to be a police informer. He had a transmitter taped to his leg and a man in the hall, I just know what I read in the paper Polly brought, the guy in the hall, he had a receiver. Can you believe it? They were all set to go before the grand jury, turn state's evidence against Bernie. I told you I had my suspicions about Frank, didn't I? You can't trust anyone now."

"I didn't realize." I said.

"I assured Bernie you didn't know anything about it. Isn't he a wonderful person! You know what made the biggest impression on him about you? Your love of children, the way you spoke about your son."

I left Sidney on the sidewalk in front of Polly's building at one thirty in the morning. I told him Ellie was kind of worried, what with Frank's picture in the paper and all, I better get home.

"Remember my advice," Sidney said, "before it's too late."

"What advice? I mean which particular—?"

"You married the wrong woman. Leave her before she kills your talent."

He was holding his side as I left.

I had no key to the new lock. I had to ring the bell.

The first words Ellie said to me after she'd locked and bolted the door were, "We're going to Florida."

"When?"

"Tomorrow, the day after, soon as I can pack."

"Where in Florida?"

"I called daddy. He was delighted. He's been so worried about Arthur going to school here."

Ellie's father lives alone in a house on Robbins Key. It's a beautiful place, right on the beach. The water is warm and clear as glass.

"He's been wanting me to come down for a long time," Ellie said and went into the bedroom. "Little Arthur's sleeping with me tonight." she said as she disappeared.

I had an eerie feeling, a mouse the owl is watching out of the dark.

She was sitting on the edge of my cot, studying me. She was not trying to wake me.

"What?" I said. It was the next morning.

She didn't answer. She was dressed in her traveling tweed.

"Well," I said, "what?"

"I didn't tell you. I had a call last night, from your director, Adam somebody. Rehearsal had just broken up, and he was worried and wanted to talk. You weren't here so he unloaded on me."

"What did he have to complain about?"

"He wanted to know what you're up to."

"For chrissake, he sees me every day."

"He still doesn't know. 'Is he trying to ruin his career?' he asked."

"I'm trying my level best—"

"He doesn't think so. He said at first he thought you were just going through the motions, mumbling your lines, feeling your way and biding your time. A lot of old-timers do that, he said. But now he's beginning to suspect you have some self-destructive wish to ruin yourself and sink the production. 'There isn't a rehearsal,' he said, 'that doesn't end with him frantically rushing off somewhere before I'm through with my notes or getting mysterious phone calls or distracting visits.' Adam doesn't know what's going on. He asked me what I knew."

"What did you say?"

" 'I don't know anything about him,' I said."

"O.K."

"What does that mean?"

"It means he's right, I don't give a shit about him or his play. All he's got to do is ask for my resignation. He'll get it."

"I may not be here when you get back this afternoon," she said. "If I can get a plane, we'll go down this afternoon."

"Why are you looking at me that way?"

"I'm waiting for you to say something."

"Like?"

"Like please don't go."

I didn't say anything, that or anything.

"It's that trip to Africa," she said. "Ever since you came back you've behaved completely irrationally."

"You used to say I was too controlled, remember?"

"You misunderstood that. I liked how you were. You weren't like every other jerky actor. But now something is controlling you. I don't know what. That's what I told Adam."

"I wish you wouldn't talk about me to other people."

" 'Something's gone wrong with him,' I said. 'It's not only the production. He seems determined to break up his marriage and his home. He lies to the police, such obvious and pathetic lies, protecting I don't know what or whom. So I'm not surprised when you tell me he's out to ruin his—' "

"Oh, come on, Ellie."

"And all because of some insane concern for—this I didn't say to him—a selfish, arrogant, vicious old man who doesn't give a damn about you or your life."

"Look, Ellie, what I don't need this morning is to be bawled out."

"I'll be gone soon. You won't have to take any more of it ever. But now I want to say this, O.K., just this."

"O.K., just this."

"You're helping to conceal a criminal. You're behaving like a lousy citizen. You are a terrible husband. You don't protect me, and you don't protect my son. You don't even protect your home. You are insulting, according to Adam, to the people you work with—"

"For chrissake, Ellie, you've read the play I'm in. You don't expect me to take it seriously, do you? When I can't believe a word of it? The whole profession I'm in is contemptible. It's nothing for a grown man to spend his life doing."

"Then why don't you get out of it?"

"And the police! They want to make everyone an informer, including me."

"How else can they catch these murderers? They didn't force Frank Scott. You heard what those detectives said, Scott came to them with his electronic scheme. Be fair. Be honest."

She was crying, so I laid off.

"And why are you against me?" she said. "What bad have I ever done you?"

"Oh, Ellie, come on, I'm not against you."

"You are. I don't know what you're thinking. You never say anything. I don't know whom you're with. Where the hell were you last night? Rehearsal was over at eleven. You came home after two."

I couldn't say I was with Sidney. She'd tell the detectives for sure.

"Who were you with? Tell me, whom are you seeing, whom are you—?"

"It's none of your business. I resent being questioned this way."

"None of my business! You goddamn son of a bitch."

She began to hit me with all her might, my unprotected face with her fists, landing on my nose bone, which rang with pain.

Suddenly I had enough. I walloped her across the mouth, and she stopped.

Blood flowed from between her teeth.

She touched the place, looked at the blood on her fingers.

Then she got up and left the room. Ten minutes later I heard her leaving the house with Arthur.

I lay in bed. I really didn't care what the end would be, let come what may. Having decided that, I fell asleep.

One of the phony phone calls woke me. Someone on the other end listened to my "Hello, hello," then hung up.

I wanted to walk to work, but for no reason I could tell I had the feeling I was being followed, so I took a cab.

Outside the theater, Polly was waiting.

"Well, how is he today?" I asked.

"He called me, said he wants you to do something for him, immediately."

"What now?"

"He would like the backstage dimensions of the Phyllis Anderson Theatre"—Polly was changed some way—"and he'd like them as soon as—"

"Polly, I'm in rehearsal. We're having run-throughs."

"This is important," she went on. "He wants precise measurements of"—she took out a slip of paper—"the width, the depth, the height of the stage, the dimensions of the forestage, the nature of the access to the auditorium. Here." She gave me the list.

Polly had taken on Sidney's imperious tone, and from her I didn't need it. "Let Prince do it," I said.

"Mr. Prince," she said with baronial asperity, "has become pretty arrogant since meeting Mr. Kasko. Mr. Prince has to be taught a lesson. For the moment, Sidney is not talking to Mr. Prince."

"I can't go down to Second Avenue today. I'll try to get the information from—"

"Not information. Sidney wants a scale drawing. I'll be here tomorrow at this same time, and you can give it to me then, O.K.?"

I didn't bother to answer.

She took that for obedience, signaled an old green Chevy waiting down the street, and it hustled up. Polly turned to me with a triumphant smile. "You know that boy I told you about? I got him."

The side door of the green Chevy was thrown open and leaning forward for Polly was the good-looking young man with the trim-cut red hair.

Inside the theater, Adam was waiting for me with a show of affection. He had perseverance, that kid, one day's supply. It ran out by the end of each day's rehearsal, but by morning it had filled up again.

"I understand you talked to my wife," I said.

"Oh, yes, she's an extraordinary woman, beautiful."

"How do you know she's so goddamn beautiful from talking to her on the phone?"

"I'm referring to her soul," Adam said. "Clasp that woman to you with hoops of steel," he said. Such pompous garbage! Shakespeare excuses all! "Because she really loves you," he said.

A new thought. But it hung in there all through that morning's rehearsal. In the lunch break, I decided to go home and say goodbye in case they'd been able to get an afternoon plane.

Our place had been burglarized.

Everything had been thrown on the floor, the contents of every drawer, the books off the shelves, the records from their stacks, the spices, cereals, condiments in the kitchen, all on the floor.

In the middle of chaos sat Ellie. She looked up at me when I came in—the front door had been left open—then looked down. She'd given up trying to preserve privacy or ownership. Her knees were apart in the final gesture of female surrender.

My bureau drawer had been turned upside down, and my good watch, my cuff links, studs, handkerchiefs, were all over the place. I stooped to pick up the gold links Ellie had given me on our fifth anniversary.

"Don't touch that," she said. "Don't touch anything."

"Why not?"

"The police will be here in a minute. They said don't touch anything."

"Why didn't you call me?"

"What for?"

"I could have—"

"What?"

I didn't have an answer.

We waited for the police in silence.

My suits, my Sunday suits, were in wrangles and tangles.

The only object which had survived the storm without a scratch or a stain was Arthur's piano.

"What did they get?" I asked.

"As far as I can tell, absolutely nothing."

"Then what the hell was all this for?"

"I don't care anymore. I'm not even going to lock the door when I go. Anybody can have anything—"

There was a knock on the door. The locksmith pushed his way in, I wish I could say apologetically, but I can't.

"I told you that lock was no good," he said.

Neither Ellie nor I answered. He examined the lock.

"There's one thing you can do for me," Ellie said.

"What?"

Suddenly she screamed at the locksmith. "Don't touch that god-damn lock."

"They picked it," he said. Then, "You don't have to yell at me that way, lady, that wasn't called for."

"There is one thing," Ellie said to me, "that you can—"

"I mean, why take it out on me? I don't have to take that from you."

"Will you try," Ellie said, ignoring the locksmith, "to get Arthur and me on a plane tonight? I don't want to spend another night of my life in this place or in this city."

"Didn't you get a reservation—?"

"I don't like people yelling at me, even when they got a good reason," the locksmith said.

"I got a reservation, but it's for tomorrow."

"When does Arthur get out of school?"

"Usually at three. I wouldn't have let him go there, but I thought it was the safest place for him, and I was right."

"They're here," the locksmith said. The arrival of the police calmed him down.

If Boruff and Bird felt any surprise at what they saw, they didn't show it. They walked around and around slowly, not touching anything.

The phone rang. It was Sol Bender.

"We're waiting for you," he said. "You're half an hour late for rehearsal!"

"I'm not coming to rehearsal," I said.

"Come on, cut it out. What's the matter?"

I caught a signal from Detective Boruff, a wave of his finger, instructing me not to say anything about the robbery.

"Because I don't feel like it," I said and hung up.

"Well, what do you know?" Boruff said. It was not an expression of astonishment.

"Who, me? What do I know?"

"What were they looking for?"

"How should I know?" I said.

Boruff made a gruff sound. What I'd thought of as a friendly casualness at our first meeting was a mask. It had dropped off.

He turned to Ellie. "When did this happen?" he asked.

"I took Arthur to school myself, so he'd arrive there without having his throat cut. Then I went to Eastern Airlines. Then I got back, and here it was. This!" She swept her arm around.

"When did you leave the house?" Detective Boruff asked me.

"Half an hour after she'd gone. About nine."

"Your rehearsals are starting pretty early now, aren't they?" Bird said from where he was toeing some of the stuff on the floor.

"What do you think, I robbed my own house?"

"Stranger things have happened," Bird said, looking at the shelves, which were clean.

"What did you do between nine and when rehearsals started—?"

"I had two cups of coffee and two sugar doughnuts at Chock Full o' Nuts. I read the *News*. I read the *Times*. I went to the theater, to my dressing room and so on."

I left out my encounter with Polly.

"What did they take?" Bird said.

"Nothing," Boruff said.

"How do you know they took nothing?" I asked.

Boruff turned to the locksmith.

"Don't look at me," the locksmith said. "I told them it was a cheap lock. You were here."

"If forty dollars buys a lock anybody can pick, what do you have to pay for a good lock?" I asked.

"They come all prices. You want me to change it again?" he turned to Ellie.

"I'm not living here anymore," she said.

"You can go now," Boruff said.

"Take my advice next time." The locksmith left.

Boruff sat down, close to me. "We've learned a lot more about that party since we spoke to you last," he began. "We've questioned some of the girls who were there. One of them told us there was a short, violent scene between one of Bernie's buffaloes and Frank Scott, you remember that?"

"No," I lied.

"Look," Boruff said, and his patience was going. It was very thin now. "I don't have to be a genius to read this scene. Somebody believes you have something that they want badly enough to take a chance like this. Now tell us what it is."

"I don't know," I said.

Bird was fed up with me. "For chrissake, mister, who you protecting?" he said.

Boruff gave him a sign, and Bird stopped.

"My partner," he half apologized, "is getting understandably impatient. Let me say this to you. You don't know it, but you're at a crossroads of your life. I mean exactly that. If you persist in not telling us what you obviously—"

"What do you mean, obviously?"

"This is our trade. We can read you, sir, so I mean obviously. They turned your place upside down not for a few bucks or a TV they could quick-hock for drugs. These were not addicts you had here. They were looking for something. They have reason to believe you have it, and I believe you have it."

"Are you calling me a liar?"

"Yes, sir."

"Well, I'll be—"

"And if you don't decide to cooperate with us—"

"If I don't become a stoolie—"

"Make your own choice of words. What I say is, if you don't come forward to help us, we have ways of making you talk, and we will use them. The government of this country has the right to the true testimony of every one of its citizens. If you refuse to testify when we bring you before the grand jury, one of two things will happen. You will either be brought down in contempt, or you will be offered immunity, which you will have to take when it's—"

"Then it's not being offered, is it? If I have to take it?"

"Come to your senses, man, before something terrible happens. You're a target—look around you—for some reason that only you know and—"

"That's all speculation."

Boruff gave up.

"You are threatening me and I don't have to take that. I know my rights."

Bird came on. "Something much worse can happen, mister, I'm warning you."

"They want what you have very badly," Boruff said.

I didn't know what to say.

"Well?" Boruff asked.

"I'll tell you," I said. "I'm going downtown and resign from that play, and as soon as they can get another leading man, I'm going to Florida with my wife."

Ellie didn't look happy about my decision to join her in Florida.

"O.K., Ellie?" I said.

"Do what's best for you," she said.

"I'll be back as soon as I can make arrangements with Sol Bender. I'm sure Mr. Bender'll be glad to get rid of me. Then, Ellie, I'll do what you asked. I'll try to get you on a plane this evening. I'll take you out to the airport."

"May I walk downstairs with you?" Boruff said.

"May I stop you?" I said.

"No, sir, you may not," Boruff said.

Boruff didn't say anything till we were on the sidewalk. Then he said, "There is one girl we haven't been able to find. She came to the party, we're told, with your friend, Mr. Schlossberg. Her name is Polly, and we want to talk to her. Whenever someone disappears in a case like this there's a reason. Do you know what it is?"

"No."

"The other girls think she lives with Mr. Schlossberg. Does she?"

"I wouldn't be surprised," I said. "The girls like the old man."

"That's all you know about that relationship?"

"That's all."

"We don't believe you," Boruff said. "In fact we know better." He turned and went back into the house.

The only person on stage was Sol Bender. The cast had been dismissed. Slouched in a seat in the last row of the orchestra was Adam Garshman, his head just visible above his knees.

'Thanks for waiting for me. Sol " I said.

"What thanks? What happened to you?"

"My house was burglarized."

"Your home was what? Did you hear that, Adam?"

"Please don't tell him. Don't tell anybody."

"What happened?" Adam came trotting down the aisle.

"Go back," I said harshly. "Go back where you were. I don't want to discuss this in front of him " I said to Bender.

"Let's go in that dressing room," he said.

I closed the door. "My wife's hysterical." I said. "She's going to Florida. I've decided to go with her.'

"For how long?"

"Ellie? She'll never come back."

"You, I mean you."

"I don't know."

"Go for a day. Set her up. Come back."

"I don't want to do that. I'm quitting, Sol."

Producers play kind old uncle, but they don't last beyond a

production or two if they don't carry a big concealed weapon. This might be threats, it might be fits of rage, it might be cries of agony. Whatever, it is always backed by a very tough lawyer.

"You can't quit," Sol said, turning his other face.

"I'm leaving tomorrow, Sol."

"Like hell you are! Don't ever talk to me that way, kiddo! This is a matter for you and me to settle together. We're in bed now, so don't talk that way to me. I've sold almost one hundred thousand dollars' worth of theater parties, and I've sold them because of you. Who ever heard of Adam Garshman? We both know what this play is, drek. But you I can sell! And did! And I got backers, friends of mine, and if you pull anything unethical on me, sweetheart, let me tell you I'll sic Mr. Manny Bloom right on your ass, and you'll never recover. However much money you got, I'll get it!"

"Do what you want, Sol."

"It's your wife, I know. You would never do this to me."

"No, it's not my wife—only basically."

"That's what I mean, basically, basically it's your wife. You wouldn't do this to the institution of the theater, shame yourself. Because if you do, you'll never play again."

"I don't care."

"It's your goddamn wife, excuse me."

"Sol, she doesn't even want me to go down there with her."

"She got somebody down there?"

"You mean a lover?"

"Why not? She's not a bad-looking head."

"Her father's down there."

"Sweetheart, let her go. In difficulties, always hold on to your profession. It will pull you through, take my advice."

"Generally I agree with you, Sol, but you've no idea, Jesus, the tension I've been under here. I'm not doing you or the play justice."

"Is it the boy, Adam? Because I can fire him quick as I can spit. He's right downstairs."

"Who? Adam? No."

"You know, I've been watching, and one thing Mr. Lee Strasberg never taught that little momser how to handle a star."

"I've begun to like him." I said in an explosion of tolerance. "I really have."

"He's got to go."

"Sol, it ain't him."

"He's out. I made up my mind. I knew all along you weren't

happy with that phony intellectual with his director's book and his hand-held tape recorder!"

"Sol, believe me—"

"You're too professional to say so, but I been watching. He hasn't been able to turn you on yet. Admit it! Of course, you can't say anything. You're a big man, and he's a mosquito." He laughed scornfully at himself. "What a fool I been. I'm waiting for you to take over the production, and he's looking in his book where he's got everything written down in red, green, and blue ink!"

"I like the kid, Sol. I really do."

"Stop being generous. I got one hundred thousand dollars here, and I'm going to have to ask another twenty overcall, and the theater is falling to pieces, and you're being generous? We all know you've been having difficulties with the smart guy. My wife Ida took one look, she saw it! Ask anybody in the cast. You don't think they come to Uncle Sol and tell him what's going on?"

"Just that one girl you're laying, Sol."

"Because I'm socializing with her, it means she don't tell me the truth? Listen. You're a big star. There ain't many left. This cast, this playwright, me, the whole shmeer, we're here for you. You're the only excuse for my existence. To make it possible for an audience to enjoy your talent. Let her go, your wife. What does she know about theater? I'll get you another girl. Name your preference."

"I don't want another girl, Sol."

"Well, now I have to say it. The truth. My friend, you're becoming, if you don't look out, a stuffed shirt. You used to be an artist, a person of spirit, sowing your seed here and there like a man. Now look at you."

"You're talking like Sidney Schlossberg."

"Don't put Sidney down. He was a great star in his time. I would be honored if I had a part for Sidney, even now, if he was in shape to play it. Because he loved the theater first. No personal-relationship shit with him! Why do you think you never became a real headliner? Forgive the truth."

"Because I'm not enough of a bastard."

"A woman says 'oy vey, I'm frightened,'" his voice pitched way up, "'I'm running home to daddy.' And what do you do? Run after her! Can you imagine Barrymore doing that? What's her father anyway, what kind of business?"

"Air Force, retired. A general."

"Oh my! So you don't think a general can protect her without your help? Your wife is taking the fun out of your life, my boy. You used to enjoy rehearsals. What happened to you?"

"Years ago I used to, but—"

"You look so worried all the time. What's the matter? You have the main thing. Talent! From God! But you won't have it forever. Now you got it. Enjoy it!"

He came to me with tears in his frog eyes, threw his arms around me and said, "I worship talent. Why? Because I have none. What I got is the privilege of helping talent. I live to serve. Just you. The others here, they have nothing. Adam? Zero! My designers? Disasters! The other actors? Please! Only you. You are my indispensable! My life is in your hands. Don't let me down. That's all I got to say."

"O.K., Sol," I said after a while, "I'll open your play."

"I never expected different," he said.

"I'll do it, and then we'll talk."

"Talk, of course! Because you are a fine professional, one of the last. A giant!"

"Just see if you can get Ellie and the kid on a plane tonight. She's hysterical."

"Sure, a woman, what do you expect?"

"Says she won't spend another night in that apartment."

"We'll get her a hotel room. Ida will stay with her."

"No, not a hotel room. Get a reservation on a plane to Sarasota, Florida, tonight. Will you do that, Sol?"

"I'll charter a plane if necessary. Your wife is leaving here tonight. You can count on it."

Suddenly he turned brisk. "Now come on," he said, "they're downstairs, waiting."

"Who?"

"The cast. They'll cheer when they see you. Leave the transportation to me. Sarasota, Marasota, you got it! Now rehearse. Be what you are. My leading man! Take the production over. Tell Adam to throw away his book where's he's got everything down in three colors. The audience is not going to pay ten dollars to read his book. As soon as I get your wife's ticket, go home, pack her up, take her to the airport, stuff her on the plane, kiss her goodbye, then, my dear friend, come back and go to work. O.K.?"

Everything went smoothly. Adam had expected to be fired. He knew it was in my power to do that. When I protected him, he was grateful. He began to like me. In fact, that afternoon there began what was to turn into hero worship. He laughed at some little comic improvisations of mine. That tinkle of appreciation did more for me than all his well-thought-out direction. I cut loose on a wave of what they call instinct. I don't know what it was, probably just a lot of ham, but the cast laughed and at one point old Sol, who was in the back of the house waiting for news on my transportation problem, and Adam and Adam's secretary all applauded something I did. In the wings the members of the cast waiting for their entrances were murmuring comments to each other and laughing, too. They were surprised, I guess, and relieved. The star of the show had come to life.

I forgot all about Ellie waiting at home.

At one point, pantomiming a pistol, I pulled the little reel of tape out of my pocket and holding it in my pistol grip, I realized what it was and burst into laughter, then whirled in place, landing with a hop, during which maneuver the reel had disappeared back into my pocket. I know it doesn't sound funny, but it brought the house down—the house, three people, but still.

It was then I decided, not till then, that I would not go to Florida with Ellie. In the midst of that thin laughter I decided I could really do a job on that play, I could be great in it. Maybe now, finally now, I could be a real star, not an actor, a star. That's what I wanted to be, what Sol called indispensable.

No one noticed Detective Boruff coming in from the stage door because they were busy looking at Sol Bender running down the aisle waving something white over his head, airplane tickets, and shouting, "I got the sons of bitches, I got them!"

As he climbed up the steps from the orchestra aisle to the stage, Boruff came up behind me and whispered, "You better go home now."

"What happened?" I asked.

Everyone was still. How did they know he was a cop?

"He didn't come home from school, your son."

"What time is it?"

"Five fifteen."

"He should have been home by—my wife?"

"She was on the curb, waiting for the school bus. She checked with the driver. He said he thought the boy got on the bus, but he wasn't sure. He's such a quiet kid, not like the others."

Little Arthur was almost three hours late now.

We left Boruff in the house while Bird, Ellie, and I went looking. Nothing. Back home we called all his friends. Nothing. Eight o'clock.

The two detectives went home. Ellie and I were left with each other.

Does disaster bring people closer? I didn't think so.

We kept the radio on to the news, WINS. Everything but.

Ellie fell asleep sitting up. I watched her. I liked her. Yes, Florida, I thought, she would live in peace in Florida.

I fell asleep sitting up.

I woke up terribly frightened. I hadn't really realized what was happening.

"I'm going out to look again," I told Ellie and left.

On Columbus Avenue, the Puerto Ricans were out. A sign of spring. They were so fucking jolly as they quarreled. What kind of people were these? Where had they come from suddenly? Why couldn't they live properly like the rest of us? They had no control. I decided I liked Ellie, how she ran our house, neat and orderly. These little brown cap pistols were always shooting off, quarreling and drinking, yelling and pounding each other. They irritated me. The blacks too. Violence is so natural to them. A new kind of creature was loose in the city. Death and killings were incidental to them. I wondered if Bernie had fucked that girl from Bennington to the music of Chopin's piano concerto while Frank was being killed?

And where was Little Arthur?

Ellie was on the phone. "No, Wilhelmina, nothing like that. We're moving to Florida. Yes, for good. Well, I'll certainly miss you, too. I'm sorry, too. And do keep up your lessons, won't you? You'll be glad you did later in your life. Goodbye, dear."

"Anything on the news?" I asked.

She shook her head. Later she gave me tuna fish and pickled beets. I ate a box of raisins.

Then it was nine thirty. Ellie lay down to sleep with her clothes on.

At a few minutes before ten, Little Arthur came home.

"I got a puppy," he said over the intercom from downstairs. He sounded fine and very excited.

"It's a toy poodle," he said, coming out of the elevator. "That's the way they look before they're clipped. I like them this way better, don't you?"

"Who gave it to you, dear?" Ellie asked.

"Your friend," he said to me, "that heavy short guy, you know."

The moment I saw the pup, I'd remembered a conversation at the Plaza party. Bernie'd told me that the one thing he wanted most when he was a kid was a puppy. Finally he'd stolen one, and, as if in punishment, it had been run over by a truck. I'd said that a puppy was what my own kid wanted too, but his mother had pointed out, and I guess she was right, that the city was no place to raise a dog.

What was Bernie telling me now? He knew where Arthur was and—what else?

Ellie was packing with the speed of a quick-change artist. "You can't make it," I said. She would have to leave for the airport within twenty minutes to catch the midnight.

Little Arthur was on the floor. He'd arranged pillows in a corner for a bed and was stroking the puppy's chest.

"If you want a dog to love you forever," he said, "you scratch him right here. It's the only place they can't reach themselves, your friend told me. See, he likes it." He looked at me. "Thanks a lot," he said. "It's the best present I ever got."

"I didn't give it to you exactly."

"Yes you did. Your friend told me it was from you."

"Don't bother with that now, Arthur," Ellie said. "We're leaving in ten minutes."

"Where we going?"

"We're going to Florida to see your grandfather," Ellie said in her cheeriest voice.

Neither of us had asked any questions. We went on as if it was perfectly natural for a kid to disappear at three in the afternoon and reappear at ten at night holding an unshorn poodle.

"Come in here. I want to wash you," Ellie called. She'd finished packing.

While they were in the bathroom, I called Boruff and told him what had happened. "I'm coming right over," he said.

"We're leaving for the—"

"Never mind for where," he said quickly, "and don't make any other phone calls. I don't think your line is tapped, but you never know. If someone knocks on your door, don't open it. I'll call from downstairs first."

"We're leaving in ten—"

"I got a car. I'll ride you out."

"Come in here," Ellie called me. I could tell she was making an extra effort to keep her voice calm. I hung up and ran to the bathroom.

She'd rolled down the boy's collar to soap his face with a washrag.

Across Little Arthur's neck was a heavy red line made by a Magic Marker.

It was jagged, and it was thick, and it was the rest of Bernie's message.

"Where did you get that?" I asked the kid, keeping my voice playful, I hoped, and unconcerned.

"Oh, we were playing around with some Magic Markers and stuff. We had a lot of fun."

"Who?" Ellie said as she scrubbed the mark away. "Who and you had a lot of fun?"

"The man he told to get me Beanbag," he winked at me. "That's the name of the dog."

Ellie glared at me.

"Did you have any supper?" Ellie asked, rinsing the washrag.

"Oh, yeah. From McDonald's! They got me everything. Gee, I like those men, Charlie whazisname and the fat one who keeps starting to smoke, then doesn't. Why? Were you worried about me? I told them to call you. Didn't they call you?"

"Did you give them our number, baby?" Ellie asked in her calming voice.

"Yes, I gave it to them. Didn't they call?"

"Oh, yes, sure, they called," Ellie said. "Now you see if you can make a movement, dear, because we're going to be on the plane for almost three hours."

She ran out of the bathroom, pushing me out ahead of her.

"He's drugged," she said. "They drugged him."

"Detective Boruff is coming," I said. "He's going to drive us out to the airport."

She changed her clothes and finished Little Arthur's packing. She was only taking two small bags. "I don't want anything they touched," she said.

All the way out she didn't talk to me. Before she got on the plane, she scribbled her father's phone number on a slip of paper. "He expected us to come down tomorrow," she said, "and land in Sarasota. Call him and tell him to pick us up in Tampa."

"Suppose he's not home?"

"Daddy goes to bed every night at nine o'clock," she said.

She didn't say goodbye to me.

Little Arthur kissed me, the first time ever. He had the "toy" in a flight bag. He was on top of the world.

"Come down quick," he said.

"Soon as the play is over," I promised.

Boruff had disappeared. As the flight's gates closed, he appeared again. "I think I'll take you to a hotel," he said.

"I'd prefer that."

He left me in the car parked before the Edison Hotel while he went in and registered for me in his name. Then he came out and took me upstairs. We ordered a couple of drinks and sat and stared at each other. He was waiting for me.

"O.K.," I said. "I'm going to do it."

I gave him the reel. He didn't seem a bit surprised.

"I'll come back in the morning," he said. "Don't go out. I'll bring you breakfast and what clothes you'll need. Make a list. Give me your key. Tomorrow I'll walk you to rehearsal. O.K.? I mean about not going out?"

"O.K."

"And don't make any phone calls. We'll call your wife's father. I looked around the airport while you and your wife were saying goodbye. I'm pretty sure no one followed us. So they won't know where she went or where the kid is. But for you there's an element of danger. You know that?"

"I'll be goddamned if I'm going to be intimidated."

"I'm glad you said it. It's what I thought you'd say, sooner or later. That's why I stuck with you."

"Did you know I had that reel of magnetic tape all the time?"

"Everybody knew it. Bernie Kasko knew it, I knew it, my partner knew it. Who else would have it?"

"Why the hell didn't you make me give it up?"

"I wanted you to. You see we need more than that reel. We need your cooperation now."

"Cooperation," I said, "that's a euphemism for informing, am I right?"

"What's a euphemism?"

"A nice way of putting a bad thing."

"It's not a bad thing," he said. "You got to remember that."

I went to bed to hide. An hour later, I was in a nightmare.

Little Arthur had fallen off the subway platform in front of a rushing train. Or had he been pushed? I was scrambling in the rush of people trying to find out who'd pushed him. Sirens sounded from every side. Ellie was there, blaming me. There was an intense light on the tracks, and they were all into his body, tooth, claw, and beak, devouring him. "Don't interfere," Jim Piper commanded. "Let nature take its course." I jumped out of the Toyota and began to pull the filthy scavengers off the boy's body.

Then I woke. I still heard sirens. Broadway was half a block away. It was very late. My sheets were soaked in sweat. I turned them back to dry, then took a shower as hot as I could stand it.

How was I to get through the night? The TV. A western, everybody killing everybody, its violence seemed so innocuous. Over to Jolly Johnny, his guest, an author peddling his ass. I watched the one o'clock news, scandals, corruption, crime, all a matter of course. That's the way we were living now. An English murder mystery, crap's better in an English accent. Finally an old-time musical. How innocent the forties were! I fell asleep, immediately woke. I was hungry, or maybe I wasn't, but food would certainly be a comfort. I decided to go out. Why should I hide? I decided against it. What about going down to the lobby and picking up the morning papers? No, I'd ask the bell captain to send them up. But when he asked me what my room number was, I hung up. I sat at the window, waited for the light. There I fell asleep.

At eight thirty, Boruff came with coffee and cake. He asked me how I'd slept. I told him I hadn't. He didn't seem surprised.

"We'll get you some pills tonight," he said.

"I don't take pills."

"Mild ones. By the way, the tape's O.K. It'll be very useful."

"I'm worried about the kid and my wife."

"I don't think anybody knows where they—"

" 'I don't think!' That's not very reassuring! I'd like them watched over. Will you arrange that?"

"Florida is not in our jurisdiction."

"Well, what about the FBI? Somebody!"

"The FBI can't do anything till there's a crime committed."

"Isn't that a little late? Goddamn it, somebody's got to watch over them before a crime's committed. What about the Florida police?"

"I'll call them if you want."

"What do you mean, if I want? Of course I want. Englewood, that's the town where they shop. The police would be there too, Englewood, Florida. Use that phone."

"There is another consideration."

"I don't care about any other—"

"That you'll call attention to them that way. It'll get around, quick."

"Well, what the hell can I do, Boruff? You got me into this."

"Wait a minute. You got yourself into this."

"Tell me what to do."

"Ask them to stay inside the house, then you move as fast as you can to help us here."

"How?"

"What we want is to put your friend, Mr. Schlossberg, before the grand jury. They're sitting now and—"

"I'm talking about today, Boruff, this morning, this afternoon, tonight. Oh, hell, I'll hire somebody myself."

"I really do think you're getting much too worked up about this. I'm almost certain no one has the least knowledge where your wife and kid are."

"How certain is almost? Tell me the truth."

"As certain as I can be of anything. I'm sure. O.K.? Now, listen, please. According to that tape, Mr. Schlossberg was in room 1708 all through the last conversation Frank Scott had with Bernie Kasko. That's his voice on the tape, Mr. Schlossberg's, isn't it?"

"I didn't hear the tape, but he was in the room."

"He keeps butting in, praising Bernie Kasko, sort of sucking up to him?"

"He was promoting Kasko."

"So I gathered. What we want is for Mr. Schlossberg to appear before the grand jury and identify the voices. Then I think we'd have enough to call Bernie Kasko before the same grand jury. Once we do that, play him the tapes, he'll either deny that's his voice, or he'll take the Fifth. Either way, we'll have what we need to get an indictment."

"Then why don't you pick Kasko up now? He lives in Jersey somewhere."

"We know where, but he's not there."

"Where is he?"

"We want Mr. Schlossberg to tell us where he is," Boruff said.

"He won't do that, for every reason."

"But if we could get him to lead us to—"

Desperation stimulates the mind. It was at this moment my scheme was born. I told it to Boruff, and he liked it. Talk about cooperation, I was leading!

At the theater, Polly was waiting.

"Come inside," I said. Boruff had told me not to stand in one place on the sidewalk. He was across the street now. I caught his eye as the stage door closed.

"I didn't have time to go down to the Anderson," I told Polly, "but I did manage to arrange to have the theater opened at ten thirty tonight. Tell Sidney I'll meet him there. We can pace off the measurements—"

"Why didn't you do it the way he wanted?"

"I didn't have time."

"You mean you have time for shit like this—" she indicated the stage with a gesture like Sidney.

"Polly, you are not an old man whom I owe something. You're just a wise-ass kid, so don't give me any lip. Now here"—I gave her a slip of paper—"I'll meet him at the Figaro East, which is at Seventh Street and Second. The Anderson is a couple of blocks down. You tell Sidney it's tonight or never, if he wants to see that theater."

"He's going to England tomorrow early. He's got to get ready, you know him."

"Fine," I said, concealing my surprise. "Tell him I hope he has a good trip. Maybe I'll see him when he gets back."

I walked away from her. She ran after me and took my arm.

"Wait a minute, don't get so huffy," Polly said. "What's the matter with you anyway?"

"What's the matter with *you?*"

"I'll try to get him to do what you say."

"Don't do me any favors," I said. "I've got to go to work now."

"Why are you so angry with me all of a sudden? Gee whiz, are you ever temperamental!"

There is nothing like arrogance to restore humility. "You're a nice kid, Polly," I said, "so don't turn bitch. Now you get that old man there at ten thirty if he wants any help from me, and if he's not going to be there, let me know so I don't—who the hell do you think you are anyway?"

She smiled at me and touched my arm. "He'll be there," she said. "O.K.?" Suddenly she was finding me attractive!

"Where's he staying, by the way?"

"I don't know. Mr. Kasko's orders. They drive him around. He calls me at home."

Ten thirty on the dot, I was sitting in the Figaro East. If anyone was watching me or watching over me, I couldn't tell. How many times people are observed these days without their knowing it!

Sidney didn't show, Polly didn't show, who did was the good-looking young man with the trim red hair, Polly's new boy friend. He didn't accept my offer of a drink.

"He's down there waiting," he said. "I think there's something the matter with that old man."

"What?"

"He keeps breathing with his mouth open, like it's an effort for him to draw in air and expel it."

The green Chevy was parked on Fourth Street at the side of the Phyllis Anderson, near the stage door. The street was deserted except for some men drinking out of bottles in brown paper bags. They sat along the side of the theater and on the stoop of the fire escape, drinking, laughing, and quarreling.

Boruff had arranged for a doorman. Now that I knew the score, he was obviously a cop in plainclothes. There were a couple of other such, seated around the back of the stage house, dressed in old clothes.

Sidney was extra glad to see me.

"She's taken up with Standard Brand," he said, pointing to Polly and her boy friend. "Look at him, an accountant. She prefers him to me. Imagine!"

It occurred to me then that Polly's new lover was a detective, too—a guess which turned out to be correct. Christ, this city was full of cops in every disguise, even lovers, that disguise.

Sidney walked me around the stage the way he used to long ago, in step, with his arm around me. "Now Bernie wants to try it out in London first," he said. "I don't think that's a good idea. What do you think?"

"This is the first time you've ever asked my advice, Sidney. I'm flattered."

"I've thought everything over, I'm referring to your lapses, and I've come to the conclusion that you are, after all is said and done, the most enduring friend and even the most trustworthy friend I have. Not saying a hell of a lot, but still! O.K.? Enough of that."

"Enough of that," I said.

"So what do you think?"

"I thought you were going into the hospital?"

"I have to, yes. You hear my voice?"

"It sounds O.K."

"Let's pace off the width first."

"Are you all right otherwise?" I asked.

We were walking across the stage together taking yard-long steps, fourteen of them.

"Now times three," I said. "Forty-two width," I called to Polly, who wrote it down.

"I'm, well, that soreness in my throat, it's beginning to affect me," Sidney said. "I get pains in other places, nothing to worry about. It's the poison going through my system."

"Well, you better have it checked," I said.

"God, how can she stand him?" he asked.

"Who?"

"That boy. Now he looks like a cop."

We had walked from the footlights to the back wall.

"Twenty-seven, make it eight," I called to Polly.

"Let's guess the width of the orchestra pit and how deep it is," Sidney said. "It's a great entrance for Neptune. You see, about these other pains I have, I take pills to quiet them, but then I've been doing that for over a year—"

"Your belly seems—somewhat bigger," I said.

"Gas!" he said, and belched. Sidney used to make a joke of belching on cue.

"Standard Brand," he called out. "get me a glass of water.'

"Please don't call me that anymore, Polly's boy friend said.

"Will you forgive me if I do call you that?"

"Yes," the boy said, "I'll have to."

"That's the most insulting thing of all," Sidney said. "Now he's forgiving me!"

We laughed together.

"Have you pocket money?" I asked Sidney.

"Oh, yes, Bernie is a very good paramour. He gives."

"I'd guess that orchestra pit to be nine feet across and maybe twelve feet deep."

Sidney tried his voice and the acoustics. "Naaiiinnnhhh!" he reverberated, "naaaiiiiinnnhhhh!"

"Nine what?" Standard Brand asked.

"Across," I said, "and twelve deep."

"See, that hurt, when I said that, 'nine,' that way, it hurt," Sidney said.

"Where, where did it hurt?"

"In my throat, the locus of my cords is in my throat, damn fool!"

"And in your belly?"

"Sympathetic, they call that, sympathetic pains. I've got to sit."

He sat on a backless chair and stared into the dark house. Then he reached out his hand, and I put mine in his, and he squeezed it.

"Thanks," he said.

"For what?"

"For taking my shit all these years."

"I've enjoyed every minute of it, Sidney."

"Bullshit!" he said, "bullllllshit! However, gladly accepted."

"About England," I said, "I guess you've got to follow that old show business rule."

"Go with the money?"

"That's what they always say."

"Not me! I have other sources of funds," he said, "though for the moment I can't recall what they are." He burst into obscene laughter.

Polly and her friend were not watching, she waiting for the next dimension, he gone for the water.

Gingerly Sidney moved to the footlights. He lifted one foot, like a cat, and placed it on the old tin lip. Then he thrust his head into the black of the dark, empty house. I heard the word *whore,* said with affection, for he still found the old cunt attractive.

Then he turned the side of his body to the footlights and began to strut, a flirtation in tight little steps across the front of the stage. His hands were in the side pockets of his suit up to where the thumbs were joined. The curved handle of his cane was hooked into one pocket and swung freely.

He was cakewalking, his hat's brim pulled low, his shoulders hunched, his knees rubbing together, each step smaller and tighter than the one before. I heard the words, sung for those who were not there and for himself,

> *Kiss me, Tootsie, and then*
> *Kiss me over again.*
> *Watch for the mail*
> *I'll never fail.*
> *If you don't get a letter*
> *Then you know I'm in jail.*

He broke off, faced the black void, and spit into it.

"Whore!" he said, this time unforgiving.

He lifted his head, and in his great rumbling voice he sang the corniest of the Jew-blues, that song whose only words are "Roumania, Roumania!" Up and down the threadbare configuration of the old tune he pushed that one word of longing, "Roumania."

Then with his head down, his arms parted, his palms out, he stood before the void and waited its judgment.

Polly and her friend applauded.

Sidney turned to them. "What?" he said. "I don't want applause from you. You have no taste."

They laughed. The red-headed lover-cop came up with a glass of water.

"Why are you laughing? Are you impervious to insult?"

"I can't get angry at you, Mr. Schlossberg," the cop said. "I respect you too much."

"Spare me your respect," Sidney said. "Go down and pace that aisle. Give me the exact distance from the edge of the orchestra pit to the last row of the auditorium so I will know how much that throw will tax my voice."

The young cop, all eagerness to please, jumped over the nine-foot orchestra pit into the unlit aisle, almost fell.

"Damn fool," Sidney said.

Then he put his arm around me and walked me into the back corner. "I have to tell you something," he said when he had me in the dark.

I was shaking, my throat was dry.

"When you hear that I have not wakened from a sleep, I want you to know that I've left everything I have to you. I'm not talking about money or real property. You know I have nothing. I am talking about the twelve productions I have, all laid out, ready to go! I'm talking about my notes and scripts and projects. These are my gift to you. I want you—this is my last wish—to have them, and I want you to do them. All! They will give you a dignity and a size you have not yet attained and which you will need for your final self-respect. Here, written in longhand," he gave me an envelope taken from the Hotel Plaza, "is my last will and testament. I have not always agreed with you, I have not always liked you, I have rarely respected you, but of a poor lot, I must say in the summing up, you're the best, and I have always relied on your loyalty."

"Thank you," I said.

We parted with an embrace. He kissed me on the cheek, and his breath was sour.

I got a cab almost immediately because Boruff was in it, waiting for me.

"Well done," he said.

"Were you there?"

"In the balcony. I watched the whole thing."

"You will be good to him, careful, gentle, respectful of his feelings?"

"We will be all those things. We will follow him to where he's staying, take him, and take Bernie. I got Mr. Schlossberg a room in the Plaza. Bernie we will have to detain under guard. They will both testify the day after tomorrow."

Up early the next morning, I continued working hard, alone in my room at the Edison. With Ellie not there, my concentration was better. The room without memories helped. I forced myself to think of nothing but the play. Later at rehearsal I found myself becoming more and more deeply involved. Working hard helped me forget what I'd done.

With the director, Adam, in his proper place, that is, subservient, I began to invent little comic set pieces, shticks, bits and turns, twenty seconds with an old watch, twenty mistying a tie, an instant where my foot falls asleep. I suddenly had the wholehearted admiration of the cast, of Adam, above all, of Sol Bender.

He called Ida in to admire me. She brought me some of her chicken soup with matzoh balls.

When I got back to my room that night, I had the bellboy heat it. A quiet evening ahead, the first for a hell of a time.

In the middle of my meal, Boruff opened the door with his key.

"We want you to go before the grand jury tomorrow," he said.

"I don't want to do that."

"I'm afraid you have no choice. We need your testimony. No one will know you were there. No one will know what you said. I promise you that. Those sessions are absolutely secret."

I couldn't finish Ida's soup.

"You feel bad, eh?"

"How's Sidney?"

"Very p.o.'d. But I believe he's enjoying the drama of it all. He likes that hotel—and room service. He's running up one hell of a bill."

"Has he any idea that I—?"

"No. You may run into him in the anteroom but only as one victim of our system of justice to another."

"And Bernie?"

"He got away. He's in England. In fact, I think he left the same night your wife did. Don't feel bad."

"I do."

"You should feel proud, and sometime later, you will. Please believe me. No one knows what you did. I will try, we will all try, to build the case so you won't have to testify in court, only before the grand jury, where it is absolutely secret."

"You will try to build what—?"

"So you won't have to testify in open court."

"What if you can't?"

"We'll cross that bridge when we—"

"Then I may have to testify in court?"

"That's a chance you always took."

"Why don't you go now?" I said. I was furious.

"I'm sorry you're angry at me," Boruff said, "but it was you who threw that party for a man who ordered two people killed. There was no way ever that you could finally have avoided testifying in court. You should know that."

Before going down to Foley Square the next morning, I went by the theater to leave a note for the stage manager.

At the stage door, Polly was waiting for me. She spit in my face.

When I entered the grand jury room, I saw why I'd been kept waiting for almost an hour. The room had been rigged so each juror had a headset with cushioned earphones at his seat. At the side of the table where the foreman of the jury and the assistant district attorney sat and where I was seated, there had been placed professional play-back equipment. The jury had twice run the tape Frank Scott had made. Now they expected me to identify the voices.

It was well past ten o'clock when I was finally seated. Sidney was due at eleven. Whatever else I thought during the replay of that tape, some bits several times over, I was simultaneously trying to figure out how I would confront Sidney.

The jurors were ordinary citizens, in their middle or late years. "They have nothing better to do," is how Boruff described them. Most of the men had long since left regular employment.

"You realize," I said to them, "that I wasn't in the room at the time this tape was made. It's as new to me as it is to you. If I try to identify any of the voices, I'll be guessing."

The assistant district attorney answered for them. "You've heard Mr. Kasko's voice, haven't you? And Mr. Frank Scott's. Make the best identification you can."

They ran the tape again.

I was amazed how ruthless Bernie was with Frank. He was not making a deal. He was telling Frank how it was going to be. Bernie saw himself as eventually dominating all policy traffic on the island of Manhattan. Talk about control! And arrogance!

After a couple of minutes I was identifying the voices without hesitation or apology. It was the way Bernie spoke that made me do this. He was so certain of the rights he was usurping, so confident of the terror he was threatening, this music lover!

The tape was played, stop and go, for over an hour. Then the assistant district attorney asked questions.

"Are you familiar with a black attaché case that belonged to Frank Scott?"

"Very well," I said. "Scott always carried that black case."

Boruff, seated next to me, showed no surprise at this turnabout in my testimony.

"When did he leave the hotel?"

"A few minutes before eight."

"How do you know the time so precisely?"

"I left with him."

"You went down in the same elevator?"

"Yes."

"And did he have his black attaché case when he left?"

"He did."

"Is it true you returned to the party after your rehearsal was over?"

"That is correct."

"And did you see the black attaché case in the room at that time?"

"Yes."

"Who had it?"

"Mr. Kasko. He was ripping out its lining with a knife. You'll get much more on that from Mr. Schlossberg. I understand he's your next witness."

Now a certain casualness was permitted. Jurors were allowed to question me directly. They'd speak to their foreman in my hearing, and with a look he'd direct me to answer their questions.

I elaborated every aspect. I had the urge to spill. I told them about my wife's fear on the streets, her brutal mugging. I showed which of her fingers had been in splints. I told how I got back the contents of her wallet, the truth this time. "Except the money," Boruff reminded me. I told how my place had been robbed and of my wife's inner collapse which followed, how she wouldn't even put anything back on the shelves before she left the city. Finally I told the story of the disappearance of my son and his return with the puppy, how I'd remembered the conversation I'd had with Bernie, so knew immediately who'd taken the kid.

Then I picked up a pencil that was on the table and drew it across my neck where Arthur's had been marked red with a Magic Marker. As I did this, I felt a fury rising in me. I exhorted the grand jury in a way that is not permitted and was soon stopped by the assistant district attorney. But he wanted the grand jury to feel the force of my feelings, so immediately led me into more details of my story. I told the jury about my wife's decision to leave the city for good, to live in Florida. I described her fear at the airport. I guessed she was still living in fear, even now on Robbins Key off Florida's west coast in a house her father, an Air Force general, guarded. I said I'd directed her not to venture outside.

"These men have to be controlled," I said. "The city either belongs to them or it belongs to us."

Then I lost all control. *Now hear my Rave Act, Sidney!* I said to him in my heart. "May I tell you one more thing before I leave," I said to the jurors. "I am a peaceable man, a good-natured man. I'm known for my mildness. My wife kids me about how controlled I am. But since these events I am not the same person. I am telling you plainly that I intend to take the law into my own hands. I have my sidearm from the war in the Pacific, and I will carry it at all times. When I came here to testify I knew I was taking a chance with my life. But in a situation where it's his life or mine, it will not be mine. When I see him, and I expect to see him because I'll be looking for him, I will shoot him through the heart."

"I hope you don't mean that," the assistant district attorney said. But again he was secretly urging me on.

"I do," I promised, "because when it gets right down to it, I don't think you will do what you're supposed to fast enough. I believe you will leave me and my family in danger."

The assistant district attorney excused me, and I left.

In the little room where witnesses for the grand jury wait their turn, Sidney Schlossberg sat, fast asleep with his mouth open. In the chair across from him was a heavy man, dressed in a stylish suit with wide lapels and high vents. Around his jowl was a mod tie.

Sidney was sedated.

I sat next to him and put my hand on his shoulder. He didn't react, he was that far under. He needed a shave. The white stubble was well-sprouted out of the coarse skin of his face. His mouth, hanging open, revealed tobacco-stained teeth. I'd never noticed how small they were. How helpless Sidney seemed, how tragic, how alone, how defeated, a dying elder of my family, as familiar as my hand.

I guess that was the first moment of my life that I wasn't some way or other afraid of him. I could love him purely and without qualification.

I'd decided to tell him what I'd done. It was going to hurt him, and he'd hate me, but there was no way out of it for either of us.

I shook him gently. Then I shook him till he woke.

"Let him sleep, for God's sake," the heavy man in the wide-lapel suit said. "He hasn't been feeling too well."

"Who are you?"

"Bernie's lawyer," Sidney said. He looked at me, then he took my hand, which was still on his shoulder, moved it to his lips, and kissed it.

"How are you, Sidney?" I asked.

"I've been better," he said. "This gentleman's Michael Meier. He's taking care of me while Bernie's in England."

Sidney yawned, stretched, roused himself.

"Isn't this shameful, this inquisition?" he said. "Isn't it barbaric?"

"I don't think so," I said. "I think it's about time."

"They are trying to turn us into a race of informers."

Sidney, of course, hadn't heard me. He never heard anyone else's opinion.

"I've decided," he said, "to try out our play in England. They still have freedom there."

"Sidney—" I started. But I couldn't continue. The man's eyes were watering, his lips caked dry. He wasn't ready for anything like I was going to lay on him.

I turned to Michael Meier. "Have you a Magic Marker?" I asked.

"Who are you?" he asked. "And whoever you are, my friend, watch yourself."

He kept buttoning and unbuttoning his coat. He wore a heavy cologne.

"I am the parent of the boy across whose neck your client drew a thick red line with a Magic Marker," I said.

"Alleged line," Meier said. "Alleged Marker."

"I am the man who informed," I said, "just now, in there."

Then I looked at Sidney. He was getting the idea.

"I am the man who connived to trap his old friend and bring him before the grand jury and who is determined not to stop before your boss is either indicted or—"

I stopped and turned to Sidney. "I don't care about Bernie Kasko. I'm going to kill the son of a bitch next time I see him, but I care about you, Sidney. I only care about you."

"You've got one hell of a way to show it," Meier said.

"Stop your kidding," Sidney said. "I'm a little tired today."

"I'm not kidding. You're here because of me."

"I don't believe you'd do that," Sidney said.

"Well, you better begin, because it's true. Now I want you to help me, not him. I want you to help all of us, not all of them. I want you to go in there, and when they ask you to identify the voices on the tape, the tape which I had—" I turned to Michael Meier again. "Your boss was right about that. I had the tape, and I gave it to them in there."

"My God," Sidney said, "have I taught you nothing in my whole life?"

"It's worse than you think, Sidney. That tape, Frank's, they didn't force me to give it up. I gave it willingly. Now I know you're sick, and I'm truly sorry to have to do this at this time, but it will be the greatest act of your life if you go in there and identify the voices on that tape, tell them who each voice is, what they're saying, and what they meant. You were the only other person in that room besides Frank and Bernie."

"Boy, do you really mean that you—" Sidney said.

"Worse than that. What I really want you to tell them is that one of Bernie's buffaloes came in a couple of hours after Frank left, and he was carrying Frank's black—"

Sidney walloped me across the face.

He was on his feet, shaking, his face tensed, red.

The door opened. A clerk came out, followed by Polly's cop and the assistant district attorney.

Sidney turned to the assistant district attorney. "Get him out of here." He pointed to me. "I don't want to see him when I come out." Sidney was directing them as he must have his stagehands in the old days.

"The grand jury's ready for you, Mr. Schlossberg," the assistant district attorney said, indicating the open door.

Sidney's right knee began to tremble as it always did before he played a scene of emotional outburst. Then he leaned forward and, using that momentum, entered the grand jury room. He was ridiculous, but everyone there admired him.

Now I had Meier to myself.

"Tell the man you work for—" I started.

"Oh, stop being silly," he said. "Stop making a fool of yourself." He coughed and got up, buttoning his coat as he did.

"Here's what I want you to tell him," I persisted. "Tell him he didn't terrorize me, but I'm going to terrorize him. I'll be waiting for him, and I'll be armed. Don't turn away, you fat putz. Listen to what I tell you."

"You know, you're ridiculous." Michael Meier said. "Can you hear what you're saying? Don't worry, I won't pass on all this shit, but be careful where you talk like that, because I really wouldn't want it to get back to Mr. Kasko. He isn't as patient as me."

We heard Sidney shouting from the other room. He was telling off the grand jury. "I don't want immunity," we all heard. And then, "Contempt! Yes! I'm contemptuous of you!" Then the door of the room was thrown open and out he came. He walked right by me to Michael Meier, shouting, "Immunity they're offering me! Immunity if I testify! I don't want their goddamn immunity. They threatened me with contempt! I said, 'Yes, I am contemptuous of all of you, you scoundrels of the system, I defy you to make me talk, I defy you to make me be even civil!' "

Now he turned slowly and spoke his judgment of me. "I declare you dead," he said. "You are not a member of the race of men. You are dead morally because no one will respect you again. You are dead artistically because you have permanently discredited yourself. And" —you could see he thought this the heaviest punishment of all— "you are dead humanly because you are no longer my friend!"

The grand jury wanted him back, of course, and one of the police who descended on him now was Polly's boy friend, presently unsaddled, I'm sure.

"And you!" Sidney turned on the young man. "So young and so treacherous! Aren't you ashamed, young man?"

The odd thing was that Polly's boy friend answered him calmly and logically. "There seems to be no other way, Mr. Schlossberg, to bring people like Bernie Kasko to justice. Informers like your friend whom you've just damned, they're a necessary evil!"

If that was intended to make me feel better, it didn't succeed.

The assistant district attorney had come up to Sidney and asked him in the most respectful tone, "May I speak to you for just a moment, Mr. Schlossberg, please, sir?"

Behind him a clerk held Frank Scott's black attaché case.

Sidney was giving consideration to the man's request for favor. He liked the respectful way the man addressed him.

"I wonder if you'd all, the rest of you, excuse us," the assistant district attorney went on. "I want to speak to Mr. Schlossberg alone."

"Nothing more about immunity," Sidney warned him.

"Won't mention the word," the assistant district attorney promised.

"No more threats of contempt!"

The assistant district attorney said, "None." Then he made a sign for us to go.

I started out, and then something about Sidney stopped me. I knew him better than the others so I wasn't as surprised as they were when there was a little flutter in his eyes, and he staggered, reaching out his hand for the back of a chair. I slid it to him, and he fell into it, breathing hard.

He looked around, his eyes met mine, and he made a sign for me to get out. "What's all this?" he said. "Get out! Now! I want to talk to this man. I want to make my"—he was breathing very hard—"my position clear. Relieve me of your presence," he said to me. "I won't miss it. Michael, wait for me, I shan't be long."

I could see he was fighting faintness and a blackout.

As we left, the clerk holding Frank Scott's case opened the door back into the grand jury room.

Michael Meier and I stood in the hall outside, he leaning against one wall and I the other, with Polly's deceitful lover in between.

"Now there is a great old man," Polly's boy friend said.

"Say it again because this time you're right," Michael Meier said. Then he looked at me. "Aren't you ashamed of yourself?" he asked. "Didn't Mr. Schlossberg make you feel—?"

"Sort of," I said. "Yes, sort of."

"Can I give you a piece of friendly advice?" Michael Meier said. "This is not a stage play playing here. So I suggest you keep your mouth buttoned. Your safety, for the moment at least, depends on your old friend in there. If he's as good a friend of yours as I've been given reason to believe, he will keep his mouth shut. That little D.A., I've had experience with him, and when he drips honey he can be very persuasive. The only thing that might get Bernie indicted is if your

Mr. Schlossberg says the wrong things in there. Then Bernie might have to go to court. He would not be in danger because he never left the hotel room that night, and we have four unimpeachable young ladies to so testify, but you would be in danger because Bernie doesn't like to be dragged through court, and he would not forgive you if he is. What does this mean? I'll tell you. The address of your father-in-law is North Robbins Key Road, just off Englewood, in Florida. The house is white stucco, and there is a raised portion, a second story in the center which is the bedroom of the general. The beach where your son plays is deserted and—"

I hit him high and very hard, and he went down. I was on him, one hand at his throat, the other holding what hair there was. I was slamming the back of his head on the floor, once, twice, three times before Polly's boy friend had me under the armpits and pulled me off.

That was the finish of my Rave Act.

Meier was a cement head. He was already sitting up, rubbing his head, and trying to stand.

"I will call down every instrument of the law of this state on your ass," he was screaming, and I could smell the cologne in the air, mixed with the smell of sweat. "Assault! Battery! Intent to kill! You are all witnesses!"

The door of the waiting room was thrown open and out came Sidney. Meier forgot his bone head and was after Sidney, quick as a cat, to find out what had happened.

Sidney was striding away already past him down the hall. Whatever was wrong with Sidney that had caused him to faint was overcome for now. He was around the corner going at a great pace, Meier following. As they disappeared, I heard Sidney writing his own notice, saying to a bruised and battered lawyer, "You should have heard me. I was unforgettable! Those whores of the system almost applauded me!"

Polly's cop-boy-friend looked at me and smiled. "Did you hear that?" he said. "You're safe."

He'd taken Meier's threat seriously.

Maybe it was serious, but whose side was that young cop on?

Boruff had followed Sidney out. "He's a terrific old guy," Boruff said. "You should have heard him talk to that grand jury. Wrong but magnificent!"

Nobody'd said I was right and magnificent. Yet it was I who'd done the difficult thing.

Boruff walked me down the hall. "You can go now," he said. "If we need you again, we'll send for you."

"Suppose something happens?"

"Like what?"

"I don't think Bernie's going to forgive me. His lawyer threatened my kid again. They've tracked down the house where Ellie and he are living in Florida."

"I'll talk to Mr. Meier. He can be disbarred for threatening you, and he's perfectly well aware of it."

"But Bernie?"

"Bernie's not going to bother you. We just got the news. He was shot."

"Dead?"

"Dead as you'd want him."

"Where?"

"London."

"By a black?"

"The police got one of those taking-credit calls. The man who killed him was Frank Scott, the voice said."

Poor Sidney, I thought. "Did you tell Sidney?"

"I didn't have the heart."

I was glad I had the theater to go to.

There was no way Sidney could outlive Bernie's death.

Our final rehearsal sessions now consisted mostly of the cast sitting around listening to Adam praise me. I was suddenly the sensation of Broadway. Actors talk and meet, they meet and they talk. It was all over the Street that I was giving the tour de force of the season. People I didn't know waved to me through the window of Sardi's Little Bar.

I knew I was good because the playwright came to me and said if I didn't stick to his lines more faithfully, he'd complain to the Dramatists Guild. "The serious side of my work is being slighted," he said. "My theme is being lost."

"What is his theme?" I asked Adam.

"First I've heard of it," Adam said.

We'd become friends. The promise of success can do that.

"Our author will feel much better when he begins to get his royalty checks," Sol said.

"Well, I'll try to say more of his lines the way he—"

"Please don't," Adam said.

We laughed, the Dramatists Guild's board should have heard us.

I decided to install a police lock on my door, which means I'd decided to stay in the apartment. Nothing told me I wasn't going to be molested, but I felt sure I wouldn't be. Bernie's death was the lancing of a boil. It would take time to develop a new one.

About two o'clock the next morning my doorbell rang. I jumped out of bed, ran into the kitchen, and picked up the bread knife.

"Who's there?" I demanded.

I couldn't make out the words, only the rumble.

Sidney looked terrible. As his belly had swelled, his face had hollowed.

I guess he knew how bad he looked because he dropped his head and walked past me into the dark apartment. When I'd closed and bolted the door, he was at the little bulletin board just inside the kitchen alcove. Ellie had nailed a pad there and hung a pencil on a string. Sidney tore off a sheet and wrote, "I will stay here on one condition, that you don't require me to talk to you. Agreed or not?"

"I wrote, 'Condition accepted.'"

I was awful glad to see him. He was terribly sick now and in need of constant attention, had no money and no one except me.

I made him as comfortable as I could in Little Arthur's room. The kid had his own TV set, and his walls were lined with pictures of rock and sports heroes, a gay effect.

Sidney didn't look at any of it, didn't use the TV. He lay in bed staring at the ceiling. Occasionally I would hear him mumbling to himself.

The next morning at about a quarter of four, he called. I hurried to his room, and he spoke to me, for the first time.

"Where is Prince?" he demanded.

"I don't think he knows where you are, Sidney, or he'd have been here long ago."

"We should inform Prince of Bernie's death," he said.

"I imagine he saw the papers."

"Was it in the papers? Oh, of course, that's where I saw it."

He floated off, then he looked at me. He might have been dying, but his arrogance was going to go last.

"Well!" he demanded. "Say something intelligent!"

"I suppose Prince was pretty discouraged," I tried, "just as you were."

"I was not discouraged. It merely confirmed my feeling for fate. I have been on a down curve, the planets, you know. Polly is deeply schooled in astrology. I brushed it off, but she predicted this, and she was right. Polly's a fine woman. I've known many fine women in my life, many!"

"You certainly have, Sidney."

"All sex objects." He burst into coarse laughter ending with a heavy cough of rheum. "Oh, God, oh, God," he said.

"Sidney, don't you think I might bring a doctor here?"

"If it will make you feel any better to show me to a doctor," he answered, "why then, don't hesitate, but I warn you, I am without financial resources."

"Do you mind, Sidney, if I do it today, the doctor, this morning?"

He weighed the problem. "I'm afraid of what he might say."

"Yes, but—"

"It's all right," he finally indulged me, "since it means so much to you, do it."

"I will," I said. "Thank you."

"Although I have still to find a doctor whom I could trust. They do not appreciate the role of the psyche in health and disease—in death, too."

"Well, you'll explain it to him, Sidney."

"I will, I will. By the way, how is your show going?"

"I think it may work."

"Well, don't be too downcast. They all finally close. You can go now. I have some thinking to do. Give me another white one before you go."

The doctor looked at Sidney's belly, then felt it, then called the hospital to reserve a bed.

An ambulance came and took the old man away. He cursed the attendants all the way to the hospital.

I went to the theater. Adam, who'd become positively sycophantic, embarrassed me now by asking me if I wanted to rehearse. I said it was up to him, of course.

"I was so pleased with the preview last night," he said, "this morning I bought my mother that Persian lamb coat she always wanted."

"You're going to jinx us, Adam."

"I was laughing so hard I couldn't dictate any notes. In all modesty, I think we've done a very good job, even the director. I wish we'd opened last night."

When I got back to the hospital, they had Sidney ready for the operating room. He was shot full of dope, barely acknowledged my presence.

I went out into the hall. The doctor and a couple of attendants were coming for Sidney with the rolling stretcher.

"How bad is it?" I asked the surgeon.

"That's what we're going to find out," he said.

They rolled Sidney out of the room, and I followed as far as the big elevator. There was a wait, and I heard Sidney calling. The doctor went to him, and Sidney said, "When you cut me open, if you see I'm not going to be able to do my work properly again don't bother to sew me up."

They were in the operating room a long time. When they brought Sidney back he was white as the sheet which covered him. Except for a slight heave and collapse of his chest at irregular intervals, he was without visible animation.

It was past time for me to be at the theater, but I had to talk to the surgeon. I caught him in the hospital cafeteria, eating a beef stew.

"What took so long?" I asked.

"Because I looked everywhere," he said. "It's everywhere."

"What's the prognosis?"

"Medically, forget it. Practically, he ought to move home in a few days. We need every bed. The pressure here is something awesome."

Of course he hadn't done what Sidney asked.

That night was our last preview. I must have been pretty good. They kept clapping after I'd signaled the stage manager to leave the rag down. Adam said I was brilliant, but then he and Sol were trying to get me to sign a new contract giving them another year in New York.

My agent was there and came back, loaded with big ideas. He wasn't keen on the proposed extension of contract. "This is the era of the TV series," he said, "not the theater."

The network boys had heard about my success, even before it happened, and were reaching for me. There was one series in particular, centering around a frontier figure, a crusty widower with seven children trying to control his amusing if decidedly eccentric brood while fighting off ruthless outlaws and equally predatory women.

"Pappy Morgan's the character's name," my agent said. "It's

perfect for you. Now's the time to move into clover," he urged. "Look at Karl Malden, thirty years nothing, then he makes a cool mil in nine months."

Then he philosophized. "The public never gets tired of a good character man. Styles in lovers come and go, but when a comic puts on twenty pounds it doesn't hurt, it helps. Sure, live in Florida! There's nothing a producer likes better than to send his secretary chasing a performer over the long distance phone. If you were living in Brooklyn he might not bother, but when his girl can't find you anywhere, he's got to come to me. When I tell him you're twenty miles off the Florida Keys fishing, he goes crazy, becomes hysterical. He's got to have you—"

"Then I wouldn't be out of touch in Florida?"

"You'll be out of touch, baby, with everyone except me. As for getting to where they're shooting the shit, always remember what that politician said, 'It's one world now, all Beverly Hills!' You put down your fishing what-do-you-call-it in the morning, you're eating dinner with the director that night. Anywhere in the world! 'How manly you are!' he says. 'That outdoor look!' "

So on and on, ending with, "Finally the ship you've been waiting for all your life has come in, so let's get on board, buddy-boy!"

The hospital lobby was deserted when I arrived, the corridors empty. No visitors were allowed in the middle of the night, so I found the fire stairs and walked up ten flights.

Sidney was awake. He scowled at me, but I was used to that. His greeting was generally some kind of reprimand. I saw his lips moving, bent over to hear.

"That son of a bitch!" He meant the doctor.

The morning my play was to open, I took Sidney home. Determined to make his last weeks or days as pleasant as possible, I fixed him up in Ellie's room, where he'd have a bedside phone. I put the big color TV at the foot of the bed, surrounded him with magazines, fluids, and a bucket of ice. I even got him an extremely pretty young nurse, thought he'd like that.

But he didn't. "She's too pretty," he said. "She reminds me! Now I can't do anything about her, and there's the bedpan. I don't want a pretty girl doing that for me."

We opened. We weren't quite the success Sol and Adam had anticipated. The critics thought exactly what I thought of the play.

That always happens. Rehearsal is a process of self-hypnosis. But, as my agent impressed on everyone, it was a personal triumph for me. I couldn't believe the newspapers!

"Something has happened to this performer," the leading paper's fellow said. "He was always a competent actor, but never before brilliant. He always seemed to lack the final spark and flare a really great actor has. But now, it's as if he were suddenly liberated. He's not just a superb technician. He's a vibrant personality who fills the theater with his presence. A new phenomenon, a legend aborning. He is no longer working within the confines of modesty and moderation, always a false place for an actor. He swaggers onto the stage, reeling with confidence, as if he owns it. He wraps up the evening and takes it home, and me with it. He could come on stage without a script, as he did last night, to tell the truth, and be totally entertaining, totally engrossing, totally beguiling in the way that Bert Lahr was before him, and before Lahr, Barrymore, and before Barrymore, W. C. Fields and Sophie Tucker and Spencer Tracy and Ethel Merman and Mary Martin and—" and so on.

The ads Sol took were totally different from the dummies he'd had prepared with blank boxes for the good quotes. What appeared in next morning's papers ignored the play. They were all about me, featuring a picture of one of my funnier moments. I looked like a dancer, not an actor.

Overnight, I was the toast of the town. The hand I got when I came on was the same size as the hand I got at the last curtain call.

At last I'd become what Sidney had always declared I couldn't become, a star.

It was a mystery, my transformation, to everyone except me. I knew just when I'd shed my old skin of constraint and busted out in this new one. It was when I'd played my Rave scene to the grand jury and in their anteroom when I'd told Sidney the score and when I'd lost control in the hall and tried to crack poor old Meier's skull on the cement floor.

It made my heart pump faster, the memory of all that!

"Think over that offer," my agent said as he left me—they were even congratulating him as he left Sardi's that night—"because it's firm now. They want you and they want you bad. We can write our own ticket, at least till the next big number comes along."

When I got home it was very late. There was an opening night wire from Sidney written on the back of our phone bill. "You're wasting your talent," it said. "Otherwise I forgive you."

Sidney needed a full-time companion-nurse so I dug up Paul Prince. I told him what the situation was and what I hoped he could do, keep Sidney calm and do the bedpan bit. Paul was moved to generosity, said he'd be glad to do me the favor. I insisted on paying him the going rate. I didn't have to insist long.

He was most respectful of Sidney, so concerned that he insisted on sleeping in. I had a roommate.

Within a day they'd taken over the place. It looked like after the robbery. Everything was everywhere it shouldn't be. I also had the impression, which I didn't pursue, that Paul Prince was stealing. Poor Ellie.

Paul, of course, was above washing the dishes. So every night after my triumph downtown, I came home to clean up the day's litter.

Sidney was heavily sedated all the time now, slipped in and out of consciousness. Still he couldn't really sleep, nor could Paul, nor could I. I began to entertain them by telling about the animals in Africa, little tales like those I might have told a child. Sidney seemed to be interested. Then he'd float away. When he came back, I'd pick up exactly where I'd left off, to the word, just as if nothing had happened.

I told them about the prancing Tommy. His behavior didn't puzzle Sidney. "I understand perfectly," he said. When I pressed him for his explanation, all he'd say was, "If you can't see it, no one can explain it to you."

One night I told them about meeting Mr. Bert Lahr outside my tent and how I'd spoken with him and that I'd thought it was a fantasy of fever but the boys next day reported finding the pug marks of a large lion. They really enjoyed that story, me apologizing to an old lion for taking his wife.

"He's got a good imagination," Paul Prince said to Sidney.

"But not in his work," Sidney said.

"I'm forced to admit he's not too bad in his present vehicle," Paul said. "I think even you'd like him. Of course he discards the text. That's how he does it. Our friend has no gift with words, none whatsoever, but he has some cute tricks."

Paul got up to illustrate. He looked so grotesque doing all my shticks! His wig was out of order. Paul'd got caught in the rain without a hat, and he'd forgot to take his rug off. I laughed as loud and long as the audience had laughed at me.

But Sidney had floated off again, and we called it a night.

A couple of days later I came home after the performance, and they were having a terrible quarrel.

"You've been the ruination of my life," Paul was screaming. "I trusted my play to you, and you delayed and delayed until this happened. You were playing games with me."

"I delayed because your script was never ready for rehearsal," Sidney lied.

"You never had the intention of doing my play, and you certainly never had the money. It was a game you were playing, and you played it with my life's blood."

They were like two kids without a TV. They had nothing to do but quarrel, make up, then scrap again.

Saturday night I had to make up my mind about the series, so after the performance I came home to think it out. I found them squabbling so I went into Little Arthur's room and closed the door, turned the news up full blast to drown out their racket.

A few minutes later, screams topped WINS, and there was Paul Prince on top of Sidney, choking him. Sidney was holding him off with what strength he had left and, when he could, spitting in his author's face.

I had a hell of a time pulling little Paul off. I told him not to come back.

"I'm initiating a lawsuit against you, too," he promised. "You were part of the conspiracy against my play."

Paul left with all his scripts, including those Sidney had marked for direction, in a Pathmark shopping bag.

Sunday was quiet. The fellow in the *Times* topped his notice in the daily edition. I showed the piece to Sidney.

"Too bad he doesn't know something," Sidney said.

I decided to talk over my TV decision with him. It was to be our last coherent conversation. His strength was almost gone.

"If I take it," I said, "I'll become what you called Polly's boy friend, 'Standard Brand,' a household puppet, Barbie Doll's father. I'll never be able to play any other kind of character again. Pappy Morgan will become me and vice versa."

"There are no plays," Sidney rumbled mournfully. All he had left was a hoarse whisper.

"If I don't take it, well, we'll run to maybe February, March, next year, then it's back to the labor pool, waiting for work, all alone at the telephone. You know? What'll I do, Sidney?"

"There are no plays," he mourned. "They're all gone, Big Bob and Little Sam, Elmer and Max, Clifford, who was like me and wanted everything, Moss with the golden garters, and George, who could fix anything. Pixie Phil Barry and Bill Inge, sweet, gentle Bill, Howard Lindsay and Sidney Howard, who remembers him now? And Gene O'Neill, the king! They're all dead, and all the others who used to give us plays every season, they're dying or their talent is."

"Sidney, there's a whole new bunch, and they're very good."

"Sure. I'm sure. But something's gone, am I wrong? Wasn't there a time of glory? Those years? How many, twenty, thirty? Every season there'd be five or six new plays you couldn't forget, and I'm not even talking about the actors we had. Who's taken their place, those actors? Who?"

He floated off, was gone, came back.

"So," I asked him, "what'll I do?"

I was asking his permission to take the series.

"Why don't you take over *Titan* and do it?"

"I don't think I'm up to that play," I said quickly. "I don't have the talent."

"You're right," he said. "Take the TV job, Sonny. That's within your range."

Later he smiled at me. I hadn't fooled him. "That play, you know, is not as bad as you think. The source is good, the central idea. The individual against authority! The independent spirit against society and its controls. Maybe both are necessary, but which is death to lose? Tell me that."

"You know the answer, Sidney. You lived it."

"It's not cleverness that gets to people, Sonny. The great plays were not great because of cleverness. Today it's all experiments in style. What counts and what endures is meaning, theme. What you have to touch in an audience is their fundamental concerns, what's worrying them now and always will, even if they don't know it, the mind's despair, the heart's hope."

He groaned and moved. "Meantime," he said, "your wife has won the war! A TV star for chrissake!"

Then he did a terrible thing. He began to laugh, spending the last of his strength in a paroxysm of mirth, the kind that gets out of control, like one of those old cars whose motor, self-firing, keeps going after the ignition's turned off. Sidney laughed and coughed and laughed and coughed and laughed and that was his verdict.

Then he was through, I thought. He'd closed his eyes, but at intervals he kept throwing heaves, as much sobs as laughter.

I sat at his side till he was quiet. Then I got Ellie on the phone and told her my news. She sounded happy, even friendly. "Wait till you see Arthur!" she said. "He's brown as a nut. And grown? You won't know him. Every morning he and daddy catch their breakfast in the gulf, bring in little Spanish mackerel for me to fry or a string of pompano. Then Arthur's off to Saint Rose's. It's a very good school, very disciplined. In the afternoon, the same bus brings him to the end of the driveway where I'm waiting." She went on and on, the point being that she felt safe down there.

"Oh, I need a quick favor," she finished. "Get hold of a moving company and send me Arthur's piano."

Two mornings later I found Sidney dead. I'd just bought a new batch of sedatives to ease his pain. He'd eased it for good.

He was spread-eagled on top of his bed, completely naked, his arms thrown over his head, his belly a grotesque.

"What part's he playing now?" was my first thought. "The Cosmic Martyr? That big ham can't even die like a normal human being.

"Or is he leaving me a message?"

Why had he pulled everything off his body that way? The halves of his pajamas were against the wall where he'd flung them.

Sidney hated doctors. Was he showing me what they'd done to him? The man was stitched from pubis to solar plexus. The scar-skin, still inflamed, glowed like neon.

I was to carry it, the memory of that burning scar, like a spring virus that keeps coming back.

When I thought of Sidney boxed in the ground, I decided on cremation.

One person came to the service, Paul Prince, but many people asked after Sidney later, especially stagehands, the old-timers who'd survived from the big days. They'd come up to me in the street and say, "Did I hear right, Mr. Castleman's gone?" I'd say yes, and they'd pay their respects, more often than not by an anecdote.

On the sidewalk outside the chapel, the author of *Titan* was forlorn and deflated. He pressed my hand and said with a pearl in each eye, "I'm sorry I said that about a lawsuit."

I told him that Sidney had instructed me to give him all his money. "Here it is," I said, "an even hundred dollars."

"Is that all?"

When I told him he could have any of Sidney's belongings, he hustled me home and went straight for the vicuña. Then he crammed a shopping bag with socks and shirts and pajamas. I was amazed how much that nimble little fellow found he could use.

Well, that's the end of Sidney, I thought, and to tell the truth, despite all that I felt for the man, I was relieved. Life would be smoother and quieter now, and much simpler.

But then came the tide of miracles.

Success in show business strikes like lightning, in a succession of bolts. After Pappy Morgan's first two shows for the new season, it was obvious he was going to take over the airwaves. After his third and fourth, it appeared he'd take over the nation.

A greater miracle was to follow, one that would settle the problem of my living expenses forever.

A great life insurance—oops—a great life assurance company decided that of all the public figures available to represent them in the public eye, the one they wanted was Pappy Morgan. Pappy embodied, it seemed to them—I might as well quote from the press release announcing the contract we signed—"those qualities of pioneer hardiness and back-country resourcefulness that made this country what it is, that inspirational ability to endure hardships, overcome reverses, persist against all odds, and come through. Pappy is courage in adversity."

You've seen me in their commercials, full of that old-time grit.

The deal we worked out was for $200,000 a year for ten years. The work required amounted to, believe me, an aggregate of four weeks a year. Those weeks, furthermore, could be adjusted within reason around the rest of my schedule. The assurance company wanted me to continue as Pappy. Of course, they'd even allow me to make a few films, asked only to O.K. my scripts. Careful. No porno.

"We're going to pull down five fat figures from Pappy Morgan T-shirts alone," my agent crowed. "What do you say to that, dreamer?"

On the first of February, my show having closed, I moved to Florida. I'd flown down for a couple of weekends in the fall, during which Ellie and I had purchased a small place on the bay side of the key, directly across from Ellie's father on the gulf. We use his beach and his boat, a Boston Whaler powered by fifty Johnson horses.

Robbins Key is nothing more than a strip of sand connected to the mainland at either end by a narrow bridge. These two bridges, Ellie's father informed me, can easily be blocked and defended by a comparatively small force. Was he kidding? A military man's quirk of humor, I suppose.

We have—"we" is the community on the key—a patrol that rides up and down the single road night and day. We've never had any trouble. Oh, once our mailbox disappeared from the head of our driveway, but I'm sure that was just a prank, college midterms. Still, that patrol makes everyone on the key feel safer.

You might not like my neighbors. For one thing they're all over sixty, and I must say, even though it's ungracious, that they look it. The State of Florida is a state of dying.

There's a lot of social life on the key, cocktail parties most every afternoon. When the conversation at these gatherings turns serious, it's about what concerns these people most, how to make the money you've spent your life accumulating last until your death.

For a while I joined right in, but then I'd catch Sidney watching me with that satyr's smile, and I'd shut my face with a drink.

I noticed that everyone around me, despite their ease and calm and grace, is scrunched up in a posture of defense. They are all every way fearful.

But my own little herd, they're blessed out! My sudden affluence and this new environment has solved everyone's problems.

Ellie? She wears translucent gowns of multicolored crepe, and you can't get her to leave our house. She's put up a vast screened-in area, top and four sides, to keep out insects and those pesky little green lizards. Life in a gazebo! And she's found a friend, a Welshman, who gives her what I never could. He plays the violin. They have a relationship which fills out her life. No, his name is not Arthur. Hugh. They do the *Kreutzer* beautifully. I don't know what else they do. Does it really matter? He makes her happy. And she doesn't demand miracles of attention from me anymore. Hugh! I give him presents.

One sunny day she said to me, "You have your needs, I have mine." Then she kissed me. Thanks, I suppose.

I got to like her old man, sort of. I mean, he's pathetic. He had never found a way to plug the hole the Air Force left in his life. Now he's got it, a grandson who's a fishing fool.

Little Arthur's a new kid. Everybody's fighting for his favor now, that little boss. And he's beginning to sprout horns. He pulled down his britches the other day and showed me. "Look," he said, "hair!" His rage is surfing. When there are waves, he goes out before dawn. There's a reef breaking water a quarter of a mile out, it fences off the big beasts. I love to watch that kid with the first sun in his face, riding in on the furl of a wave.

As for me, I'm set for life.

I am an icon of the tube.

I had introduced Sidney's favorite line at least once in every show. At the darkest moment of their darkest hour, Pappy would say to the besieged, the cornered, the demoralized, the apparently defeated, "Don't worry, you're with me now, kid."

And the tables would turn. Every episode has that story. Popeye's spinach brought up to date.

What do I represent? Freedom from Fear. Fear of what? The future. Debilitating old age. Being left alone by the death of a mate. Failure in business. High blood pressure. Algebraic inflation. Galloping arthritis. Ulcers due to tension. Ulcers due to keeping too many secrets. Another nineteen hundred and twenty-nine. Another Nixon. Everything that worries everybody. Yes, death, even that. Pappy brings them back from the grave.

What I am in one word is Assurance.

Something worrying you? Courage, man! See my show! Got a problem? Write me. I have a staff. They answer all letters. Feeling threatened? Call me. We pay the toll. Let it all hang out. Be with me!

And they were. In Florida, whoever heard of the Broadway stage? But they sure as hell heard of Pappy Morgan. Everywhere I went folks used to ask about my brood as if they were living people. I threw out the first ball at the opening game of the Pittsburgh Pirates training season at Bradenton. I was introduced from the center ring of the circus at their winter headquarters in Venice Florida. You should have heard that crowd yell 'Pappy! Pappy! We re with you, Pappy!'

Yes, I had everything any man could want.

But here is where the trouble started.

Who was Pappy Morgan? You guessed it. I'd taken my whole character from that old man, his swagger. his irreverent humor. his sudden, overwhelming tenderness, his insane optimism, his everlasting resilience, his balls, the old lion, Sidney with the twitching tail.

I was him at last, which is all I ever wanted to be.

But suddenly something I wasn't prepared for happened. The sharp tongue of the man began to come out, his arrogance, his scorn, his impatience, his insufferable superiority to everybody, his irascible truth-telling, his short-fuse temper—all the "bad" sides of the old fellow.

Yes, the Titan, his defiance of authority.

The engineers sitting in their glass box had to listen carefully, bleep me out a couple. three times every program.

Something was cooking that I couldn't—or didn't want to—control.

Maybe the stuff just got too heavy for my shovel. I began to go plain old bananas from the crap I had to say and pretend to believe.

Between jobs it was even worse. I would walk up and down that empty goddamn beach—our neighbors prefer their filtered pools—and revile the Gulf of Mexico. Most days it was like a lake, lapping up with those feeble little waves. It irritated me, that continuous rhythmic wash of old pebbles and the teeth of dead sharks.

I'd go into the house, and sure enough there'd be Ellie and Hugh sawing away at an Old Master with a reverence that compelled them to go over and over each passage numberless times. I'd climb two flights to my air-conditioned, soundproof study, close the door. The silence was deadly. I'd sit by the telephone and wait.

For what? Believe it or not, a call from my agent.

What he called about when he called was employment, work somewhere else. Maybe a guest shot in Los Angeles, where I've got buddies, fun-loving old show business degenerates. Maybe a personal appearance at a big convention in San Francisco. That spaced-out city always makes me feel young again. But best of all, my hope and my salvation, a film in Europe.

No one ever heard of Pappy Morgan over there. I can be myself.

What happens? The usual. Nothing glorious.

Those big cities are crawling with malcontents. I find them congenial.

And celebrity-fuckers.

For a time I was with a Noirette from North Africa, rebellious and intemperate, her frizzy hair shooting out as if her head had exploded in one of those stop-action photographs taken at a thousandth. She calls me Sheik. What do you know!

I'd go any old way with any old thing.

I'd developed an irresistible compulsion to muck up my life.

I knew whose fault it was. He was dead, one way. Not another.

There were incidents, fights and frolics.

The assurance company covered for me a few times. They did everything anyone could ask.

But then I'd developed a drinking problem, too. I didn't think it was too serious but—

Well, it was bound to happen. Like the Tommy, sooner or later he had to take one hop one inch too close.

One night in New York, when I was there taping commercials, I made the mistake of going to a show at night, loaded. The theater always makes me disgruntled, too many memories. I knew I should never have gone, especially to the Ethel Barrymore, where I'd played so many times.

In the intermission, walking up the aisle, I suddenly passed someone I thought I recognized. I walked back a step or two and stood over this man, staring at him till it came to me who he was.

"Hello," I said. "Remember me?"

He didn't.

"I've always wanted to ask you something," I said, kneeling in the aisle at the side of his seat.

He gave me two blanks.

"Remember you cut a friend of mine open," I said, "a Mr. Sidney Schlossberg? Then you stitched him up, because you saw he was beyond saving. You're that same doctor, aren't you?"

"I'm a doctor," he said, "but I'm not sure I remember any Mr.—"

"Yes you do," I said. "Try. He asked you something. Remember that old man with the enormous belly and the arrogant—?"

"Oh, yes," he said.

The word *arrogant* did it.

"Remember waiting for the elevator to the operating room, he asked you that if you saw he couldn't continue to live in his own style—?"

"Oh, yes, yes," he said.

"What did he ask you then?"

"Don't bother to sew me up."

"You see, you do remember!"

"Nothing could have been done for that man. I believe I told you—"

"That's the point. Why didn't you do what he asked?"

I had my hand on his arm, and I suppose I was holding him harder than he cared to tolerate because he said, "Would you mind releasing my arm?"

"Why didn't you do what he asked?" I said. "That's the way he wanted to go. And when. Why did you sew him up again if you knew that?"

"I'd have been breaking the law if I'd done what he asked."

"Fuck the law. Why didn't you do what that dying man asked?"

I was talking, they told me later, louder than necessary, besides making no sense, and people were watching us, and the doctor was looking around with that call-the-cops look on his face.

Then he made a mistake. He called, "Usher!" And when he didn't see one come running, he called, "Police!"

I grabbed him by the shoulders, they told me, and was shaking him, saying something or other, and people had to rush up and pull me off.

I left the Barrymore escorted by a darling old usherette, a friend from the days when I'd played that theater. She accompanied me to the street, like my mother would have, turned me loose with a kiss.

I wasn't disposed to think any more about the incident, but the next morning a column had it. Never would have except Pappy was this big national symbol.

Toot suite, the assurance people asked me would I come into their executive offices for a talk with the head man and his staff.

I knew if I said the right thing at that conference, I could patch everything up.

But for the longest time they didn't say anything, just sat drinking coffee out of cardboard containers and looking at me with those tight little executive smiles.

They were waiting for me to crawl.

So I said that what had happened had nothing to do with that doctor. I'd spent the whole day making commercials, I said, and "When you're that cheerful, that reassuring, and that phony for that long, what other way can you be at night?"

This explanation did not satisfy them.

They waited for something more.

I wondered what Sidney would do. Apologize? Are you kidding? Especially if that was what they were waiting for with those "or else" looks on their faces.

So I said I was going to trip over to the bar across the street for a refresher. Did anyone care to join me?

No one did.

The next day, the assurance folks had a very friendly chat with my agent—that's what agents are for, to be friendly no matter what—and he assured them a settlement of my contract could be worked out.

He tried to call me at my hotel to discuss details. By then I was nine miles off the west coast of Florida in a Boston Whaler.

The following day, my agent found me and asked if I had any last words.

"Don't bother to sew me up," I said.

I was already riding another compulsion, to speak up for Sidney, what he was, and what he meant to me.

And what was gone when he was gone.

They tell me there's been some crap in a column about my being what Jim Piper used to call "not myself."

But people who come down from New York for one of those frantic six-day vacations, they compliment me on how well I look. "You're the only man I know," one of them said, "who does not age. How do you do it?"

I gave him that Schlossberg half smile, half sneer and said not a goddamn thing.

What the hell is there to say, except tell the story.

I have bowed my head in respect.

Now may he rest in peace.